Penguin Books
Other Women

KU-794-788

Lisa Alther was born in Tennessee in 1944 and attended college
in Massachusetts. She has lived in New York City, Cambridge,
Massachusetts, Cincinnati, Ohio, and London, and now lives in
Vermont, though she retains close links with the South.

She wrote for twelve years before *Kinflicks* was published to
international acclaim in 1976. Doris Lessing praised her 'strong,
salty, original talent'; *The New York Times Book Review* found
'an energetic intelligence, an absence of self-pity, an appetite for
experience' and 'a true comic genius'; *Harpers* greeted the work
of 'a most powerful and remarkable talent'.

Kinflicks and Lisa Alther's second novel, *Original Sins*, became
bestsellers and have been translated into many languages. Both
are published in Penguin.

Lisa Alther

Other Women

PENGUIN BOOKS

Penguin Books Ltd, Harmondsworth, Middlesex, England
Viking Penguin Inc., 40 West 23rd Street, New York, New York 10010, U.S.A.
Penguin Books Australia Ltd, Ringwood, Victoria, Australia
Penguin Books Canada Limited, 2801 John Street, Markham, Ontario, Canada L3R 1B4
Penguin Books (N.Z.) Ltd, 182–190 Wairau Road, Auckland 10, New Zealand

First published in the U.S.A. by Alfred A. Knopf, Inc., 1984
First published in Great Britain by Viking 1985
Published in Penguin Books 1985
Reprinted 1986

Made and printed in Great Britain by
Hazell Watson & Viney Limited,
Member of the BPCC Group,
Aylesbury, Bucks
Typeset in Plantin

For Nancy Magnus

Heartfelt thanks to the following friends, without whom this book wouldn't exist: Nancy Magnus, for our endless discussions of therapeutic technique and the meaning of life; Carey Kaplan, for extensive assistance and unstinting encouragement; Richard Alther, Blanche Boyd, Stephanie Dowrick, Alice Reed, Bill Reed, and Shelton Reed, for careful readings and fruitful suggestions; Bob Gottlieb and Martha Kaplan, for their usual sound editorial sense; and all the above for their kind support on days when this project felt to me like the worst idea since nuclear warheads.

'Is life so wretched?
Isn't it rather your hands which are too small,
your vision which is muddied?
You are the one who must grow up.'

Dag Hammarskjöld

Part One

One

Caroline switched off the ignition of her red Subaru, gripped the steering wheel with both gloved hands, and gazed across the parking lot down to Lake Glass. Raindrops rolled like tears down the windshield, and dripped off the bare gray branches in the yard. 'God is crying,' she used to explain to her younger brothers on rainy days in Brookline. 'For all the sad and suffering people in the world.' Once-vivid leaves lay in sodden heaps around the tree trunks. Lake Glass looked cold in the fading afternoon light. It was hard to believe that a couple of months earlier power boats had dragged water skiers around it. Gusts had driven sailboats across it. Swimmers had churned through those murky waters, and fishermen had lounged on the banks. Soon the lake would freeze solid, the way chemical solutions used to crystallize in test tubes during her laboratory experiments at nursing school in Boston.

In her dream last week the lake was already frozen solid, and dotted with acres of human heads, mouths wide open in silent screams. Faceless men in army uniforms marched among them, halting to split some open with bloody axes. The ice was strewn like a packinghouse floor with brains and gore and shards of bone. Caroline woke up with her mouth wide open, her hair soaked with sweat. For a moment she was unable to move or to think. Gradually she realized she was in her own bed, in the cabin in New Hampshire she shared with Diana. She climbed out of bed and went into the next room. Her sons and Arnold, their black Labrador puppy, lay asleep, breathing noisily. Diana and her daughter, Sharon, were asleep upstairs. Caroline rubbed the floor by Jackie's and Jason's bunk beds with her big toe. Wood, not ice, and the boys' heads were evidently still attached to their necks.

The next day a little boy was wheeled into the emergency room, his head split up the back, his light brown hair matted with blood. His father had grabbed him by the feet and swung him against the edge of a stone fireplace for tracking mud on the rug. As Caroline stared at the wound, her mouth fell open and her limbs went rigid. Brenda, an Emergency Medical Technician name badge shaped like an ambulance pinned on her uniform pocket, was too busy snipping away the clotted hair to notice Caroline's paralysis. But Caroline finally understood that she had to do something about herself. It was one thing to awaken terrified in the night, but something else again not to be able to perform your job. She had two sons and no husband, had to keep bringing home paychecks. Even if what she really wanted was to lie swaying among the blue gill on the lake floor, seaweed entangling her hair, as a skin of thickening ice above shut off all contact with this repulsive world in which people tortured and maimed each other with pleasure.

A couple of weeks earlier, as she chopped kindling in the woods beside the cabin, she watched a man in waders, a red plaid wool shirt, and a green Homelite chain saw cap walk across the brown meadow to the lakeshore. He assembled a cairn of small stones. Then he dropped each stone into his waders – and lumbered into the lake. When his head disappeared, leaving the green cap floating on the gray water, Caroline first grasped what he was up to. It took her a few moments to shake off her admiration and race to the cabin to phone the rescue squad. For several hours she sat on the hill and watched scuba divers scour the lake floor, amphibious wasps in their sleek black wet suits and yellow tanks. The man had been clever: this was the deepest part of the lake. The rock ledges dropped off abruptly into hundreds of feet of frigid water. A gray state police boat circled slowly, trolling with grappling hooks, the snowcapped White Mountains as a backdrop. Along the shore sat relatives, eating Kentucky Fried Chicken beside beat-up Chevies. A child with Down's syndrome lurched back and forth along the shoreline howling mournfully. Leave him alone, Caroline kept thinking. For Christ's sake, leave him alone. She was sorry she'd told anyone in the first place.

Would it look like an accident, she wondered, if she revved her engine and shot across this parking lot, over the cliff and into the lake? Then she remembered Jackie and Jason. Tall, skinny, shy Jackie, his joints as loose as a jumping jack's, his voice starting to crack. And Jason, built like an armored truck, with a personality to match. Jackson was all wrapped up in his second wife and new babies. Jackie and Jason had no one but herself. She'd have to kill them too. But she'd put too much effort into keeping them alive all these years. It would feel as unnatural as picking green tomatoes each September before the frosts.

Before Jackie and Jason existed, after Arlene and prior to Jackson (she catalogued the phases of her life according to what person disrupted her days and dominated her dreams; just now she was in her Diana Period), she used to assure herself that if things got too dismal on the evening news, she could exit early. Lined up on the dresser in her Commonwealth Avenue apartment were pill bottles she'd stolen from the Mass General supply room, and she studied them thoughtfully whenever traffic through the ER seemed too grim. But the arrival of Jackie and Jason had sealed off that escape hatch. She still had the pills, but she kept them on a closet shelf now, out of their reach. She no longer consulted the bottles daily to determine whether to continue to participate in such a disappointing world.

She'd tried all the standard bromides: marriage and motherhood, apple pie and monogamy, bigamy and polygamy; consumerism, communism, feminism, and God; sex, work, alcohol, drugs, and true love. Each enchanted for a time, but ultimately failed to stave off the despair. The only bromide she hadn't tried was psychotherapy. Members of the helping professions were supposed to pull themselves up by their bootstraps. But she'd recently been forced to concede that she was barefoot. Which was why she was sitting in the Lake Glass Therapy Center parking lot, planning her suicide and being late for her first appointment.

She climbed out of her car and walked past a copper-colored Mercury with a broken taillight, bits of red glass crunching under her boots en route to the entrance to the large gray turreted structure that had served as a guest house when the town was a summer colony for Edwardian Boston.

'I have an appointment with Hannah Burke,' announced a young woman in a faded Boston Irish accent to Holly, the receptionist.

Hannah, standing behind Holly, looked up from her phone call. There was tightness around the woman's mouth, bafflement in her eyes. God, she's in so much pain, thought Hannah. But at least she's attractive, if I have to look at her for however many months. The woman looked familiar, but Hannah couldn't place her. Putting her hand over the receiver, she said, 'Hi, I'm Hannah. Be right with you.' She recalled the woman's voice from their conversation over this same phone last week – faint, polite, apologetic . . . and somewhat belligerent. After the request for an appointment, Hannah had remained silent, waiting for her own answer. She never knew why she said yes or no to someone. Probably an instinctive sense of whether she'd be able to work with the person. If you cut your losses before taking them on, you could skew your success rate and feel more capable. But this time she said yes. If the woman had bothered to track her down, probably there was a reason, since Hannah didn't believe in accidents.

Except ones like smashing the taillight of her new Mercury in the parking lot that morning. She inquired into the phone about the cost of replacing it. She'd backed into Jonathan's Scout while trying to quell the irritation she felt on days when a new client was scheduled. It was a strictly mechanical thing: her routine was being disrupted by an unpredictable element. But each time the irritation felt real and personal, and this morning she'd been feeling impatient with the timidity of this woman's voice on the phone. Was she going to be one of those women who asked to be stepped on, and then complained that there were boot prints on her back?

She glanced at Caroline. Tall and slim. A graying Afro. Nice tan. From skiing or from a trip south? A lady of leisure? We should all be so lucky. Don't be a martyr, she reminded herself. You like your work, apart from not liking to starve in the streets. Navy blue parka and Frye boots, faded jeans and a plaid flannel shirt. A tiny ivory sea gull on a gold chain at her throat. Those clothes are too youthful for her. She looks like a student, but she must be thirty-five. Where is she stuck? By what? Please not another wilted flower child. She'd already seen one that morning – Chip, a cross between Che Guevara and Peter Pan, a bearded, overalled refugee from the sixties who clutched his tattered idealism around himself like hobo rags. In a permanent funk that the world hadn't improved in the last fifteen years just because he wanted it to. He seemed to feel he couldn't get his own house in order until he'd tidied up everyone else's.

The woman was standing with her hands on her hips, her weight on one leg. An athlete. Probably a lesbian. I wonder how long it will take her to tell me. I wonder if she knows.

Hannah's eyes registered information like a mother hen scanning the skies for a hawk. This need of hers to know what was going on at all times was awesome in its voracity. But she'd been taken by surprise too often. Four years old and your mother dies of typhoid. Abandoned by your father at five. Nineteen, and your husband is killed in battle. Two children dead in their beds from carbon monoxide. No more surprises in her life if she could help it. Which she knew she couldn't.

Caroline felt impaled by the woman's blue eyes. Their expression wasn't unkind, just relentless. Not unlike her voice over the phone last week. A clipped British accent. This woman didn't mess around. She had a big reputation around town. Several nurses she and Diana worked with thought Hannah Burke was Wonder Woman. But Caroline had been expecting a mix of Mary Poppins and Aunt Jemima, not a gray-haired housewife in a polyester pants suit with a gaze like a police interrogator.

I can always split, Caroline assured herself. One lousy hour, and I walk out her door forever. Let her refer to herself just once as a healer, and I'm off like a shot. Last week at the Wellness Clinic, in the converted tannery at the top of town, a bearded man in a 'Love Me – I'm Italian' T-shirt had gazed at her with a meaningful smile: 'I hear you, Caroline. Thank you for sharing with me. I feel really good about this hour. How has it been for you?'

Please God, get me out of here, she'd prayed. And God had. Only to land her here with this woman with eyes like blue laser beams, who'd just lit her second cigarette, a thin brown brand. She was coughing like someone auditioning for a black lung commercial. So apparently she didn't have it all together either. Besides, she's short, Caroline reflected. I can handle her.

Alarm bells went off in her head. This was what she'd told herself when she first met Arlene, and Diana, and Jackson, and David Michael. That she needed to reassure herself indicated she was in some doubt. And in fact she hadn't 'handled' the others – each had disrupted her life in a major way.

Caroline followed Hannah down a shadowy corridor past several closed doors. On Hannah's door was a sign that read, 'Thank you for shutting up while I smoke.' Caroline plopped down on a brown tweed couch, glancing around at piles of books and papers on the desk and bookshelves. Photos of several towheaded children with missing teeth were pinned to a cork bulletin board along with a scramble of greeting cards, memos, children's crayon drawings, pictures torn from magazines. Objects hung on the white walls – a primitive painting of a creepy-looking little demon or something, an abstract black-and-white photograph. The ferns hanging in the windows, framed by elaborate Victorian molding and orange plaid curtains, looked limp and pale. If Bach stimulated plant growth, would witnessing misery all day stunt them? Caroline stifled her need to offer to take them home, set them in the sun, and feed them fish emulsion.

Hannah sat down in a padded metal desk chair and put her feet up on a rush footstool. Her hands hung off the chair arms, two fingers holding a brown cigarette. Caroline knew it would be inappropriate to describe what smoking was doing to her lungs, how smokers staggered into the ER coughing blood.

'So tell me why you're here.'

Presumably the same reason anyone's ever here, Caroline thought. The world's a mess, and I want to be dead. 'Well, I've been depressed a lot.' She wondered how to convey the atmosphere inside her head. The morning after Diana decided they should stop being lovers, she'd woken at dawn, alone in her double bed, and watched the mother-of-pearl sky, streaked with angry red. And thought about the infected flesh of a baby girl in the ER the previous day, whose father had been burning her with cigarettes. After cleaning and binding the angry wounds, she suggested other methods for getting the baby to stop crying, and the father stomped out, insulted. Caroline had spent several nights since dreaming of a vast ice field, with the severed limbs of little children frozen beneath the surface. Last week the ice field had been littered with shattered human heads. She was falling to pieces. She'd lost so much weight that bones were appearing she'd never known she possessed.

Wimp! she snapped at herself. War, starvation, nuclear

weapons, torture. Only an idiot wouldn't be depressed in a world like this. Whenever she or her brothers whined as kids, their mother would drive them down to the Salvation Army in Dorchester. As they watched the hungry and homeless wander in, she'd inquire, 'And you think *you've* got problems?'

Hannah drew on her cigarette and watched the struggle begin – between a new client's wish to trust her and maybe get some help; and fear of getting hurt, based on past experience. Caroline was sitting with her legs crossed and her arms folded across her chest. She wasn't about to let anybody in.

'What are your depressions like?' asked Hannah.

Caroline studied Hannah, who was exhaling a shroud of smoke. If you'd seen one depression, hadn't you seen them all? Was she paying good money just to educate this expert on depression? 'I have bad dreams. I wake up sweating in the middle of the night and can't get back to sleep. I have a grinding feeling in my stomach most of the time. I cry over dumb things. I snap at the people I care about. I lie face down on the floor and can't move. I feel like a pustule somebody ought to pop.' She gazed out the window opposite her, past the ailing ferns to the gray lake. Maybe that guy in waders was still walking around down there somewhere. The temptation to join him in his stroll was strong.

Yup, thought Hannah, sounds like the big D. 'Tell me about your family when you were a baby.'

Caroline frowned. Apparently she hadn't conveyed how awful she felt. How could you, anyway? Either someone knew what you were talking about, or she didn't. Evidently Hannah Burke didn't, or she wouldn't react so blandly. Family? If she wanted to wallow in all that Freudian shit, she'd have gone to a psychoanalyst. Her misery had to do with a life sentence in this hellhole of a world. She began talking in a monotone about being born during World War II, about her father's departure for the South Pacific and capture by the Japanese, about her mother's work for the Red Cross.

Hannah felt herself flip the switch that, on her good days, allowed her to listen without relating what was said to herself. She stripped away the details of Caroline's early experiences as though shucking corn, focusing on the ear, not the individual kernels. Upheaval, an absent father, a remote anxious overextended

15

mother, younger siblings whom Caroline tried to mother, a succession of melancholy maids. Not an unfamiliar story for Caroline's class and generation.

Caroline had dropped her stance of polite boredom and was struggling to remember what she'd been told about those three years when her father had been halfway around the world in battle and POW camps. '. . . my mother always says what a good baby I was during the day. I'd sit so still in the grass that bees would crawl around my fingers, inspecting the crumbs from my cookies but never stinging. She'd put me in a jump seat, suspended from a doorjamb, and I'd just hang there, holding my pink blanket and sucking my thumb. But in the middle of the night I'd scream bloody murder.'

Caroline paused to watch the woman watching her with those icy blue eyes. In her dark blue polyester pants suit, she looked fresh off the contract bridge circuit. Fuck this self-indulgent shit, Caroline thought. Millions of people starving out there, and I'm blathering to some foreigner because I feel a little down. What does my playpen behavior have to do with the resurgence of fascism in western Europe? This woman is too respectable. She wouldn't have a clue what I was talking about if I said, 'I don't like this world. I don't want to fit into it better. I just want to be more comfortable with not fitting in.'

'I'm a lesbian,' Caroline announced, sounding more certain than she felt, since things with Diana hadn't worked out any better than with Jackson or David Michael.

Hannah shrugged. Oh yes, she thought, and what did you have for breakfast? All of a sudden she recalled where she'd seen Caroline: on TV and in the local papers, lobbying for abortion rights at the state legislature a few years back. She'd been impressive standing on the capitol steps in Concord with the sun in her eyes, confronting the taunts of her opponents with humor and conviction.

'Would that be a problem for you?' Caroline asked. Surely someone so respectable would be appalled to be trapped every week with a living breathing queer.

Is it a problem for you, wondered Hannah, pursing her lips and shaking her head no. Homosexuals seemed to feel this revelation was a big deal. Probably it was for them. Probably it had gotten each of them rejected several times.

'How old do you feel?' asked Hannah. She'd just pictured Caroline as a frightened infant, tapping into the horrors loose in a world at war, and the anxieties loose in her fatherless household; being handed over to indifferent maids; trying to be still and quiet and 'good' so that somebody would care for her. Hannah remembered her own babies, gazing up from her swollen breasts with dark blue eyes, reaching out to clasp her little finger with tiny pink hands, smiling toothlessly, wanting only to adore and to be adored. The babies who weren't able to charm someone into falling in love with them – she saw them as adults all day long in this office. At least her own babies had never had that particular problem, however else she'd failed them later on.

Hannah lit another cigarette and switched off her emotions, glancing out the window beside the couch to the smashed taillight on her new Mercury. It felt like the time Simon knocked out Nigel's front baby tooth during a fight over a tricycle, and Hannah had had to accept that the world of disintegration had claimed her perfect little bundle. 'Maintenance,' her husband, Arthur, often insisted. 'Life is nothing but maintenance.' Jonathan's Scout had escaped without a scratch. An unfamiliar red Subaru station wagon with a 'Club Sandwiches Not Seals' bumper sticker sat beside her Mercury.

Caroline was gazing at Hannah, disconcerted. Horror at her perversion, yes. Outrage, fear, curiosity. But not indifference. She tried to consider her age. 'I feel like a seventeen-year-old, trapped in a decaying thirty-five-year-old body.'

Hannah studied Caroline, who clutched upper arms with opposite hands. Quiet, still, and good. Witty and self-effacing. Obedient and entertaining. These would be her ploys. The aggression and rage had gone underground, where they could blast a hole to China.

'Try eleven, going on twelve.' She knew she couldn't get away with telling Caroline she was probably eighteen months old emotionally. Though not on the capitol steps in Concord. There she'd been every bit of thirty. These two aspects cohabited. The trick was to introduce them to each other.

Caroline frowned. Eleven? For this I'm paying thirty-five dollars an hour? Where does this bridge-playing chick get off? These goddam suburban housewives with their boring little split-level lives. Caroline knew all about that scene – the sailing yachts on the lake, the cocktail party flirtations, the attention devoted to matching flower arrangements to place mats, the play groups and car pool and coffee klatsches. She'd done that trip with Jackson in Newton for eight years. And she'd ended up immobile, face down on the plush rose-colored living-room carpet, agonizing over the corruption of such a life when American tanks were rolling through Cambodian jungles. Jackie and Jason pulled her hair, poked Tinker Toys in her ears, and rode horsey on her back, but she was too busy picturing American helicopters napalming Vietnamese children to respond to her own.

'Glad you came?' asked Hannah with a smile. She had to establish who was running this show if the show was to happen at all. On the capitol steps Caroline could be in charge, but in this office Hannah had to be. Someone about to explore a swamp needed to know her scout had a general idea where the alligators hid out, or she'd be too terrified even to begin.

Hannah realized she had to get either a smile or a yes pretty soon, or Caroline wouldn't return. Usually she didn't care if they returned, but she was challenged by Caroline's timid truculence. It reminded her of her own stance at the same age, after the children had died, when she'd shake her fist at the universe and defy it to yield up some meaning. But she now knew that it simply wasn't necessary to live with Caroline's current level of misery.

'Your mother tells you you cried a lot in the night?'

'Yes.' This was the most incoherent conversation Caroline had ever had. How could it help her feel better if she couldn't even follow it?

'You do realize that's just her version? Maybe you cried a few times, like all babies, and it seemed like all the time because she was so busy and tired and lonely and scared.' She remembered those years when her own house was crammed with babies as one long night full of children's nightmares, tears, and vomit.

Hannah watched Caroline's strained face register the struggle to identify the truth about her past. But there wasn't any such thing – only Caroline's own personal truth, shared by no one, but valid for her nonetheless.

It suddenly sounded to Caroline as though Hannah was on her side. Unnerving, because they had nothing in common. Caroline couldn't even play bridge.

'Why did you pick me?' asked Hannah.

'You're about the only shrink in town I don't already know. And most of the others are in worse shape than I am.'

Smiling faintly, Hannah glanced at the clock on her desk. 'So how do you feel about our working together?'

'How do you?' Caroline certainly wasn't going to express interest first. One of her earliest memories was of Maureen, the orange-haired maid from Galway, hissing at her in her crib, 'I know what you want and you can't have it!' Caroline couldn't recall what she'd wanted, but she'd learned since that you don't show what you want, because then you deprive others of the satisfaction of denying it to you. You had no business wanting anything anyway if you had food on the table and a roof over your head, when half the world lacked even that.

'I feel very comfortable with you,' said Hannah.

Caroline looked up. Slowly she uncrossed her legs and arms, and rested her arms by her sides on the tweed couch. 'Well, I guess I'd better think it over and give you a call.'

'Fine.' Hannah suppressed a smile. She'd just gotten her yes from Caroline's body, which was now sprawled on the couch in a posture that said, 'All right, I'll try, but it isn't going to help.'

Hannah replied silently, Yes, it will too. You just don't know it yet.

Driving out of the parking lot, Caroline shoved a cassette from the hospital library on new developments in burn therapy into her tape deck. The sunset, blotches of scarlet and purple, reflected off Lake Glass as though off a mirror, which was where the lake had gotten its name, back in the eighteenth century from trappers and loggers. Tourists marveled over these sunsets, but Caroline had to squint even to look at one. Because the sky looked the way her brain felt – bruised and mangled, a cut of raw beef pounded flat by a cubing hammer. She'd felt like this a lot. But of course there had been a lot to feel bad about – Selma and Watts, Kent State and Watergate.

Too late, she realized she'd run the stop sign at the entrance to the lake road. A driver crossing the intersection had thrown on his brakes and was blaring his horn. Jesus, one way or another she was going to kill herself off.

This therapy stuff was a big waste of time, Caroline decided as she headed home, south down the lakeshore. She was a nurse, she could diagnose her own malaise: she inhabited an insane asylum called earth. Do something about that, and she'd be fine. But what could anybody do about this ghastly world? She, her parents, most of her friends had spent their lifetime trying to stanch the hemorrhages of misery from the body politic. But wars still raged, tyrants ruled, and torture flourished.

She pulled into the driveway of the two-story log cabin, which had been built from a kit of giant Lincoln Logs by Diana and her ex-husband, Mike, during their back-to-the-land days. It fit snugly into the contours of the hillside so that both stories were at ground level with views along one side of the lake and mountains. Mike had simply walked out one day five years ago, announcing that he had to find himself. He followed his star to Ann Arbor, where he now ran a men's clothing store.

The sunset was bathing the honey locusts out front in shades of purple. The swollen clouds behind the curly branches reminded Caroline of those Jonestown corpses on the news last night, bloated on poison grape Kool-Aid. This was the worst time of day for auto accidents and domestic violence. The ER was chaos from sunset through twilight.

Climbing the steps, she stopped abruptly. On the landing was a ragged bundle. An infanticide? Two weeks of back newspapers? She tried to examine it without touching it. A huge bird. She turned it over with the toe of her boot. A Canadian goose, its white breast brown with caked blood from a bullet wound. She drew a sharp breath. Her relationship to nature had always been problematic. A diseased raccoon once crawled out of these woods to expire at her feet. One afternoon she picked up a puppy staggering alongside the road and drove it to the vet, who informed her it was a rabid fox. Snakes swallowed toads nearby as she lounged in the grass in summer. Owls swooped down from trees onto scurrying field mice when she snowshoed in winter. In spring wild cats pounced on shrieking fledglings beneath her open windows. She tried not to take it personally.

Removing a glove, she placed her hand on the feathers. The flesh was cold. She picked it up by a wing and heaved it to the ground, too tired to deal with it in the twilight. As she wiped her boots on the doormat, Diana called for her to come in.

'Did you know there's a dead goose on the doorstep?'

Diana looked up from the couch, where she sat knitting a dark green turtleneck sweater for Sharon. Still wearing her white uniform pants and top, she looked exhausted and rumpled. Her curly red hair was even more scrambled than usual, and there were dark circles under her green eyes. Good. Maybe she was having trouble sleeping alone too.

'Honestly,' Caroline told her, standing in the doorway, hand resting against the jamb.

'How come?' Diana's hands subsided into her lap.

'You've got me. It's got a bullet hole in its chest. I guess it just fell out of the sky.'

'How unpleasant. What do you think it means?'

'Don't fly too low over a hunter,' said Caroline.

Diana smiled. 'Come in. Sit down. Do you want some wine?'

Caroline hesitated, wondering if she should go downstairs to her own apartment. It was hard to figure out what was okay between them these days. They'd gone from being best friends in nursing school, to being pen pals while serving as the little women for big men, to being roommates, to being live-in lovers, to being – what? The past weeks had felt like living on the San Andreas Fault. One thing was certain: Working together all day and sleeping together all night had been too much togetherness. Especially for two nurses. They fought constantly over who got to bring the other coffee in bed, who got to baby-sit the kids during parties, who got to tend a vomiting child in the night. Joan of Arc would have had to drive them both away to die on her own hard-won pyre. Jesus Christ would have found Himself on Golgotha without a cross; one would have taken His place while the other stitched His wounds.

Their relationship wasn't working, they finally concluded, because each had an equivalent need to be needed. In relationships with men, each had been exploited to her heart's content. But with each other life was a constant struggle to outnurture. The cabin filled up with their greeting cards. Banks of flowers were always dying on the tables. Each put on ten pounds from the candies and pastries the other brought home, which were dutifully devoured to please the donor. During lovemaking each would wait for the other to climax first, until both lost interest altogether. They fought over who got the most burnt toast, or the lukewarm

21

second shower. They would have fought to be the last off the *Titanic*, or the first off Noah's Ark. Eventually they were compelled to address the issue of what to do about two people in whom thoughtfulness had become a disease. Diana felt the cure involved learning to do without doing things for each other, including holding each other through the night.

'So how did it go?' asked Diana, handing her a glass of white wine.

'She's a nice woman, but I'm not going back.'

Diana hugged her with one arm. 'I've never seen you so decisive. See what a little therapy can do?'

They stood with their arms around each other, looking out the picture window past the locust trees to the mountain range beyond the lake. It undulated to resemble a reclining female torso. In the old days merely looking at it had triggered bouts of lovemaking on the beige shag carpet. Caroline rested her chin atop Diana's head. Hard to believe someone so small could trigger such overwhelming feelings. But of course thousands had gone to their deaths for Napoleon. She found herself studying Diana's large breasts, which strained against the fabric of her uniform top. Off limits now. How were you supposed to make that switch from one day to the next?

'You know,' said Caroline, 'I like celibacy fine. The only part I don't like is not having any sex.'

Diana laughed. She'd said she hoped Caroline would bear with her. Maybe she'd get over it. And maybe she wouldn't. In the meantime, they were to fall back on their friendship of many years, the safety net under a high-wire act. Caroline had replied, 'Yes, of course we can still be friends. Not very good friends, but friends.'

'What's she like?' asked Diana, pulling away and walking to the couch.

'Who?' Caroline restrained her wish to dump her wine on Diana's curly red head.

'Hannah Burke.'

'Smart. Nice. But suburban.' Caroline studied the tapestry above the couch, which she'd woven for Diana several years earlier. The Garden of Eden, both people women, both smiling and eating apples.

'What does that mean?'

'Going for safety and comfort. No political analysis. Protecting herself from reality.' Caroline plopped down beside Diana, sloshing wine onto her own hand.

'Well, you've always insisted on staring down the horrors. Sometimes I wish you'd just poke out your eyes and have some fun.'

Diana insisted Caroline took pleasure in her depressions, regarded them as evidence of superior perception. Caroline couldn't entirely deny this. 'With you as my Seeing Eye person?' asked Caroline, blotting the spilled wine on her jeans.

'Right.'

'As you know, I'd rather be your Seeing Eye person.'

'I think we've been over this before,' said Diana. Her grin looked like the grimace of a patient receiving an injection.

'Ad nauseam. Oh yeah, I came out to her.'

'That was fast. How did she react?'

'She didn't seem particularly interested.'

'How disappointing.'

'Yeah. It was.'

Diana stood up. 'Want some soup?'

'No you don't. You're not feeding me.'

'It was worth a try.' She sat back down and reached for her knitting.

Caroline shrugged off her dark blue parka, then walked on her knees past Diana's spinning wheel, a relic from the grueling days with Mike when she raised sheep and processed her own wool. Caroline turned on the Sony to find Walter Cronkite tracing the life of Jim Jones. His flock called him Dad. As she crawled back to the sofa, she learned that the main industry in his Indiana hometown was casket-making.

'What I can't figure out,' said Caroline, sinking back into the sofa as a frazzled denture wearer disclosed her most embarrassing moment, 'is why it turned out so badly when Jones apparently meant so well.'

'It's like Arnold,' said Diana, scratching her own back with a knitting needle. Arnold, the new puppy, was having difficulty grasping toilet training. 'His intention exceeded his aim.'

Smiling, Caroline gave Diana a quick kiss to one side of her mouth and headed for the stairs, leaving Diana, hands frozen in midstitch, looking taken aback by the abruptness of the departure. But if she stayed, Caroline knew her hand would stray over to one of Diana's breasts.

Caroline turned on the lamp on her bedside table and glanced around the room. Her loom stood in the corner next to a picture window that looked down to Lake Glass. Exterior walls of logs and chinking, interior walls of pine paneling. These downstairs rooms were supposed to house the six children Diana and Mike had planned on. Diana and Caroline knocked down a couple of walls and turned them into an apartment for Caroline, Jackie, and Jason.

Caroline pulled her Lanz nightgown out of her pine chest, studying the framed collage of obscene French postcards Diana had done for her, which hung on the pine paneling above the chest. Her cheery demeanor was slipping like an ill-fitting toupee. Miss Congeniality offstage. It was a strain to be cooperative in enterprises to which she couldn't see the point, like therapy and celibacy. But her role in life was to help others feel better. Her parents used to come to the dinner table exhausted from their welfare work, and she'd tell every new joke she could think of, whatever her own prior mood. It had been worth it to watch them smile reluctantly, then laugh. As satisfying as watching the color return to patients' faces as you resuscitated them.

Her apartment was uncharacteristically silent because Arnold, Jackie, and Jason were sleeping over at friends' houses. All she could hear was the hum of the refrigerator and Diana running a bath upstairs. She pictured Diana in the tub, head back, eyes closed, faint smile on her lips. The water rising slowly over her pale freckled skin, which was smooth as butter to the touch. They used to lie in the bath together, the head and back of one on the other's chest and abdomen. She removed the gold chain with the ivory sea gull from around her neck. One afternoon last spring she and Diana sat in the thick new grass holding hands and watching hundreds of sea gulls descend on a neighboring farmer's newly manured field to feast on worms and insects. Diana and she defined the different groupings as rival sororities and laughed themselves sick inventing stories about their machinations. The next day Diana came home from town with the ivory gull.

As she hung up her plaid shirt, Caroline looked across her closet shelf to the cluster of pill bottles in the back corner. She shoved a pile of sweaters Diana had knit for her in front of them.

Walking into the dark living room, she stumbled over a hockey stick and stubbed her toe on the gateleg of the dining table. She didn't need a calendar; she knew what time of year it was by which sports equipment she tripped over in her living room. Last month it was soccer balls and cleats. Currently she was lacerating herself on skate blades. Before long she'd be dodging baseball bats and catchers' masks. Unhooking the boys' video game, she moved the TV into her bedroom. She piled up pillows and crawled under the huge gold and brown afghan spread Diana had knit for her. As she sipped her coffee, she watched a movie about two career girls on the make in New York City. She realized she'd seen it before. The good-looking one got Jimmy Stewart and the other one got promoted to editor. If only once the girls would get each other. But probably that was asking too much of Twentieth Century–Fox. Didn't David Michael once say they were owned by a conglomerate that also marketed infant formula? She switched channels to a documentary on drought in the sub-Sahara. Her brother Howard was in Chad at that very moment with an international relief agency. Howard had been a scrawny little boy. It made sense he'd grow up to be a famine fighter. She looked at the little children with their swollen bellies and fly-coated lips and eyes for as long as she could stand it. Then she turned off the TV and fell asleep.

She dreamed she was lying in a putrid swamp surrounded by poisonous snakes, her eyes and lips covered with insects that were half bee and half leech. They clung to her and stung continuously. Her face throbbed and burned. Jim Jones appeared through the tangled vines and matted trees in his red robe and sunglasses. He carried a syringe and a pitcher of grape Kool-Aid. He injected her as she struggled to escape. Hannah Burke appeared. She dismissed Jones. Then she methodically plucked the insects from Caroline's face.

Caroline sat up, flesh burning, hair soaked with sweat. The sheets were tangled and damp. The clock read 3.00 a.m. She took several deep breaths, determined not to run upstairs to Diana. She got up and brewed chamomile tea. Sipping it in bed, she itemized the ways she'd failed that week – screaming at the boys for pasting autumn leaves all over their clothes as camouflage in their war games; throwing the blender at Arnold for climbing on the dinner table and running off with the pork roast; losing her car keys so Diana couldn't get her car out to have dinner with Suzanne, the new young nurse on the children's ward who gazed at Diana with mindless adoration. Caroline was not a nice person. She was selfish, impatient, and jealous. She was a bad mother, a worse friend, and a hopeless lover.

Shivering, she turned on her electric blanket. She and Diana had generated so much warmth together that they never needed the blanket. But these last weeks it had been on nonstop.

The house was still without the mumbling, sighing, and tossing of the sleeping boys, the growling and twitching of the dreaming puppy. Before long they'd be gone for good. Jackie and Jason, Diana, they'd vanish, just like Arlene and Jackson and David Michael, leaving her here alone night after night, as snow piled up outside the windows and buried her in an icy cocoon. Her stomach clenched. But what had she ever been if not alone? She must have known that even as a baby. Probably that was why she'd screamed at night. Since then she'd come together with people for illusory moments of companionship, only to watch them fade away like cinema images as the house lights go on.

The sky outside her window was black, but she was awake for good. She got up, put on her down bathrobe and slippers, and sat at the loom in the corner, on which she was weaving place mats in shades of brown and black. Her napkins, place mats, and tablecloths always sold best, ever since she'd started weaving in Jackson's house in Newton. She'd done so many she was getting sick of them, but she couldn't think what to weave instead. She could weave at night only when the boys were away because the thud of the beater woke them up. But weaving was the only thing that could stave off her despair. When her feet and hands finally found their hypnotic rhythm, she had no time or attention for her own misery. She'd always woven in stealth, like someone sneaking away to perform unclean acts, because pursuing a private pleasure seemed irresponsible in a world full of collective agony.

She thought about those bizarre clinging, stinging insects in her dream. Hannah Burke had helped her remove them. But it was just a dream. Was there really any point to another appointment? What could Hannah do about the human condition? You just had to grit your teeth and make the best of it. Or bow out.

She thought about the pill bottles behind her sweaters. Out of sight maybe, but not out of mind.

Grimly she pedaled her loom and threw the shuttle back and forth through the warp.

Two

Hannah drove through town, across the falls, past the renovated factories which now housed specialty shops, restaurants, a health club, condominiums, offices. Lake Glass had evolved as an outpost for fur traders and loggers. Transport down the lake proved inefficient, so factories were set up to process the furs and timber in situ – a tannery, a shoe factory, a furniture factory. When the factories were lured south by cheaper labor, the town took on new life as a summer resort for the wealthy of Boston, drawn north by the remoteness and beauty of the lake. When Hannah and Arthur arrived thirty-five years earlier, the town was sleepy and dumpy, full of dilapidated factories and deserted summer cottages. After London it felt to Hannah like exile to Patagonia. In its current incarnation, the town hosted tourists and skiers, and had also acquired a couple of electronics firms. A small private college had grown into a university. The streets were crawling with well-dressed strangers; the restaurants were crammed with exotic delicacies – felafel and knishes, burritos and sushi. In some ways Hannah preferred the dear dead Patagonia days.

Heading north through the ranch houses of the electronics executives, Hannah watched the sky above the lake perform its time-lapse pyrotechnics. The colors faded in and out so slowly that each configuration seemed permanent. But if she pulled over for a nap, she'd wake up to pitch black. Sunsets annoyed her. She'd driven this road twice a day for twenty years, ever since Mona and Nigel died. After three thousand hours of watching sunsets, she'd discovered they were shell games. All that turmoil, and in the end nothing was left. Much ado about nothing.

As she turned onto the lake road, she remembered her left rear blinker was bashed in. What was that new client's name? Why did she have such a hard time with names when she could keep a couple of dozen life histories straight at once? At a staff party recently, as she began to introduce Arthur to Mary Beth, the new young counselor at the office, she couldn't remember Arthur's name. He studied her with amazement. She'd only known him for thirty-eight years.

Caroline, it was. Yes. She tried to imagine being an infant arriving as war engulfed the globe. If you couldn't delight your parents with your appearance, at least it could be your fault that Daddy was going away, that Mummy was frantic. Ever after you'd carry around a vague sense of responsibility for disaster. If you couldn't locate ready-made disasters to feel guilty about, you'd concoct your own.

Her son Simon was in the same boat. Colin, his father, left to fight in Belgium before Simon was one, and never returned. Simon had been a frail, anxious little boy, and was now a tyrannical adult, who ran his Federal Housing Agency office like a penitentiary. The flower children. An entire generation sensitized as infants to loss and terror, as adults acting out their indignation in the streets on behalf of the dispossessed, who were actually themselves. You didn't have to be run over by a tank to be harmed by a war.

Glancing at the savage sunset, Hannah recalled the sunset she'd watched with Arthur from Hampstead Heath, not long before Caroline's father was sweating it out in the South Pacific. London, steeped in blood red, spread out below them to the Thames. Arthur was with the U.S. Department of War, negotiating delivery of equipment to replace what Britain had left behind at Dunkirk. She'd met him several weeks earlier at a diplomatic reception her grandmother had dragged her to, to cheer her up in her plight as war widow. What she noticed first were his straight white teeth, which gave him away as an American even if his uniform hadn't. His flat accent was also American, though she couldn't then identify it as a New England one.

She and Arthur sat on the grass on a hill in the Heath, wrapped in his olive army overcoat, greasy newspapers from fish and chips rustling in the autumn gusts. Then it was dark, and the Luftwaffe arrived to dump its load of fireworks. They watched in grim silence as sections of London and assorted Londoners were blown to bits and consumed in flames. Then they walked hand in hand past the deserted fun fair, down through the Vale of Health, feet scuffling among clumps of damp leaves. She wore Arthur's overcoat with the sleeves turned up, a bit like Charlie Chaplin.

'People came out here from London in the fourteenth century to escape the Black Death,' she announced, to fulfill her grandmother's instructions to 'show Arthur London.' His American manners were so different from Colin's East End ones. He asked her opinions and waited for replies.

'I guess things don't change much from century to century.'

'I suppose not.' She was wrestling with herself over whether or not to 'give in.' It was a very short wrestle indeed. Colin was rotting in a grave along the Meuse. Her grandmother was in Somerset with Simon. Most of London huddled in underground stations. She didn't know then that Arthur had a wife in America. And neither was certain of surviving to see another day in which to regret the events of that night. In a world gone mad, the sensation of flesh on flesh, sweaty and insistently alive, was the only thing that made sense.

When they reached her grandmother's brick house at the edge of the Heath, with deserted houses on all sides, Arthur asked, 'How come you didn't clear out with the rest of your neighbors?'

She looked at him, tall and solid in his American uniform. He would take care of her, as her father and Colin in their British uniforms had not. 'Because I was hoping if I stuck around,' she replied, lowering her eyes, 'you might take me to bed.'

His soft brown eyes looked alarmed, but a wry smile spread across his face as he murmured, 'Brave woman.'

They went inside, pulled down the blackout shades, and made love by candlelight, in the mahogany Victorian sleigh bed from her girlhood.

She pulled her Mercury into the driveway. Walking up to the remodeled yellow Victorian summer house, she wondered for the hundredth time if she and Arthur ought to move to something smaller. When Simon and Joanna finally got places of their own in town, she and Arthur had closed off half the rooms to save heat. No point in paying taxes now on bedrooms and a playroom for children who no longer existed. But there were memories connected with the place. The hidden meadow enclosed by birches where Nigel had been conceived one hot May afternoon. The huge twisted cedars along the cliff above the lake, which the children planted as seedlings. The rock caves where the children hid to smoke cigarettes stolen from her pocketbook. The marsh where they staged roiling mud fights. Memories and some photos were about all she had left of Mona and Nigel. She and Arthur used to talk of moving so as not to be reminded constantly of that horrible night. But she was reminded constantly in any case. And she eventually concluded that the horrors were offset by the memories. So here she and Arthur remained, half their house empty and unused, the ghost limb of an amputee.

Arthur took her martini from the refrigerator freezer as she walked in and handed it to her after she hung up her London Fog. 'How was your day?'

'Fine, thanks.' She relaxed into his embrace. It was pleasant to find she still got hugged, even if her answer to his inevitable question wasn't 'terrible.' As they sat down on the brown leather couch in the cathedral-ceilinged living room to watch the sunset's finale, she lit a cigarette with matches from Ron's Steakhouse in Kansas City. She inspected the matchbook, which featured a bull's head with a wide smile and a winking eye. A charming young colleague had used it to light her cigarette at dinner during a conference last month, just before asking her to sleep with him. She'd been surprised and flattered. She didn't often affect young men who weren't her clients like that anymore, now that she was into the heavy maintenance decades, with teeth, eyes, lungs, and stomach all giving faint warnings of eventual collapse.

She gave the invitation a moment of serious consideration, based on the three martinis she'd just drunk. Then she pulled herself together and replied, 'If my life were different, Charles, I'd say yes in a minute. But since it's not, please accept my thanks and my sincere regrets.' If she wanted to complicate her life, there were easier ways than an affair with a married man from Toledo.

'And please give my best to your parents?' added Charles.

'Exactly.' Hannah smiled and toyed with her cigarette in the ashtray.

'Don't say I never asked you.'

'I won't, Charles.'

'I thought you were quitting,' said Arthur as she inhaled deeply on her cigarette.

'I probably was. I quit all the time.'

'I've noticed.'

'I had a new client today whose father was a Japanese POW. It got me to thinking on the way home about that night on the Heath.'

Arthur smiled. Hannah loved his wry smile, the wrinkles around his eyes that got more indelible with each passing decade. More wrinkles, less hair. Otherwise he was pretty much the same as all those years ago on the Heath, when she first felt such passion for him. He still had all his Ipana-white American teeth. But when she was younger – and dumber – she sometimes regarded his reliability as boring. Excitement in those bad old days consisted of chasing men at parties in other people's living rooms, men whom she treated as cavalierly as Colin and her father had her. But when Mona and Nigel died, it was Arthur's steadiness that got her through – and that was when she began to regard staying power as a virtue, and one Arthur had developed slowly and painfully in his private struggle to come to terms with having left behind one family in order to form a second with her.

'One thing does lead to another.' He sipped his gin.

'Did you think about consequences?'

'Are you kidding? With bombs falling all around me? You'd have to be crazy to turn down a gorgeous woman groping in your greatcoat at a time like that.' He caressed her cheek with the back of his hand.

'Me groping?'

'Well, it certainly wasn't my idea. After all, I was a married man.' He draped his arm across her shoulders.

'You didn't bother to tell me.'

'Would it have made any difference?'

'Probably,' she replied primly.

He laughed. 'Tell me about it. Well, it's worked out okay, I'd say. You don't even talk too funny anymore. If only you'd get rid of some of these plants. It's like living in an oxygen tent.' He nodded toward the greenhouse window, beyond which the mauve sunset was losing its struggle against the night.

'So what do you think is going to go on in here?' asked Hannah, sitting back in her metal desk chair and lighting a brown cigarette. Caroline was wearing a rumpled white uniform and white shoes. Evidently she was a nurse. Or a Good Humor man. She looked sallow, with dark circles under her eyes, as though her mascara had run, only she wasn't wearing any. Hannah hadn't been surprised to hear her voice over the phone again. But Caroline had sounded both surprised and reluctant. Hannah remembered early in her own training analysis insisting to Maggie that she was absolutely fine and was in Maggie's office only to earn her degree. Maggie's mouth twitched, but she managed not to smile.

'I don't know,' replied Caroline. 'I assume you've got techniques and stuff.' Please don't make me be a chair or beat a pillow, she thought, recalling accounts from Jenny, with whom she played poker every week, who was an acolyte for the Growth Movement. I don't want to own my wild child or explore my beingness. I just want to wake up not wishing I were dead.

'No, we're just going to have an extended conversation.' She watched Caroline rub the bridge of her nose with thumb and forefinger. Then Caroline gave a wan smile. A good omen. Usually clients took their miseries so seriously that you couldn't get a smile out of them for weeks. 'What's the most painful thing that's happened to you lately?'

Caroline sighed. How could she choose? Celibacy? A dead goose on her doorstep? Norman Rockwell's death? 'The Jonestown thing, I guess.'

'Why is that so painful for you?'

'Well, I mean, aren't nine hundred cyanide-soaked corpses rotting in the jungle painful for *you*?'

'It's not too pleasant. But I'm not one of them. And I don't have to think about them for very long unless I choose to. And I don't. So why do you?' She considered the symbolism and gave a nod of respect to Caroline's unconscious.

Caroline looked with weariness at Hannah in her red plaid Pendleton skirt and sweater. It was a mistake to have come back. She'd thought that dream was a message from her unconscious, but clearly her unconscious was as out to lunch as usual. Hannah was hopeless. She lacked a political analysis. You didn't need one to play bridge. 'It tears me up, the gap between what they were trying to do and how it all turned out.' Jones as a young man, with all his concern for the downtrodden, sounded not unlike herself, her parents, her classmates at nursing school, her colleagues at the People's Free Clinic and the abortion referral service and the ER. The same wish to serve and to save. What had gone wrong? What always went wrong?

'Ah.'

'Ah what?'

'Did you hear what you just said?' asked Hannah. She tapped her cigarette into a hollow stone Nigel had given her years ago. He found it on the beach one afternoon. 'Mommy, come look at the gray grapefruit,' he called. Splitting open this unlikely gemstone with a hammer and chisel, he discovered a hollow interior studded with quartz crystals and lined with mica, which flashed in the sun like fish scales.

'Yes.'

'Can you apply it to *your* life?' Hannah was seeing that infant, trying so hard to please and failing so consistently. A normal baby didn't just hang in a jump seat. Nigel practically tore the doorjambs down, swinging like a parachutist in a windstorm. During her internship at the state hospital, she tried to work with a teenage girl who did nothing but sit in a corner with her knees to her chest, her sweat shirt drawn up over her head and down around her ankles. The girl seemed to feel if she could remain perfectly still and silent, she'd offend no one and stay safe.

'What?' Screwing up her face, Caroline studied the pale, limp asparagus fern in the window. It was criminal to treat your plants like that. She'd bring Hannah some Miracle-Gro.

'What about in your personal life? What was the most painful thing at home this week?'

Caroline twitched. This was going exactly nowhere. How could this British housewife understand American genocide?

'Think,' suggested Hannah. These failed revolutionaries sometimes pissed her off, projecting their inner state onto the world and then insisting it constituted objective reality. Chippie the Hippie had been in that morning moaning about lack of world peace. She'd asked if it wasn't hypocritical to demand world peace when you hadn't even achieved personal peace. 'There must have been something.'

They sat in silence as Caroline, ankle resting on opposite knee, traced the red rubber tread on one white shoe with her finger.

Hannah shifted her gaze out the window to the parking lot. Jonathan walked by, fluffy snowflakes falling on his gray Afro, which looked like a dandelion gone to seed. He climbed in his Scout and drove off. Hannah struggled not to smile at his new bumper sticker, which read 'Eat More Lamb. 50,000 Coyotes

Can't be Wrong.' A part-time farmer, he was also cofounder and codirector, along with herself, of the Lake Glass Therapy Center. They'd gravitated toward each other in graduate school because they were older than their classmates, and they'd worked together ever since, despite times when they irritated the hell out of each other.

The silence was oppressive. Caroline cast around for something to placate Hannah. 'My sons, Jackie and Jason, got into a fight and broke their video game.'

'Why was that painful?'

'Because it was brand-new.'

'So get it fixed.' Any minute now Caroline was going to shoot off into some complicated evasion, a startled quail catching sight of a hunter. 'What else?' Caroline was right to be scared. Some of the things she'd have to face about herself would be painful.

Caroline pinched the bridge of her nose. 'Nothing else.'

'You've had a pleasant week?'

'I guess so.'

'Then why are you here? You must have better ways to spend your money?'

'Yeah, actually I've been saving up to build a sauna . . . '

Here came the digression. Hannah raised her eyebrows ironically to stave it off. The stronger the defenses, the more devastating the wounds underneath, she reminded herself to reclaim patience.

Caroline observed the raised eyebrows and fell silent, aware that she wasn't trying. She glanced out the window to the lake. Snowflakes the size of goosedown were swirling around, as though Jackie and Jason were having a pillow fight in the yard. Eventually she began to talk in a low voice: 'Diana, my lover, or my ex-lover, left out a letter she was writing that said I was difficult to live with because I was a taker.' She fiddled with the ivory gull at her throat.

Stubbing out her cigarette, Hannah suppressed a smile at the ease with which Caroline acknowledged reading someone else's mail. She was beginning to like this woman. Once she got through the bullshit, she was alarmingly straightforward. Hannah made a mental note of the ex-lover bit. Her sex life was messed up. That was enough to depress anyone. 'You don't see yourself as a taker?'

'I'm a nurse, for God's sake. A mother. Anyhow, last month Diana complained I was cloying because I did things for her all the time.' She ran her hand distractedly through her Afro.

'How *do* you see yourself?'

'Huh?'

'List some adjectives that describe you. Tell me what you're like.' Hannah was pleased they'd gotten to the heart of the matter so quickly: Caroline didn't know who she was.

Caroline sat silent. Jackson said she was too intense. Howard insisted she was cruel when they were kids because she lynched his teddy bear and let the air out of his bicycle tires so he couldn't follow her. Of course he also said the worst day of his life was when he realized he couldn't marry her. Cloying. A taker. Which was she?

'Does it occur to you that Diana sees you as a taker because she's afraid she is herself? Otherwise, why would it be an issue for her?'

Diana a taker? Wrong. Diana sent her friends solstice cards, went to the mall to hand out extra vegetables from the garden, knitted ski caps for the Special Olympics, put stranded tourists in her spare room during foliage season. Then she remembered Diana's mother, a shrill woman in pink plastic rollers and thin white socks, who was always phoning from Poughkeepsie to complain that Diana was an ingrate. Diana laughed sourly after each conversation, but maybe she was secretly worried her mother was right.

'Do you see the link?' asked Hannah.

'What link?'

'Between your reaction to the Jonestown thing and to Diana's letter?'

Caroline frowned. 'What?' Where was this woman coming from? Nothing she said made sense.

'Think about it. Your assignment for next week is to make a list of adjectives that describe you.'

'My assignment?' She didn't realize she'd indicated an interest in returning. 'How long does this usually take?'

'Does what?'

'Therapy.'

'If I can't get somebody back on her feet in a couple of months, I ought to be in another profession. I don't want my clients to become my breadline.' Caroline probably wouldn't even try if she knew how long it sometimes took to unravel patterns woven over thirty-five years.

Caroline looked at her. Everyone she knew had been in therapy for eight years. Hell, she could stand anything for two months. Even this nonsense. Then she could tell Jenny she'd tried and it hadn't helped. There were always those pills in her closet.

'So you're a nurse,' said Hannah, as Caroline wrote a check. 'Where do you work?'

'In the emergency room at Lloyd Harris. It's my lunch hour.'

Hannah nodded. 'Just like home, huh?' She stretched her feet out on the rush footstool.

Caroline looked up. 'What is?'

'It sounds as though you're accustomed to being surrounded with crisis.'

'It does?'

'That's how it sounds to me.'

'No, I had a very happy childhood.' Caroline stood up, handed Hannah the check, and took the appointment card Hannah held out to her.

'Good. I'm glad.' Folding the check in half, Hannah felt Maggie's smile tug at the corners of her mouth.

As Caroline walked out, Hannah stood up, stretched, and thought about Maggie, a fierce old lady with a sharp brain and an even sharper tongue. She had trained at the William Alanson White Institute in New York and hung out with all the famous Sullivanians, prior to retreating to her summer house on Lake Glass after the death of her husband. Where she went into a funk for several years, from which her own therapeutic skills couldn't rescue her, emerging eventually with some new techniques hammered out in the forge of her own private hell. Upon her return to the land of the living, she split her time in New Hampshire between private practice and teaching at the university in town, where she helped the clinical psychology department develop its Ph.D. program, from which Hannah was one of the first graduates. Born in Czechoslovakia, Maggie had lost most of her family to concentration camps, which gave a certain credibility to anything she might say about human suffering. Her house on the lake near Hannah's had been filled with antiques, carpets, and art objects purchased on her world travels. She was one of the few people in the area with whom Hannah had been able to discuss England and Australia.

Arms folded across her chest, Hannah strolled down the

carpeted corridor picturing Maggie, glasses on a chain around her neck. She put them on, not to see better, but to conceal her eyes, which were always revealing inappropriate reactions to clients' dilemmas, such as amusement or fascination. But Maggie had poked and prodded with delicate restraint to get Hannah to face her own pain and rage. Watching them finally gush out like amniotic fluid during labor had been a sobering experience. Years later, after she and Maggie became colleagues and friends, Maggie used to maintain that doing therapy was simply a question of raising the child concealed within each client, and then disillusioning the client about the extent of your own powers.

Hannah visited Maggie at Lloyd Harris every day as she was dying of cancer. Maggie retained her sharp mind and tongue, but her body wasted away. Her eyes, which had so often sparkled at Hannah with amusement, were clouded with a pain her glasses couldn't conceal. The corners of her mouth, which had twitched with suppressed smiles, now twitched with grimaces. It was the ultimate in disillusionment. Among her last words, spoken in a raspy voice as she lay in the hospital bed surrounded by life-support equipment with dials like hyperthyroidal eyes, were, 'So you see, my dear Hannah, as wonderful as I may be, I die just like everyone else.'

Discovering from Holly that her next appointment had canceled, Hannah returned to her office, sat in her chair, lit a cigarette, and gazed out the window. An orange Le Car crept up the street beyond the parking lot. Hannah exhaled. The driver, a former client named Harold Mortimer, was one of her most outstanding failures. She could see his strained white face gazing at her office window, hoping for a glimpse of her. Sometimes he stopped to leave messages of undying devotion under her windshield wiper. Maybe her new car would fool him.

As the orange Le Car turned the corner, Hannah speculated on Caroline's emerging pattern. She'd probably try to win Hannah over, then try to get Hannah to reject her. And at that point Hannah would refuse to cooperate. The one useful skill she had learned at the Sussex boarding school her grandmother had shipped her off to was fencing. She did the same thing in here all day – exchanging thrusts and parries, until one day she'd drop her foil and allow a client to plunge right at her. And she'd observe their bafflement when she neither crumpled to the floor nor slashed back. But of course she'd learned to do this by sparring with Zorro during training.

Hannah's shoulders sagged. She propped her elbow on the desk and rested her chin in her hand. Her grandmother probably programmed her for this tedious profession by telling her all the time how gifted she'd be at working with troubled people, if only she'd get her own garbage out of the way. She smiled faintly as she thought about her grandmother, white hair in an elaborate bun, corseted bosom jutting out like a Victorian sideboard as she ran jumble sales for charity behind a stall in the High Street. Hannah had always predicted the old battle-ax would outlive them all, but she hadn't. And no doubt raising an angry, rowdy granddaughter hadn't prolonged her stay. She recalled how the old woman's white eyebrows fluttered with dismay when Hannah spent afternoons after school racing her bike down the sidewalks through the Heath with a pack of boys and dogs, while other girls went to ballet lessons. Or balancing along the high garden walls of neighboring houses, peering into upstairs windows at neighbors changing clothes, taking baths, or making love. Or careening down Christ Church Hill on roller skates with pedestrians leaping out of the way. Or using her pocket money to ride a double-decker bus to the end of the line and back. Or making kites to fly from the high hill on the Heath out of the *Financial Times* before her grandfather had read it.

Hannah's father had gone to Australia as a young man to convalesce from tuberculosis on a sheep station owned by a family friend. There he met Hannah's mother, a daughter of the owner. They married and produced Hannah. Hannah had hazy memories of straining to interpose herself between her parents while her father shouted. Her mother died of typhoid picked up while tending an aboriginal who camped on the station. Her father brought Hannah back to his parents in Hampstead prior to departing for service with the British High Command in Trinidad. She remembered him as a handsome, breezy man who turned up in Hampstead every few years with a deep tan and smiling teeth like tiny white tombstones. All he ever said to her was a phrase he'd picked up in Australia: 'So how's it going then, mate?' He'd pat her awkwardly on the shoulder while gazing at a far wall.

Hannah glanced at the bark painting on her office wall. The aboriginal gave it to Hannah's mother before he died, and

Hannah's father brought it back to Hampstead. Her grandmother thought it was hideous and kept it in a closet under the stairs. In white on reddish-brown bark, it featured a bizarre leaping creature called a mimi spirit, with hollow eyes and sticklike limbs. It had terrified, yet fascinated, Hannah. Whenever her grandmother found her looking at her, she'd shake her head and sigh, 'My wild aboriginal granddaughter.'

Looking at it now, Hannah remembered a farm pond encircled with ghost gums, in whose branches kookaburras laughed; a lamb named Mutton, who gradually turned into a sheep and wandered across the wide verandah of their cottage, shitting little round turds on the flowered parlor carpet; flocks of garish galahs, flashing flaming waistcoats; small dark children tumbling with her in a dusty paddock; flies buzzing incessantly; her father's hat, with corks hanging from the brim on strings, to keep the flies away; the winter rains drumming on the iron roof. She remembered a hand pushing damp hair off her forehead when she was half asleep. But she couldn't remember her mother's face. The only face she could summon was from a faded photo, sad and strained. A little girl, Hannah, clutched her arm, as though aware her mother was about to vanish.

'Why so somber?' asked Jonathan from the doorway, holding out a wrapped sandwich.

Hannah looked up. 'I was just thinking about my mother.'

'That'll do it.'

'Come in. Sit down. Thanks. Is this ham?'

Jonathan nodded his bushy gray head. 'What's happening?' He sat down on the tweed couch and unwrapped his own sandwich.

'The usual.' Hannah picked up half her sandwich. 'Loss, sorrow, betrayal, and deceit.'

Jonathan smiled. Mary Beth appeared from the next office. She wore a high-necked ruffled blouse, Mao slippers, and generally resembled Little Miss Muffet after forfeiting her curds and whey to the spider.

'What's wrong with you?' asked Jonathan.

'I've just realized I don't like clients giving me all this power.'

Hannah took a large bite. Mary Beth was fresh out of graduate school and still thought real life was an ongoing seminar. Hannah knew the upcoming conversation by heart. A client had split with his wife because he thought Mary Beth had told him to. Now he was miserable and was blaming Mary Beth. Jonathan was making all the usual responses about clients hearing what they wanted to hear, not having to come back, etc.

'Call it trust instead of power,' suggested Hannah between bites. 'It'll help you feel better.'

'It doesn't matter what you call it,' said Mary Beth, leaning up against the doorjamb. 'It's still power.'

Hannah shrugged. 'So be a veterinarian.' When they were interviewing, she hadn't been sure about Mary Beth, who seemed a trifle earnest. But Jonathan insisted they needed another woman, someone young, with credentials as impressive as Mary Beth's. It was hard to tell if she'd work out because she still had what Hannah called novice nerves, took everything that happened with clients too seriously and too personally. Sheer exhaustion would no doubt cure her of that.

'A client has to relinquish a certain amount of power for the process to work,' Jonathan was saying.

Hannah watched him look up at Mary Beth with a patient smile. He felt Hannah was too harsh. Hannah felt he drowned people in honey. They used to argue over this issue of power. But she was still convinced clients didn't hand over any power at all. All they did was to use the therapist as a stand-in for the strong part of themselves, until they were ready to face their own strength.

Three

Caroline went through the lunch line, taking salad and coffee. Holding her plastic tray, she glanced around the large, drafty tiled room. Diana was sitting at a table with Brenda, Barb, and Suzanne, all dressed in white uniforms. Feeling no wish to be pleasant to Suzanne, who'd spent the past week lurking behind oxygen tanks in the halls to pop out for chats whenever Diana passed, Caroline walked to a table inhabited by Brian Stone in light green scrub clothes and plastic booties. Brian was a young surgeon whose wife had recently left him, taking their children to Boston without a backward glance. Caroline had assisted him several times in the ER, and they'd sometimes drunk coffee together between cases. She admired the delicacy and deftness with which he tied sutures, as though assembling a sailing ship in a bottle. He struck Caroline as a touching fellow, with his receding hairline, his mournful eyes, and his endless grief over Irene's departure. Although she scarcely knew him, she'd become his confidante. It was impossible not to because Irene was all he ever talked about.

'Mind if I join you?'

Brian looked up with bloodshot eyes and a pained smile. 'Delighted.'

Taking the dishes off her tray, Caroline asked, 'So how's it going?'

'Fine. Just fine.'

Caroline sat down and picked up her fork. 'Pretty day?'

'Not bad for December.'

'What's new?'

Brian sighed. 'Nothing much. Same old grind.'

'As the burlesque queen said to the bishop.'

'What?'

'It's an old joke.'

'Sorry. I guess I'm pretty out of it today.'

'Please don't tell your patients,' said Caroline.

'They're out cold. They don't know the difference.'

'What's wrong?'

'Oh, I talked to Irene this morning.'

'How's she?'

'All right, I guess. But I really don't understand women.' Brian was handling his knife and fork as adroitly as he did a scalpel, with long graceful fingers.

'Don't look at me,' said Caroline, her mouth full of lettuce. 'That makes two of us.'

'I mean, for example,' he said, gesturing with his fork, 'Irene loved to buy all this stuff – clothes, furniture, cars, trips. And I had to bust ass to pay for it. But then she complained I was never home. I don't get it.' He shook his head.

Caroline thought she got it, but she wasn't sure it would be kind to explain that maybe all those purchases were an attempt to fill the gap where a husband should have been. 'Sounds like my marriage.'

'I didn't realize you'd been married.'

'Many years ago.'

He laughed. 'Come on, you can't be that old.'

'Some days I feel older than King Tut.'

He sighed. 'Yeah, I know what you mean.'

Do you, wondered Caroline. If only they had more time, it might be interesting to find out. Besides, she'd just seen Diana glance in their direction.

'I always wondered why an attractive woman like you wasn't married.' Brian studied her with his sad eyes, resting his chin on his fist.

Oh, give me a break, thought Caroline. She stood up. 'Gotta run, Brian. Nice talking with you.'

Caroline sat down behind the ER admissions desk and picked up a pencil from atop a stack of patients' charts, intending to make the list for Hannah and hoping no one would come rolling through those swinging doors on a stretcher. She used to feel such delight at the People's Free Clinic when a woman hemorrhaging from a coat hanger abortion or a student on a bad trip staggered into the cluttered storefront office in Somerville. She was needed. She could help. Now she wished they'd leave her out of it. She'd lost her nerve. She was terrified she'd freeze with horror at some crucial moment, as she had that afternoon over the little boy with the gaping head wound. Who was she to think she could help anybody? It was all she could do to keep *herself* alive.

She wrote the word 'kind,' just to prime the pump. But what about the hats of street musicians she hadn't tossed coins into, the hitchhikers she'd driven past, the Muscular Dystrophy cannisters she hadn't deposited change in, the phone market surveys she hung up on, the times she pretended not to be home when Jehovah's Witnesses knocked? She crossed out 'kind.'

Brian was being paged over the PA: 'Dr Stone, Dr Stone, fourth floor, fourth floor . . .'

Caroline wrote 'honest.' But was it honest to pretend that she and Diana were just roommates simply in order not to lose their jobs and cause their children harassment on the playground? Was it honest to sit behind this desk and dread the arrival of patients? She drew a line through 'honest' and scribbled 'unkind' and 'dishonest.' She studied those words. That was the effect of her behavior, but it wasn't the intention, any more than Jim Jones originally intended to poison his followers.

Marking out 'unkind' and 'dishonest,' she wrote 'well-meaning.' But was she, she wondered as she chewed her pencil eraser. To eat she allowed plants and animals to be slaughtered in her behalf. When she walked, she squashed insects. When she breathed, she butchered bacteria. Her white blood cells were destroying germs every second. Even to live was to be a murderer.

Diana sauntered down the corridor, her head with its scrambled red hair turned toward Suzanne, her bedroom eyes laughing. Suzanne looked as thrilled and expectant as Arnold when he confronted his first dead woodchuck. They wore street clothes – corduroy jeans, parkas, boots. As they headed out the door, Diana called to Caroline, 'Don't worry about me if I'm out late.'

Pencil poised, Caroline considered this remark. If Diana stayed out late tonight, it would be no comfort to know she was doing so with Suzanne. It would be preferable to have her dead on the highway. So Diana wanted to play hardball? Maybe Brian Stone should be encouraged. Too bad he had to be a man.

Inspecting these thoughts, Caroline added 'ungenerous' to her list. But damn it, she'd usually done her best. When Maureen, the Irish maid who told horror stories about British rule, sobbed with homesickness, Caroline patted her orange hair and told her everything would be all right. When her father limped home with colitis from fighting court cases for minority groups, Caroline ran his bath and rubbed his temples. As he bathed, she polished his shoes. When her mother returned from the welfare office where she began working after the war, Caroline brought her tea, turned on the opera, and covered her with a blanket in her armchair under the seal from her college that read 'Non Ministrari sed Ministrare.' Not to be ministered unto but to minister. Which was what Caroline had always tried to do. While her parents rested, she kept Howard and Tommy quiet by locking them in the playroom and making them play medical missionary.

For Christmas one year their parents gave them each sponsorship of a Save-the-Children child. Caroline's, from Kentucky, was named Stanley Horton. In his picture he had no shoes and very few sound teeth. He wrote every month and sent a picture of his house, a shack sided with tar paper and roofed with tin Nehi signs. At dinner she, Howard, and Tommy would pass around the pictures and notes, and their parents would explain that because they were so privileged, they had a responsibility to those less fortunate. Caroline began saving her baby-sitting money to buy Stanley special treats, like Band-Aids in the shape of stars.

Sandra removed the stack of charts from under Caroline's elbow, saying, 'Let me get these out of your way, sweetie.'

Caroline studied her list, most of which was crossed out. She erased 'ungenerous' and examined 'well-meaning.' But what about when she used to place Howard at the bottom of the stairs and dangle his teddy bear on a noose by its neck just out of his reach, hissing, 'I know what you want and you can't have it'? What about the time she bit Maureen so that she had to have four stitches? She crossed out 'well-meaning.' Nothing was left. Fuck it, she wouldn't do the list. She didn't see the point anyway. She tore it up and dropped the pieces in the gray metal waste can.

Brenda leaned on the desk with both fists. 'Ready to roll a few strikes, babe?'

Caroline looked up. Brenda reminded her a bit of Arlene, her favorite teacher at nursing school – the same massive build, like a vertical iron lung; the same mindless dedication to her profession. But unlike Arlene, Brenda played as hard as she worked, always organizing sports leagues and excursions to nearby bars.

'Sure thing,' Caroline replied without enthusiasm. She'd forgotten this afternoon was bowling. This was her week to tend the kids. She picked up the phone and called the cabin. Sharon answered. Yes, Jackie and Jason were home. Yes, she was baby-sitting them. Logistics were simpler now that Sharon was in the eighth grade and required unending supplies of money for her constantly expanding wardrobe. It made a big difference to her set whether the tag on the back of Levi's was red or orange. But baby-sitting Jackie was no easy task. A sixth grader himself, he insisted he was too old for a baby-sitter. He was, but he also was too young to be without one, since he sometimes forgot to turn off stove burners or tried to blow-dry his hair while sitting in a tub full of water.

'Shall I bring you a pizza or Big Macs?' she asked Sharon.

Sharon yelled to Jackie and Jason. 'Jackie wants a Quarter Pounder, large fries, and a medium Coke. Jason wants Kentucky Fried Chicken, fries, mashed potatoes, and rolls. And I want a pepperoni pizza.'

'Forget it. Take a vote. I'm not driving all over town.' Sounds of loud argument came over the phone. Participatory democracy. Caroline sighed and rested a hand on her hip.

'Be with you in a minute,' she said to Brenda. 'The Kentucky Colonel is being routed by Ronald McDonald.' She heard Jason howling with pain and calling Jackie a 'motherfucking faggot.' She'd spent her whole life rearing little boys, first her brothers and now her sons, and she still didn't understand them. Didn't understand their fascination with constructing elaborate machines for destruction from their Legos and Tinker Toys – tanks, intergalactic warships, fighter planes, aircraft carriers, missile silos. When she gave them dolls, as *Ms* magazine recommended, they used them for target practice.

Sharon came back on the phone. 'Jackie and I want Big Macs, but Jason says he doesn't want anything if he can't have chicken.'

'Okay, but tell him I'm not fixing sandwiches in the middle of the night.' When she'd given birth to Jackie and Jason, she'd had no idea she'd spend her next twelve years scheduling – meals, rides, baby-sitters, dentist appointments, hockey practices. And juggling her work hours, and enduring the anxiety when everything fell through and the boys ended up alone. Any mother could perform the jobs of several air traffic controllers with ease.

In the staff room she and Brenda changed into orange team shirts that said 'Lake Glass Kennels' on the back. The husband of a former team member, who ran the kennels, had sponsored the team last year. Brenda smelled sweaty, and huge breasts strained her shirt buttons. She was an old-style nurse, referred to any doctor she was working with simply as 'doctor': 'Doctor will see you right away.' She approached human suffering with gusto, rubbed her hands at the challenge of stitching the pulpy remains from motorcycle wrecks into human beings again. She lived in a small ranch house in Idyll Acre Estates with Barb from Intensive Care. They bowled all winter and played slow-pitch softball all summer. They had fun. They seemed at ease with their work and their lives. When they asked Caroline to join their bowling league, she accepted, thinking if she spent time with them, she'd acquire that same ease. So far she hadn't.

Brenda's green Torino had an 'Emergency Medical Technician' license tag above the New Hampshire plate that read 'Live Free or Die.' As Caroline climbed in, Brenda was fiddling with her CB radio. She belonged to the town rescue squad. Whenever she picked up word of an accident, she raced to the scene to offer help. Several times a month she was on call as ambulance crew.

Looking out the car window as they passed Maude's Corner Cafe, Caroline saw Diana and Suzanne at a table, engaged in intense discussion under the light from a low-hanging Tiffany lamp. They had pink drinks in front of them, probably strawberry daiquiris, Diana's favorite. One afternoon just after they'd become lovers, Caroline spent hours in the neighboring field picking enough wild strawberries to make a pitcher of daiquiris. She and Diana lay in the sun drinking them until they were so drunk they made love in the open meadow. A herd of cows arrived to watch, munching placidly on all sides. Caroline recalled thinking as she lay there surrounded by the sound of cuds being chewed, This is it. This is happiness.

How could Diana prefer Suzanne's witless hero worship to honest interaction with an old friend? It was incredible. Suzanne wasn't even attractive. She was gawky. With buck teeth. And slightly crossed eyes. And a hunchback, Caroline added in an unsuccessful attempt to cheer herself up.

'You're awfully quiet tonight,' said Brenda as they pulled into the parking lot at Lake Glass Lanes, a low building sided with asbestos shingles that were supposed to look like bricks. It sat on the highway next to the new mall.

'I guess I am.'

'Something wrong?'

'No, I'm fine.' You couldn't complain about a little insomnia to someone who'd spent the day rigging IVs, pumping stomachs, and jump-starting stalled hearts. A gold medallion at Brenda's throat glinted in the streetlight. A gift from Barb, who, like Brenda herself, was from a French Canadian family, it read, *'Plus que hier, moins que demain.'* Caroline and Diana used to mock Barb and Brenda's devoted coupledom, saw it as a parody of Irene and Brian Stone. Two flagging swimmers in a death grip, dragging each other under. Even at the height of their honeymoon she and Diana had retained separate friendships, separate flirtations, separate apartments, and separate checking accounts. But this afternoon Barb and Brenda's symbiosis struck Caroline as touching, if the alternative was abandonment. Better to suffocate in sweetness than to drown in despair.

Barb was taking a practice frame on lane four. She slid up to the foul line and stumbled over it, setting off the buzzer. Brenda cheered and applauded. Lucille from Coronary Care, whose rows of finger curls made her head look like the roof of someone's mouth, was setting up the score sheet. Brenda and Caroline changed from boots into red, white, and blue spangled shoes. As Brenda unzipped her ball from its padded case, Caroline went in search of one of the alley's balls with finger holes the right size. When she returned, Brenda was splashing rum from a bottle in her pocketbook into her teammates' Cokes, glancing around to be sure the manager wasn't watching.

Caroline sat on the smooth red plastic bench, getting up for her turns, making the proper responses to teammates' chatter, and reflecting that bowlers sometimes turned up in the ER with dislocated shoulders and thumbs, or broken ankles. As the game progressed, she felt she was being packed in a cocoon of sterile cotton wool, like the batts for casts. The voices of her teammates were the cackling of a flock of migrating birds during a rest stop. The balls down the alleys and the clatter of falling pins were the hollow thundering cracks of distant rifles, killing geese in mid-flight on gray fall mornings. Watching the pins scatter, get swept away, then set up again, only to be knocked down again, she felt exhausted. What was the point? It was exactly like her life – she'd set it up, it would fall apart, she'd set it up again . . . There was no point.

She watched her teammates critically as they howled at Barb's story about Dr Watson at the urinal in the men's room, being paged for ICU: 'Dr Watson, Dr Watson, ICU, ICU . . .' Brenda spewed her rum and Coke all over the score sheet. Caroline smiled weakly when Lucille looked her way.

Caroline continued to study these women, her teammates, her colleagues, as they ate powdered doughnuts, slid to the foul line in spangled shoes and orange shirts, jumped and squealed over strikes. She finally concluded they were simpletons. If not, they'd be as appalled as she over the futility of it all – throwing absurdly heavy balls at distant wooden pins while the world drowned in grief and gore. She fought a longing to lay her head on the ball return, so when one arrived it would split her head wide open, like a pumpkin thrown on a sidewalk. Like the head of that little boy whose father swung him against the stone fireplace. Her brains would spill out on the shiny wooden floor like a Jonestown corpse exploding in the jungle heat . . .

'Hey, are you okay?' asked Brenda, standing above her and bending down with a look of concern, the gold medallion swaying hypnotically from her throat. More than yesterday, less than tomorrow, bullshit.

'I'm fine,' Caroline replied, wishing she could fight through the wall of cotton wool between them, but knowing it was impossible. They inhabited one world, and she another – a place of deep dark pointlessness. That was why she couldn't do Hannah's damn list. How could you describe someone who didn't even exist?

Leaning forward from the tweed couch, Caroline searched through her National Abortion Rights Action League totebag on the carpet. Driving down the hill from Lloyd Harris without a list, she'd been seized with anxiety. That list was her assignment, and she hadn't done it. God knows she'd tried. There where a self-image should have been was a great charred crater. But if she didn't hand over a list, Hannah would be displeased. So in the parking lot she scribbled, 'Kind, honest, well-meaning, mean, devious, ungenerous, possessive, wimpy . . .' Let Hannah figure it out. That was what she was being paid for.

She looked up at Hannah, who sat in her swivel chair watching Caroline's rummagings with a faint amused smile. Wearing a tan pants suit and a blouse with attached cravat and tigereye stickpin, Hannah looked like a truant from a Tupperware party. Caroline did a double take: Hannah was in stocking feet.

'Ah yes, the list,' said Hannah, taking it. She glanced at it, then handed it back and lit a brown cigarette with matches from Corinne's, a new restaurant in the tannery where she and Arthur had eaten rack of lamb last night. If Caroline had done the list to please her, she wanted to convey that Caroline's compliance or noncompliance was a matter of indifference to her. From the perplexed look on Caroline's drawn face, she suspected this assessment was correct. Therapy was theater. You tried to restage scenarios from the client's past so the outcomes were different. She remembered a boy at the state hospital who spent his days plucking invisible bugs out of the air. But the one time she persuaded him to stop, he ended up in a straitjacket.

'For next time why don't you divide your list into categories?' said Hannah, picking up Nigel's stone and cradling it in one palm as she flicked her cigarette ash into it.

Caroline frowned. The list had occupied her entire week, only to be dismissed in fifteen seconds. Why bother? 'What kind of categories?'

'Whatever ones you see.'

Caroline heaved a sigh. Now she'd have to spend next week figuring out what categories Hannah had seen. As though she didn't have report cards to sign, laundry to fold, dressings to change. She didn't have time for these games. Let housewives with nothing better to do play them. Her eyes returned to Hannah's bare feet.

'What's wrong?' asked Hannah. These ritual enactments struck her as transparent, but most clients seemed not to see through them. This was where her British heritage came in handy. Nobody was so gifted as the British at pageantry – coronations, corteges, royal marriages, the changing of the guard, masterpieces of fantasy that participants and observers alike believed were real. But at least she was aware of being a fraud.

'That list was really hard to do,' Caroline said. 'All I could come up with was what other people have told me I'm like. But their versions contradict each other. I felt canceled out.'

'So why did you do it?'

There was a long pause. Good question, thought Caroline. It hadn't occurred to her not to. She lowered her eyes to the box of IGA tissues on the carved wooden chest beside her. 'Because I wanted you to like me.'

They both blinked. Caroline froze, not daring to look up. Why in hell had she said that? It was a firm rule with her not to let people know what she wanted from them. *I know what you want and you can't have it.* If you pretended you didn't care, sometimes what you wanted came to you unasked. But in this particular case, she really didn't care. Why should she care whether this aging British housewife liked her? She absolutely didn't.

Hannah felt herself blush, whether from embarrassment at such vulnerability or from a hot flash, she wasn't sure. She fought an urge to assure Caroline that she did like her. It wasn't the right time for reassurance. But how could anyone who'd been a mother not give it right then?

'Do you feel you need to make lists for people to like you?' Hannah asked kindly. She felt a stab of pain for that infant, so eager to please.

'I feel I'd better do what they want, or there's not a chance in hell,' Caroline was surprised to hear herself say.

'Do you see where that comes from?'

'What?'

'That feeling. Do you remember telling me about trying all the time as a child to be helpful?'

Caroline closed her eyes and squeezed the bridge of her nose. It looked to Hannah like a direct hit. After many direct hits, the point would begin to sink in.

Gazing out the window across the yard where the stubble formed a five o'clock shadow on the dusting of new snow, Caroline recalled how the various maids used to set her mother's hair. Caroline would stand in the corner of her dressing room, one foot atop the other, wishing she could help. Her mother laughed and gossiped with the maids, and almost purred when they massaged her neck. Her brown satin dressing gown would fall open at the throat to reveal sculpted collarbones and soft hollows. If Caroline could do the things the maids did, her mother would act like that with her too.

As Hannah watched Caroline's eyes cloud over and narrow with pain, she reminded herself not to go too fast. If the pain was too great, Caroline would shut down. You had to balance their developing trust in you with the unveiling of their ancient sorrows. 'You've been thinking this week about how people see you. Do you want to hear what I see?'

'Yeah. Okay.' Caroline dug her fingers into the tweed sofa. What was the woman going to bitch about? She'd done the assignment the best she could. She couldn't help it that she was a nonperson.

'I see a kind, gentle, vulnerable person who's been through some difficult stuff without losing those qualities.'

Caroline looked up. For a moment her eyes met Hannah's. Then she looked away quickly and studied the brass doorknob, frowning. It didn't sound right. She remembered the radio program she, Tommy, and Howard listened to as kids, sitting as close as possible to the large wooden box with its fabric front, and shuddering with delicious terror as a voice leered, 'Who *knows* what evil lurks in the hearts of men . . . ' If gentleness was what Hannah saw, she was less perceptive than she seemed.

'What makes you say that?'

Hannah shrugged. This assessment was so remote from what Caroline was used to that she couldn't even take it in. She would have argued with St Peter that she wasn't fit to enter heaven. 'Your face, your expressions, the way you stand and sit, how you speak.' And not just Caroline, but most clients. She tried to hold that image in her mind as she worked with them – of affectionate, capable people, with an overlay of crap from things other people had laid on them when they were too little to protest. She shifted her gaze from Caroline's troubled eyes, which were assessing her bare feet, to the small gray stone Willendorf Venus on the windowsill, with its huge thighs and swollen belly. She'd bought it at a stall in Camden Lock the last time she was in London.

As she studied a run in the foot of Hannah's stocking, Caroline itemized her failings for the past week. She forgot a lunch date with Pam. She argued with Jackie over his messy room. He yelled, 'I never asked to be born!' She yelled back, 'And if you had, the answer would've been no!' She snapped at Diana about the electric bill when she stayed out until 3.00 a.m. with Suzanne, leaving her lights blazing. Caroline knew she could pass herself off as polite and charming. But her true self was a raging virago. Harpy. She'd add that to her list. Diana had seen this true self often enough. It was probably what had driven her away. Diana said she was a taker. That was the least of it. She was a selfish, self-centered nightmare of a woman. Kind and gentle? It was what Hannah was being paid to say.

'You wouldn't think that if you really knew me,' Caroline said.

It seemed to Hannah there were only two types of behavior in all the world. One said 'come here,' and the other said 'go away.' 'All right,' she said with a smile, 'reveal to me all your true flaws and failings.' You could go away angry, or you could go away amused.

Caroline shook her head no. And studied the red tread on one white shoe, feeling irritated. 'Nobody in this nation is entitled to see herself as kind and gentle,' she announced. 'America is looting the world, and all Americans are beneficiaries.'

Hannah studied Caroline. What a panicked reaction to hearing something nice about yourself. 'And you, of course, are personally in charge of American foreign policy?'

Caroline looked up at Hannah. Then she looked back to the tread on her shoe. Her parents, David Michael, her comrades at the abortion referral center and in the hospitals where she'd worked had all taken for granted that they were responsible for their nation's behavior, that collectively they were the nation. This woman was British, so maybe she didn't understand democracy. But it did sound as though Hannah was on her side. She sat in silence for a long time, tracing the stitching on her shoe with her fingertips. Unfamiliar sensations having to do with relief and gratitude flickered on the horizon of her awareness like the northern lights over Lake Glass on a clear winter night.

'What about transference?' Caroline finally asked. She knew from psychology courses at nursing school that this was how therapy worked. She recalled reading about it in her text. But then it had actually happened, with Arlene. The bland textbook description had very little to do with the real thing.

'What about it?'

'I don't want to do it.'

'If you don't want to, you won't.' Unfortunately, it had to happen for the process to work. Caroline had to accept Hannah as an authority figure so she could rehear things she'd misheard as a baby – such as the notion that she'd caused World War II.

'I've already done it once, and that's enough.' The last thing she needed right now was to lapse into that state of doglike devotion and dependency.

'I didn't know you'd done therapy before.' The fact that Caroline was bringing up transference probably meant it was happening. Hannah made a mental note to do what she could to undercut it, which usually involved telling lots of bad jokes.

'I haven't. I mean in my personal life.'

'Well, what do you mean by transference?'

'Turning someone into God.' She haunted Arlene's office. Her every waking moment became devoted to Arlene's service. She cleaned the windows in her office and waxed her VW, brought her sandwiches from the deli down the street and sharpened her pencils, took her uniforms to the laundry and typed up her reports. She copied the angle at which Arlene wore her starched white cap, the purposeful stride with which she marched down corridors dispensing mercy. It had been terrifying having people's lives depend on your delivering the right medications at the right intervals. Aping Arlene gave her the illusion she was equal to her job.

Hannah nodded. 'Well, I don't like it any better than you do. Imagine what it feels like having someone do that to you.' When she was first doing therapy, it freaked her out. A client's eyes would take on a milk-sated glaze, and he or she would start laughing at all the bad jokes, and repeating her comments from previous sessions as though they were the Ten Commandments. It was a strain to have her every remark scrutinized for hidden meaning, when most of the time she was just goofing off. But she eventually realized she could have propped a dust mop in her chair and the same idolization would have occurred.

She glanced out the window to the street just as the orange Le Car crept by. Transference run amok. On the other hand, Maggie used to point out from time to time, 'Face it, my friend: Sometimes you adore being adored. We all do.' And Hannah couldn't deny it.

'You sound British or something,' said Caroline. Hannah's clipped accent was reminding her of her mother, who thought that because her father was British, she was entitled to sound like Queen Victoria: 'We are not amused . . . ' She could just barely remember her grandfather, delivering a sermon in his Shaker

Heights church when Caroline was four, dressed in a black bathrobe with a huge purple satin bookmark around his neck. Caroline started hiccoughing and couldn't stop. Her mother kept glaring at her. Later she made Caroline apologize to her grandfather. He died a week later. For years Caroline thought his death was her fault for hiccoughing during his sermon.

'I was born in Australia and moved to London when I was four,' Hannah explained. To disclose things about herself was to open herself up to a real exchange; real exchanges led to caring; each person you cared for was one more you might lose; and there had already been so many. She understood the appeal of Freudian detachment: 'Let's look at why you're interested in my accent . . .' Appealing, but counter-productive if you were trying to downplay transference, which fed on mystery and remoteness. Caroline had had too much remoteness already.

'So how did you end up here?' A gray stone statue of a bulbous naked woman sat on the windowsill across from Hannah. Had it been there all along? Caroline hadn't noticed it before.

'I married an American during the war.'

'Oh.' It hadn't fully sunk in for Caroline that Hannah had a life outside the hour they spent together in this room. She wasn't crazy about the idea. 'My grandfather was from England. He was an Anglican priest.'

'Really? Where in England?'

'Dartmouth.'

Hannah pictured the lovely little town, on hills around a harbor, the closest England could come to the Mediterranean. She'd gone there once with her grandparents. They marched along the cliffs above the harbor, her grandmother leading, an ocean liner flanked by two tugboats. They ended up at an inn on a narrow twisting road, where they had a wonderful cream tea with fresh strawberries.

'But your accent is Boston Irish, isn't it?' asked Hannah.

'My father is Irish. Our neighborhood was mostly Irish. My mother must have felt like a missionary among the heathen. She used to make fun of our accents. 'Good mawning,' she'd say when we came down to breakfast. She'd make us repeat 'heart' and 'bar' time after time until we got them right. My brother Howard didn't speak at all for about four months when he was five. It was wonderful. Except that he hasn't shut up since . . .'

Hannah was watching and listening closely. Caroline was smiling, but what she was saying wasn't funny.

'. . . we used to have this parrot named Cracker, and everybody said his vocabulary was bigger than Howard's. When the phone rang, Cracker would say, "Hello?" When you walked in the door, he'd say, "Hi!" If you called his name, he'd say, "What?" Did you ever hear the joke about the man who went into the pet shop and asked for an armadillo?'

As she told it, Caroline searched her brain for her best jokes. Hannah was probably exhausted from dealing with loonies all day. Why not give her a break? As she told another joke, about a frog taking out a bank loan, she watched Hannah's face carefully and thought she could detect color rising into her pale cheeks. As Hannah smiled, then chuckled, Caroline felt a surge of pleasure. Good sense of humor. Maybe she could add that to her list?

After the third joke, Hannah glanced at the clock, realizing that if Caroline was already somewhat transferred, this was probably how she tried to charm her mother. And Hannah had to confess to being charmed as she tried to memorize the punch lines so she could tell Arthur the jokes at supper. But being charmed wasn't part of her job, she reminded herself. 'I've really enjoyed this hour, Caroline. But I feel I should point out that these are probably the most expensive jokes you've ever told.'

Caroline looked at her, bewildered.

As the boys watched 'Welcome Back, Kotter,' Caroline fried pork chops and thought about transference. Gradually she realized Arlene wasn't her only case of it. Her first case actually involved her pink blanket, whose miraculous powers she discovered when she was three. She remembered waking in the dark with a full bladder, pleased not to be surrounded by a warm puddle. She got out of bed, dragging her pink blanket, and started down the hall to the bathroom. There were terrifying shadows. She wasn't absolutely sure they weren't monsters. She stuck a thumb in her mouth, but it didn't help. Drawing a deep breath, she raced into her parents' room, where her mother lay sleeping on her side. Alone in the bed because Caroline's father had been captured by the Japs. Caroline shook her shoulder, whispering, 'Mommy, got to go potty.'

After the third shake, her mother began sobbing. Caroline

froze. What had she done? She thought her mother would be pleased she wasn't wetting the bed. 'I'm too tired, Caroline. Go by yourself. You're a big girl now.'

She had to do something fast. Dancing on her toes, she wrapped herself in her pink blanket and assured herself that no monsters could get her as long as she was encased like that. She dashed to the bathroom, arriving unharmed.

Feeling awful to have made her mother cry, and knowing she'd be pleased to learn that Caroline had negotiated the monster-filled hallway and the toilet all by herself, Caroline pulled some tissues from the box on the toilet tank, wrapped herself in her blanket, and returned in triumph to her mother's side, where she dabbed at her mother's tears with the tissues. Her mother pushed her hand away and said, 'Stop it. Get back in bed and go to sleep.'

After that, Caroline knew that as long as she was wrapped in her pink blanket, nothing could harm her. Never mind that her mother and Maureen complained it was smelly and dirty, she knew it possessed magical powers inaccessible to adult scrutiny.

She glanced at Jackie and Jason, who lay on their stomachs on the hooked rug with their feet in the air and their chins on cushions, giggling at Barbarino on the TV. Jason held his hockey stick in one hand. Caroline wouldn't have been surprised to discover he slept with the stick. Jason took after Caroline's father, was short and compact with auburn hair, green eyes, and lashes so long they looked fake. He laughed a lot and had a blustery self-confidence. Jackie was more like herself – tall and slim with curly dark hair and tortured blue eyes. He took everything too seriously, and covered that up with a pained but pleasant social manner. It amazed her that both boys had the same father and had emerged from her body.

Arnold was daintily chewing one of Jason's new blue Nikes. 'Stop it, Arnold!' she called. 'Jason, don't let him chew up your new shoe, honey.'

'He can if he wants to, Mom.'

'No, he can't. I paid for those shoes, and I'm not – ' She halted, already bored with the upcoming lecture. 'Jackie, would you please put some more wood in the stove for me, honey. It's getting chilly in here.'

As Jackie stood up slowly, eyes fixed on the TV, Caroline returned to her memories of Pink Blanky. Usually she dragged it with her wherever she went. But one morning her mother persuaded her to leave it behind when she went to nursery school. She folded it carefully and laid it on her pillow, patting it reassuringly. All morning long, as she cut and pasted construction paper, she kept clutching at thin air for Pink Blanky with her left hand. When she got home, Maureen announced she'd needed cleaning cloths and had cut Pink Blanky into four pieces. Caroline climbed into bed for her nap in a state of shock. As she pulled up the patchwork quilt her mother had purchased by mail from the blind wife of an Appalachian sharecropper, she assured herself that this quilt would also safeguard her from fire in the night, thieves in the closet, monsters under the bed, Japs on Okinawa, and British rule in Ireland.

But the quilt smelled like the cedar chest where it lay in summer, rather than mildew, snot, and saliva. It lacked Pink Blanky's limp threadbare kneadability. Sucking on its corner was like sucking cardboard. Pink Blanky would yield to the caresses of fingertips, but the quilt just lay there like a tin washboard. As she sought safety in its stiff, clean folds, she thought wistfully of the disgusting delights of Pink Blanky, who now lay surrounded by her father's old jockey shorts. How had she caused this? She should never have left Pink Blanky behind, even if its presence did make her look like a baby at nursery school. If she hadn't clung so insistently to Pink Blanky, maybe they'd still be sleeping together. *I know what you want and you can't have it.* If you didn't let them know you wanted something, they wouldn't have to take it away. She shoved a thumb in her mouth and fell asleep, comforted by this insight into the curious workings of the adult world.

A couple of nights later, she sneaked at midnight to the cleaning closet, rummaged through the dust rags, and rescued two of Pink Blanky's four pieces. Racing upstairs to bed, she caressed one piece. It was smooth and stiff, coated with floor wax. Grabbing the other piece, she buried her nose in it. It smelled of lemon oil furniture polish. She began to cry. Not only could Pink Blanky not save her from the loss of its magical protection, it couldn't even save itself from this humiliating dismemberment and exile. She had to face it: Pink Blanky was merely mortal.

The next morning she shoved the pieces under her mattress, but Maureen found them when she was changing the damp sheets.

As she carried them away, Caroline buried her teeth in Maureen's forearm. Maureen had four stitches and returned to Galway with many bad memories of the New World. Caroline was sent to her room for the rest of her life. Maureen was replaced by Esther from Poland, who told bedtime stories in broken English about being a teenager in Buchenwald.

Caroline studied her sons as they gazed with adoration at Gabriel Kotter. Jason periodically asked her to marry a man like Gabriel Kotter so he could be Jason's dad.

'You've already got a dad,' Caroline would point out.

Jason would screw up his face with distaste, and Caroline could no longer summon enough loyalty to Jackson to reprimand him.

Jackie and Jason had both had special blankets, but giving them up hadn't been a big deal. They just gradually lost interest. Maybe they felt secure enough with her not to need substitutes? Maybe she wasn't such a flop as a mother after all? She speculated on how much she'd damaged them by dragging them from house to house. Out of Jackson's neo-Tudor manse in Newton, and into David Michael's van with a scene from Mao's Long March painted on the back window. To the Somerville commune, then up here to this cabin in the woods. Each time they made a bad grade or fought with a friend, she assumed it was her fault for burdening them with so much instability. Of course she herself had spent her first eighteen years in the same rambling Victorian heap in Brookline, and she was no paragon of mental health. Good mother. Could she add that to her list?

She thought about her list as she opened the oven door and poked the baked potatoes with a fork. If Hannah could tell her to divide it into categories, evidently she'd seen some herself. But what? *Kind, honest, ungenerous, possessive, wimpy* . . . . She hadn't a clue. Good sense of humor, she was going to add. But Hannah hadn't liked her jokes. Or rather, she responded to them, then told her she was wasting her money. Fine. She wouldn't tell any more. Let Hannah sit there all day like Buddha, getting exhausted by other people's problems.

She remembered saying to Hannah that she felt she had to do what other people wanted for them to like her. Would she tell Hannah her problems just because this was what Hannah wanted? But she didn't care whether Hannah liked her. Then she recalled telling Hannah she did care. Why the hell had she said that?

Because she really didn't. That Betty Furness look-alike meant nothing to her. She'd add 'liar' to her list.

Was it even true she felt she had to do what others wanted for them to like her? She thought about Jackson, his pager strapped to his belt like a mountain man's hunting knife. When she finally voiced despair over the fact that she never saw him, he stayed at the hospital more than ever. What about David Michael? She pictured him drawing on a joint, his ponytail tucked under an operating cap, a fleck of marijuana flaring in his mustache. When she complained about his other women, he took up with Clea, one of her best friends, who lived right there in the Somerville commune. Whenever she failed to be long-suffering, people withdrew. But Diana had withdrawn too, and Caroline had always tried to do everything Diana wanted. Including this god-awful celibacy.

As Caroline tore up lettuce leaves and tossed them into the wooden salad bowl, she resumed her memorial service for Pink Blanky, the only object of her adoration whose departure had been involuntary. No, that was incorrect. What about Marsha? Caroline remembered pedaling her tricycle down the block one summer afternoon, grieving over Pink Blanky. She was pedaling with her eyes closed, hoping to fall into a manhole or get hit by a bus. Probably she would without Pink Blanky to protect her. It was all her fault. She'd left Pink Blanky home alone with a murderess.

A girl riding a red tricycle in the opposite direction pulled in front of Caroline and said, 'Don't cry, little girl. I can be your friend.' She had a short ponytail on each side of her head, like pig's ears, tied with narrow pink ribbons.

It turned out Marsha knew everything worth knowing except what penises were for. She knew which neighbors' gardens you could pick flowers from without getting caught; how to crush the flowers to manufacture perfume (which you put in emptied pill capsules and forced the younger neighborhood children to buy); why there were cracks in sidewalks; how to fasten playing cards to tricycle wheels with clothespins to make flapping sounds as you rode; why certain graves had sunk in the cemetery down the street (grave robbers had stolen the coffins); where baby brothers like Howard came from (you bought them at a hospital), and why you shouldn't hurt them. Caroline ceased to be a scaredy cat who couldn't even get to the bathroom alone at night. Marsha was the Lone Ranger, and Caroline was Tonto. Marsha was the Cisco Kid, and she was Pancho. Marsha was Roy Rogers, and she was Dale Evans. Their tricycles were stallions, and they rode them all the way to the end of the block.

Practically the only thing Marsha hadn't known was how not to die when hit by a Bunny Bread truck in sixth grade. Caroline had known to trust no one, even when the light was green in your favor. If she'd been with Marsha that afternoon, instead of at a meeting of a school club Marsha couldn't join because her grades weren't high enough, Marsha wouldn't have been run over. Caroline hadn't even wanted to join a club that didn't want Marsha too. Marsha's feelings had been hurt.

The neighborhood kids spent a lot of time searching the crosswalk and curb where Marsha had been hit for bloodstains. When Caroline walked by, they'd call for her to come look at a pebble they insisted was one of Marsha's teeth. But Caroline could see it all too clearly in her head already – Marsha's body bloody and mangled, limp and lifeless on the concrete.

Caroline saved her baby-sitting money and bought a potted lily for Marsha's grave. Esther had been replaced by Geraldine, who told bedtime stories about fleeing Mississippi after her husband was lynched by the Klan. Geraldine, head wrapped in a flowered scarf, agreed to take Caroline on the bus to Marsha's grave. But she looked at the lily and said, 'Have mercy, child, you don't want no real flowers. Shoot, that old thing'll rot just like her. You want you some plastic ones that'll stay pretty from here to yonder.' So she and Geraldine stopped off to buy some purple plastic hydrangeas. As she looked at the marble headstone of a lamb, Caroline reminded herself that Marsha's death was her fault. She hadn't been with her that afternoon. She hadn't known until too late that Marsha needed her protection as much as she needed Marsha's.

When she got home, she locked herself in the bathroom with a box of Uncle Ben's Rice. Marsha's mother was an ex-nun who'd left her order because it denied her an electric heating pad when she developed arthritis. Marsha had often told Caroline about doing pennants for being bad, like you waved at football games. As pennants for causing Marsha's death, Caroline sprinkled a layer of rice on the tile floor and knelt on it with her arms outstretched, like Jesus on the cross. After several such afternoons, her knees rubbed raw, she ran out of rice. She considered watching 'American Bandstand,' but instead took her allowance to the store for more rice. Because if she wasn't someone who deserved punishment for causing her best friend's death, who was she? No one.

As Caroline flipped the pork chops and began slicing apples into the iron skillet, she speculated on whether those purple hydrangeas were still on Marsha's grave, fresh as the day they were bought. After Marsha came Rorkie, then a series of gruesome boyfriends, then Arlene, Jackson, David Michael, Diana. Ever since Pink Blanky, she realized, there'd been someone she'd endowed with its wisdom and benignity.

As she set the tan stoneware plates on the table, which were among the few relics other than Jackie and Jason from her marriage to Jackson, she remembered Hannah's saying this afternoon that she was a kind and gentle person. Was there any truth to this? After all, the woman had a Ph.D. and a British accent. Even if she did run around barefoot.

Looking up from the floor in front of the TV, Jackie asked, 'What's so funny, Mom?'

She realized there was a bemused smile on her face. Oh God, no. Please not another Pink Blanky surrogate. 'Nothing,' she snapped.

Four

Dressed in a nightgown and rose flannel robe, Hannah sat in an armchair by the Franklin stove in her bedroom reading *Love Comes Fast* and drinking a dry martini. She could hear the rustle of Arthur's *Wall Street Journal* in the living room. Her paperback was tattered and dog-eared, having passed through the hands of three friends who traded gothic romances with the enthusiasm with which her children used to trade baseball cards. She'd begun reading romances years ago, to find out what many of her female clients saw in them. She quickly understood they devoured them to convince themselves of the glamour of dreary marriages and boring or abusive husbands. Having discovered this, she also discovered she too was hooked. The damn things turned her on. Clients often complained their relationships went stale, as though it were their partners' faults for not being transformed into exciting new people every few years. She'd reply, 'That's why God gave you an imagination.'

Maggie used to chide her for her taste in reading matter. One morning when Hannah stopped by Lloyd Harris, she found Maggie watching 'The Price Is Right' on TV. 'Aha, I caught you!' said Hannah. 'I'm not supposed to read romances, but you can watch game shows?'

'My dear,' said Maggie in her quilted bed jacket, 'when you're dying, you can watch anything you like.'

Hannah lingered over the last several pages, pleased *Love Comes Fast* was ending as she'd known it would: boy gets girl, boy fucks girl, boy and girl display every symptom of living happily ever after. She laid the book on the floor and lit a cigarette. Closing her eyes, she felt the warmth from the stove. Another reason she read romances instead of *Madame Bovary* was that they had happy endings – unlike many of her clients. After listening all day to reports of child abuse and wife beating, rape and incest, she was too tired for any more realism. She needed stories in which good guys got what they wanted – and bad guys what they deserved.

Standing up, she stretched and walked to the window, which had a panel of stained glass across the top. Cold seeped in around the caulking. Way down the lake the lights of town lent a faint aura to the night sky. Simon and Joanna were down there somewhere, doing whatever they did. They'd formed in her womb and clung to her skirts for years, and now they bounced checks, cooked quiches, played racquet ball, and conducted love affairs entirely without her assistance. She looked at the portraits on the wall of Nigel and Mona. She couldn't so easily imagine their current state, though God knows she'd tried. Wherever they were, she hoped they too were managing all right without her.

She studied all four pictures, painted from photos by a man in town. Each child her product, yet each so distinct. Simon good-looking and bossy, with the features and gestures of a father who vanished when he was one – the same fair hair and pale skin, the same arrogant tilt to his head and jut to his jaw. Nigel, a slight, wacky little boy in thick glasses who used to run down to the lake at dawn to skip stones, terrifying her when she found his bed empty. Once she sent the uniformed game warden down to find him, hoping it might frighten him into staying in bed in the future. He fell to his knees, raised clasped hands, and said, 'Arrest me, sir!' Mona, pudgy and cuddlesome, friend to new children at school, savior to injured pets. She'd have grown up to be a mother, a nurse, a therapist, a social worker, burdened as she was with her mother's sympathy for anything weak or injured. And Joanna, brisk and efficient as a little girl, the librarian when the kids played library, head nurse when they played hospital. A successful stockbroker now, president of the Lake Glass Business and Professional Women's League, New Hampshire Business-woman of the Year last year. The game warden once gave them an abandoned fawn. Joanna planned how to shelter and feed it, but it was Mona who nursed it with a baby bottle day after day.

As to how Hannah was managing without them – well, it certainly was different now in this perpetually neat and quiet house. She kept waiting for the empty nest syndrome to arrive, but so far it hadn't. Occasionally she felt lonely, but it was easy to convert that into a sense of delicious solitude. She had only to recall the chaos of a house crammed with small children; the piles of laundry and dirty dishes and broken toys; the fights and blaring music. Of course during that raucous phase she maintained her sanity by reminding herself that one day soon they'd all be gone and she'd miss their mad chaos. That time arrived, much sooner than she'd imagined, and miss them she did. But not to the point of not savoring this sudden stillness, broken only by the snapping of the fire in the Franklin stove and the rustle of Arthur's *Wall Street Journal*. That was probably the difference between her and some of the mothers who landed in her office. They felt frantic during the chaos, lost when it was over.

She strolled into the living room and fixed herself another martini in the antique pine dry sink that served as a bar, wondering if she drank too much. It was true that a night without a martini seemed to her like a birthday without a cake. But she never claimed to be an ascetic. She sat down on the leather couch across from Arthur, who smiled at her over his paper. He wore his favorite tattered green sweater with leather buttons and elbow patches, which made him look like Mr Chips. She began sorting through that day's clients. She tried to identify and detach from the emotions that swirled through her office so they didn't distract her. Early in her career it had been tempting to regard them as real and to leap into the fray, but eventually she realized that the emotions clients sparked in her were important only as clues to the reactions they'd elicited from previous significant people in their lives. If she felt anger, probably that client was accustomed to inciting anger.

Ed, an engineering student with a double cowlick and lanky legs, had been in that afternoon. Gentle, whimsical, and attractive, he struck her as the kind of young man Nigel would have become. He talked about his sexual attraction to older women. She'd guessed this was coming and had felt the attraction too. These attractions tended to be fleeting. Apart from her devotion to Arthur, to lose interest she had only to think about how much training a young person would require. Training in physical lovemaking, since the enthusiasm of youth couldn't compensate for the expertise of long experience. But especially training about what one could reasonably expect from another person, training about the space and freedoms you had to allow so as not to kill off the qualities that drew you to someone in the first place. She'd been through all this with Arthur – the frantic demands for proofs and declarations of devotion – in the course of learning to let love alone, to wax and to wane, to heave and shift and settle and heave again, without endless dreary dissection. Learning to come as close as possible for two people lodged in separate bodies, but then to accept the necessities of that separateness and move away, sadly perhaps but without rancor, knowing you were merely setting the stage for reenacting the pleasure of breaking down the separateness once again.

'How much older?' she asked Ed with a smile, teasing him to defuse the issue.

'A lot older.' He blushed and gazed at her.

Fuck you, kid, you just blew it, she thought. 'Ed, let's look at why you bring that up now . . .'

Sipping her martini, she considered Caroline's wariness about transference. Quite right. They couldn't just replace their parents with her as their magical protector. They had to find protection within themselves. But how to get them to switch from looking out to looking in? Transference was so delicious at first, like being in love.

Probably it was the same thing. At the time, in her grandmother's house overlooking the Heath, she'd have said she was 'in love' with Arthur. But in retrospect it certainly resembled the transference she felt later toward Maggie, and that many clients now seemed to feel toward herself. The same hunger for acceptance – and the same eventual fury at feeling such need, longing, and gratitude. After she and Arthur had been going at it for several weeks in her Victorian sleigh bed, she sat up one morning and announced, 'You miserable bastard!'

'What?' He rolled over, his brown hair scrambled, and opened his eyes in alarm.

'You're going to leave me.'

'What?' He sat up, clutching the covers to his chest.

'Get out of here.'

'Huh?'

'I said go away.' She shoved him out of bed with her feet.

'What are you talking about? I love you.' He stood there on the cold oak floor, naked and vulnerable in the early morning light.

'Oh, do shut up!' She began sobbing.

'I have to return to America. But I'll come back for you.' He climbed under the covers again.

As he tried to hold her, she swatted him over the head with the folded London *Times*, snarling, 'Don't bother. Just scram and get it over with.' She wrapped her arms around herself and rocked back and forth, thinking of her handsome father in Trinidad with his bright white teeth, thinking of Colin rotting in his mossy Belgian grave, thinking of her mother turned to dust in the Outback. Loving people wasn't worth it.

Arthur did scram that day, but he came back – and kept coming back. God knows why, since she insisted on punishing him for the others who'd run out on her. Except that he always acknowledged she was the best piece of ass he'd ever had.

Stubbing out her cigarette and setting her martini on the end table, she called sweetly, 'Arthur.' They'd had no further problems once they established that he made the big decisions, like whom America would go to war with, and she decided everything else. 'Get over here.'

'I recognize that tone of voice,' said Arthur, lowering the *Wall Street Journal*. 'I believe it's my wild aboriginal rose.'

'Damn right,' she said, patting the couch beside her.

Standing outside her office door, hand resting on the doorjamb, Hannah closed her eyes and tried to regain her composure after an hour with a banker who'd been sodomizing his son. Doing therapy had gotten easier since her discovery that she wasn't running the show. When she first started, fresh out of graduate school, she took notes, analyzed them in accordance with whichever theory had her in its grip, and plotted a course of action. Then, when clients failed to conform to her plans, she wanted to kill them. But over the years, as she struggled to make sense of Mona's and Nigel's deaths, she was forced to choose between cracking up and accepting that events occurred at their own pace and for reasons that were often opaque. You tried to learn from whatever happened, however little enthusiasm you might feel.

Caroline sat on the tweed couch feeling alternately alarmed and pleased that she hadn't divided her list into categories. Would Hannah kick her out? But Hannah hadn't seemed to care about the list last week. Doing the list hadn't pleased her. Telling her jokes hadn't. For God's sake, what did she want?

Caroline's glance shifted to the gray stone Venus on the windowsill. Swollen belly, hands resting on huge breasts. Seemed like a dykey object to have in an office. Was that why Hannah hadn't been shocked when Caroline came out to her? She was a lesbian too? No, that was ridiculous. She was far too respectable. Besides, she'd mentioned some repulsive husband. Caroline didn't care for the idea of Hannah with a man. But she was probably too old to sleep with anybody.

What's it to me whether Hannah sleeps with her husband, Caroline reflected. She'd better stick to the topic at hand – herself. Should she reveal her meditations on Pink Blanky? It seemed a bit much.

Hannah walked in dressed in a wool skirt, navy blazer, and pinstriped shirt open at the throat. And no shoes. 'Hi.'

'Hi.' Caroline nodded toward the Venus. 'That thing's neat. Where did you get it?'

'Bought it at a stall in a market the last time I was in London. It was a blustery day, and she looked so exposed I felt I had to rescue her.' The last time she'd been in London had been for her grandmother's funeral, at Christ Church down the street from the house on the Heath. Probably she bought the statue in a vain attempt to replace the old woman. A portable mother figure that would never die.

'How come you have it in here?'

How come you want to know, wondered Hannah. 'The originals of those statues were used in fertility ceremonies. The community held the image of a fruitful female in their heads, and then their flocks and herds and crops and families prospered. And that's more or less what I do in here. So I keep it around to remind me.' She sat down and rested her stocking feet on the rush footstool.

'What?' Caroline thought they were doing therapy in here, not hocus-pocus.

'What what?'

'I don't see what you mean.'

'I hold an image of a healthy happy coping client in my mind, and that's what I work toward. If I held the idea of a depressed dependent client in my mind, then that's what I'd work toward.' Hannah shook a brown cigarette from a pack of Mores on her desk and put it between her lips.

'I disagree.'

'You disagree that's what I do?' Hannah raised her eyebrows. The lady was combative today. Good. Hannah could use a nice set-to. She was still a bit agitated from her sodomist.

'I disagree it's that simple.'

'Well, that's certainly your privilege.' She'd had enough success with her methods not to have to defend them. 'It's also your privilege to stay depressed if you want to.' Flicking her lighter, she drew the flame into the tip of her cigarette.

'Want to?'

'It's your choice.' Hannah exhaled a steady stream of smoke into the beam of weak winter sunlight coming through the window.

'Choice? If you really look at this world, you can't help being depressed.' Apparently Hannah had never been depressed. She didn't know how it felt for the air to turn too heavy to breathe.

'That all depends on what you see when you look. What do you see?' Hannah arranged both arms along her chair arms, hands hanging over the ends.

'Injustice, brutality, war, hunger.'

'True. But it's also a place of incredible beauty and intricacy. Inhabited by some people capable of great generosity and decency.'

'Tell me about it.' Didn't this woman read the papers?

'I just did,' said Hannah. 'Why are you so pissed off today?' Caroline's mouth looked pinched, and there was a slow blue burn to her eyes.

'Who's pissed off?' Hannah had dumped on her jokes last week, and she was right to. They were here to deal with Caroline's depression. Caroline was determined to keep it businesslike. Hannah seemed to have some skills, and maybe Caroline could benefit from them, but she didn't have to start liking her. She'd regard these sessions as visits to the dentist, appointments with the plumber.

'You want to know why I think you're pissed off?'

Caroline heaved an impatient sigh.

'Because you're starting to like me.' She looked at Caroline matter-of-factly.

Caroline was astounded. Like her? She didn't even know her. She hadn't been angry before, but she was certainly getting angry. 'The real reason I'm angry is that when I told you I was a lesbian, you changed the subject. It took me a long time to face that, and you just shrugged.' She remembered her horror when she woke up naked in bed with Clea, whose golden hair fanned out across the pillow like harvested wheat in the summer sun. She'd made love with a woman. She'd taken to it like a hog to mud. She practically wore David Michael to a stub in the ensuing weeks trying to prove that she wasn't a pervert. Surely lesbianism couldn't descend unheralded onto such a vigorous heterosexual. But it had. Which was why Hannah kept fleeing the topic.

'I didn't know you still trusted me so little,' said Hannah, glancing out to the parking lot. Jonathan stood talking to a man leaning on a shovel who'd just scraped ice off the sidewalk. Sometimes she wished she had a nice straightforward job like shoveling snow.

Caroline felt a stab of remorse. Hannah wanted to be trusted, and Caroline had let her down. But what did trust have to do with anything? 'What makes you think I don't trust you? What I just said?'

Hannah nodded, drawing on her cigarette.

'See? You did it again. Changed the subject.'

'I didn't change the subject. I was trying to address what was really going on.'

'What was really going on,' said Caroline, 'was that I was trying to talk about my sexuality, and you changed the subject.'

'What was really going on, from my point of view, was that we got pretty close last week, and now a reaction has set in.' Hannah felt at an unfair advantage. She'd been through this so many times. Whereas to Caroline it was all new, real, and in earnest.

Was this true, Caroline wondered. Hannah told her last week she was kind and gentle. But she hadn't really meant it. It was a ploy, something to do with that stone Venus. 'Why can't you just accept my lesbianism?'

Hannah laughed and shook her head. 'But I do accept it, Caroline. You make love with women, and I make love with men. Fine. Who cares?'

So she did screw her husband, reflected Caroline. Men? Who besides her husband? Maybe she wasn't as respectable as she looked. What about those bare feet? 'You don't really think it's fine.' Caroline knew that a woman who hadn't felt desire for another woman regarded lesbianism as an inferior form of sexuality, fit only for the unfeminine and the immature. This was incorrect, but you couldn't tell hardened heterosexuals anything. They had biology and the pope on their side.

'Who else in your life hasn't thought it was fine?' asked Hannah putting her cigarette between her lips and leaning forward to shrug off her blazer, which she folded and lay on the desk. The sunlight through the window was baking her left shoulder.

As they sat in silence, Caroline reflected that hardly anyone knew, to think one way or the other. David Michael had been appalled and had done his best to dissuade her from a life of bourgeois decadence, but she never saw him now. Jackson probably had a clue because on the rare occasions when he showed any interest in Jackie and Jason, he grilled her about her living arrangement. Her parents carefully avoided that topic. She was going home for Christmas, but without Diana. There was no one in her life who thought lesbianism was fine except her lesbian friends. Which was why she spent as much time as possible with them. Though she'd had some lunches lately with Brian Stone, who kept dropping by the ER admissions desk in his scrub clothes while she was on duty. His sad dark eyes were starting to take their toll. She felt a growing need to cheer him up, bolster his shattered ego, make everything all right. A time or two she found herself wondering if lesbianism could be just an interlude in a lifetime of rampant heterosexuality.

'What are you so afraid of?' asked Hannah.

Caroline looked up. 'Why would you assume I'm afraid?'

Hannah pursed her lips and shrugged, stubbing out her cigarette in Nigel's stone.

Caroline heard words coming from her mouth without her permission: 'That I'll open myself up to you and get clobbered.'

Hannah drew a sharp breath. Caroline's candor, when it came, was painful. She left herself wide open. Hannah said nothing, unbuttoning and rolling her shirt sleeves to her elbows. Wanting Caroline to feel her wish to confide, cling, collapse – feel it, expose it to the air, find it didn't frighten or appall Hannah, and needn't Caroline herself. Caroline put on a brave show of tending everyone else. Doing for others what she wished someone would do for her.

'Well, I can't promise that won't happen,' Hannah finally replied, lighting another cigarette, 'because someone who's determined to get clobbered will see a clobbering even when the other person intends nothing of the kind. But let's set this aside for a while. How was your week?' Jonathan sometimes encouraged massive explosions, like emotional electroshock, but Hannah preferred to deplete the stockpile little by little. Most of her clients still had to function in the everyday world, and they couldn't if they were in pieces.

Caroline slumped into the sofa, the armpits of her white uniform clammy. 'I thought a lot about transference.'

'What about it?'

'About why I'm not going to do it again.'

'What was it like for you before?'

'Do you think it's possible to transfer onto objects?'

'Sure. People transfer onto anything. Ideologies, pets, shoes, pills. This world can seem a very scary place. Most people search for someone or something to make everything all right.' Mary Beth yelled in the next room. Hannah glanced at Caroline, who didn't seem to have noticed.

Caroline studied Hannah in her oxford cloth shirt, her eyes squinting from cigarette smoke that drifted on the sunlight through the window. Maybe she understood more about the misery of the world than she let on? 'I had this pink blanket when I was a kid, and I used to think if I covered myself with it, the knives of invading murderers would be deflected.'

Hannah nodded. 'Sounds like a useful item.'

Caroline smiled.

'What happened to it? Or do you still have it?' Mary Beth yelled again. Hannah frowned. What was this, Yankee Stadium?

'The maid cut it into cleaning cloths.'

Hannah grimaced, closing her eyes. 'That's bad.' She tried to avoid value judgments, but she was remembering how her children clung to their bottles, stuffed animals, and blankets, anchors in a turbulent sea of objects. Simon used to stand mournfully in front of the washer while his blanket went through the cycle. Each child had disrupted at least one vacation by forgetting a cherished object and insisting they turn the car around to retrieve it. She bought Mona three identical stuffed lambs because she was always misplacing one and getting frantic. Nigel had dragged around a pink plastic bottle for years.

She glanced at her gray stone Venus, then at her mimi spirit.

Was their function any different, however much classier their appearance? Whatever got you through the night. She glanced at her brown cigarette. If she gave these things up, what unattractive habit would she replace them with? Maggie used to say in her Eastern European accent, 'My dear Hannah, effryvun is queer for somezing.' The trick was to get someone to replace fucking his son with stamp collecting.

'That must have been painful,' said Hannah.

Caroline thought this over, looking out the window. Lake Glass was doing its thing, reflecting in its still waters the sun overhead and a solitary bird in flight. It must have been painful, though she couldn't recall feeling anything. 'I was thinking this week about my best friend when I was a kid . . .'

As Caroline talked, Hannah reflected that Caroline's reality was a vacuum of fear, insecurity, and longing for affection and protection – which she'd attempted to fill with a parade of people, objects, and projects. The color guard in Hannah's similar parade included her parents, her grandparents, Colin, Arthur, Maggie. All dead now except for Arthur.

'Do you realize,' asked Hannah, 'that your feelings for Marsha were the same as for your blanket?'

'Yeah, the other night it hit me that I've felt like that towards a bunch of people. Time after time. Like angina attacks.'

Hannah smiled and nodded. 'Very good. And so what happened with Marsha?'

'She got hit by a bread truck and died.'

Hannah flinched. Caroline's expression was so bland that Hannah wondered if she'd ever mourned her friend.

'I should have been with her that day. She'd probably still be alive if I had been.'

Hannah shrugged. 'Whatever happens, happens. I think your pattern of feeling responsible for disaster was set much earlier.' If you'd caused World War II, subsequent disasters must seem like small beer.

Caroline pinched the bridge of her nose and frowned. This hadn't elicited the sympathy she'd expected. Once again Hannah had just shrugged. 'I was talking to a guy at the hospital yesterday. He smiled, and I felt this pang. I realized his smile was just like Marsha's. I thought, God, the girl's been dead over twenty years.'

'She's part of your program now. In that sense she's still alive for you. But it's got nothing to do with her. You use the memory of her smile as an excuse to feel bad.'

Caroline looked at Hannah. Did she have any normal human emotions, or was everything just an intellectual exercise?

Hannah observed Caroline's look of indignation, one she was accustomed to. But it was one way to jar a client out of a twenty-year rut. She remembered feeling similar outrage one day at the hospital when Maggie, dressed in a quilted bed jacket, meal tray on the bed table before her, eyes clouded with pain, said, 'One nice thing about dying is that you don't have to be on a diet.'

'Do you have any childhood photos?' asked Hannah, rolling down her shirt sleeves, suddenly chilled. Her internal thermometer was haywire today. Must be about time for some hot flashes.

Caroline nodded yes.

'Why don't you bring some in next week?'

Caroline frowned and said nothing. They were moving to another assignment, and Hannah hadn't noticed that she'd failed to complete the last one.

'It helps me if I can picture whom we're talking about,' explained Hannah, knowing Caroline would do it if the request was made in terms of helping someone else. Poor sap.

Hannah walked along the lake, which spread out still and silent to the snow-covered mountains on the horizon. The cold air stung her cheeks. As she wrapped her arms across her parka, she reflected that there was nowhere on earth she'd rather be. But she hadn't always felt this way. Compared with London, rural New England had seemed, as it must have to Arthur's forebears in the Massachusetts Bay Colony, like a barren wilderness inhabited by savages. In her first months here, recently wed to Arthur, she experienced the sudden stillness as emptiness. And she proceeded to fill that emptiness – with babies, belongings, and emotional intrigue. She thought about the many flirtations she conducted at parties – the glances and innuendos, the phone calls and notes, the displays of outraged innocence on the bedroom threshold. Time after time through these unsuspecting men she punished her father and Colin for leaving – and Arthur for not leaving as he was supposed to. Arthur watched it all with a wry expression and still didn't leave. And she felt contempt for his weakness, not having the sense to realize that his staying came from a strength she knew nothing about. Besides, he couldn't leave her. He'd given up too much to be with her in the first place.

She filled the house with china, silver, linens, and antiques. She filled her closet with expensive clothes. She insisted Arthur buy a Lincoln Continental and a sailing yacht.

And then Mona and Nigel died, and the antiques were stolen. The children were missed. The antiques were not. Her previous life fell away like a dried-up husk. The yacht was sold. The silver was put into storage. She continued to wear the clothes, not noticing or caring as they went out of fashion. She avoided parties; and when she couldn't, she avoided past and potential male prey.

Her clients talked about the complications of their lives as though divinely ordained. They were unimpressed when she suggested they'd devised many of the complications themselves, and could therefore simply drop them. But five-year-old children knew this. On the shale beach where she now stood, she used to give her children sparklers on the Fourth of July. They traced elaborate designs on the night sky and yelled for her to come look. In no time the sparklers burned out, and the designs vanished without a trace. The children too. But thirty-five-year-old children had lost track of the fact that it was their hands that waved the sparklers.

She strolled over to the flat gray rocks where her children had flopped and scrambled like small white seals. Ice coated the bare branches of the huge old oak at the water's edge, from whose branches her children had swung on knotted ropes. Those had been frantic years, with four young children and a husband often away on business. She'd had very little idea what she was doing. Like Caroline with her pink blanket, Mona had clung to her stuffed lambs and Nigel to his pink bottle. She could recall times when she scowled at Nigel's jokes and rebuffed Mona's hugs. If she'd known then what she knew now about a parent's impact on a child, she'd have behaved differently. But I didn't know, she insisted to herself. How could I?

She pulled herself up short. This particular routine was too tedious. She'd done pretty well, especially considering that she had no parents to copy. Witness how well Simon and Joanna turned out. And Nigel and Mona had happy times and lots of love while they were here. She looked down into the still gray water and saw a middle-aged woman, nearly old, in an overstuffed parka and Wellingtons, with a pleasant face and curly gray hair. She watched the woman touch her face with her gloved hand. Feeling her fingers against her face, she smiled and shook her head – and saw the woman in the water do the same. There was no question about it: life was a strange experience. No doubt death would be even stranger.

She looked up to the icy oak branches, which were gleaming in the late afternoon sun. In spring the ice would melt and sink into the earth, be absorbed by rootlets, and erupt on a branch as an oak leaf. Which would turn dull purple and fall in the autumn, to rot and be devoured by earthworms . . .

And so on, until she got bored following the permutations of the initial drop of water, and went home for a martini and a cuddle with Arthur by the fire before the Sullivans arrived for bridge.

Hannah had just won the bid at five no-trump when the phone rang.

'Julie Byington,' Arthur whispered in her ear.

Hannah groaned and gazed wistfully at her hand full of face cards and aces. She took the phone behind the refrigerator so Allen and Harriet couldn't hear. 'Hi.'

'I'm sorry to bother you at home,' a frail voice said.

Then why are you, turkey, Hannah wondered, carefully not saying it was okay. Even members of the helping professions needed their nights of bridge.

'I hope I'm not interrupting something?'

Only an orgasm. 'Only a five no-trump hand.'

'What?'

'I'm playing bridge.'

'Oh.'

Hannah could imagine her thoughts: You're playing bridge while I'm here all alone mixing a Drāno cocktail. 'What can I do for you, Julie?'

'I feel awful about interrupting you.'

'It's okay.' They needed you not to reject them, but they were so accustomed to rejection that they did everything they could to trigger it – like calling on a Saturday night during a five no-trump hand.

'I feel really awful.'

'What's the problem?' Holding the phone against her ear with her shoulder, Hannah crossed her arms, one hand holding her drink, and leaned against the refrigerator.

'Terry's left me. He kicked me in the stomach and walked out.'

Hannah took a sip of her martini and thought wistfully of those three aces. 'Do you want to talk about it now, or can it wait until Monday?' Just then a hot flash hit her. The burning sensation spread across her back and chest like a prairie fire. Sweat popped out on her forehead and began dripping down her sides from her armpits.

'It can wait, I guess.'

'Call me Monday morning at the office and we'll set a time. And remember: You've been doing fine, and you'll be fine again.' The receiver trembled in her hand.

'I don't know how you stand it,' Harriet murmured as Hannah studied Arthur's hand, spread out on the oak pedestal dining table in the light from the Tiffany lamp, and decided they'd make the bid easily. They'd played bridge with Harriet and Allen once a month for over twenty-five years. Allen was a partner in Arthur's law firm and had been a Deke at Cornell two classes behind Arthur. Harriet had a silver Marie Antoinette hairdo and a small painted mouth.

'It makes me feel important.' Her turtleneck was damp, but she didn't want to take the time to change it when there were tricks to be won. She just hoped she didn't smell.

'Is it worth it?' asked Allen, sucking on his pipe to get it going.

'Oh yes,' Hannah said, taking tricks rapidly. 'I like knowing what everybody in town is up to. That way nobody can take me by surprise. I like it almost as much as I like knowing that you have the king of diamonds, Allen.'

'Right,' he said with a smile, putting down his pipe to fling down the king and take the last trick.

As Arthur in his tatty green Mr Chips sweater swept together the cards, Hannah looked back and forth between him and Allen. White-haired and distinguished, they got better looking with each passing decade. Whereas she and Harriet were sagging from repeated childbirth, and wracked with hot flashes, night sweats, and anxiety attacks. It simply wasn't fair. Arthur came by his steadiness biologically. Women, with their hormone storms, were in constant flux. In therapy she often prodded the men to allow themselves a wider emotional range, whereas the women usually needed to discover the part of themselves that didn't change along with the hormones each month. Until they found this inner pole star, they clung to relationships, or to anything else that seemed to promise external stability. Like poor old Julie with that creep Terry. But at least she could count on his beating her up every other week, as regular as clockwork.

She made a face at Arthur.

He gave a startled laugh. 'What's that for, my pet?'

'Because you're so damn attractive. Isn't he?' she asked the Sullivans. She'd just realized that in any earlier era, Allen and Arthur would have had new twenty-year-old wives, and she and Harriet would be dead in their graves from puerperal fever. 'You two are "older men," but Harriet and I are little old ladies.' Everyone laughed.

'That's a lot of garbage,' said Arthur, shuffling the cards. 'There's still lots of life left in you, old girl.'

'Take comfort from the fact that you'll both probably outlive us by many years,' said Allen, getting up to mix more martinis in the pine dry sink.

'Yes,' said Arthur, dealing. 'And you can go on exotic cruises and pick up young deckhands.'

'Spare me,' said Hannah, picking up her cards.

'What are you smiling about?' asked Arthur.

'I remember Maggie told me she was walking home from a show one night down West Forty-third Street, and this prostitute came stumbling out of a seedy hotel calling for a doctor. So Maggie went upstairs with her, and there was this naked man lying on an iron bedstead. Gray-haired, well-groomed, a businessman or something. Maggie checked him over and he was dead. When she told the woman, the woman looked at her and said, "Well, Doc, I thought he was coming, but I guess he was going." '

'I bet she made that up,' said Arthur between laughs.

'I wouldn't put it past her.'

'She was some lady.'

'She sure was.' As Hannah watched her three old friends chuckle and shake their heads, she wondered if the pain of losing them was worth all the good times they'd had together. It was an equation that was harder to balance as you got older. Because you knew for a fact, as you hadn't when you were young, that before long your friends would start dying on you. Or you on them. One way or another, you had to part. It made one reluctant to let new people in. There was no way around it: Life was a painful experience. All pleasure faded, and everyone had to die. But meanwhile, there were compensations. For example, Arthur had just dealt her another fine no-trump hand. She sipped her martini to conceal her expression of delight from Allen, who played bridge like poker, reading people's hands from their faces.

'Oh no you don't, Allen,' she said, raising her hand in front of her face.

He grinned. 'Sorry, babe. I've already read you.'

Hannah glanced at the others, sitting around the pedestal table under the circle of light, with a wind off the lake battering the windows. Night fallen, winter looming, senility pending. The gift from middle age was the ability to enjoy the moment without expecting it to last.

Five

Jackie and Jason were so far ahead that Caroline could hear only the faint roar of a distant snowmobile and the swish of her own skis. She poled along in the boys' tracks, watching the new snow sparkle in the sun – as though some planter had sown multicolored glitter. The wind had sculpted the drifts into scallops. As she took a deep breath, her nostrils stuck together from the cold. Today would be busy at the ER. Frostbite, fractures from skiing, back spasms and heart failure from shoveling.

She passed a huge gray dead elm. From its branches last winter an owl had swooped down and carried off a field mouse as she skied past. Someone ought to cut the tree down. Limbs kept falling. One shaped like a giant wishbone hung over another near the top. One day it might land on someone's head. Of course anyone trying to cut down such a huge tree might bring the whole thing crashing down on himself, or on an innocent hiker. Also, chain saws sometimes kicked cutting dense, tangled elm. A couple of years ago a man in the ER lost a leg that way.

Suddenly it occurred to her she didn't have to think about ravaging owls or amputated legs on such a beautiful afternoon. She could think instead about sculpted snow gleaming in the sun. Halting, she stood still. Hannah said whether you were depressed depended on what you saw when you looked around. You could see that dead elm as a potential accident, as a supply of firewood, as a natural sculpture. She leaned forward on her poles and studied the tree. Hannah also said she used the memory of Marsha's smile as an excuse to feel bad. Maybe there was something to this. No, it was ridiculous. Hannah was a zombie.

It was time to return to the cabin for a fire. 'Okay, guys, where are you?' she yelled. Ahead, one set of tracks went to the right, the other to the left. Obviously a trick. Whichever path she took, the other boy would accuse her of loving him less.

The afternoon silence was broken by a hollow thumping. Her eyes traced the noise to the elm. Way up in its gray branches a woodpecker maybe a foot high with a bright red head drummed on the wishbone limb. She watched with astonishment as the huge bird threw down a shower of sawdust and dead bark onto the snow drifted against the trunk. It paused to turn its head, inspect its work, and devour whatever it was uncovering.

Shouting boys raced in on skis, poles flying. Arnold leaped alongside them barking, his dark fur dusted with powdery snow. The woodpecker lifted off, circled with a raucous cry, then floated across the field toward the far woods.

'Look!' said Caroline. 'A pileated woodpecker. You hardly ever see them.'

'Big deal,' said Jason, pushing off with his poles like a slalom racer. 'Race you home, dummy!' Arnold barked happily, trying to grab a pole in his teeth.

Jackie glanced in the direction of the departing woodpecker, strictly from politeness.

As Caroline poled along back to the cabin in the boys' tracks, she studied the view through the trees of the cabin down below, a plume of smoke waving from the chimney, windows flashing in the sun. Glistening white meadows stretched down to Lake Glass, which spread out to hazy mountains on the far horizon. And over all, a deep blue sky. She had to admit it was breathtaking. Tourists knew what they were doing flocking up here to exclaim over these views. It occurred to her she could make a shawl like that – tie-dye the warp in blues, grays, and purples. Weave bands of those same colors. It would be stunning. A landscape shawl. The loom was empty. She'd start this weekend.

Caroline sat watching the fire in her stone fireplace and thinking about her new shawl idea, as she drank a Michelob and listened to the boys play Space Invaders on their video game. Arnold lay dozing, firelight reflecting off his glossy black coat. He was pleased with himself, having just chewed Jason's hockey stick to pulp. Wet ski socks hung steaming on the arms of a ladder-back chair beside the fireplace. Caroline had a shoebox of photos in her lap, and from time to time she looked at one, trying to select a few for Hannah. Herself, her parents, Howard and Tommy, various maids and clients, Jackie and Jason, Jackson, David Michael, Diana. Different backdrops, at different ages, in different outfits.

81

Ranks of ghosts. Even those infants and toddlers called Jackie and Jason no longer existed. They were big boys now. The earnest little girl named Caroline, the anxious nursing student, the harassed housewife, the rabid revolutionary, all had vanished. Yet apparently whatever made Caroline Caroline remained, because here she sat. Maybe that was what Hannah was trying to get her to define with that wretched list?

Whenever he lost at Space Invaders, which was often, Jason stumbled over, knelt beside her, and rested his head on her lap. She smoothed his auburn hair for about twenty seconds, marveling at the length of his eyelashes, before he raced back cheerfully for another defeat. Caroline realized as she gazed at the flames that was what *she'd* like to do, sit on the carpet by Hannah's desk chair and rest her head in Hannah's lap while Hannah smoothed her hair. God help us, she thought, jumping up.

As she furiously scrubbed potatoes for supper, she assured herself there was no way she was going to do that tired old transference trip again. She was afraid of getting clobbered, she'd heard herself tell Hannah. Well, it was a valid fear. Witness all those faces, now departed, in the photos.

After supper Jenny and Pam arrived for poker, and Diana came down from upstairs. They evicted the video game to the boys' bedroom, but the bleeps continued to bounce through the living room as the four women sat at the gateleg dining table, which they'd covered with green felt.

'So the last of the great therapy holdouts is getting her head shrunk?' asked Pam, adjusting her hand-tooled leather eyeshade.

'Yup.' Caroline was having trouble with Pam's new hairdo, almost a brush cut in front, but long in back. She'd known Pam for five years with a wild tangle of hair that almost hid her pale blue malamute eyes. They'd all four met while working on an abortion referral project in the bad old days before abortion was legalized. They'd scrounged money, driven sobbing teenagers to Canada, talked hysterical housewives out of douching with Black Flag, picketed wet T-shirt contests. Together they'd faced down anti-abortion groups on the statehouse steps and interviewers on the evening news. But one day Caroline sent a welfare mother to a doctor in New Jersey for a saline abortion. He administered the injections and turned her out on the street. She checked into a

Holiday Inn and miscarried, sobbing and screaming at Caroline over the phone while holding the dead fetus in a blood-soaked bed. Caroline dropped out of the project and descended into despair.

As the image of the woman alone in the motel with her dead fetus floated though Caroline's head, she felt a funk gathering like pigeons around popcorn. She reminded herself she didn't have to think about that shit any more than she had to see the dead elm this afternoon as an eventual accident. She shrugged a couple of times in imitation of Hannah. She was surrounded by old friends in a warm cabin with a glass of cold Michelob before her. All was well.

'So how is it?' asked Pam.

'Fine,' said Caroline. 'I feel sheepish for having said so many awful things about it.'

'You were pretty obnoxious,' said Jenny, dividing up the poker chips and taking their money. Jenny and Pam were close friends and occasional lovers. They devoted themselves to working for wages as little as possible, and to conducting as many simultaneous love affairs as they could. By not working they felt they did their bit toward undermining the patriarchy; by sharing the sexual wealth, they did their bit toward building the matriarchy. Caroline found their philosophy appealing, but was unable to overcome her Boston Puritan heritage enough to practice it.

'But it was obvious you were so down on it because you were so drawn to it,' added Jenny, who was wearing a Red Army cap with a red star on the front, acquired on a recent trip to China with her parents and a group of Presbyterian missionaries from Georgia, one of whom Jenny claimed to have bedded in Nanjing.

'That sounds like the assessment of someone who's done a lot of therapy,' said Diana, turning up cards to determine who would deal first.

'Years and years of it. I was a regular therapy junkie. My parents spent a fortune on my shrinks, hoping I'd get cured of my perversion. Instead I spent my sessions trying to seduce my female therapists. And succeeding once, I must add. She wanted us to stop therapy and continue the affair. I pointed out that one of my presenting symptoms was my inability to sustain a sexual relationship. She threw her letter opener at me, and it stuck in the wall beside my head. As I left, she was dialing her therapist for an extra session and muttering that at least now she understood countertransference.'

'Is that a true story?' asked Pam, dealing seven-card stud. 'Or are you being apocryphal?'

'I'll let you know when Caroline's finished,' she said with a sly smile, tossing her ante into the pot. She reached over and took some peanuts from Pam's pile, as though they were a married couple of long standing.

'Go right ahead and enjoy yourself, girls,' said Caroline. 'I know I deserve it.'

Caroline watched the fire, sipped her beer, and won at seven-card stud as they chatted about who was sleeping with whom. The funk had departed as abruptly as it appeared. What a luxury it was to spend time with old friends with whom it was okay to talk about nothing much. They had watched each other's hair go gray, each other's stretch marks sag, each other's disposable incomes shrink with inflation. Snow floated by outside the window. The odor of damp wool socks wafted over from the fireplace. Enemy lasers bleeped in the next room. The boys' voices accused each other of cheating and lying. A visceral feeling of well-being crept over Caroline so stealthily she didn't have a chance to fend it off. The ghosts hovering behind her became wispy and faded. Whoever and whatever were here and now were enough. More than enough – an unexpected gift from nowhere. Like the woodpecker in the elm. This is peace, she informed herself with surprise.

'What's wrong?' asked Diana, after Caroline failed to trade in cards on five-card draw and lost the hand.

'I'm becoming middle-aged, right before your very eyes.'

'Why do you say that?'

'I feel peaceful.' Surely peace couldn't be this easy – just being grateful for what was present, rather than dwelling on the dead and departed, the diseased and distressed?

'Don't worry,' said Pam, pulling on the brim of her eyeshade. 'It won't last.'

'But I'd like it to. And I always used to think contentment was irresponsible in the world where so much needs changing.'

'Everyone gets religion in the first weeks of therapy,' said Jenny, poking through her army surplus knapsack on the floor to remove a second deck of cards. 'It's a high having someone listen to you.'

'I listen to her,' protested Diana.

'You don't count. You're free.' Jenny shuffled the new cards and shoved them in front of Caroline for cutting.

'What are these?' asked Caroline.

'Got them in Hong Kong,' said Jenny, dealing Anaconda.

When Caroline picked up her cards, she was confronted with seven naked women in obscene poses. She and Diana started laughing.

'You're really disgusting,' Pam informed Jenny, studying her hand.

'Fun, though,' said Jenny.

'I'm serious. This is really offensive to me.'

'Even if we remove the ones with men in them?' asked Diana, trying to arrange her cards.

'I could wrap them in plain brown wrappers,' said Jenny.

Pam shot them both looks of contempt.

'Your missionary must have loved this one,' said Caroline, holding out the three of spades, which featured a woman wearing only black stockings and a cross on a gold neck chain.

Jenny grinned.

'But I can't even see what suits they are,' said Diana.

'Birthday suits,' suggested Caroline.

'I refuse to play with these cards.' Pam threw hers face down. 'I can't stand seeing women exploited like that.'

'Oh, all right,' said Jenny, sweeping them up. 'But don't you get bored with being so goddam politically correct all the time, Pam?'

'Don't you get bored with your bad-girl act?'

Jenny pulled down the brim of her Red Army cap and shuffled the old deck without replying.

Caroline tried to decide whether to feel ashamed for not being as horrified as Pam over Jenny's cards. Pam was studying Caroline's stacks of red, white, and blue chips with veiled resentment. 'Look, Pam, I can't help it if I always beat you turkeys,' Caroline said, to break the strained silence.

Everyone gave a startled laugh. 'I think the therapy is already working,' said Pam, tilting back her head to look out from under her eyeshade with malamute eyes. 'You're getting butch.'

'She's always been butch,' said Diana. 'We both are. It's why we can't get along. We try to outbutch each other by outfemming each other.' She reached over to pat Caroline's forearm.

'Christ, are you two still squabbling?' said Pam. 'Cut it out. Life is too short.'

Diana's touch felt like a jolt of electricity. Caroline's arm twitched so sharply that she dropped the queen of clubs. She and Diana looked at the card, then at each other. Jenny and Pam also exchanged a glance. 'Well,' said Jenny briskly, in imitation of June Allyson on some late-night movie, 'we must be off. I'm sure you two have a lot to talk about.'

Diana washed the beer glasses and put away the peanuts while Caroline put the boys to bed. Then they sat down on the sofa by the fire.

'It's nice to see you feeling so well,' said Diana.

'Thanks. It's nice to feel it.'

'Hannah Burke must know her stuff.' Her voice sounded stiff.

'I wouldn't know. I haven't been to another shrink.' Their corduroy-clad thighs were touching. Caroline increased the pressure slightly. They both studied the dying fire.

'The thing is,' said Diana, 'I guess I'm jealous. I wish I could have helped you feel better.'

'But you did. You do.' All Caroline's attention was focused on the spot where their thighs touched.

'No, I know I'm part of the problem, rather than the solution. But that isn't what I want.'

Caroline couldn't think what to say. She knew both statements were true. But what *did* Diana want? 'How's it going with Suzanne?'

Diana looked at her, green eyes hooded in the firelight. 'She and I are just friends, you know.'

'For now.'

Diana shrugged irritably and shifted her thigh away from Caroline's. 'She admires me. I like that. I need it right now.'

'Well, it looks like you've got it.'

'Ah, Caroline, look . . .' She took Caroline's face in both hands and kissed her mouth. Caroline kissed her back, and pulled Diana's body against her own.

After several minutes of kissing, Diana murmured, 'We're not supposed to be doing this.'

'Who says?'

'Me.'

They resumed kissing. Caroline ran her hands under Diana's chamois shirt and up her smooth bare back.

Diana stood up abruptly, combing her scrambled red hair with her fingers. 'I'm sorry. I shouldn't have started that. Sweet dreams, my lovely friend.'

As Diana dashed up the steps two at a time, Caroline smiled faintly from where she sprawled on the sofa. Goddam tease. Caroline knew she should feel annoyed or miserable, but the peaceful mood from earlier that evening was still with her, reinforced by the new information that Diana still wanted her. The message was encoded in her body, whatever her silly little mouth insisted on saying. Diana was one ghost who was still very much flesh and blood.

Caroline went into her room and began experimenting with dyes for the warp of her new landscape shawl. She worked happily into the night, bunching, twisting, tying, and dipping bundles of natural yarn into dye solutions, splattering dye around the room.

That night she dreamed of sitting in the dark in an overstuffed armchair watching TV. Hannah came on the screen. She was young, with dark hair and a tormented face. She talked in a lackluster voice about the difficulties of being a young mother. At the far end of the room, a door opened. In marched a middle-aged Hannah with graying hair and cheeks flushed from the cold, a vibrant smile and piercing blue eyes like sapphires in the sun. Caroline was pleased to see her and wanted to greet her. But she was unable to stand up. Apparently she had to continue watching the distraught Hannah on TV.

'Hi. Be with you in a minute, Caroline.' Hannah, sitting at her desk, studied her appointment book. She wrote in one name and erased another.

Caroline sat down on the tweed couch, crossed her Levi'd legs, and looked out the window to Lake Glass. The snow in the trees in the yard had melted and refrozen, branches gleaming in the bright sunshine like crystal filigree.

Hannah swiveled around in her chair and smiled. Caroline looked tanned. She must have skied over the weekend. The habitual tightness around her mouth and eyes had relaxed a bit.

A slight puffiness to her cheeks was gone. It was astonishing to watch their appearances change as they began to feel better.

'I dreamed about you the other night,' Caroline said, folding her arms across her stomach.

'Oh yes? What?' This process never ceased to amaze Hannah. Two people sat talking in a small room for several weeks, and things started happening. They began thinking about each other; one would dream about the other; they copied each other's mannerisms. What was it really all about? She liked to think she had a firm hold on the reins at all times, but the truth was that often she was just along for the ride.

'I used to be a harassed housewife,' said Hannah, after hearing the dream. 'Four children, no outside work, a husband who was gone a lot.' She propped her feet on the footstool.

'You?' That was how Caroline had seen Hannah initially. But since then she'd come to see her as a skilled professional. It was hard to fit the two together.

'Yes. But what do you make of the dream?'

Caroline hesitated. Hannah was the expert. What was the right answer? 'I wondered if I was trying to fit you into the mold of lots of the people around me.'

'Who are how?'

'Since I'm a nurse, I'm always surrounded with the sick and depressed.' If she could see Hannah as just another potential patient, she'd know what to do with her.

'Sounds reasonable. But also in dreams other people usually represent different parts of the dreamer herself. It sounds to me as though you're trying to move away from that depressed part of yourself.'

'Huh?'

'What about the rest of your week? How did it go?' If only it were as easy as just explaining in so many words. Then she could hand clients a list of psychological principles as they walked in the door and send them away as functional human beings.

'Pretty well. On Saturday I went skiing with the boys and saw this incredible pileated woodpecker. We went home and had a fire. Some friends came over to play cards. And for almost the whole evening I felt – peaceful or something.'

'How nice.' There was an open, trusting expression on Caroline's face that Hannah hadn't seen before.

'Well, not that nice . . .'

Hannah laughed. Caroline's face had just contracted into its old expression of pained distrust, like a hermit crab withdrawing into its shell. 'Come on, it's nice. Let it alone.' They got scared when they started feeling good, just because it was so unfamiliar. Like chronic prisoners facing release from their cells.

There was a long silence. Finally Caroline said, 'I don't have a lot to talk about. I've been feeling pretty good ever since. Maybe I shouldn't have come today?'

'I'm delighted,' said Hannah. 'We don't have to talk about anything. Let's tell jokes. Or tell me about your friends. I was playing cards Saturday too. What were you playing?' She had to combat the notion that she was interested only in Caroline's problems. Otherwise Caroline would knock herself out fabricating ever more exotic problems.

'Poker. You?'

'Bridge.'

Caroline looked at her. So she did play bridge. But she didn't seem like the type anymore. Whatever that meant.

'Did you win?' asked Hannah.

'Yes. I usually do.'

'I can see you would.'

'How come?'

'Your face takes on a certain impenetrability when you don't want people to know what you're feeling. Especially if they don't check out your eyes.'

Caroline was flattered someone had observed her so closely. Her eyes dropped for a moment to Hannah's bosom, ample under a yellow turtleneck sweater. She felt a longing to rest her head there and feel Hannah's arms around her. Oh, please God, no.

'Did you win?' Caroline asked quickly. She searched for something to dislike about Hannah, now that labeling her a bridge-playing housewife carried no clout. She ran around her office in bare feet? But Caroline liked that. She glanced at the towheaded children in the photos on the bulletin board above Hannah's desk and was swamped with jealousy. The little bastards. They got held in Hannah's arms.

'Yes, I always win too. Same impenetrability. That's probably why I recognize it in you.' She felt the sickening lurch that told her a client was beginning to ingest her. 'What are your friends like?'

'I've known them for years. They're aging hippies. They don't work if they can avoid it, and they love to hang out.' Hannah's desk was a mess, Caroline reflected, with books, papers, coffee cups, and sandwich wrappers all over it. She was a slob. But so was Caroline sometimes.

'The part of yourself you've never acted on?'

'What?'

'You've been so busy taking care of everyone, in hopes they'd then take care of you, that you've never done much hanging out, have you?'

Caroline lowered her eyes. Had she always taken care of everyone? If so, was that her motive, and not disinterested altruism?

'So you live it out through your choice of friends,' continued Hannah in an offhand fashion, looking out the window as Mary Beth walked past in a chinchilla coat and boots with ridiculously high heels. How did she avoid breaking her neck on the ice? 'Like in your dream: Me on TV is that responsible, depressed part of yourself. Your friends are your lazy, fun-loving side. But we're both actually you.' The orange Le Car crawled up the street past the office like a particularly unappealing insect.

Caroline felt her brain sizzle trying to take in more than it could handle. Then it shut down entirely, and she sat in bewildered silence, watching motes drift in the shaft of sunlight that came through the window. When the silence became oppressive, she said, 'I thought we were going to tell jokes.'

'How many therapists does it take to change a light bulb?' Hannah asked. It usually took a while to get someone to see the elements of her life as pieces of the jigsaw puzzle that was her own psyche.

'How many?'

'One, but the bulb has to really want to change.'

Caroline smiled, and Hannah thought about how much she enjoyed helping people feel better. If it took shrinking their heads, fine. If she could do it by telling jokes, so much the better. Applying her formula, she acknowledged that to help other people feel better was to do that for the depressive part of herself.

'Do you know what's going on in here, Caroline?' Hannah lit a cigarette.

Caroline looked up. A cloud of smoke was obscuring Hannah's eyes. Not much was going on today. Which was just fine with her.

'You're getting the acceptance you didn't get as a baby. And when you've had enough, we'll move on.'

Caroline felt a stab of indignation. Who said she wasn't accepted as a baby? Hannah thought she knew everything. Caroline focused righteously on Hannah's arrogance. 'I've got only a couple more sessions before two months are up.'

'We'd better get busy then.'

'So you're really going to kick me out in a couple of weeks?' Caroline asked belligerently.

Hannah looked at her with mock surprise. 'As I recall, the original issue was whether you'd be trapped into coming here for the rest of your life. You can come forever if you want. It's your money.' She reached for Nigel's stone ashtray.

Caroline was irritated. Hannah didn't seem to care one way or the other. But she herself had started to care, she realized with alarm. This was supposed to be a visit to the dentist. She sat in terrified silence. Hannah mattered to her. She wanted to keep coming, wanted to see Hannah every week, wanted Hannah to want to see her. If Hannah found out, she'd go away in disgust. *I know what you want and you can't have it.* Caroline would have to play it cool, reveal none of this, do as she was told, or Hannah would withdraw like all the others. She felt her features assemble themselves into the bland mask she used for poker. The photos! She'd done her assignment!

Reaching into her tote bag, Caroline announced, 'I brought you some pictures.'

'Great,' said Hannah, stubbing out her cigarette and setting the ashtray on the desk. Glancing through the photos, she saw confirmation for her original diagnosis in shot after shot. Obvious to anyone not blinded by the emotions associated with those individual personalities. Two anxious little boys clung to their older sister, whose head was usually turned down as though awaiting a blow. The father was absent or gazing off-camera; the mother was usually turned slightly away from the children, a literal cold shoulder. One photo was of a baby, Caroline presumably, hanging listlessly from a doorjamb in a jump seat. In more recent photos two little boys again clung to Caroline, and a shifting array of men and women stood beside her, turned slightly away.

'Are these all you have?' asked Hannah.

'No, I have a whole boxful. Do you want more?'

'No. Just curious.' Caroline had selected these photos from many to tell her tale. Whether this was the 'real' situation from anyone else's perspective was irrelevant. A different selection would have told a different story. But rejection and abandonment were Caroline's inner ambience, probably shaped in those first months when Daddy went to war and Mummy went berserk with abandonment and terror. But consciously Caroline knew none of this. And telling her in so many words wouldn't work.

'Do you see any patterns in these photos?' asked Hannah, leaning forward to hand them back.

'Patterns?'

'Take them home and look at them every now and then.'

Caroline frowned. She thought the point was for Hannah to picture the people they were discussing. Patterns?

'What are you doing for Christmas?' asked Hannah.

'Going to my parents in Boston with my sons.'

Hannah blinked. The showdown at the OK Corral was coming sooner than she figured. 'Will that be fun?'

'Yes. The boys like lots of activity at Christmas, and there'll be parties and stuff.' She rubbed the bridge of her nose, then was startled to hear herself say, 'I'm scared.'

'What of?'

'I've been feeling so good lately.'

'You can't feel good on a sustained basis by avoiding things that cause you pain. You have to come to terms with them. And you will.' She smiled at herself for sounding so sure.

'I don't know why I said that. I get along fine with my parents. Always have. I had a very happy and privileged childhood.'

Hannah held her face expressionless, remembering the many times Maggie fought to do the same with her.

'I did,' said Caroline, looking at Hannah defiantly.

'I wasn't disagreeing.'

'You just said they caused me pain.' She stuffed the photos into her tote bag.

'All right, so they don't. Fine.'

'They've done a lot of good for a lot of people.' Throughout her childhood clients and neighbors collared her on the street to tell her what wonderful people her parents were. And it was the truth.

'Great.'

'Well, they have, damn it!'

'Whom are you trying to convince, Caroline? Not me. I'll go along with whatever you tell me. After all, I don't even know them.'

They sat in silence. Finally Hannah said, 'Call me while you're down there if you want to.'

Caroline looked at her with surprise, wondering why Hannah would think she might want to. Then it came back to her in a rush, the times she phoned from school for rides home when she was sick, to have maids and secretaries reply that everyone was out doing good. The times she phoned Jackson at Mass General for advice on the boys' health or for an errand on the way home, to be told he was in surgery. The times she reached out for David Michael in bed, to find he'd gone to Clea. And Diana? Who knew what she was up to? Courting Suzanne one minute and coming on to Caroline the next. She announced last night that she was staying in Poughkeepsie after Christmas to meet Suzanne in New York City for New Year's Eve, the first they wouldn't be spending together since they became lovers.

'Thanks,' she said to Hannah in a choked voice. 'Nobody's ever done something like that for me before.' Her hand fluttered on the couch, wanting to reach for a Kleenex from the box on the chest. She pulled the hand back to her side. Her fingertips stroked the tweed cushion cover.

'It sounds as though you *have* surrounded yourself with people who haven't valued you properly.' It took a real leap of the imagination to call someone as doggedly determined to please as Caroline a 'taker.' Hannah noted the near-lunge for a Kleenex, pleased self-pity had appeared on the scene. The battlements must be tottering.

Caroline struggled with Hannah's remark. What had Caroline said to convey the impression people hadn't treated her properly? She'd led a privileged life. What had Hannah seen in those photos?

'You didn't pick your parents,' Hannah replied to Caroline's look of confusion, 'but you've picked everybody since.'

Caroline stood up abruptly, feeling like a wimp. 'I picked you, didn't I?'

'Yes, and it was a smart choice, too,' said Hannah.

Caroline unloaded cardboard boxes of the boys' outgrown clothing and L. L. Bean boots from the back of her Subaru, as the boys raced to the corner drugstore to squander their allowances, a luxury country living didn't afford. Her mother had asked for stuff for a Boat People Relief Fund rummage sale. Caroline carried the boxes into the empty garage. There were two large oil stains on the concrete floor where the cars were usually parked. Her parents had evidently gone to their offices despite her arrival. But it had always been understood in their family that disaster had priority. Vacations had been postponed, Brownie Flying Up ceremonies missed, as her father went to jail to post bond, as her mother tracked down a runaway. It went without saying that clients' needs came first, because their own family was so fortunate. Her parents were good people. She resented Hannah's skepticism. How could Hannah feel so free to pass judgment on people she didn't even know?

As she stacked boxes, Caroline reflected that her father had always brought things into this house, whereas her mother had always taken them back out again. Their marriage was a perfectly balanced ecosystem. He'd had clients who could get anything wholesale. One managed a salvage store in Dorchester that sold the contents of wrecked trucks and trains. The beige wall-to-wall carpeting through the house had survived a thirty-five vehicle pileup on Route 128. Whenever her father locked the keys in his car, he'd phone a client he'd gotten off a breaking and entering charge. Every fall they'd driven to Maine to gather bushels of potatoes too small for harvesting by the machines. On weekends they'd go to a fish market at Boston Harbor. In front were trays of fish under a sign reading 'Catch of the Day.' They'd buy the limper, smellier catch of yesterday out back. On the way home they'd stop at the Haymarket for unsold vegetables at reduced prices.

His forebears came to Boston from a farm on the Bay of Dingle during the potato famine. He put himself through BU Law School during the Depression by loading freighters and delivering laundry. He met Caroline's mother at a mixer at Wellesley College. She used to talk regretfully of the other young men who'd pursued her at Wellesley. Though what she wanted that he'd failed to deliver had never been clear. Caroline's mother's father, the Anglican priest, reared his daughter to a life of service. As did her mother's mother, who ran sales at the Shaker Heights church with the finesse of a casino croupier. Here in this rambling wreck of a house on Walnut Street in Brookline Village, Caroline's family lived alongside those who needed service. Apparently Caroline's mother's notion of service was more genteel. You served, but you retreated at night to your Shaker Heights comforts.

Caroline walked out into the driveway and inspected the huge Victorian structure with its peeling white paint, on its street of similarly dilapidated houses. Exterior woodwork had fallen off the turrets and from under the eaves throughout her childhood, and hadn't been replaced, so the house looked still under construction, a hundred years in the making, like a Gothic cathedral. The evergreens out front were rust-colored from salt spray from the street, and the grass had been trampled by passing schoolchildren. There were patches of dirty snow where the house cast shadows. Her father had grown up down the street with nine brothers and sisters, children of an Irishman with a minor position at the municipal housing authority. Their mother worked as an aide at Beth Israel, which was where Caroline first got the idea of becoming a nurse. When Caroline was sick, her grandmother would stop by in her white shoes, uniform dress, and hairnet. Caroline liked getting sick because her grandmother would rub her shoulders with alcohol and bring her meals on trays. Also she got to stay in bed all day instead of following Howard and Tommy around the neighborhood, rescuing them from falls into manholes and rides with strangers. She used to be terrified something awful would happen to them while she was in charge.

Entering the house, Caroline was glad for a few moments alone. She looked at the stairwell, where she hanged poor Howard's teddy bear. He'd gone to Penn State and joined the boxing team. It was probably she whom he was pulverizing in the ring each match. He wouldn't be home for Christmas. He was still in Chad in connection with the famine. Tommy was with the Public Health Service on a Sioux reservation in South Dakota, and wouldn't be home either.

As she crossed the Route 128 carpet, she looked around the living room. The shelves and tables were devoid of the personal objects other people crammed their houses with. Her parents were ascetics, didn't clutter up their lives with the insignificant, focused all their attention on important issues like disaster relief. It was admirable. But this house was so different from the ones she'd lived in since. Jackson's neo-Tudor place had been a new bride's wet dream – every appliance and decorator touch imaginable. David Michael's Somerville commune had been its own kind of masterpiece – auto seats as couches, curtains of American flags liberated from government flagpoles, silk-screened posters about freeing this and saying no to that on every bare surface, glasses made from wine bottles, utensils stolen from Waldorf's cafeteria at Harvard Square. Diana and she tended toward the rose-covered cottage motif – hooked rugs, fresh-baked bread, and laundry on the line. Each style was distinctive, unlike this living room, which could have been a motel lobby.

Her father walked in the front door, heavy-set and florid-faced, with auburn hair like Jason's, gone to yellow-gray at the temples. He had a scar across his forehead above one eyebrow, from a bayonet wound when he'd fallen on a forced march as a Japanese POW. His tie was an inch wide. As a teenager, Caroline used to be humiliated by his ties and lapels. Since he bought everything on sale, when width was fashionable he was buying narrow ones, and vice versa. He'd advance on Filene's Basement like a soldier on an enemy trench, emerging with marked-down factory seconds. 'It's fine,' he'd insist, hunching a shoulder as his wife inspected a new jacket with appalled disbelief. 'You just have to hold one shoulder higher than the other.'

'Hello there, darling!' He hugged her awkwardly. The boys burst in, mouths stuffed with gum, hands full of Star Wars cards. 'Why, who do we have here?' demanded her father, shaking the boys' hands as they juggled Star Wars cards. 'How was your trip, darling?'

'Fine, thanks, Dad. Uneventful.'

'Sorry no one was here. I had to go Dorchester. And your mother had an emergency. How about you three going with me to Filene's to pick out presents for the secretaries?'

The crowds on the MTA were daunting after the New Hampshire woods. The boys stuck close to Caroline's side, and grabbed her hands as they fought their way through writhing ranks of half-dressed women trying on blouses in the aisles of Filene's Basement.

Her father decided on Chanel No. 5 for the secretaries. As Caroline helped him take bottles from a damaged carton, she was inundated with the scent. Her mother had always worn it. Caroline, Howard, and Tommy used to gather around her as she dressed for work. Whoever had been best behaved got to fasten her stockings to her garters. Caroline's fingers twitched recalling the pleasure of fitting the silk stocking over the garter button and sliding both into the wire fastener. Meanwhile, her mother dabbed herself with Chanel No. 5. And Caroline gently ran her fingers over the ridges of pelvic bone that distended her mother's silk slip. Breasts and bones, that was what you grew when you became a woman. They never had a clear idea what her work was. She talked about orphans shivering on street corners whenever Caroline or her siblings whined about anything. Maureen used to read them 'The Little Match Girl,' and Caroline got it into her head that her mother went around to street corners handing out matches for orphans to sell.

'Do you think they'll like this all right?' her father asked as the saleslady rang up the Chanel No. 5.

Caroline looked up at him from where she squatted by the battered carton handing him bottles. She wasn't accustomed to his asking her advice. 'Mother loves it. So do I. I'm sure they will too.' She studied his ruddy, jowly face. Hannah implied he caused her pain. But she recalled him in terms of his absence. He was hardly ever home. And when he was, he was on the phone, or reading depositions, or lying in bed moaning with colitis. She couldn't remember their ever having a disagreement, or even a conversation.

Washington Street was jammed with holiday shoppers who moved from window to window outside Filene's and Jordan Marsh. Caroline, her father, and the boys halted before a display in which mechanical mice in red bow ties scurried through presents under a huge Christmas tree, as an alarmed mother in a nightgown threw up her hands time after time. Caroline sniffed the sample of Chanel No. 5 on her wrist and thought about her five senses. The more she entangled them with another person, the more rapidly a bond turned into bondage. As long as she merely yearned with her eyes, as she had at Jackson in his white lab coat and tie in the corridors of Mass General, she was okay. She had entertained fantasies about what his skin would feel like, but they stayed inside her fevered brain. Actually talk to a person and detachment became more difficult. Snatches of conversation recurred to you when you weren't prepared. When your sense of smell became involved, your troubles really began. Everywhere you went, you picked up hints of the person's cologne or aftershave, which triggered memories of the face or voice. Lately she'd become aware of Brian Stone's English Leather. This wasn't a good sign. To touch the person was to feel the slack go out of the chain, as when a wrecker is about to tow your car to the junkyard. And God help you if your tongue began to insist on tasting the person's sweat and saliva. When all five senses were fully engaged with those of the other person, you were done for. The two sets of senses began to spin their own tangled webs of intrigue, with no regard for the best interests of those originally employing them.

As they were carried along by the crowd to a second display window in which harnessed reindeer did a softshoe on someone's rooftop, Caroline reflected that that was why this celibacy shit was so difficult. It was like drug withdrawal. Diana was at her mother's in Poughkeepsie. She and Caroline had never spent a Christmas together, and now they probably never would. It hadn't seemed worth ruining everyone else's Christmas over. If you were black or crippled, at least your family still loved you. But if you were homosexual, you went it alone, as despised by your family as by the rest of society. They created you in their crucible, then loathed you for turning out as you'd been programmed. Maybe that was why there was a note of such desperation to her and Diana's perplexing relationship. Each other was all they had.

But of course now Diana had Suzanne any way she wanted her. They were meeting in New York for New Year's. Caroline tried to decide if they'd check into a hotel. It was none of her business anymore, but it still felt like her business. When Brian asked her out for New Year's Eve, she accepted. And Diana raged around the cabin like Elizabeth Taylor in *Who's Afraid of Virginia Woolf?*

'Why are you acting like this?' Caroline asked. 'I thought you wanted us to date other people.'

'So who's annoyed?' snarled Diana. 'Other people doesn't mean men,' she added from the next room.

In the first flush of new love, she brought Diana to Brookline, thinking her parents would be relieved to know she'd finally found happiness. Her mother, tall and angular, eyed Diana with tight-lipped, narrow-eyed disapproval and spent the weekend at her office. Her father chatted with them uneasily about abortion rights, then slipped out to his office, leaving them with the Vietnamese maid who'd fled the collapse of Saigon. She spoke no English except words like Lemon Pledge, Drāno, and Comet. Trying to talk with her was like watching a TV commercial. 'Need Vanish now,' she replied koanlike to every query.

Walking home from the MTA, Caroline, her father, and the boys passed Caroline's old high school, a sprawling red brick place where she'd been in a four-year anxiety state over the labels on her clothing. Rorkie, the leader of her crowd, decided who was in or out. Caroline imagined her marching up to an 'out' and ripping the Villager labels off her blouse and sweater.

'I went to school there,' she informed Jackie and Jason, who were balancing along the curbstone.

'Were cars invented back then?' asked Jason.

Caroline's mother was lying on the couch in a wool suit with her shoes off. 'Hello, dear, how nice to see you,' she murmured.

'Hello, Mother.' Caroline bent and kissed her forehead, smelling Chanel No. 5. Her hair, which Caroline remembered as silky chestnut, was mostly wiry gray now. Her mother had fine features and high cheekbones. Her blue eyes narrowed to make her seem suspicious and critical. Caroline recalled pleading when she was ten, 'I'll do anything you want, Mother, if only you'll stop being angry.' And she replied, 'But I'm not angry, dear.' Her mother had seemed breathtakingly glamorous to Caroline as a child. Sometimes people on the street would say, 'You look just like your mother.' And her mother would reply, 'I've never seen the resemblance myself.' Caroline would feel as though the cracks in the sidewalk had just yawned open.

'How are you, Mother?' asked Caroline, realizing all of a sudden that Diana had those same fine features and high cheekbones, though not the silky chestnut hair. And when Diana's eyes narrowed, it was with lust.

'As well as could be expected, considering.'

'Considering what?'

'Considering it's Christmas, which is a depressing time of year.'

'I think I'll go upstairs and lie down until time for church,' said Caroline's father, loosening his too-narrow tie.

'Are you tired, dear?' asked Caroline's mother.

'I am a bit. I went to Dorchester to talk to the parents of a first offender this morning. And I was out this afternoon buying presents for the secretaries.'

'I spent the day collecting clothes for a rummage sale.' She closed her eyes and rested her forearm on her forehead.

'You must be tired too.' He rubbed the ridge of scar tissue above his eyebrow.

'Oh no, not too bad,' she said wanly. 'But you look tired, dear.'

'Well, my bowel is tightening up.' He removed his jacket and hung it on the newel post.

'Go have a rest. I'll bring you some tea.'

'No, you're tired, dear. Let me bring you some tea.'

Caroline had forgotten about the Great Exhaustion Sweepstakes. It had always been understood that those who spent their days relieving human suffering were more evolved and deserved to be waited on when they got home. But problems arose on the maid's day off.

'I'm not tired,' said Caroline wearily, hitching up her gray cords. 'Why don't you both lie down and I'll make the tea?'

'But you must be tired, dear,' said her mother, glancing up from the couch, 'after your long drive. Why don't you lie down and I'll bring you some tea?'

'But I'm not tired and I don't want to lie down!'

'I was just trying to be nice.'

'I'm sorry. Please let me bring you some tea, Mother.'

'No,' she said coolly, turning on her side with her back to Caroline. 'I don't want any tea.'

Caroline's skin crawled with anxiety. She restrained herself from begging to make tea and ushered the boys into the playroom so her parents could rest in peace, as she had Howard and Tommy so often all those years ago. But Jackie and Jason began playing Space Invaders, not medical missionary.

As she brewed herself some tea in the kitchen, on the harvest gold stove that had survived a warehouse fire, she felt tightness in her shoulders. She shrugged a few times to loosen the muscles. Why was she so exhausted? Probably from all those shopping crowds.

Sitting in a pew at St Bartholomew's Episcopal Church, as she had most Sundays of her life until she moved into David Michael's

Somerville commune, Caroline glanced at Jackie and Jason, who sat on either side of her, wearing blazers and ties and looking perplexed by the hocus-pocus going on around the altar as communion was readied. When she was married to Jackson, she went to this church alone because he was usually either at the hospital or on call. The boys had been christened here. But when she left Jackson, she also left the church, adopting David Michael's scorn for anything organized, and discovering she enjoyed sleeping late on Sundays and waking to lovemaking and breakfast in bed.

Her father in his too-narrow tie and lapels sat beside Jackie. He'd been excommunicated from the Catholic Church, and very nearly from his own family, for failing to raise his children as Catholics. As a child, Caroline had often wished she were Catholic, like Marsha, like the neighborhood kids, like the most popular kids at school. She coveted Marsha's prayer cards and rosary, her candles and catechism classes. She watched enviously when Marsha took candles from the holders on Caroline's dining table, crossed them over her own throat, and described how on St Blase's Day the priest did the blessing of the throat so no one would choke on fishbones. The Catholics had blessings for anything that could go wrong. The priest even blessed Marsha's mother's new Amana range against grease fires and short circuits. Of course none of this helped Marsha. Though maybe the priest had simply forgotten to insure against careless Bunny Bread trucks.

Caroline had never seen this particular priest before. Tall and stooped in his black robe, he looked like a crow at rest as he perched at the lectern and delivered his sermon: '. ... just like the Israelites, who were unable to receive the living word of God from Moses as he came down off the mountain. They were dancing around a golden calf, having forgotten the instructions from their Lord God: "Thou shalt have no other gods before me." Just so do we fail to experience in our hearts the arrival of the newborn Christ. So preoccupied are we with gifts, food, and family. And not just at Christmas but all year long. We are obsessed with our relationships and our achievements, our new cars and the decoration of our houses, our golf scores and the labels on our clothing . . .'

From the way he said 'we,' Caroline could tell he was just humoring them. He knew he himself had transcended all this. There was a reason she'd stopped going to church.

'. . . and put aside all the false idols of your own making. For just a moment, look into your naked soul, unadorned by the tawdry trinkets of this sinful world, and see what you can find . . .'

Here was a boy who knew how to take all the fun out of Christmas, reflected Caroline, glancing at her mother in her hat and veil, who sat beside Jason eyeing him grimly as he scribbled infinitesimal amounts on the pledge cards in the hymnal rack. Did her mother cause her pain, as Hannah implied?

They walked home through the cold night, along Cypress Street past darkened storefronts and through circles of light from street lamps, footsteps muffled by new-fallen snow. Caroline glanced at her parents, bundled in overcoats, their breath steamy white, both slightly stooped from carrying the weight of the world on their shoulders for all these years. How had they kept on decade after decade? She herself was about to give out after only a few years. Maybe she should join the Catholic Church at long last. Attend altar guild meetings at Our Lady of Sporadic Mercy. The saints in the pictures in Marsha's house and church – St Sebastian full of arrows, Jesus on the cross with thorns ripping his forehead, St Stephen bruised and bloody from stones – were always looking upward, as though they saw something that cheered them up. As though they'd managed to make peace with the savage ways of their fellow citizens.

On Christmas morning they sat around a cedar tree Caroline's father had bought at half price the night before from a man eager to shut down his lot to go to mass. Jackie took an envelope with his name on it off the tree and ripped it open. Inside was a partially filled March of Dimes card. He looked at it questioningly, turning it around and over.

'You fill the blank slots with dimes from your allowance,' said Caroline's mother, who sat on the sofa in her brown satin robe. 'When it's full, you mail it to national headquarters.'

'Neat,' said Jackie, glancing under the tree for another gift.

'Won't it be fun to help some crippled child walk again?' asked Caroline's mother, sipping her coffee.

'Yes, I guess so.'

'He certainly doesn't seem very excited,' said Caroline's mother.

Caroline felt a twinge of anxiety. Jackie wasn't showing enough gratitude. Her mother would think she'd reared a greedy ingrate. 'I'm sure he is,' said Caroline as Jason opened an identical card and displayed even less enthusiasm. They'd asked for cartridges for their video game. Evidently no trucks carrying such cargo had wrecked lately in the Boston area.

Inside the UNICEF card addressed to Caroline, her mother had written the usual message – that the card represented a donation to the charity of her choice. Caroline had been told that other families sat around on Christmas discussing the merits of the Buffalo Bills over the Dallas Cowboys because of their running offense. Her family had always discussed the superiority of the Salvation Army over Planned Parenthood because of low administrative costs.

'Which are you going to pick this year, Caroline?' asked her mother, extending her arm along the back of the sofa. Caroline studied her satin robe. It seemed so elegant when Caroline was little, something Loretta Young would wear. Caroline had watched it fall open at the throat as the maids set her mother's hair and rubbed her neck. Now it looked as though it ought to be donated to the Boat People Relief Fund rummage sale.

'I've been thinking about Amnesty International.' She sat cross-legged in her down bathrobe on the beige Route 128 carpet.

'Bunch of masochists,' her father, wearing his red plaid wool robe, said from the corduroy armchair. 'Spending their lives discussing how horrible torture is.'

'But it probably is,' said Caroline.

'But who'd want to make a career of researching it?'

'But that's what you do, Dad – spend all your time rescuing people.'

'So do you.'

'I never said I wasn't a masochist.'

He smiled. 'Masochists, are we? Maybe so. But I couldn't live with myself if I didn't do what I can to make this world less of a hellhole.' He was rubbing the scar above his eyebrow.

Caroline nodded. 'But isn't that what Amnesty's doing?'

'You're probably right.'

Jason knelt on the rug by the tree, tearing open a present as though shucking corn. Holding up a pair of L. L. Bean boots, he said with suspicion, 'Hey.'

'Got them at a sale,' said Caroline's father. 'Good as new. It's amazing what some people give away.'

Caroline inspected them. They were Jason's own outgrown boots. His initials were inside in Magic Marker.

'Try them on,' her father said.

Jason pulled them on, a perplexed expression on his face, and walked over to his grandfather.

'What sale?' asked Caroline.

'The Boat People Relief Fund rummage sale.' He leaned over and felt Jason's foot. 'They fit just fine.'

'Too tight,' muttered Jason, glancing at Jackie questioningly.

'Yes sir, just fine,' said Caroline's father, slapping Jason on the shoulder.

Jason screwed up his face and looked at Caroline. This was nothing new to her. She and Jackson had been married under a funeral tent erected by a client of her father's who ran the Ready Funeral Parlor. The boys might as well become acquainted with their heritage. 'Did you thank Grandpa, Jason?'

'Thank you, Grandpa,' he said in a bewildered voice. He came over and plopped down in Caroline's lap. She put her arms around him, feeling the warm flannel of his Dr Denton's under her hands.

'You're welcome, Jason. I hope you enjoy them.'

'By the way, how is poor Jackson?' asked her mother. She always preceded his name with that adjective.

'Fine, as far as I know. He and his wife had another baby this fall.' Resting her chin atop Jason's head, she remembered wanting to rest her head in Hannah's lap. She looked at her mother, self-contained on the sofa in her satin robe. Caroline couldn't recall ever resting her head in her mother's lap, or sitting in it as Jason was now in hers.

'Are you still living with that woman?' asked her mother.

'Diana. Yes.' She restrained an urge to add that they weren't lovers anymore. No need to let a dead cat out of the bag. Whether her parents knew they'd been lovers was unclear. It had never been acknowledged. Nor had her divorce, David Michael, Clea, her depressions. What had been discussed during this visit was the fate of humanism in the twentieth century; interracial knife fights at South Boston High; the threat posed by killer bees and aerosol cans; relief efforts in behalf of families involved in a West Virginia mining disaster; starvation in Chad, and floods in India. Personal disaster was insignificant by comparison.

Her mother looked so unhappy from the mention of Jackson and Diana that Caroline felt a need to cheer her up. 'Mother, how many therapists does it take to change a light bulb?' She could use this as an opener for telling about Hannah. Surely they'd want to know about such an important development. But maybe it would upset them to hear she'd been unhappy?

'One, but the bulb has to really want to change.' She watched with pleasure as her parents' faces softened into smiles.

'Speaking of which, I've gone into therapy myself.' Too late she remembered they didn't approve of therapy. They belonged to the Bootstrap School. They'd think she was a wimp.

'Why?' asked her father, looking up.

'I've been depressed a lot,' she said in a low voice.

'Depressed?' said her mother. 'Who isn't depressed? How could you not be with all the dreadful things going on in the world? Did you read in the paper about Vietnamese troops amassing on the Cambodian border? That could be World War Three.'

Caroline sat in silence. How could she had forgotten the trips to the Salvation Army? She adjusted her poker-playing face. Then she noticed what she was doing. She glanced around the room at the doorways. From which jamb had she hung in similar silence as a baby?

'People like us have no right to be unhappy,' her father said. 'We have food, shelter, clothing, good health, relative safety.'

Caroline knew her parents were right. One individual's despair wasn't important in the light of Vietnamese troops poised to invade Cambodia. If she were Cambodian, she might be starving, homeless, raped, murdered right now. Depression was a luxury of the American middle class, just as David Michael always used to insist. She should be grateful to have the leisure in which to feel so awful. Guilt over her ingratitude wrapped around her like Dracula's cape.

'One more thing,' her mother called to the boys as they departed to the playroom to hook up their video game and try out the cartridges Diana had given them. 'We got carried away and invited more people for dinner than we have food for. So could I ask you three please to eat small portions and skip dessert?' They all nodded.

'Who's coming?' asked Caroline, recalling past holiday dinners, jammed with her parents' clients. Her father had been known to scour the streets on Christmas Day searching for people with nowhere to go. Once he brought home a hitchhiker named

Bradley, who entertained them by swallowing a spoon, a skill he developed in jail. He'd swallow a spoon, they'd rush him to the emergency room, and he'd escape when no one was looking. How he retrieved the spoon wasn't explained. A regular named Lionel, a tall sad man with a tic, had no family to eat holiday dinners with because he murdered them all by putting laxative in their food over many months. A woman named Bertha used to sit on the couch and open and close a pair of scissors all afternoon.

'You don't know most of them,' her mother replied.

'What's happened to the old gang?'

'Bertha's coming.'

'Does she still play with those scissors?'

'No, she took up knitting.'

'That's a nice thing you've done all these years, Mother. Now that I'm an adult, I realize how much work it is.'

Her mother's shoulders sagged under the brown satin robe. 'Well, poor people. Life isn't easy for anyone, but it's easier for us than for most.'

Every chair in the house was crammed around the mahogany dining table. Caroline had a son on either side, and her parents presided at either end. Bertha had knitted throughout the meal, on what looked like either a narrow blanket or a wide scarf in shades of red and brown. Occasionally she put down a needle to stuff a hasty bite into her mouth, never taking her eyes off her handiwork. A tattered man who lived somewhere in the Park Street Under MTA station sat next to Bertha and tried unsuccessfully to strike up conversations about people he'd seen electrocuted on the third rail. A woman from her mother's office wore her hair on top of her head in a large bun, which she'd encircled with holly like a Roman emperor with his wreath of laurel. The barmaid from underneath her father's office kept flicking her crystal goblet with a long mauve nail, to hear the tinkling noise like a tiny jingle bell. Caroline found herself staring at the polished nails, thinking the fingertips had been severed, like those of the drill press operator who'd come into Peter Bent Brigham during her ER rotation at nursing school.

Bradley, the spoon swallower, had been replaced by Sidney, who had the illusion he was a magician. He kept laying his linen napkin across the turkey and mumbling spells. Jackie and Jason watched with wide eyes, worried it would vanish while they were still hungry. But each time Sidney whipped off the napkin, the turkey was still there. He'd retreat himself in a funk, rehearsing spells, trying to see where he'd gone wrong. A mother in a baby blue argyle pullover and plastic Pop-It beads was trying to prevent her son from thrusting his drumstick obscenely in and out of the turkey's neck cavity.

Caroline glanced at Jackie and Jason in their sports jackets and ties, their hair parted and slicked down. She'd never seen them so quiet. For one thing, the other little boy had demolished their video game. When he couldn't get his lever to function as he wanted, he simply tore it out of the box. Caroline recalled that feeling of bafflement on holidays, never knowing who'd be there, knowing only that they had nowhere else to go and that her family could afford to include them because her family was so fortunate.

She wondered what Hannah was doing right then. Was her house also full of the homeless? Was Hannah correct that her parents caused her pain? She wasn't feeling so great, but that certainly wasn't their fault. And she could see for herself how the sad people at this table gazed at her parents with admiration. Her parents had served on the school board and the city council. They'd been heart fund volunteers. They'd raised money for the community ambulance. They were good people.

Her mother was right: there wasn't enough food. The boys had copied Caroline's example and taken only a thin slice of turkey, a small spoonful of mashed potatoes, and a few peas. The rolls were gone before reaching their side of the table, and the pies went just as quickly. The abstinence required no effort on Caroline's part. She wasn't hungry. In fact she felt nauseated. As she cleared the table, the guests moved into the living room, and her father began to stoke the fire.

'How about some carols?' her mother was suggesting as Caroline entered the living room. These were among the few occasions on which she saw this cheery side to her mother. Usually she was exhausted from having spent all day being cheery at the office. Jason was pulling his grandmother's arm, trying to get her attention about something to do with the video game. She shook him off, whispering, 'Not now, Jason. I'm busy.'

Jason plopped down beside Caroline on the Route 128 carpet and looked up through his absurdly long Minnie Mouse eyelashes.

'Mommy, I'm hungry.' He wrenched off his blazer and wadded it on the floor.

She patted his thigh hopelessly. He shoved a thumb in his mouth. He hadn't sucked his thumb for years.

'Jason, why are you sucking your thumb?' asked Caroline's mother as she handed him a carol book. 'You're a big boy.'

'Hungry,' he whimpered.

Caroline felt her stomach tensing. He didn't know he was supposed to pretend he was fine even if he wasn't. She hadn't trained him properly. Her parents were seeing her as the bad parent she in fact was.

'Hungry? But we've just finished dinner.'

Jason gazed at his grandmother over his fist, sucking the thumb with furious defiance.

'Look at Jackie,' said Caroline's mother, gesturing to the fireplace, next to which Jackie stood looking awkward and shy, hands clasped behind his back. 'He's not hungry and he's a bigger boy than you are.'

Caroline watched a tear begin to swell in Jason's right eye. Why couldn't the kid just play the game and get it over with?

'At least you're not cold,' said Caroline's father, joining them. 'What about the millions of children all over the world right now who are cold as well as hungry?'

'At least he has a house and a family,' said Caroline's mother to Caroline's father. 'Unlike several of our guests today.'

'And he has nice new boots,' said Caroline's father to Caroline's mother. 'What about children in Kentucky who are barefoot at this very moment? Up in the snowy mountains.'

Caroline's parents studied Jason, perplexed. He jumped up, raced to the front door, flung it open, and dashed out.

'What in the world?' said Caroline's mother.

Caroline knew she should do something, but she couldn't think what. She was in the grip of an overwhelming inertia. All she wanted was to stretch out face down on the Route 128 carpet and let events wash over her like waves over flotsam at high tide. Instead, she unfolded herself and stood up, as though in slow motion. She went out the door and glanced around the yard in the light from the colored Christmas bulbs over the door. She trotted around the house, maternal instincts on automatic pilot. No Jason. God, her parents must be thinking she'd reared little barbarians. When she returned for her coat, the room was silent, the guests looking at each other and straining forward in their seats. Bertha had even stopped knitting.

'He's gone,' said Caroline. 'Jackie, please help me.'

They searched the neighborhood for fifteen minutes, calling for him into the dark. Damn kid. Why did he have to be so melodramatic? Why couldn't he just do as he was supposed to, be quiet and polite and sing carols until time for bed? Finally they climbed in the Subaru and drove toward Cleveland Circle. She was getting really worried. The terror she used to feel as a young girl when she lost track of Howard or Tommy was setting in. Anything could have happened to him. Cities were full of creeps. Jason was so young and vulnerable. Goddam it, where was he?

A mile away they found Jason, shivering by a lamppost, shoeless, coatless, sucking a thumb. Caroline got out and hugged him. Then she squelched a wish to hit him for terrifying her.

As he climbed in the car, he asked, 'Mommy, can we go back to our own house now? Grandpa and Grandma don't like me.'

Caroline said nothing.

The route back to her parents' house took them past her old high school again. Caroline glanced at the darkened hulking old building feeling dread. When she led Jason into the house, she was aware her parents were studying him critically. He was an ill-mannered little boy, and it was all her fault.

'What was that all about?' asked Caroline's father of the sniffling Jason as Caroline rubbed his frozen toes. All Caroline wanted was to be alone in bed, lying as still as possible. A grave would be even better. She eyed a doorway and pictured herself hanging silently in it – from a noose.

Caroline sat up in the spool bed from her girlhood, suddenly wide awake, flesh burning. She pinched the bridge of her nose, trying to recall what she'd been dreaming. Something about rowing in a leaking boat with Jackie and Jason in an effort to escape a nuclear fireball. The sun was white hot, and the water still as glass. They reached a beach, but every time the boat landed, a man in an ill-fitting army uniform pushed them back out to sea and threatened to split the hull with a bloody ax.

Wiping the sweat off her forehead with the back of her hand, she tried to quell her anxiety. She used to lie in this bed and cover herself with Pink Blanky for protection. But where was her pink blanket when she really needed it? She was definitely losing it. She tried to remember where she'd put Hannah's phone number. But she couldn't call in the middle of the night. But by daybreak she wouldn't need to call because either she'd feel better, or she'd have killed herself.

She tiptoed into Howard's old room to be sure Jackie and Jason were still breathing. Kissing them, she inhaled their healthy boy smells. How often had she put everyone else's interests ahead of theirs, she wondered. Leaving them long hours with unfamiliar baby-sitters while she worked late. Ignoring their requests for time and attention so she could save the world. Slaving for suffering humanity while her own sons suffered. She'd done the same to Diana – worked late, canceled dates, rushed out in the middle of intimate dinners, expecting her to understand that patients' needs came first because she and Diana were blessed with such a rich love. But maybe Diana hadn't understood. Maybe that was why she'd withdrawn. Maybe that's why she called Caroline a taker. Maybe Suzanne put Diana ahead of suffering humanity. Caroline was a lousy mother, and an even worse lover. Diana was right to have left her. Her stomach clenched rhythmically like labor pains.

She remembered Hannah's saying she was kind and gentle. But what did Hannah know? That was what she was being paid to say.

Climbing back into her bed, she struggled to picture Hannah, her quiet strength and composure. Her calm face, graying hair, and blue eyes. She gave an exaggerated version of Hannah's shrug. It had worked last weekend to banish the woman miscarrying in the motel room. If she tried, she could rid herself of that vision of little Jason, barefoot and coatless, shivering all alone in the dark. She shrugged several more times, searching desperatel· for the state of mind that went with such a gesture.

Six

Hannah's feet hit the carpet next to Arthur's and her four-poster bed. Grabbing her throat, she ran for the bedroom door. By the time she reached the living room, she was fully awake and able to stop herself from flinging open the door to Simon's old room to shake him awake, as she had from time to time when he was a teenager. At least if storm troopers arrived to carry him off, he'd think it was just his crazy mother having her bad dream again. She remembered that Simon wasn't even home. He and Joanna had come out on Christmas Day but had returned to their apartments in town after a turkey dinner.

Hannah sank into the leather couch and lit a cigarette with trembling hands. Drawing the smoke deep into her lungs, she closed her eyes and tried to relax into the cushions, which felt icy through her nightgown.

The dream came less often, but no less convincingly. In it, she awoke with a band of pain around her forehead. She staggered to the bathroom and vomited. On her way back to bed, thinking she had flu, she checked the children, as she had since they were infants, to be sure they were breathing. And Nigel and Mona weren't. Their faces were cold to her frantic fingertips, and slightly blue in the moonlight. In disbelief she raced around throwing open windows. As frigid air howled through the house, she fainted. When she came to, she vomited on the Oriental carpet in the living room. She crawled to the phone, called the operator, and then passed out again.

She drew on her cigarette and exhaled. Slow suicide, these cigarettes. But smoking them, she could at least control her intake of poisonous fumes and die at her own chosen rate. The wind swirling off the lake was rattling the storm windows. She could hear waves slapping the gray rocks along the shoreline. She inhaled the fresh scent of the balsam tree in the corner, which was also dying quietly.

The town rescue squad arrived that night and rushed them to the emergency room at Lloyd Harris. From which only three of the five emerged on foot. A freak accident. Impossible, the furnace dealer said. An east wind had driven the exhaust down the chimney. The rescue squad left the door unlocked, and before Arthur could get home from his business trip to Des Moines, the antiques were stolen. She felt sure, life being the ongoing delight it was, one day in someone's house she'd look into a corner and see her pine cupboard.

She could have – what? She began to review her responses in obsessive detail, trying to see how she might have prevented the outcome. She should have smelled the exhaust, should have gotten up sooner, should have had the furnace checked out for this possibility. How had she brought this on? What crime was she being punished for? She'd broken up Arthur's first marriage. Mona and Nigel were a result of the breakup. Therefore, they had to be taken away from her . . . .

She knew this was crazy, what clients came to her about. There had been a time when she'd have picked up the phone and called someone, as she now suggested clients do with her, had there been anyone to call. But she quickly realized she was stuck with this horror. Even Arthur – as much as he mourned the children, as often as he comforted her in the numb months that followed – hadn't been there that night. Her friends and colleagues looked at her as though she were the Ancient Mariner, a rotting albatross cradled in her arms. When she tried to speak matter-of-factly of the accident, they looked embarrassed or pitying. Maggie came closest to hearing her out, poking at the wounds in her office at her house on Lake Glass. She forced Hannah to rehearse the events of that night time after time as though Hannah were a soldier with shell shock. 'Describe what they looked like,' insisted Maggie from her tapestry-covered wing chair, thick glasses concealing her eyes. 'How did their skin feel when you touched them?'

'What are you – some kind of bloody ghoul?'

'Tell me again about crawling to the phone, Hannah.'

'No! I won't! Goddam you, Maggie!' At one point Hannah hurled the box of Kleenex at Maggie, who caught it and threw it back.

Once it was over, some of the horror had been depleted. But even Maggie had been ad libbing. Her three children were alive and well, called every week and came to visit on holidays.

Having no one to call wasn't an unfamiliar feeling to Hannah. In the Hampstead house, with her mother in the grave and her father in Trinidad, she often woke from bad dreams and padded into her grandmother's room to watch the old lady snore in her black eyeshade and ear plugs, longing to wake her up but afraid to. Loss and abandonment, guilt and terror. The same primal atmosphere her clients inhabited. Probably that was why she was such a good therapist.

Listening to the crashing waves, she tried to switch off her emotions. It was easier to silence them when she had to in order to perform her job. So she began to run through her clients from the previous week. Ed, the engineering student, had found himself an older woman, since his campaign to seduce Hannah had failed. He was flaunting it, yawning and sprawling open-legged on the couch with coy remarks about how little sleep he was getting.

Hannah felt her tense mouth soften into the beginnings of a smile. Caroline was with her parents in Boston. She hadn't phoned, so she must be getting along all right. Those parents of hers. To have a daughter like that and not dote on her. Her smile turned bitter as she realized Mona would have been only a few years younger than Caroline had she lived. Then she reminded herself that therapy was like a trial with only one witness. Caroline's parents' versions of what had gone on in that household would be entirely different, from Caroline's and from each other's. And they'd all be telling the truth – each his or her own individual truth. Hannah had been outraged the entire time Joanna was doing therapy by the scenario Joanna constructed from their shared past, which involved negligence Hannah had no memory of. Finally she accepted that this was how Joanna needed to make her break from home.

Well, there wasn't any such thing as an adequate parent anyway. It was an impossible job. If their parents had been present, clients felt suffocated. If absent, clients felt deserted. How could one flawed mortal protect another from all the ghastly things this world dished out? She hadn't been able to protect Mona and Nigel. Even if you could protect your children, you'd probably be doing them a disservice. She had a feeling this world wasn't meant to be settled into like a comfortable old sofa; it was meant to be experienced, then discarded like an empty tin can.

She wondered if her clients had any idea how much she needed to see them become healthy happy adults, needed to know she was doing everything she could to help this happen. The process had been interrupted with Nigel and Mona, leaving her with all these thwarted instincts. It was like being pregnant with a dead fetus. Somehow you had to get it out. She'd tried to get pregnant shortly after that awful night, with the pathetic notion of replacing the irreplaceable, but it hadn't worked. So she'd gotten her degrees and devoted herself to rearing other people's grown children. Lately she'd begun to wonder how much longer it would take to work through this. Eventually she'd move on. But to what? Probably to an aluminum walker.

Sucking on her cigarette, she watched the tip flare and sputter in the dark. The wind whined through the cedars along the cliff. She was shivering. Squashing out the cigarette, she stood up and walked to the greenhouse window. The cold had etched an icy forest of prehistoric ferns on the panes. The pattern stood out in the moonlight like the rickshaw-pulling coolie on the lantern globe in that house on the Australian sheep station so many years earlier. Sitting on her mother's lap playing with her gold wedding band, Hannah used to watch moths flutter around the candle flame that illuminated the coolie, watch them immolate themselves with a sickening odor. Her mother, Maggie, Mona and Nigel . . . Grief sliced through her like a scalpel.

Taking a trembling breath, she pressed her fingertips to the glass. If there was a design to frost crystals on window panes, she reminded herself resolutely, who was she to say there was none to human events, even if the shape wasn't always detectable in the gloom?

Back in bed she wrapped herself around sleeping Arthur and waited for morning, pleased with herself for staving off the despair. Sometimes it took a pitcher of martinis and nice slow screw.

Oh my God, thought Hannah as she looked at Caroline's face in the waiting room. Numb and puffy, eyes squinting with pain. Back to square one. As they walked down the shadowy corridor,

Caroline carrying her parka, Hannah observed the tightness in Caroline's shoulders beneath her white uniform top and geared up for combat with Caroline's devils.

Caroline sat on the couch in silence, examining the tread on her snowmobile boot with the fingers of one hand. From time to time she looked up and opened her mouth, but no words came out.

'Just say anything,' said Hannah. 'It doesn't have to make sense.' They continued to sit in silence. Hannah was seeing that little baby, hanging motionless in her jump seat, trying to be inoffensive by appearing nonexistent.

Finally Caroline looked up and said, 'I've lost it. I felt good last week. But it's gone.'

'You may have lost it, but you can get it back if you decide to.' Hannah realized she was grateful for her own bouts of despair like last night's, if only to confirm that the techniques she offered clients could work.

'You make it sound as though I enjoy feeling bad.'

'Is that what you hear me saying?'

Caroline didn't reply. She felt too shitty to play Hannah's word games today. Added to her despair was a new element: terror, that Hannah would find out Caroline had come to depend on her, summoned her image and gestures to feel better when she woke up in an anxious sweat. Hannah would see her neediness and be repulsed. *I know what you want and you can't have it.* Caroline couldn't let her know how important she'd become to her. If she kept perfectly still and silent, Hannah wouldn't be able to tell.

'So what happened in Boston? How did you lose it?'

Caroline sighed and folded her arms across her stomach. 'It's too boring.'

'You don't look bored. You look like you're in pain. How do you feel?'

Caroline looked at Hannah's blue eyes and felt exhausted, her poker-playing expression slipping like a denture wearer's upper plate coming unstuck. 'Not too good.'

Hannah shrugged, sat back, and lit a cigarette. Okay, feel bad if you insist, kiddo. She waited, watching Caroline sit as motionless as a corpse, concentrating on maintaining her own sense of well-being, and willing it to communicate itself to Caroline. Sometimes she thought anything that got said in here was irrelevant. What she really had to offer was an attitude, which a client picked up, if at all, by osmosis.

Studying Caroline's anguish, she concluded that parents and grown children should make a pact to stay out of each other's lives. Let the parents retire to Fort Lauderdale and play shuffle-board. Let their children set up households and repeat their parents' mistakes, until they developed enough understanding of the difficulties of being parents to forgive their own. She didn't see much of Simon and Joanna anymore, even though they all lived along Lake Glass. They checked in regularly, but not for long. The tug of the past was too compelling.

Caroline started talking in a monotone about Christmas. Hannah heard another variation on what she already knew about Mother and Dad Kelley. Therapy reminded her of the bell tower at Christ Church, down the street from her grandmother's house in Hampstead. On weekends carillonneurs rang the changes, their equivalent of piano scales, a slight variation on the basic pattern being introduced every few minutes.

She was left with the image of a humiliated little boy running barefoot through a winter night.

'Do you understand why what happened was so upsetting for you?'

'I was terrified something awful had happened to Jason.'

'And?'

'I thought my parents would think I was a bad mother to have raised such a rude child.'

'And?'

Caroline frowned and rubbed the bridge of her nose. These sessions were like a TV game show. When Caroline guessed the right answer, she'd hear an inaudible buzzer.

Hannah raised her eyebrows.

'How Jason felt was how I felt as a child in that household?' Caroline heard herself say.

Hannah pursed her lips. Bingo. 'Did you?'

Caroline was stunned by what she'd just said. She had a happy privileged childhood.

'Take another look at those photos,' Hannah said.

Caroline sat in silence, gazing out the window to Lake Glass. Hannah felt a twinge of envy. Her clients got to see the lake. She got to see the parking lot. Was this any way to run an office?

'You're entitled to feel pissed off, you know,' said Hannah. 'I would have. Lousy gifts, not enough food, a houseful of loonies.'

'They're good people.'

'If you say so.' Caroline wouldn't touch her anger with a ten-foot pole.

'They mean well.'

'But it's not good enough, is it?' If Caroline wouldn't get angry at her parents, maybe she'd get angry at Hannah.

'I realized I've treated Jackie and Jason like that all these years.'

'Whom did you learn it from?'

'I've been a terrible mother. I didn't defend Jason – not over the gifts, or the food, or the broken game. I was only concerned with whether my parents would see me as a bad mother.'

'Rubbish. You're doing beautifully.' Rather than face her parents' imperfections, she was playing up her own. In these regions of the soul, all events were simultaneous: Caroline was at once the infant and the thirty-five-year-old mother.

'How would you know? All you know is what I tell you.'

'My friend, I pass many a delightful hour in here with child abusers. If child abuse is your ambition, I'm afraid you're a dismal failure. Look, at least your son was able to run out of the house. He didn't just hang there in his jump seat trying to be good. You must be doing something right.'

Caroline felt a flicker of gratitude. Hannah always insisted on seeing her failings as virtues. But it was just a technique. Having something to do with that Venus. Her eyes rested on the gray stone statue on the windowsill. She smiled wanly.

'What's so funny?' asked Hannah.

Caroline nodded toward the statue. 'Her expression is so calm and kind. I think I have Venus envy.'

Hannah gave a startled laugh. A touch of color had returned to Caroline's cheeks. Still grinning, Hannah asked, 'What do you suppose your parents get out of filling their house with loonies?' She knew the answer from observing herself at various times: They got to avoid contact with their own family, and they got to feel sane by comparison. But she wanted to find out how far Caroline had come.

'I wish you'd stop calling them loonies. They're sad troubled people with nowhere to go.'

Hannah shrugged, pleased Caroline was feeling enough better

to get irritated. That corpse imitation was unnerving. 'Maybe they should get together and set up a fund for the neglected offspring of servants of humanity. Might give them a sense of purpose.'

Caroline's face began to twitch. Hannah tried to think of something even more obnoxious. What would it take to get Caroline angry at someone beside herself? She felt like a banderillero planting darts in a sluggish bull.

'Something I've just realized,' said Caroline. 'Maybe it's not just me who's crazy. Maybe it's them too.'

Bravo, called Hannah silently. 'Scapegoats always feel whatever goes wrong is their fault.' She drew on her cigarette and waited to see if Caroline would accept this label.

Caroline blinked. Scapegoat? That didn't sound right. Those were people who got stoned or crucified or something. The worst that had happened to her was that she hadn't gotten her fill of turkey.

'When my two children died from carbon monoxide poisoning,' said Hannah, lowering her gaze to a spot on the carpet damp from Caroline's boots, 'there were even a few friends who implied it was my fault. People need to believe in cause and effect. Random disaster is too scary.' She watched this information sink in.

'Your children died?' Caroline stared at the photos on the bulletin board of the towheaded children with missing teeth and Hannah's eyes. Jesus.

'A while back. From a faulty exhaust on our furnace.'

'I'm sorry.' Caroline felt suddenly sheepish. She was unloading her troubles on someone who'd been through something like that? She remembered the trips to the Salvation Army. *You think you've got problems?* She glanced at the children on the bulletin board and felt guilty for hating them so much.

'Thank you. But the point is, awful things happen. You can't control that. But you can control how you respond.' With a lot of practice and effort, she added silently, remembering her seizure of despair last night, and all the years of numbness and nightmares. Hannah rubbed the bridge of her nose. Then she noticed what she was doing – plagiarizing Caroline's stress gesture. This modeling process worked both ways. Just as long as she didn't pick up sodomy with young boys or heroin addiction.

Caroline studied Hannah's face as though seeing it for the first time – the patina of wrinkles like a piece of fired pottery, the curly gray hair and sharp, clear eyes. If Hannah could get through the death of her children, presumably Caroline could get through a failed dinner party with her parents.

'How do you feel?' Hannah didn't want to send someone back out on the street for another week feeling as bad as Caroline looked when she came in.

'Better,' said Caroline, realizing it was true. The funk had lifted like the lid of a coffin. She drew a deep breath, her first in several days.

'And one of these days you won't even need the example of someone with more to cope with than yourself to feel better.'

Part Two

One

Brian ushered Caroline into the Eliots' house, a low-slung natural wood structure with lots of glass, furnished with what looked like the latest in dental chairs. Chrome gleamed in lights that seemed too bright. Sitting on a hill overlooking Lake Glass, the house could have been featured in *House Beautiful*. Randy Eliot owned the local Peugeot dealership out on the highway next to Lake Glass Lanes. For Christmas his wife, Connie, had given him silicone implants in her breasts. Connie wore a low-cut red satin gown that served up her amplified breasts like cheese balls. Caroline tried not to stare at them as Connie shook her hand and took her coat.

Caroline had been anxious all day over what to wear and how to act. It had been years since she'd been to a party involving anything other than women in Levi's and running shoes. In the back of her closet she found an emerald-green velvet cocktail dress from her days with Jackson, so outmoded it was just coming back into style. She couldn't imagine how she'd had the foresight to save it. Wedging herself into it, she hoped her body would conform to its coverings and replicate proper dinner party behavior.

Brian brought her a Scotch and water, and she clinked the ice cubes in her glass and nodded as he discussed the fuel ratio in the carburetor of the new model Peugeot with Randy Eliot and a Nationwide Insurance man in a bow tie named Curtis. Randy, Curtis, and Brian were evidently in a racquetball league together, and they moved on from Peugeots to three-wall serves.

A tall man in a red blazer with an elaborate college crest on the pocket walked up to Caroline and murmured in her ear. 'Smashing dress.' A button on his lapel read 'Beer Drinkers Get More Head.'

'Thanks.'

'Haven't I seen you somewhere before?'

Probably I gave you an enema the last time you were in the hospital, thought Caroline. 'Have you?'

'I've got it.' He was studying her cleavage thoughtfully. 'Weren't you in the finals of that tennis tournament at the club last summer?'

'No.' Was this for real, or was it a come-on? She simply couldn't remember how to play these games. She felt as out of it as if she'd been dumped in Tibet without a translator.

'I could have sworn it was you. In the doubles semifinals with Betsy Burns.'

'Nope.'

'I haven't been able to take my eyes off you since you walked in the room,' he said in a low voice with a guilty glance in Randy's direction.

'Who, me? Look, would you excuse me? I have to find the . . . ah, powder room.' Did this man know there was a famine in Chad? That a woman had been carried into the ER last night with the initials of the six men who'd raped her carved on her thighs?

'I love your house,' Caroline told Connie as they stood beside a chrome and glass table spearing shrimp on toothpicks.

'Thank you. How do you know Brian?'

'I work with him at the hospital.' Caroline was concentrating on looking directly into Connie's eyes and ignoring the reports of her peripheral vision on Randy's Christmas gifts, which were swelling out of Connie's red satin bodice.

'So you're a nurse?'

'Right. I work in the emergency room.'

'How interesting.'

'Yes, it is.' Caroline searched for something to say. She'd really forgotten how to do this.

'Randy and I think Brian's pretty special.'

'Yes, he certainly is.' Caroline speared a shrimp and dipped it in cocktail sauce.

'We've partied with him for years.'

Caroline nodded as she raised the shrimp to her mouth. It fell off the toothpick and landed on Connie's left breast, the sauce splattering across the smooth brown flesh. Caroline stood still, holding her empty toothpick in midair as though conducting a symphony with a miniature wand.

'I'm sorry,' Caroline finally thought to murmur. She reached out to pick up the shrimp, then thought better of it and retracted her hand.

Connie plucked the shrimp off her breast, and popped it into Caroline's mouth.

'Uh, shall I . . .' Caroline gestured with her cocktail napkin, which read, 'Old Sailors Never Die, They Just Get a Little Dinghy.'

'Here, I'll do it.' Connie took the napkin and blotted her breast, giving Caroline a frank, amused smile.

Caroline reminded herself that flirting with the hostess wasn't acceptable cocktail party behavior for a woman. Evidently she couldn't rely on her automatic pilot. She looked around for Brian, thinking she'd better sleep with somebody soon or she'd be a menace to polite society. Murmuring to Connie about the powder room, she escaped into the hallway.

Next to the bathroom was a coat closet. A powder-blue Princess phone sat on a stand between the two doorways. Looking around, she grabbed the phone and retreated into the closet, closing the door behind her and settling down among the boots, a Persian lamb coat hanging in her face. She considered phoning Hannah for some hints on how to resume being respectable. After all, she hadn't called her from Boston in the middle of the night, so Hannah owed her one.

Instead she dialed Jenny.

'Why, I do believe it's Saint Celibate,' said Jenny. 'Listen, I can't talk right now. Pam and I are watching "Dallas." J.R. and Sue Ellen are having a terrible fight. Can I call you back?'

'No, you can't,' said Caroline, shifting her head to get the coat out of her face. 'I'm sitting in a Peugeot dealer's closet.'

'What?'

'I'm at a party.'

'At a Peugeot dealer's?'

'Yeah.'

'How come?'

'This guy at work invited me, and it seemed like a good idea at the time. But I haven't spent much time lately with people who have joint checking accounts, and I've forgotten how to act.'

Jenny didn't reply. Caroline could hear J.R. yelling in the

background. Was Jenny's silence disapproval of Peugeot dealers, or absorption in 'Dallas'?

'Where's Diana?' Jenny asked, sounding distracted.

'Probably in some New York hotel screwing her child nurse.'

'Jesus, I wouldn't mess with you, Caroline. You'll do anything for revenge.'

Caroline considered whether this was her motive for being at the Eliots'. Diana had certainly been upset, flouncing around the cabin hurling Sharon's scattered belongings into her bedroom. But also Caroline liked Brian. He was a nice man. She just didn't like respectable heterosexual parties. 'Well, don't worry. It's taking its toll. These people are insane.'

'Look, do you want me to come pick you up? You could catch the tail end of "Dallas." '

'No thanks, Jenny, I just want some sympathy.'

'Well, you're not getting any from me, darling. Anyone who goes out with a man when she should know better deserves whatever she gets.'

'Thanks a lot,' laughed Caroline. 'It's nice to have a friend to count on in troubled times.'

'You think you've got troubles? You should see the mess J.R.'s gotten himself into.'

'See you, Jenny. Say hi to Pam. Happy New Year to you both.'

'Bye, sweetie. And stay out of those closets. They're not good for you.'

Caroline emerged from the closet as the guests were filing toward the dinner table.

'So tell me about your sons,' said Brian as they ate salmon, spinach mousse, and scalloped potatoes off Limoges china with enough silverware beside each plate to perform a hysterectomy. Brian had met Jackie and Jason when he picked her up at the cabin. They'd rolled up the hooked rug and were hitting a hockey puck around the living room, bouncing it off the walls and furniture. They paused to inspect Brian. A potential Gabriel Kotter?

'There's not a lot to say. They're healthy young boys. I like them a lot.'

'The older one, Jackie, looks like you.' He flaked his salmon with delicate scalpel-like movements of his knife.

'So everyone tells me.'

'Does Jason look like his father, or what?'

'More like my father. What about your kids? Do you see them much?' The man in the red blazer, on her right, was trying to catch her eye, so she gazed resolutely at her crystal goblet, and listened as Brian described the arrangement with Irene in which he hosted his children every other weekend and on assorted holidays. His voice was low and pained.

This could work, Caroline realized. Brian liked children, her sons wanted a father, she could use a husband's help. He was a pleasant man, gentle and thoughtful. Why the hell not? Her hand trembled as she raised her wine glass to her lips.

Just before midnight Connie turned on the TV, and they watched the crowd at Times Square as the ball descended. At midnight, as Times Square erupted like bees swarming, Brian put his arm around her and kissed her on the lips, and she felt a stirring in her abdomen that was unmistakably lust. The other guests, who'd welcomed in many New Years together, embraced and kissed with abandon. Most pecked her on the cheek or squeezed her arm. Red Blazer tried to grind his hips into hers, but she stepped sideways, leaving him to lurch forward of his own momentum. Connie enfolded Caroline in her arms, rubbing her large breasts against Caroline's. Caroline's twinge of desire from Brian's kiss became a major spasm. Connie's eyes narrowed with amusement, as though she was aware of what she was doing. But maybe this was just good hostess behavior. Caroline couldn't recall from the days when she and Jackson used to conduct such functions in Newton.

As Brian drove the baby-sitter home, Caroline sank into the couch, eyeing her hockey rink of a living room and trying to decide what to do. The boys were asleep. Sharon was in Pough-keepsie with Diana's mother. Diana was in New York with Suzanne. She and Brian could go upstairs and make love in Diana's own bed, if Caroline wished to stoop so low. It was a luxury having someone to drive the baby-sitter home. If she played her cards right, Brian would stick around, shovel the steps, change the faucet washers, prepare the tax returns. Life would be easier with a man. The roles were defined: Brian would bring home the bacon, and she'd make the BLTs. Jackie and Jason would be ecstatic to have a live-in dad. Her parents would be pleased. With two salaries she and Brian would have money for trips, nice clothes, Peugeots.

She realized she had no birth control. It had been years since she'd thought about pills, coils, loops, foams, creams, caps. Except to mop up the side effects in the ER. As she was counting days in her cycle, Brian walked in, his face flushed from the cold. He stumbled over a hockey stick.

'Would you like a drink?' she asked in a subdued voice, as Brian regained his balance and removed his fur-lined gloves. 'Or some coffee?'

He sat down on the sofa beside her. Caroline realized she should have built a fire, if she were really into the scenario she'd just mapped out.

'I'd rather kiss you,' he replied.

He took her in his arms hesitantly, waiting to be stopped. She leaned against his chest with a feeling of relief. Just take care of me, she thought. His mouth found hers. His hands, which moved with such precision during operations, moved delicately across her neck and face. It would be so easy just to let it all happen. She was probably fertile. She'd get pregnant. She could quit her job, stay home with a new baby, raise her children and his, make their home a haven in a threatening world . . .

Abruptly she pulled away and sat up straight. She'd already done this trip with Jackson. It was like trying to cram herself into this green velvet cocktail dress. Any minute now the damn thing would come apart at the seams. Brian looked startled and hurt. 'You're a very attractive man, Brian. But there's a lot you don't know about me.'

'I know all I need to.'

'No, you don't. You don't know that my lover for the past five years has been a woman.'

He frowned and looked down at his elegant hands.

'I should have told you sooner. I guess maybe I wished it weren't so.'

'But you're so attractive.' He spread his hands palms up in a gesture of bewilderment.

'Thanks. But please don't insist on saying the wrong things, because I don't want to stop liking you.'

'I mean, maybe you just never met the right man.'

'Maybe *you* never met the right man,' she said, standing up in her too-tight dress, hoping it would hold together long enough to get him out the door.

'But you seem so normal,' he said in a dazed voice, also standing.

'Trust me, Brian: I'm not.'

He looked at her as though seeing her for the first time. 'I'm sorry. I didn't mean to insult you.'

'It's okay. I'm used to it.'

'Look,' he said, taking her hands with both of his, 'there's a strong attraction between us. I know you feel it too. I'm not giving up.'

Caroline pulled her hands away, unable to decide if this was true. She walked to the door. 'Do yourself a favor and find another woman.'

'No,' he said with a stubborn set to his jaw, 'I've rushed you. You just need more time.'

'Suit yourself,' she said with a sigh, opening the door and letting in a blast of icy air. She closed the door behind him, leaned against it and heaved a sigh that caused some stitches in the side seams of her dress to break. So much for respectability. In high school she had an Irish Catholic boyfriend named Kevin with whom she necked and petted in the balcony of the RKO and in the parking lot behind the Stop 'n Shop every Saturday night. Obligatory behavior for every member of Rorkie's gang, along with Bass Weejuns and Villager shirtwaists. But she didn't have to do obligatory sex anymore because Rorkie was long gone. And there had to be an easier way to torment Diana.

An image of Diana's and Suzanne's naked bodies, sweaty limbs entangled across a bed, floated through her head. Her stomach clenched. How could she compete with a nineteen-year-old body, splitting the seams of her dress as she was?

She went into her room, sat at her loom, and inspected her new shawl, which was nearly finished. With bands of white, gray, blue, and purple fading into each other, it really did resemble the view from the hill above the cabin of Lake Glass, the White Mountains, and the sky. She pushed at the weft with her fingertips. How could a five-year-old romance compete with a brand-new one? It couldn't. Several times she herself had experienced the incomparable thrill of breaking down the barriers, one by one, with an unfamiliar person – the looks, the remarks, the touches, the kisses, the caresses, the sucking and writhing and thrusting and moaning.

Grabbing the beater, Caroline began pedaling her loom. Diana had a new playmate. It was as painful as when Rorkie kicked her out of the Girls' League and picked Mandy Carrigan to sit beside her in the lunchroom.

In time, she remembered the thud of the beater would wake the boys. She stood up and struggled out of her cocktail dress like a scuba diver removing a wet suit. She shrugged on her flannel nightgown, climbed into bed, and picked up the list of adjectives for Hannah on her nightstand. *Kind, gentle, generous, mean, devious, malicious* . . . Taking a pencil, she scrawled, 'lonely.' Then 'horny.' And 'cuckolded.' But she was supposed to be dividing the list into categories, not expanding it into incoherence. She turned it over and upside down, trying to discover what pattern Hannah had seen. Finally she plunked it down on the stand and turned out the light.

Lying in the dark waiting for sleep, Caroline pictured Diana's scrambled red head between Suzanne's legs, green eyes looking up past Suzanne's breasts to her face to check out her response. Caroline fought to replace this image with Hannah and her shrug. But Hannah wouldn't materialize.

Oh well, happy New Year, she said to herself, moving her hand up under her nightgown.

Caroline handed her bedraggled list to Hannah, saying, 'I don't know if you noticed, but I didn't do it last month.' It had taken the past two days. She'd divided the adjectives in half a dozen ways – positive versus negative qualities, 'male' versus 'female,' opposites.

'I noticed,' replied Hannah, sitting back in her desk chair and studying the list.

'Were you angry?' Caroline sat down on the tweed couch.

'I don't feel angry very often, and certainly not over something like that.'

'Disappointed?' Caroline asked, straining forward, feeling the tweed under her palms. If she couldn't make Hannah want her to keep coming, if she couldn't please her by doing assignments and telling jokes, maybe she could at least annoy her.

Hannah looked up and studied Caroline, head tilted speculatively. 'If an assignment is helpful and a client wants to do it, fine. If not, that's also fine. I'm not a schoolteacher.'

Caroline felt defeated as Hannah handed back the list without comment and lit a brown cigarette with a Bic lighter. Caroline sat back and looked out the window past the anemic ferns to Lake Glass, which had frozen solid during the holidays. The ice gleamed like an opaque mirror, whimsical designs etched into it by the runners of skates and iceboats. 'Which category did you see when you told me to divide it into categories?' If nothing else, she could force Hannah to earn her fee.

'The same one you saw. The qualities that are opposites. Generous and possessive. Kind and mean.'

'Yeah, they pretty much cancel each other out.'

'Do they?' Hannah held Nigel's stone in her hand and studied the mica that lined the hollow.

'Don't they? Aloof and intense. Which one am I?'

'You're both. We all are. Being aloof doesn't preclude being intense. And other people interpret what you do according to their own histories and how they're feeling at the time. Next, why don't you assign percentages to the qualities, to indicate how much of each describes you?' Getting a client to construct her own self-image was like trying to persuade her children as toddlers to build something with their blocks rather than hurling them around the room.

Caroline grimaced.

'What was that?'

'I don't know. A frown, I guess.'

'What for?'

'I'm sick of this fucking list.' Looking at Hannah, Caroline tore the list into tiny pieces, then tossed them into the air like confetti. As she watched the pieces flutter to the carpet, she was appalled. Clutching the tweed sofa cover, she waited for Hannah to ask her to leave, or at least to clean up the mess.

Hannah watched the pieces settle on the rug like dandruff on a coat collar. It was always a relief when the stalled aggression began to ooze through the skin of docility, like pus from a lanced boil. 'The cleaning lady will hate you.' Hannah glanced at her bark painting on the wall. Mimi spirits, with their hollow eyes and skeletal limbs, lived in rock ledges and came out only at night, to dance wildly, make love, and cavort across the Outback.

Caroline glanced at the mimi spirit. 'That thing's really creepy.' She couldn't believe her ears. If Hannah had it in here, it was probably important to her. And you don't tell people things they cherish are creepy. What was happening to her? Ever since Christmas, her manners had been unraveling.

'Do you think so? I like it. It's Australian. I guess it reminds me of my origins.'

'I'm sorry.'

'What? Sorry you don't like it?'

'Sorry I said it was creepy.'

Hannah gave a startled laugh. 'But why shouldn't you? Just because I like it is no reason for you to.' Hannah retained a perplexed smile. How did someone get so invested in placating others? 'What do you want to talk about today?'

Caroline studied the mess on the carpet. Apparently Hannah really didn't care about the list. Or about Caroline's calling her painting creepy. Or would she take it out on her later? 'I've been thinking a lot about high school.'

'What about it?'

'About what a nightmare it was.'

'Oh yes? Continue.' Hannah always listened to clients' accounts of American high school life with fascination, probably the same fascination her mother felt observing aboriginal rites.

Caroline talked about her clique, run by a girl named Melanie O'Rourke, who was called Rorkie. Hannah had noticed that the queens were usually known by their last names. The 'Yankee' girls who rode horses and went to summer camp on Cape Cod had nicknames, like Cricket or Muffin or Crumpet. 'Yankee' in England meant any American. 'Yankee' to someone from the American South meant any nonsoutherner. 'Yankee' here in New England meant someone from a Puritan family.

Rorkie was a cheerleader, secretary of the student council, guard on the basketball team. Caroline was delineating the school pecking order – the Jewish intellectuals and activists, the Irish jocks and politicians, the Yankee socialites and do-gooders. ' . . . Rorkie and I became friends in sixth-period study hall. I was thrilled when she started asking to borrow things – pencils, paper, class notes. Then she began to pass me notes with gossip about people in the study hall. Then she invited me to join the Girls' League, and I thought I'd died and gone to heaven. Mostly the Girls' League staged slumber parties and dances. Rorkie decided whom the club would ostracize. Whenever she turned on someone, the club would go to that person's house and strew toilet paper around the yard. Then at school the pariah would cry and ask why Rorkie hated her, and Rorkie would tell me, and I'd pass along the word. I don't know what Rorkie saw in me.' Caroline was picturing Rorkie, who was Black Irish with dark hair, creamy skin, and green eyes. She sauntered in her tasseled Bass Weejuns rather than walked, a Mafia don, minions surrounding her like bodyguards.

'Maybe she was scared of you because you weren't completely under her thumb,' said Hannah, watching out the window as the orange Le Car drove past. If she rearranged her office, she wouldn't have to see that vehicle.

'I certainly wanted to be under her thumb,' said Caroline, running her hand through her Afro.

'What stopped you?' Hannah tapped her cigarette ash into the hollow stone.

'They were Irish. My father was Irish, but my mother was Yankee. My Boston Irish accent was pretty mild, and they thought I was stuckup. At school I'd talk Boston for them, and at home I'd talk Yankee for my mother. I made good grades, and they were flunking. I was Episcopalian, and they were Catholic. I was going to college, and they were husband-hunting. I tried to conceal all this, but I guess I wasn't too successful. The other girls put up with me because Rorkie made them. And Rorkie put up with me because . . . I don't know why.' Caroline was feeling nauseated recalling the constant anxiety over what to do, say, and wear.

'Because you were the only one who stood up to her,' said Hannah. Caroline was refusing to hear anything about her own strength of character. What about those aspects of herself that had faced down the Right-to-Lifers on the statehouse steps, that tore up lists and tossed them in the air, that told jokes that would have gotten a laugh from a corpse, that raised two sons single-handedly, that coped with death and mayhem every day of the workweek? It was bizarre to realize such a forceful woman saw herself as an outcast and a victim. Hannah almost laughed out loud, as Maggie once had at her during a strained patch in her marriage when she told Maggie she had to stay with Arthur because she needed someone to take care of her.

'Because I helped her with her term papers,' Caroline was explaining. 'Let her drive my parents' car. Lent her money. She liked my house. There was a recreation room in the basement where the Girls' League had parties.'

'So you did nice things for her?'

'Yeah.'

'Does this sound familiar?'

'Does what?' asked Caroline, rubbing the bridge of her nose with two fingers.

'You as servant and lackey.' Hannah was seeing Caroline as a child, waiting on her parents, representing their wishes to the other children.

Caroline frowned. All these leaps backward and forward in time were so confusing. What did high school have to do with her family?

'Are you aware of the oldest-daughter syndrome?'

'It sounds like a disease.'

Hannah smiled. 'It is, in a way. The oldest girl in a family is often turned into a little mother for the other children. Sometimes she's expected to mother her own mother. She goes out into the world and searches for the nurturing she didn't get when she should have. But if she finds it, she doesn't know how to accept it because it's so unfamiliar.'

Caroline was pinching the bridge of her nose. So she'd tended Howard and Tommy. So what? That was twenty years ago. 'I'd have fit in with Rorkie's crowd if I'd been on the basketball team . . .'

Hannah raised her eyebrows. Maybe her assessment was too close for comfort?

'. . . but my mother thought basketball was tacky. She insisted I be in the Junior Service Club instead, which raised money for college scholarships for Roxbury students. But I was really good at basketball. I'm sure I'd have been a varsity starter.'

Hannah shrugged. 'It's not too late to be a basketball star. Why don't you go out and hire a lot of short people?'

Caroline gave a startled laugh.

Hannah smiled. Caroline's and her eyes locked. A charge of amusement flickered between them like heat lightning.

Caroline dropped her eyes to the box of tissues on the chest. Hannah wasn't taking her difficulties seriously. It had been painful to watch Rorkie and the others flock to the gym for basketball practice after school. . . .

She recalled she was complaining to someone who'd lost two children to carbon monoxide. *You think you've got problems?* Guilt washed over her as she looked at the toothless, towheaded children on Hannah's bulletin board. But goddam it, she never asked to know about those little creeps.

'Hannah, if you can't cope,' Caroline said in a low voice, 'I don't want to know about it.'

Hannah studied Caroline through narrowed eyes, trying to follow her train of thought. 'But I can cope.' Usually, she added to herself. She shifted her gaze out the window to the 'Club Sandwiches Not Seals' sticker on Caroline's bumper, still in the dark about how they'd gotten from basketball to Hannah's coping abilities. They sat silent for a long time, Hannah uncertain what was going on. Something about her joke, and that moment of contact afterwards, but what? When in doubt, ask, she finally decided.

'What are you thinking, Caroline?'

Feeling silly, Caroline said nothing.

'What's going on?'

'I don't know, it seems ridiculous all of a sudden. People are starving and dying, and I'm moaning about basketball.'

Hannah looked at her thoughtfully, in her white uniform with the ivory sea gull at her throat. Once a client got started, usually she wouldn't shut up about the many injustices she'd endured. Caroline's approach was refreshing, but was it therapy? 'Your pain is as real as anyone else's, however trivial the triggers seem. Don't belittle it, or it'll continue to kick you in the teeth.'

Caroline sat looking perplexed and plucked at her ivory gull.

'Just take my word for it. Basketball is important for now. I'm sorry if my joke made you think it wasn't. So what happened with Rorkie?'

Startled into cooperation by Hannah's apology, Caroline struggled to recall. 'One day at school I got this citizenship award, and the next night they rolled my yard with toilet paper. When I asked Rorkie why, she said my Christmas card had been too Protestant.' A snowman in a top hat, as Caroline recalled.

'Probably she didn't like competition as queen of the school.'

'But that's the only award I ever got.'

'She didn't get it, did she?'

'I thought she'd be pleased for me.'

'How quaint. Hitler had Germany. Why would he want France?' Hannah raised her eyebrows.

'Hitler?'

'Every group has its Hitler. Also its Jews.'

Caroline sat in silence for a long time. Last week Hannah called her a scapegoat. Now she was on about Hitler and the Jews. What was she trying to say? Why didn't she just say it?

Caroline thought about the months after Rorkie ditched her, when she sat by herself in the lunchroom watching Rorkie and her pals in their madras Villager shirtwaists at their usual table as they carefully avoided looking at her. Mandy Carrigan now occupied Caroline's former chair at Rorkie's right hand, and got the privilege of bringing Rorkie her waxed half pint of milk from the cooler. It felt as though all Caroline's internal organs had been removed, leaving a hollow shell of flesh that performed the activities expected of it by day, and that lay awake all night wishing for a careening Bunny Bread truck. If only there were some way to decline the citizenship award, or to have it awarded to Rorkie instead. If she wasn't Eva Braun to Rorkie's Hitler, who was she? No one.

One morning she took Tommy to Jordan Marsh to buy his first jockstrap. Afterwards as they walked to the MTA station, they saw some SANE pickets in the Boston Common. A man in a clerical collar handed her some literature, which she read in her room when she got home. The human race had had it. Her personal grief over Rorkie was irrelevant. The world was about to end. Raging infernos would incinerate most living things. Whatever was left would sicken and die. The next weekend she returned to the Common and joined the pickets. It soon became clear she had a duty to humanity to go to nursing school. If she herself survived the firestorms, she could tend the maimed and scorched. . . .

As she smoked, Hannah gazed out to the bank of dirty snow on the far side of the parking lot. Why not rearrange this place? The couch could go where the desk was now, and the desk against the opposite wall so she could see the lake from her chair. Brilliant. Why hadn't she thought of this fifteen years ago?

'You'll no doubt be pleased to hear I had a date with a man for New Year's Eve,' said Caroline, shaking off the past.

Hannah squelched her first response of 'I'd appreciate it if you wouldn't tell me how I feel.' 'Since you know I don't care about the sex of whom you date,' she said instead, 'you must be pleased yourself?'

Caroline shrugged. 'At least Diana's annoyed.'

Hannah smiled. 'For someone so intent on being a good girl, you certainly have your ways of getting even.'

Caroline smiled. 'I do, don't I?'

'So how did your date go?'

'I ended up in the closet talking to a friend on the phone. I thought about calling you. But I figured you were probably out shooting it up.'

'No, I was home. Asleep probably. This time of year is hard on me. My children died right around now.' It felt as though it was time to step up the Great Disillusionment.

Caroline looked at her. She wasn't crazy about knowing this. But Hannah did look pale and tired. Caroline felt an urge to cheer her up. She made tea for her mother, covered her with a blanket, turned on the opera, baby-sat her brothers. None of these were appropriate with Hannah. She told her mother amusing stories: 'At the end of the evening I told Mr Right I was queer.'

'That must have enchanted him.'

'I think it turns him on. He's been phoning ever since, and dropping by to see me at work. I believe he thinks he's going to save me.'

'From what?'

'From a lonely middle age.'

'Do you think he is?'

'The only thing I know for sure is that whenever I say, "I'll never do that," it means I'm about to do it. So my answer is: I don't know. But I doubt it.'

Hannah laughed. She liked the quirky ways Caroline's mind worked.

Caroline was pleased by the way Hannah's face had just relaxed and lit up.

As the door closed behind Caroline, Hannah got up and went over to the tweed couch. Beyond the ferns in the window Lake Glass stretched out to the mountains on the horizon. Definitely a nicer view than the parking lot. She must have set things up this way in her more self-sacrificing days. View Therapy, or something.

She lay down on the couch, head on a cushion, stocking feet on the couch arm, and acknowledged to herself that she had in fact felt a twinge of gratification at hearing Caroline had a date with a man. In theory and on principle she was impartial, but in practice she was constantly having her nose rubbed in her own assumptions: since she was happy, unhappy people should live as she did.

How would she feel if Joanna were lesbian? Maybe she was. She'd certainly picked a gruesome series of young men so far, the most recent being a violinist with the Boston Symphony who was constantly in rehearsal or on tour. But she'd probably worry even more if Joanna were homosexual. It took so much energy to be unconventional in this culture. Her homosexual clients spent about half their time fending off or coming to terms with all the social disapproval.

The receptionist buzzed her. Chip was here. The show must go on. She sat up, glancing out to Lake Glass, smooth and still under a steel gray sky. When she had a chance, she'd rearrange this place.

As Joanna and Hannah split a carafe of white wine at a small table in Maude's Corner Cafe, Joanna kept trying to advise Hannah on how to invest her retirement fund. 'Mother, you can't just let it sit there. You've got to manage it.'

'Why do I?' When Joanna was in high school, she used to advise Hannah on her wardrobe with similar despair.

'Every day you leave it in those CDs, you lose the extra return you could be earning in the market.'

Hannah smiled at this earnest young woman who had Hannah's blue eyes and widow's peak, and Arthur's ruddy coloring and long legs. She wore a tweed suit and cowl neck sweater. 'Yes, dear, and now tell me how your Boston fiddler is doing. Clark?'

Joanna frowned, just as she used to when the other kids failed to return books to her library on time. 'Mother, this is serious. Over the years, a few dollars of lost interest each week adds up to an enormous sum. Surely you must see that?'

As Joanna outlined alternatives to CDs, gesturing with her hand, Hannah watched her expression of exasperation and thought about the oldest-daughter syndrome she had just described to Caroline. She herself had coddled Simon and Nigel more. They seemed so frail and vulnerable. She felt sorry for them, knowing they'd have to prove themselves in such a brutal world. Whereas Mona and Joanna seemed more self-contained. Even if they never used their nubile wombs, they had the awesome capacity to bear new life. Nothing the boys could do would compensate them for that lack, and certainly not their funny little nubs of penises. So during the chaotic years, she sometimes leaned on Joanna, who responded with such efficiency and enthusiasm that Hannah had to remind herself that Joanna too needed cuddling and pampering. She probably hadn't given her enough. Hence her brittleness.

'What is this, honey?' Hannah finally asked. 'My pension is fine the way it is. How's your modern dance class going?'

'Fine. But, Mother, somebody's got to take care of you.' Joanna poured some more wine into her mother's nearly full glass.

Hannah smiled, charmed. Everyone else saw her as Brünnhilde. After Nigel and Mona died, Hannah spent a lot of time trying to persuade Joanna the accident wasn't her fault. One night at supper around the oak pedestal table during Joanna's own therapy, Joanna screamed, 'It wasn't my fault your precious Mona died, Mother!'

'Nobody ever said it was,' said Hannah, turning pale.

'I took good care of them.'

'Yes, you did.'

'I know you wish it were me instead of Mona!'

'Don't be ridiculous, Joanna,' begged Hannah, sweat breaking out on her upper lip. . . .

'Your father usually does a pretty good job taking care of me,' said Hannah.

'He won't always be . . .' Joanna stopped and looked down to trace the grain of the pine table with her fingertips.

'He won't always be here? No, he won't. But neither will I. Maybe neither you nor I will leave this restaurant alive. So why worry about it?'

Looking up, Joanna heaved a sigh. 'You have an answer for everything, don't you, Mother?'

'I appreciate your concern about my pension, Joanna. I'm sorry I don't share it. I'm sure you're right.'

'Well, it's *your* lost interest.'

'That's right.' She and Joanna often ended up in a stalemate neither of them wanted at this time of year, close to the anniversary of the accident. Usually they had enough sense to stay away from each other until February. 'Speaking of your father, I've got to get home.'

Joanna shrugged, gazing into her wine.

'Take care of yourself, darling.' Hannah stood up and patted Joanna's padded shoulder.

'You too, Mother.' Joanna looked up with a strained smile.

'I love you, you know.'

'Yes, I know, Mother. Me too.' They exchanged helpless looks.

Driving up the lakeshore, Hannah thought about how much easier it was to cope with surrogate daughters. They stayed in her office only an hour or two, and she could kick them out as failures if they wouldn't open up.

Shrugging, she began thinking about the bizarre folkways of the American high school. Caroline spoke in such life and death terms about those years – the anxiety over whether she was in or out with some teenage tyrant named Rorkie, which was determined by constantly shifting cues like clothing, hairdos, accents, Christmas cards. Maybe Hannah had never felt these pressures because she never fit in anywhere in the first place. Not as a white Australian among aboriginal playmates, not as an Australian among English schoolmates, and not now as Job among the sybarites. She was quite comfortable with being out. In fact, she became uncomfortable whenever there was a hint she might be in.

At boarding school in Sussex the girls were required to wear identical gym slips, striped ties, and navy blue blazers. Hannah always left her tie unknotted. Most of the girls, who had names like Philippa, Nicola, and Phoebe, wore headscarves knotted on their chins. They laughed by raising upper lips to uncover teeth, and tossing back their heads like horses whinnying. Hannah used to go bare-headed through the Sussex drizzle. She exaggerated her Australian accent. The other girls politely avoided her, except for her best friend, Carla, from Kenya, who had similar problems.

She traced that pattern into the present – like Gretel following bread crumbs out of the forest – to the staff meeting that morning, around the large square walnut table in the sunny conference room, at which everyone else had been struggling to find ways to become a more cohesive group. Sylvia, who drove everyone crazy fingering worry beads, suggested a group meditation to harmonize themselves. Mary Beth, flashing her brittle smile, proposed a monthly pot luck supper with spouses. Louis, in his inevitable army surplus camouflage pants and parachutist boots, wanted them to reveal their perceptions of each other's flaws as a way of feeling closer. Jonathan vented his anger about the lack of salt on the ice in the parking lot, and the others said they heard him, and supported him in owning his anger, and appreciated his sharing with them.

Leaning forward on his arms on the walnut table, Louis said to Sylvia, who was getting married, 'I experience in you a lack of affect in terms of how you're relating to this marriage, Sylvia, that I find it difficult to deal with. I know you're hopeful, anticipatory, but is there a part of you that's excited?'

Hannah excused herself to go to the bathroom. She actually just stood in the hall and grinned. On the archery range at boarding school, girls had asked, 'What pound bow do you pull?' At the kennel where she and Arthur bought their collie, the owner said, 'Sometimes this dog's sire throws undesirable traits.' All these tiny worlds, each with its own language, none of which she fit into. But it was hard to believe a roomful of therapists, whose careers revolved around decoding the private languages of their clients' worlds, could be so unaware of their own as to speak it with straight faces. Why would I want to harmonize with a bunch of turkeys, she wondered as she composed herself and returned to the staff room.

As her car hit a pothole and clattered like a New York taxi, she concluded that you never got rid of your tired old patterns. You simply began to recognize them as they cropped up. Some you valued, as she did her inability to fit into groups. Maybe she'd be able to resist joining the current equivalent of the Hitler Youth. The more obnoxious patterns, like her conviction that anyone she became involved with would leave or die, you learned to ignore most of the time. You could fill in potholes until they looked like the rest of the road, but the wound in the asphalt was still there, ready to heave open again in the next hard freeze.

As she pulled into the driveway, she saw Arthur standing in the greenhouse window in his Mr Chips sweater, putting a golf ball into a plastic hole on the carpet that flipped the ball back to him whenever he sank a putt. Recently retired, he'd begun cooking supper every night. She felt a surge of emotion that was half pleasure and half pain. Now that he'd finally convinced her, after only thirty-eight years of effort, that he wasn't going to leave like all the others, he'd be leaving in spite of himself one day soon. Joanna was right. But it wasn't fair. He got to do everything first – retire, get root canals, draw social security, die. Her conviction that loved ones would vanish – it was based on reality. It was just that it could sometimes take fifty years.

When she walked in the door, Arthur stood stirring something on the stove with a spoon. 'I see I've got you right where I want you, Arthur,' she said. 'Barefoot and in the kitchen.'

'But blessedly not pregnant,' he said, putting down the spoon and taking her martini from the refrigerator freezer. 'How was your day?' He handed her the martini and put his arm around her.

'Very much like my other days, thank you. How was yours?' They sauntered from the kitchen across the living room.

'Wonderful. I stayed in bed reading all morning.'

'Fucker.' They sank down on the leather couch. Coming home from work to a neat, quiet house and a cooked supper was still a shock. She felt as though she were playing hookey.

'Your time will come, my darling.'

'Yes, but will I be alive to enjoy it?' She sipped her martini, looking at him over the rim of her glass.

'I'd say you've got a few good years left, old girl.' He patted her thigh.

'What is this "old girl" business?' The sky beyond the jungle in the greenhouse window was a luminescent coral.

'I read it in a British novel last week. I thought it would help you feel less homesick for the motherland.'

'It's been about thirty years since I missed that place. I'm just like the rest of you rootless American riffraff now.'

'If it weren't for us rootless American riffraff,' said Arthur, 'your people would be speaking German right now.'

She laughed, drinking her gin as dark purple jet trails spread across the coral sky.

'I just had a drink with Joanna.'

'How's she?'

'Fine, I guess. She wouldn't tell me anything. Except how to invest my retirement fund.'

'Can't complain about that.'

'But I want the gossip.'

'You'll have to rely on your clients for that.'

'But what's the point of having grown children if they won't tell you the dirt?'

Arthur laughed. 'Is that why you had them? A subscription to the *National Enquirer* would have been cheaper.'

Hannah gave a pained smile and took his hand in both hers. 'No, that's not why I had them.' She studied Arthur's freckled hand and recalled how gently he used to hold each newborn baby, one hand under the head and shoulders, the other under the buttocks and thighs, gazing into the dark blue eyes with amazement. He'd take them into the bath with him, his hands cradling their tiny bodies and rocking them in the water. She would feel stabs of jealousy watching the tenderness on his face. He'd missed out on so much with his first batch – busy with his career, away at war, sneaking around with Hannah – and was determined to do it right the second time around.

As she patted his hand, she reflected that many clients believed everything would be fine if they could just find the right partner. You had to be with the right partner awhile to discover that was only half the battle. Next you had to learn how to let him go when the time came. She was still in kindergarten on that one.

Two

'I've made lentil soup and rye bread,' Caroline told Diana over the phone from downstairs. 'Want some?' They'd scarcely seen each other since Diana's return from Poughkeepsie. Except to exchange coy, hostile inquiries about each other's New Year's Eve. Diana's had evidently been a success, which Caroline was sure involved a New York hotel room. She portrayed her evening with Brian as a similar success. And Brian's phone calls and detours past the ER desk seemed to confirm her story. Today he appeared in light blue scrub clothes, wordlessly handing her a single yellow rose in a specimen bottle. Diana, who was also behind the desk, made a great point of not noticing.

Diana hesitated. 'Do you think we should?'

'Haven't we gone cold turkey long enough?' Caroline sat down in the gray plaid easy chair beside the phone table and took a sip of wine.

'God, I couldn't bear it if we got back into all that old junk again.'

'Me either. But let's assume we won't.' They'd gone from trying to do everything for each other to doing nothing. Surely there was some happy middle ground. They hadn't had a meal together in weeks.

'All right. I'll come down there. But only if I can bring the salad.'

'You're on, babe.'

The boys and Sharon dipped their rye bread in the soup, making a swamp of the rust-colored homespun tablecloth Caroline had woven when she was living with David Michael in the Somerville commune. Brian's yellow rose sat in its specimen bottle in the middle of the table, flanked by two beeswax candles. Diana was carefully avoiding acknowledging its existence.

'There's chocolate chip ice cream in my freezer,' Diana told the children. She wore a gray sweat suit and green terry cloth headband, just back from losing to Suzanne at racquetball. Her red hair was spiky from dried sweat.

'Hey neat!' said Jason. They raced upstairs with the thundering of a small earthquake.

'Anything to get them in a different room from me,' said Diana, pushing back her chair and stretching out her legs.

'Jesus,' said Caroline putting her elbow on the table and her chin in her hand. 'It's like living with a dairy herd.'

Diana smiled sourly. 'You're in a good mood. I bet you saw Hannah today?'

'Correct.' Caroline ignored the unpleasant edge to Diana's voice. 'Want some coffee?'

'I'll make it.' Diana got up.

'I'll make it. You're the guest.'

'I thought we were going to give this routine a miss.'

'All right, you make it.' Caroline sank back into her ladder-back chair.

'So what's new, stranger?' Diana measured coffee beans.

'Report cards. Did you see them?'

'Yeah, pretty dismal. But if we ground them, we're stuck with them underfoot more than ever.'

Caroline smiled. 'How come nobody ever tells you what parenthood is like beforehand?'

'The species would go to extinction.' Diana was grinding the beans in the hand grinder.

'Hannah and I talked about Rorkie today, my friend from high school.' The kettle began whistling like a factory at high noon.

'Never heard of her,' said Diana, pouring water into the filter.

'She'd rejected me by the time I met you.'

'Rejected you?' Diana handed her a tan mug with cats on it.

'Yeah, my Christmas card was too Protestant, so she and her friends rolled my yard with toilet paper.'

Diana choked on her coffee. Caroline grinned. But she hadn't been amused that morning she looked out her bedroom window at the toilet paper woven through the budding elm trees. Spelled out in toilet paper on the front lawn was CITIZENSHIT AWARD. 'Rorkie rolled Caroline!' buzzed through the halls at school. Caroline convinced the nurse she was sick. She walked home and spent the afternoon unstringing the toilet paper, like popcorn chains from Christmas trees. It felt like the end of the world. Only gradually did she realize the world didn't end so easily.

'Where do you think she is now?' Diana propped her chin on her fist and gazed at Caroline with her green eyes.

'She's probably had twelve children and a hysterectomy.'

'Maybe she runs a toilet paper concession for Boston rest rooms.'

'Let's hope she's profoundly unhappy.' It sounded as though Sharon were beating Jason's head on the shag carpet upstairs. He was screaming epithets Caroline had never even heard of.

'How could someone like that be happy? Imagine the kind of mind that gets off on tormenting people.'

'Yeah. I guess viciousness is its own punishment.' Caroline folded her arms across her stomach, remembering Rorkie in study hall one afternoon with a huge purple bruise along one jaw. Caroline passed her a note asking, 'What happened to your face?' Rorkie's reply read, 'My father hit me with a Four Roses bottle.' After a while Caroline passed her a note that said, 'I'm really sorry.' Rorkie's reply said, 'I'm used to it.' Applying Hannah's formula, Caroline realized Rorkie treated her classmates as she herself had been treated.

'I'm starting to feel it's my fault because I was so privileged and she wasn't,' said Caroline.

'That's the most convoluted logic I've ever heard. You must be a real challenge for Hannah.'

'Probably.' There was that strained timbre to Diana's voice again. Diana said she was jealous because Hannah cheered Caroline up. But surely Diana couldn't want her to stay miserable just so she wouldn't have to feel jealous? Caroline started wondering what Hannah did think of her – that she was a nut? Did Hannah like her as a person, or was she just doing her job?

'Do you remember the first time we ever saw each other?' asked Diana, as Caroline got up to pour more coffee.

'Yeah, we were watching Arlene give a bed bath, weren't we? And she said if a male patient got an erection, to hit it with a spoon.' Caroline chuckled, picturing Arlene, large and solid like the leg of an elephant, a thick braid of hair wound into a bun that sat on her head like a cow pile.

'Yes, and you and I burst out laughing, and everyone else looked at us like we were criminals.'

Caroline remembered watching Diana throw back her red head, close her green eyes, and give a husky laugh. And Caroline knew she wanted to be her friend. After class each lingered in the corridor, trying to engineer an encounter. They went for lunch, and Caroline spilled her coffee on the Formica table in the cafeteria, in amusement over the bed bath. Diana held a bunch of green seedless grapes in one hand like a softball. From time to time, she raised the bunch to her mouth and took a grape between her lips. Caroline was enchanted, never having seen grapes eaten like that. 'I probably loved you right from that lunch.'

'Well, it was mutual. But you were besotted with Arlene, don't forget. You spent most of your spare time waxing her car, as I recall.'

A door upstairs slammed so hard the whole cabin shook. Jason screamed, 'I'm telling Mommy!'

'Please don't,' Caroline said, closing her eyes in prayer. She and Diana exchanged long-suffering glances. What would she have done all these years without Diana as co-mother?

'I was besotted with Arlene. But in a different way than with you – for one thing, Arlene didn't laugh much.'

'She sure didn't. "Ladies, you have a mission." Remember? But I used to be terribly jealous. Of you both probably.'

'Well, you shouldn't have bothered.' Caroline was picturing Arlene, her bulk and her bun, her grim mouth opening like a knife puncture to announce in a broad Boston Irish accent, 'Ladies, you have a mission: to relieve human suffering. My mission is to show you how.' Caroline floated through the days of emptying bedpans, changing dressings, making beds, on wings of purpose: If she herself survived the holocausts, she'd be one of the few citizens of the postnuclear world with the skills to save others. She'd salve their burns, stitch their gashes, wipe sweat off their brows as they perished of radiation sickness.

Then she remembered the last time she ever talked with Arlene, in a deli over a pastrami sandwich. Arlene said, 'I don't know what you want from me, Caroline, but you'll have to find it somewhere else. I'm a very busy woman.'

Caroline's warm feelings from dinner with Diana began to drain away like a jaw going numb from Novocaine.

'I wonder what she's up to now,' said Diana, green eyes finally settling like two flies on Brian's yellow rose.

'God knows. Probably still molding young missionaries.'

'You sound bitter.'

'I don't mean to. She was good to me. For as long as it lasted.' Caroline studied her hands. Her nails needed clipping. No, they didn't. She clipped them so she wouldn't hurt Diana during lovemaking. But they weren't doing that anymore. She could grow them long as letter openers. The numbness spread across her face. Her stomach clenched into a fist.

It's over, Caroline reminded herself. Like Marsha's smile, like Rorkie's toilet paper, Arlene was long gone. Lovemaking with Diana was finished. Yet according to Hannah, she used these painful memories to feel lousy in the present. Resolutely she dismissed Arlene in her white stockings and bulging white uniform, and Diana naked on her back in bed reaching out for Caroline. She summoned instead the image from that afternoon of Hannah's eyes locking with her own in mutual amusement. She smiled faintly, the numbness halting its march down her neck toward her shoulders. Like a dozing driver trying to wake herself, she shook her head abruptly.

'What's so funny?' asked Diana.

'This afternoon I was complaining to Hannah about not being on the basketball team in high school. She said, "It's not too late to be a star. Why don't you hire a lot of short people?" '

Diana smiled. 'Funny lady.'

'Did I tell you two of her kids died in their beds from carbon monoxide poisoning?'

'God, how dreadful.' Diana peeled a piece of wax from a candle and melted it in the flame. 'I don't know how a mother would survive that.'

There was a loud crash and the sound of running feet upstairs. 'Try me,' muttered Caroline.

'You're awful.' Diana tried not to smile. She nodded toward Brian's rose. 'Is she pushing you to date men?'

Caroline looked at Diana. 'She doesn't push me to do anything. Except to feel better.'

'Are you in love with her yet?'

Caroline said nothing, holding her face blank.

'Look, I've done therapy. I know how it works. You fall in love with the therapist and copy her every twitch.'

'What's it to you anyway? I thought we weren't having this

kind of relationship anymore. I thought you had a new child bride.' She slammed down her cat mug harder than she intended, sloshing coffee onto the rust tablecloth.

Diana lowered her eyes, then tried to shrug. 'Well, it's nothing to me really. I just hate to see you leading that poor man on. After all, I've been to bed with you, Caroline. And you're *no* heterosexual.'

'I'm sure Brian would appreciate your sudden concern.' Caroline tilted a candle to let wax dribble down the side.

'Now you're getting sarcastic. But it's something to think about. Because you're not being fair to him. You're just using him while you try to parody Hannah.' Diana tipped her own candle and gathered the hot wax into a little ball. 'What do you see in him anyway?'

'He's a nice man, Diana. He's gentle, thoughtful, attractive.'

Diana looked at her ironically. 'He's a man, isn't he?'

Caroline lowered her head, arms spread out on the rust tablecloth. 'It's easier, Diana. I'm getting older. I'm not sure I can take the strain of defying society anymore.' Her voice was tired.

'It's easier to deny your true self? Is that what Hannah's teaching you?'

'Who says my true self is queer?' Caroline looked up, eyes narrowed with pain.

Diana glared at her. 'Look, babe, you got me into this.'

'Yeah, and you took a lot of persuading, too.' Glaring back, Caroline recalled the first time they made love – on the shag carpet in Diana's living room, late at night after two bottles of wine, after weeks of struggling to keep their hands off each other. In the morning we can blame it on the wine, Caroline remembered thinking as she buried her tongue in Diana, and felt Diana's hands lock around her head, refusing to let her reconsider. But Diana was right. She'd been more experienced. She probably did have some kind of responsibility. But fuck it, Diana was on her own now.

'You know,' said Caroline, 'every time you use Hannah's name there's this tension in your voice. I keep wondering if you really want me to feel better.'

There was a long silence, broken only by Jackie's imitation of a submachine gun upstairs. Diana had collected more wax and was molding it into globular shapes. She looked up, green eyes flashing in the candlelight. 'Can't you see I'm scared?'

'What of?'

'If Hannah helps you see what a neat woman you are, why would you want to be with me?' Her face looked haggard in the candlelight.

Caroline felt a rush of emotion. 'Because I love you, Diana.' They looked into each other's eyes as intently as during love-making. Diana reached over with both hands and took one of Caroline's.

'You can't believe I'd be with you unless I needed you?' Caroline asked.

Diana slowly shook her head no.

'That's a nurse for you,' Caroline said softly, adding her other hand to the heap on the table. 'Diana, do you think we'll be lovers again?'

Diana looked startled. 'Nothing could surprise me about us. We've been through every permutation in the book.'

'Well, I want us to be,' said Caroline. 'I'm tired of these games.' There. She'd said it. She felt her shoulders tighten. *I know what you want and you can't have it.*

'That makes the vote two to zero.' Diana looked pleased. 'Now if our brains would just shut up and let our bodies do what they're so good at.' She added, 'Please don't give up on me, darling. This thing with Suzanne will pass.'

'I'd give up on you if I could,' Caroline said, looking into the candle flame. 'But apparently you're stuck with me.'

'Good.'

'For whom?' She looked at Diana with sudden belligerence.

'Look, you've got Hannah to lean on. Who do I have?'

'Suzanne, it looks like.'

'She's young. She'll move on.'

'Oh, goodie. And then I can have you back?'

'No promises.'

'Fuck you.' Caroline got up to do the dishes. Was that all there was to it, she wondered as she ran water in the sink and fended off Diana's attempts to scrape the dishes. Asking for what you wanted? It seemed too simple. What if Diana had said, I know what you want and you can't have it? But she hadn't, Caroline realized, a smile spreading across her face, dispelling the remaining numbness.

★

Hannah was sitting in her chair, stocking feet on the rush footstool, when Caroline walked in and handed her a loaf of rye bread wrapped in Saran Wrap. Hannah looked at it.

'I made it.'

'Thanks,' said Hannah, tossing it on the desk behind her among the books, papers, and coffee cups. She felt bad about not responding more warmly to what looked like nice bread. 'Sit down.'

Caroline sat down. That bread had taken three hours. She'd given Hannah the most perfectly shaped loaf of the batch.

'So what's up?' Hannah put clasped hands behind her head, elbows out.

'Nothing much.' Caroline folded her arms across her chest. She was sorry she bothered to bring the damn bread. Children in Chad were starving, and Hannah tossed it aside without a second glance. She was just a spoiled American. Except she was British . . .

'How was your week?' asked Hannah.

'All right.'

Hannah leaned forward to light a cigarette, inhaling deeply, then looking at the thin brown cigarette. All this effort she expended helping clients break their habits, like Caroline's of trying to control people through taking care of them. How come she couldn't break her own?

Caroline was looking down at the tweed sofa cover, noting its weave and feeling humiliated. Maybe Hannah made bread night and day herself. Maybe she was swamped with moldy old bread from other clients. Maybe she was allergic to rye.

'What's wrong?' asked Hannah, remembering the time she brought Maggie a sandwich. Roast beef on whole wheat with Russian dressing, lettuce, and onions. She'd spent hours trying to decide what Maggie would like. Maggie looked at it for a long time. Then she put on the glasses that hung around her neck, looked up, and asked, 'What am I supposed to do with this?' Hannah felt as baffled as Caroline now looked.

'Don't you like rye bread?'

'I can't eat it. I'm on a diet. But Arthur will love it.'

'Who's Arthur?'

'My husband.'

Caroline glared at her. She hadn't made that bread for some creepy man. God, what atrocious manners. At least she could pretend to be delighted.

'What did you think I'd say?' asked Hannah.

'I thought you'd be pleased.'

Hannah shrugged. 'And now you're upset because I'm not?'

'Who's upset?' She was studying her palm intently, noting the spot where her lifeline ominously veered off into several branches.

'You are.' Hannah laughed. 'You should see your expression. You look like someone took away your lollipop.'

Caroline looked up. She was thirty-five years old, for God's sake. Hannah thought she was childish? How adult was it to be rude? She studied Hannah's face – kind, with a wry smile – and remembered Hannah was out to help her. 'I feel like a fool.'

'You feel foolish because I didn't react the way you wanted. You want to control my reactions so you can feel okay about yourself. Wouldn't it be easier just to eliminate me and feel okay without relation to what I do or don't do?'

'Fuck it, Hannah! Why do you have to turn everything into such a big deal? I was just trying to be nice.'

'Uh huh, the way you and Diana are nice to each other? Trying to outnice each other?'

Caroline clutched the sofa, looking as though she might tear the place apart. Hannah was impressed. What had happened to the meek woman who'd sat across from her all those weeks? 'Look, you bring me bread. Then I bring you a pork roast. Then you bring me a Black Forest cake, and I bring you English trifle . . .'

Caroline smiled reluctantly. 'Okay. I get the point.'

'But thank you for the bread.' Hannah reached behind her to pat the loaf with affection.

'You're welcome. Enjoy it, because you aren't getting any more.'

They laughed. Hannah put her stone ashtray in her lap. Caroline released her grip on the sofa and stretched out her Levi'd legs, her snowmobile boots as cumbersome as an astronaut's.

'What were you up to this week beside kneading?' asked Hannah, drawing on her cigarette.

'I've been thinking a lot about this teacher at nursing school named Arlene.' Caroline glanced out the window and could scarcely see Lake Glass through the swirling snow. It felt like looking into a paperweight.

'Oh yes?'

'I guess you'd call her my mentor. I thought she was fantastic – as a nurse and as a person. I thought if I imitated her, I'd be fantastic, too. She was huge – tall, big-boned, tough, with this gigantic bun on top of her head. She used to say, "Ladies, you have a mission." '

'Did you have a relationship with her?'

Caroline hesitated. 'You mean sexual?'

Hannah nodded.

'Well, no. I mean, she was twenty years older than me.'

So? thought Hannah.

So was Hannah, Caroline realized. And she had wanted to rest her head on Hannah's breast, feel Hannah's arms around her. She recalled maneuvering to stand close to Arlene during training sessions, and the tingle of excitement when Arlene's hands corrected hers as she changed a dressing.

Caroline said in a dazed voice, 'Now that you mention it, I would've gone to bed with her. But I wasn't a lesbian then. Neither was she, as far as I know.' That she would have liked to make love with Arlene seemed so remote she hadn't even considered it before. It should have seemed even more remote to this respectable bridge-playing non-lesbian.

'So what happened?'

Caroline described her graduation, and Arlene's apparent pleasure at Caroline's new job at Mass General. At first Caroline was worried: If she wasn't around to wax Arlene's VW and sharpen her pencils, maybe Arlene would lose interest in her. The nursing school was en route to Caroline's apartment from the hospital, so she stopped at Arlene's office in an old sandstone building on Commonwealth Avenue every week or two. A surly young woman named Dusty, two years behind Caroline, was usually present, sometimes sharpening pencils. Caroline and Arlene would chat and part, agreeing to have supper soon. Caroline was good at her job. She felt like a karate master, poised to cope with any horror that might roll through those ER doors. Good practice for a nuclear holocaust. She was quickly promoted. She stopped to tell Arlene, and to suggest a time and place for the long-proposed dinner, feeling bold now that they were colleagues in this business of relieving human suffering.

They met at a sit-down deli near the hospital one afternoon after work. Arlene shifted her large frame in the small bentwood chair and toyed with her fork with fingers like hotdogs. 'Look, Caroline, I don't know what you want from me,' she said. 'But you'll have to find it somewhere else. I'm a very busy woman.'

Caroline stared at her.

'Don't look at me like that.' Arlene patted her huge bun, removing and replacing some hairpins.

'Like what?' Caroline asked in a faint voice. She was correct: If she didn't do things for Arlene, Arlene had no use for her.

'You've done pretty well out of this relationship. You got your fancy job at Mass General.'

'That must have been painful,' said Hannah.

Caroline felt herself going numb. She couldn't recall feeling anything.

'Caroline, who else in your life used to say, "I'm a very busy person"?'

Caroline frowned.

Hannah wanted to tug at her ear as though playing charades: 'Sounds like . . .'

'I give up,' said Caroline in a flat voice.

Hannah sighed. Why did this stuff take so long? 'It sounds to me as though that was the message your parents were always putting out.'

Caroline frowned again.

'Does it occur to you that you pick people *because* they put out that message? And if they don't, you try to manipulate them into it?'

'What?'

Realizing she was going too fast, Hannah tried to figure out how to backtrack.

'But I didn't give a shit about that job,' said Caroline, saving Hannah the effort. 'I'd done it all to be more worthy of her friendship. I couldn't believe she didn't know that.'

'Did you just hear yourself?' Hannah shifted in her chair, propping one hand on the chair arm.

'Yes. I mean, no. What?' Caroline narrowed her eyes in concentration.

'You feel you have to figure out what people want and do it, for them to like you.'

'Is that what I said?'

'That's what it sounded like to me.'

'Maybe.'

'Do you see where it comes from?' Surely she couldn't avoid seeing much longer? Feeling impatient, Hannah lit another cigarette.

'My parents?'

Hannah nodded encouragingly. She realized if Caroline had guessed wrong, she'd have made no response, which was a response in itself. 'You say you did well at nursing school and in your job just to please Arlene. But I suspect you had reasons of your own as well. It sounds to me as though you've always been competent and assertive.' Caroline blinked. This assessment clearly didn't fit her picture of herself as a messy drag. 'So did you leave it like that with Arlene?'

'I said, "But I thought we could be friends once I stopped being your student." And she said, "Things have been bad between you and me for a long time." This was news to me. Christ, I adored the woman. We finished our pastrami sandwiches. Out on the sidewalk I said, 'Thanks for all your help.' She said, "Not at all." And climbed on the trolley. I vomited in the storm sewer and walked home. That's the last thing we ever said to each other.'

Caroline glanced at the Kleenex on the chest. Another new box. Apparently a lot of crying went on in here. Caroline was damned if she'd cry. She described to Hannah how each day for several weeks she stood in a doorway across the street from Arlene's second-story office window after work and watched Arlene at her desk as students came and went. One evening Caroline, her eyes on Arlene in her office, sidled over to Arlene's VW and looked in. On the seat was a box of yellow Kleenex. The door was open, so Caroline grabbed the box and faded back into the doorway. Arlene stood up and moved over to her window. Looking out into the dusk, across the commuter traffic up Commonwealth Avenue, she looked tired and sad. She folded her arms across her stomach. Her shoulders sagged, and her head drooped. Maybe she was missing Caroline as much as Caroline missed her? Caroline fought an urge to run up there and tell her jokes.

Arlene appeared to jump slightly. Her arms fell. Her back and head straightened. She smiled. Dusty appeared at her side, gesturing excitedly. They turned and left the office. Shortly they emerged from the building and walked to the VW, Dusty talking and gesturing, Arlene smiling. As they drove off, Caroline pulled a yellow Kleenex from Arlene's box and tried to cry. But her tears wouldn't flow. The next day she stole some pill bottles from the Mass General supply room. She lined them up on the dresser in her apartment and stared at them every morning, deciding whether to continue for another day. If she wasn't parrot to Arlene's Florence Nightingale, who was she? No one.

As Hannah listened, elbow propped on chair arm, chin propped on fist, she examined the dynamics of the rejection, knowing she herself was next in line. Mummy, Pink Blanky, Marsha, Rorkie, Arlene, a couple of men, Diana . . . God knew who else. At some point, as Caroline continued to feel better, she'd try to get Hannah to reject her too, so she could move on, free of the dependency. Hannah wasn't sure how. She herself had tried every trick in the book with Maggie – not showing up for appointments, going to another therapist in midstream, accusing Maggie of planning to retire.

She tried to imagine Arlene's version for some clues as to Caroline's tactics: 'I taught this kid everything I knew, and it still wasn't enough. She kept hanging around. I couldn't figure out what she wanted. She'd already landed a good job, was getting paid more than me. She kept implying I wasn't doing enough . . .' Hannah had seen it time after time in couples therapy. The two people's accounts of an event were scarcely recognizable. The husband thought he'd offered to take out the garbage, and the wife thought he'd criticized her housekeeping.

'Did you get paid more than she?'

'I guess so. I never thought about it.'

'Wouldn't it piss you off if some kid who'd worked for a few months was getting paid more than you, who'd worked for twenty-five years?'

Caroline was startled by Hannah's language. She talked like a barmaid, but in that fancy British accent. 'But that wasn't my fault.'

'None of this is anybody's fault. It's just how the world works. People can be noble and generous, but we can also be petty. You've got to protect yourself from other people's pettiness.'

Caroline said nothing. Arlene jealous of her success? What a bizarre notion. Arlene was a big strong competent woman.

'Do you see any parallels?' asked Hannah.

'To what?'

Hannah raised her eyebrows.

'To my family?'

Hannah smiled. Raised eyebrows had come to equal her family. Like one of Pavlov's dogs, Caroline was so responsive to subtle clues signaling approval. 'How old were you when your brother was born?'

'About four, I guess.' Nine months after her father's return from the South Pacific, to be specific.

'So you've begun walking, talking, growing teeth, using the toilet, going out to play, feeding and dressing yourself. And Mummy replaces you with a charming and helpless little baby. Must make you want to shed all your achievements as quick as you can.'

Caroline frowned. That was what she'd felt, all right: that she wanted to be Arlene's student again instead of a supervisor at Mass General. But had she felt this toward her mother? She couldn't remember.

'How do you feel about your brothers?'

'I liked them a lot. Still do. I took care of them.' But according to her mother, a few days after Howard's arrival home from the hospital, Caroline gathered all his clothes and toys into a pile and asked, 'Can we take him back to the hospital now, Mommy?'

'But I guess I was mean to them sometimes,' said Caroline. 'I used to lynch Howard's teddy bear. And let the air out of his bicycle tires so he couldn't follow me.'

Hannah laughed. 'Well, it couldn't have been easy, being expected to take care of someone who'd replaced you. After all, he meant more work and less attention for you. You'd be entitled to dislike him.' Each of her children turned into a total dingbat as the next arrived home from the hospital – wetting the bed, stammering, forgetting how to tie shoes, sucking thumbs, trying to nurse again. Poor little maniacs.

'But I didn't. I was crazy about Howard. Still am.'

'Good,' said Hannah, watching one side of Caroline's face contort into a grimace that contradicted her words. 'And what's just happened with Diana? Didn't you say she's been flirting with a new young woman? Just as you're starting to feel happier and stronger?'

Caroline gave a dazed smile and looked down at her fingernails.

'I don't know, it sounds far-fetched to me.' But what had Diana said the other night? *If you realize how neat you are, why would you want to be with me?*

'I agree.' Hannah still found it astonishing, even after all these years of helping clients excavate their patterns and of watching her own in operation. 'If you felt a sexual attraction to Arlene, she probably felt it too,' said Hannah, trying to make the most of Caroline's confusion. 'And lots of heterosexuals are terrified of their homosexual impulses.'

Caroline looked up from her study of her fingernails. 'Are you saying everyone is homosexual?'

'One of my clients used to say she was trisexual – she'd try anything sexual.' Hannah reflected that at various times she'd have fucked anything – trees, dogs, vegetables. It had a lot to do with hormones and very little to do with true love.

Caroline was laughing. Then she stopped abruptly. Hannah was not only not respectable, she was downright kinky. Caroline studied her bare feet with bewilderment.

'I think we're all bisexual,' said Hannah, 'and make choices based on social pressures and family dynamics.'

'Choices?'

'That's what life is all about.'

'Becoming a lesbian sure didn't feel like a choice.' She studied Hannah in her natty blazer and gray flannel slacks. This respectable middle-aged lady was apparently acknowledging her own bisexuality. But had she felt desire for a woman so compelling that she couldn't eat, sleep, or concentrate, so all-encompassing that when she dreamed it was of nothing but caressing a naked female body? As Caroline had in relation to both Clea and Diana. Hannah always looked calm and cool. Caroline tried to picture her face flushed from passion, her sharp blue eyes unfocused with desire. She realized with a jolt that she'd like to take Hannah to bed and make her care whether Caroline returned for her next appointment, make her feel sexual obsession so strongly she'd be compelled to doubt her own bland convictions about 'choice.'

Caroline lowered her eyes. Jesus. Hannah said Arlene would have felt Caroline's attraction to her. Did this mean Hannah was aware of it too?

'Caroline, do you understand you're going to try to get me to reject you?' Sometimes just saying this was enough to subvert the compulsion. Other clients wouldn't have been sidetracked by Armageddon.

'Why would I do that?'

'Because it's what you're used to, what you're geared for. What you *need* in order to move on.'

'But that's about the last thing I want, and I thought it was all a question of choice,' Caroline threw out tauntingly.

Hannah looked at her for a while, then smiled faintly. 'Conscious choices aren't always in agreement with unconscious ones. That's why we're trying to bring the unconscious ones out for an airing. To see if they're what you really want.' She drew on her cigarette and flicked the ash into the hollow stone, reflecting that it was even more complicated than that.

'Diana thinks you've put me up to dating Mr Right,' said Caroline, to break the silence.

'I don't care whom or what you date.'

'That's what I told her.'

'Does Mr Right have a real name?'

'Brian Stone.'

Hannah nodded and said nothing. She'd done counseling with him and his wife while they were splitting. A nice man, dedicated to his profession, but remote and workaholic. Caroline was zeroing in on Daddy again, just like a homing pigeon. And no doubt about to shed Diana in the process.

'And Diana's not too pleased?'

'Nope,' said Caroline with a grin. If Diana was coming around, she was certainly taking her time. She'd been out with Suzanne last night, coming home early in the morning to shower and change before leaving for work.

'Whom do you want?'

'I don't know. Both maybe.' Caroline jutted out her jaw defiantly.

Hannah smiled and gestured with her cigarette hand. 'Be my guest.'

Caroline looked at her. She didn't really mean that. She talked a good liberal line, but she'd had the same husband for eighty-six years or something. However she sounded, she was a pillar of conventionality. If Caroline called her bluff and came on with her, she'd flip out.

Hannah watched Caroline eyeing her speculatively. Asking her if she'd had a relationship with Arlene had probably put ideas in her head. Maybe that question was a mistake? She remembered her own horror at finding herself attracted to Maggie during therapy. She told herself it was disgusting, she a middle-aged mother and Maggie a grandmother. But the feelings kept coming. One day out of the blue Maggie asked, 'Is it really so terrible to want to be close to someone you care about, Hannah?'

'What?' asked Hannah warily, sitting on the couch in Maggie's office studying the pattern of the wine and blue Oriental carpet.

'Look, I know what you're feeling for me, and it's okay. It's normal in therapy. It's normal whenever people open themselves up to each other. Normal, and not very important. Just because we have the misfortune to live in a culture that says it's abnormal doesn't make it so.'

Gradually the urgency faded, and the issue was never referred to again in the subsequent fifteen years of close friendship. Maggie had always gone for the jugular as a therapist. She claimed once in New York a man in a raincoat exposed himself to her on the street. She grabbed him by the arm, saying, 'Don't be ridiculous. You can't do anything with that.' And dragged him upstairs to her office for an hour of therapy. Being British, Hannah tended to operate with more guile. So she smiled pleasantly at Caroline and allowed her to exit, still in the grip of all those disturbing and revealing feelings.

Caroline was walking down a sidewalk. In the grass sat a small boy holding a wild thrush. He tossed it into the air. The bird flapped its wings frantically. The boy held a string tied to its leg, with which he hauled it back in. Caroline walked over to him. 'Is that your bird?'

'Yes.'

'Where did you get it?'

'Trapped it.' He clutched it in one fist. She realized if she angered him, he'd tighten the fist.

'Don't you think you should let it go?'

'Nope.'

Caroline looked around for his parents, or a policeman.

Hannah marched up and yelled, 'Let that bird go, you little creep!'

Startled, he did so, the bird's leg trailing the string in flight. Hannah looked at Caroline with raised eyebrows.

Sunlight on Caroline's face prodded her awake like a cat's paw. She tried to remember her dream. Which had left her feeling hopeful. Something about a bird. As she stretched, she realized she was getting middle-aged. For the past fifteen years she'd usually managed to wake up next to someone, but these days she actually preferred waking up alone. You could stretch without disturbing your bedmate. You could drift on the wind currents of your dreams without rolling into someone's insistent earth-bound arms. You could feel the sunlight creep across your covers leaving patches of warmth, without having to put into words how billowy the clouds out the window looked, how blustery the wind that was shaking the window next to the loom. Waking up with someone was the ultimate in intimacy. She recalled people toward whom she'd felt, If you want sex with me, fine; but if you want to wake up next to me in the morning, forget it.

Caroline could hear Suzanne and Diana giggling upstairs. She could be giggling with Brian right now, if she too had the ethics of a skunk. They'd gone for dinner last night to an old stone inn on the far side of town. As they walked in, across wide pine floorboards, Caroline spotted Hannah at a table in the corner, with a distinguished-looking man with thinning white hair. Hannah wore a tailored pin-striped suit with a skirt, and a coral silk blouse. She was leaning forward, smiling into the man's eyes.

Caroline gripped Brian's arm convulsively. 'What's wrong?' he asked.

'I just saw someone I don't want to talk to.' The tune 'I Only Have Eyes for You' was running through her head. Only it wasn't true. Hannah turned those dazzling blue eyes onto a host of other people. Caroline felt swamped with jealousy. This is ridiculous, she told herself as the hostess ushered them into another room, with a low ceiling, hand-hewn beams, and a huge stone fireplace with a mantel lined with pewter plates and tankards.

As Caroline drank a Manhattan and chatted with Brian about his operations for that day, she reclaimed her composure. In the middle of a hysterectomy, she saw Hannah and the man walk past the window next to her table and over to Hannah's copper-colored Mercury. The man unlocked her door and opened it. As Hannah turned to get in, he pinched her ass. She laughed and poked him in the ribs with her elbow. Caroline watched, outraged. How dare he demean her like that? How dare she enjoy it?

'. . . if you don't have ovaries, you don't need a uterus,' Brian was saying, 'so I take out the entire shooting match.'

'I see,' said Caroline, intent on the departing Mercury. Marriage, that grotesque institution Caroline felt such contempt for, worked for Hannah and her husband. Caroline could see from their faces and gestures that they were happy. She sat in shocked disbelief, playing with the maraschino cherry in her drink.

'. . . that way you don't have to go back in again a few years later to remove a cancerous uterus.'

'What?' asked Caroline. 'Oh yes, I see.' She was thinking about her own marriage to Jackson. It had consisted almost entirely of waiting. Waiting around the phone hoping he'd return her calls, waiting for the boys to wake from their naps so she'd have someone to talk to, waiting with supper in the oven to see if he'd come home, waiting to go to sleep in case he showed up wanting a late-night meal, waiting in bed for him not to be too tired to make love, waiting in the soft gray light of the Newton dawn with her arms around a king-sized pillow for him to return home after dashing out in the middle of the night to an emergency, waiting for the man who'd courted her with such flair and enthusiasm to reemerge. She'd been an expert at waiting, until she couldn't wait any longer and walked out.

'What about you?' asked Brian, cutting his ham.

'Excuse me?'

'I said what about you?' He raised a piece of meat to his mouth on his fork.

'What about me?'

'What was your day like?'

'Fine, thanks. Nothing unusual.' She'd thought that was the nature of marriage. But Hannah's marriage wasn't like that.

'Tell me about your ex-husband.'

Thinking Brian must be telepathic, Caroline said, 'There's not much to tell. We met while I was working at Mass General. He was a resident. The usual: We dated, fucked, married, had kids, and divorced, in that order.' She poked at her butternut squash with her fork, recalling the first time she ever saw Jackson, at the ER admissions desk in his white lab coat and tie, dark hair falling into his eyes. He looked at her name tag and called her Miss

Kelley, whisking around issuing orders with brisk efficiency. Absorbing his commands, Caroline thought to herself: It's okay, I can handle this guy. As he strode away down the corridor, the nurse beside her said in a low voice, 'I wonder if that man ever takes time out to eat pussy.'

Caroline was at one of the many low points in her life. Without Arlene she had no magic. When the bloodied victims of car wrecks or knife fights rolled through the ER doors, she wanted to run the other way. A young girl with meningitis died in her arms one morning at dawn. She didn't know whom she'd been trying to kid passing herself off as a healer. She developed a rash all over her body and began lying around her darkened apartment missing work. Her colleagues started to notice her listless distraction and kept asking if she was all right. Night after night in her apartment, pill bottles lined up beside her, she watched on the evening news as one American city after another flared up in flames of racial frustration. Soon whites would be butchering blacks in the streets, the gutters clotted with blood. It wouldn't end until the black race was extinct. It was summer, and after the news she'd lie on her carpet in a pool of sweat as through her open windows drifted noises from car crashes on Route 9, and the screams of muggers' victims. But there was nothing she could do except eye those pill bottles.

At the hospital Jackson and she nearly tripped over each other several times turning corners. Eventually he exchanged a sentence or two with her during such a collision. And late one night they sat on a stretcher outside an X-ray room and talked long enough for Caroline to learn he'd grown up in a tract house in Springfield, where his father worked in the Smith and Wesson factory, put himself through Tufts on scholarships and part-time jobs, lived alone in a Back Bay apartment. He looked startled to hear himself inviting her to dinner at Jimmy's Harborside that weekend.

As they ate clams casino, lobster, Caesar salad, and drank Château Lafitte, they looked out on the harbor, where gulls mewed and swooped among the masts of docked sailing yachts. Jackson talked about his plans to buy such a yacht someday. Caroline could see the fish market where she helped her father buy the catch of yesterday throughout her childhood. Soon she was so busy being courted that she had no time to watch cities go up in flames on Walter Cronkite . . .

Brian smiled. 'Your marriage wasn't much fun, I gather?'

'When we were dating, it was daffodils and chocolate ice cream sodas, the Boston Symphony, Jimmy's Harborside, weekends of passion in Hyannis. We read Emerson and Thoreau and discussed them, listened to Bach fugues together. But after we married, that man vanished. Jackson became a phantom. I went to sleep alone and I woke up alone. The only way I'd know he'd been there was from the pile of dirty clothes on the floor. I felt like a piece of furniture. I couldn't figure out where I'd gone wrong. I cooked well, kept the house neat and comfortable, ironed his shirts the way he liked, polished his shoes, made love whenever he wanted. Dressed carefully, exercised at a figure salon, rinsed with Scope. It was almost as though Jackson wanted to outfit a house with wife, children, and accessories, so he could move on to his next project.'

'What was that?'

'I have no idea. I never saw the man.' Her appetite had departed. She poked listlessly at her roast beef.

'I wonder if Irene would say the same thing.' Brian rested his elbow on the table and his chin on his fist.

'Is that what your marriage was like?'

'I never thought about it that way before, but maybe it was. Maybe that's just how marriage is.'

'Maybe so,' said Caroline, thinking about Hannah and her husband.

'But maybe it doesn't have to be.' Brian inspected her like a broker eyeing the Dow after the crash.

Back at the cabin, Suzanne's Toyota was in the driveway, along with Caroline's Subaru and Diana's Chevette.

'Looks like a used car lot,' said Brian, sitting with his gloved hands on the wheel and the motor running, waiting to be asked in.

Caroline considered it, because if he accepted, he might end up staying the night. But revenge against Diana didn't seem a worthy motive for such a serious move. It wouldn't be fair to Brian, and she found she was starting to care about his well-being. 'I'd ask you in,' she said, 'but I don't think it's a very good idea right now.'

'I understand,' he said, taking her hand. 'You need more time. And so do I probably.' Holding her face in both hands, he kissed her.

It might work, her heart whispered as she kissed him back. If I can't have Hannah, maybe I can be Hannah . . .

More giggling cascaded down from upstairs. As Caroline gazed past her loom to the bright blue sky outside the window, she realized her ode to waking up alone was sour grapes. There was nothing to equal the pleasure of looking in the early morning light at the sleeping face of someone you cherished. She remembered her feeling of bemused wonder the first time this happened for her – with Jackson in his Back Bay apartment. She sat up and leaned on her elbow, studying his stubbly jaw, dark tousled head, and curly chest hair. Reaching out her fingertips, she touched his lips, firm and smooth. He smiled without opening his eyes and caressed her fingertips with the tip of his tongue.

Then his pager went off. He jumped up and raced to the hospital, leaving her to change the stained sheets in a haze of purpose and well-being. She'd marry him, bear his babies, devote her life to making his home a haven of comfort, to which he could return from his missions of mercy. Arlene, who had vanished from her life a few months earlier, on a trolley without a backward glance, had been mistaken. Caroline's mission was to facilitate Jackson's. She'd be Miss Kitty to Jackson's Matt Dillon.

There'd been boyfriends before Jackson, though none with whom she'd seen in the dawn. Kevin in high school, with whom she groped in the RKO and behind the Stop 'n Shop. At nursing school she dated a Harvard man named Ned Rollins III, whom she met at a mixer. One night he took her up to his rooms in Adams House. All she wanted was to roll around with him on his sitting room carpet. But he insisted she read John Stuart Mill's 'On Liberty.' Then they discussed how everyone was entitled to pursue his own pleasure so long as it didn't harm other people. On subsequent nights, as snow piled up outside, he had her read Malthus, D. H. Lawrence, and Simone de Beauvoir. After several tedious weeks they finally rolled around on the carpet. And when she persuaded him to relieve her of her virginity, he attributed her enthusiasm to the framework of emancipated ideas erected by his reading list. For her part, she first understood the world population crisis that her parents had explained at the dinner table for years: a regrettable by-product of an act that yielded more pleasure than any other she'd yet discovered.

Lying on her bed listening to Diana and Suzanne giggle,

Caroline examined the new shawl on her loom. Inspired by the blue and purple Lake Glass shawl, which now hung on the wall above the loom, she had started a second shawl based on the view out her window of the winter sunset over Lake Glass. It featured strips of oranges, purples, and reds, which faded into each other on a tie-dyed warp. In the past she'd worked mostly with earth tones. These new colors were so bright she sometimes had to stop work sooner than usual to rest her outraged eyes.

Maybe she'd give this new shawl to Hannah. No, wrong. She wasn't supposed to bring Hannah presents. Hannah wouldn't be impressed in any case. She spent her days saving people from suicide. Handicrafts would strike her as trivial.

Love. Was she in love with Hannah, Diana asked. Probably. Marsha, Rorkie, Arlene, Rollins, Jackson, David Michael – she'd been in love with them all. With every breath, she'd sighed the name of whoever was current. Sometimes she lost track and sighed the wrong name. With each one she'd known it was always and forever. Until here she was now with an entire chorus line preserved in the wax museum of her memory. Why hadn't these loves lasted? Hannah and her husband had been together since the Gold Rush. She pictured Hannah smiling into her husband's eyes at the restaurant last night, poking him playfully with her elbow. But everyone had problems. But maybe not Hannah. She seemed so together. Despite her children's deaths.

Maybe she and Brian could make it work too. But it never had for her before. There must be something wrong with her. She began itemizing her failings. She hadn't scrubbed the grouting between the bathroom tiles when she lived with Jackson. She wanted too much sex from David Michael. Or too little? Too much with him, too little with Rollins? Or the other way around? What was the point of all that passion and pain, all those pledges and promises, if now she couldn't even recall what she'd promised to whom? That was how it would be soon with Diana. And no doubt with Brian if they continued. Pointless. It was all pointless. She was alone, always had been, always would be. Companionship was a mirage. The reality was this gnawing loneliness. Why pretend otherwise?

Upstairs Suzanne and Diana shrieked with laughter. No doubt they were wrestling naked in bed, as Diana and she used to, the covers tangled and pillows heaved around the room. Caroline had woven the spread on Diana's bed – two interlocking female symbols with happy faces. It had taken weeks. She wanted to stomp upstairs and grab it off the bed, and the Eden tapestry off the wall above the living room couch.

Caroline wrapped her arms around her pillow and rocked side to side, thinking about the bottles of pills on her closet shelf. Jackie and Jason were almost teenagers. They wouldn't miss her as much now as when they were toddlers . . .

A feathered red head appeared outside Caroline's window. It was attached to a long black and white body that marched up the gnarled locust trunk like an Alpine climber with a red felt hat. Halfway up the window it stopped, studied the bark, and began drumming, its head vibrating like a jackhammer. Caroline watched in amazement as wood chips flew in all directions.

Three

While Hannah waited for a prescription for Arthur's strep throat in the mall drugstore, she took off the rack a paperback murder mystery called *Never Say Die*. After reading the first several pages, she guessed the adopted son had done it, then read the ending. She was correct. She replaced the book and picked up another. She couldn't bear to read one the whole way through because she hated suspense. Real life involved more suspense than she could handle. Would Erwin the banker rape his son again this week? How would Caroline engineer the attempted rejection?

She glanced around the brightly lit store, where several ordinary-looking people in winter clothing browsed through greeting cards, magazines, and toiletries, also waiting for prescriptions. Ordinary-looking, just like the people who walked into her office. And like them, everybody in the store had geysers of untapped fury and 'perversity' beneath a bland exterior. Just like in the mystery novels, any character in this place was capable of a murder, including herself. Today she felt this so vividly it was tempting to stay under the bedcovers with poor Arthur, who was huddled in a heap of misery, unable to speak or swallow with his raw throat.

As she picked up a *National Enquirer* with Dolly Parton's picture on the front and began to read an article entitled 'Is Your Pet a Space Alien?,' the four walls of the store seemed to cave in all at once. She felt trapped in a shrinking room, like a James Bond character. She paid the clerk behind the cash register for the *Enquirer*, and hurried out the door into the parking lot. Taking several deep breaths, she leaned against the brick of the storefront, fanning herself with the tabloid. Menopause was such a treat. Who would wish a body on anyone? She unhooked her Berber cape, which Maggie had brought her from North Africa, and folded it across one arm.

As her claustrophobia receded, Hannah breathed deeply and opened the *Enquirer* to an article headlined 'Cheerleading Pyramid Attacked by Swarm of Killer Bees.' Reading it, she reflected it was a wonder anyone lived long enough to go through menopause.

Returning to her post near the prescription counter, Hannah ran through her clients for that afternoon. Caroline scheduled for right after lunch. What would go on today, Hannah wondered. How Caroline tried to win over a parent figure was becoming clearer, from hearing about that nursing teacher and from observing her behavior toward Hannah. She turned herself into a servant, did nice things, admired one, agreed with one. It was most seductive. *Face it, my friend: You adore being adored.* If only Hannah wasn't aware that, like all slaves, Caroline had swallowed so much resentment that it seeped out her pores. But how she'd try to get Hannah to reject her remained opaque.

The pharmacist called her name. As she wrote a check, she decided when someone asked what her therapeutic orientation was, she ought to claim membership in the Drugstore Murder Mystery School. She conducted therapy like that game her children played on cold winter evenings on the carpet in front of the fireplace – Clue, in which they guessed from assembled evidence who'd committed the murder, where, and with what instrument.

Driving downtown through heavy traffic to meet Simon for lunch, Hannah thought for the first time in years about Mrs Abner, the housemother at her Sussex boarding school. Her grandmother deposited her in the neo-Gothic dormitory amid a horde of frightened adolescents, with a perfunctory hug and a 'Chin up, then.' Hannah took one look at Mrs Abner's white head and knew they were pals. Mrs Abner, a cameo brooch at the throat of her high-necked silk dress, was aloof, just like her grandmother. The other girls were terrified of her sharp tongue and fought over who had to sit at her table at meals, but Hannah adored her. She knew Mrs Abner, for all her brisk efficiency, was watching over her.

This myth wasn't dispelled until one afternoon a couple of years later during room inspection. Hannah had brought her mother's bark painting from Hampstead and kept it in her closet, bringing it out when she was homesick. That afternoon she forgot to put it back. It sat on her oak desk.

Mrs Abner looked at it, white eyebrows raised. 'This is the most barbaric object I've ever seen.'

'It's *not* barbaric,' said Hannah. 'It's Australian.'

Mrs Abner's eyebrows fluttered. 'And are you Australian, young lady?'

'Yes, I am.' She thought Mrs Abner knew this about her, knew everything about her.

'And how would you like to go back to Australia?'

Hannah looked down.

'This room is frightful,' Mrs Abner said. 'We've never had a colonial who knew how to keep a decent room. It must be those mud huts you're reared in.'

Hannah clenched the muscle in her jaw.

'No pudding at dinner until you attain the level of personal civilization befitting a British subject. And do get rid of that ghastly object, won't you, dear?'

Overnight Hannah went from adoring the woman to loathing her. No months of silent agony outside Mrs Abner's office window for her. Deserted by her parents at an early age, she'd learned to cut people off abruptly. She began to look at 'British civilization' with an eye too jaundiced for her years. Was it civilized to call other people's paintings barbaric? Was it civilized to send children off to boarding schools run by witches? She lay on her narrow lumpy bed and reflected on what she'd observed about British civilization through her neighbors' windows from their mossy Hampstead garden walls. The Honourable Montgomery James drank sherry every afternoon until he passed out on his Oriental carpet. Sir Freddie Munson, who yelled at her for bouncing her ball against his garage door during rounders, had a retarded daughter who took tradesmen into the back shed when they made deliveries. Lady Austin-Stanforth masturbated with an ivory candle from the ornate silver candelabra on her mahogany Sheraton dining table. Once she caught Hannah watching her. She went to Hannah's grandmother and accused Hannah of stealing jewelry from her au pair. In Hampstead and Sussex Hannah first learned to ignore what people said about themselves, and to watch how they behaved instead.

Mrs Abner and Hannah's boarding school chums knew when during a meal to use their fish knives. They knew where a china underliner went when setting a table. Hannah didn't know these things because she refused to pay attention when her grandmother tried to teach her. They were civilized, she was barbaric. So be it. She hung her bark painting on the wall of her room. And when she sat at Mrs Abner's table, she blew her nose into the linen napkin. She began sneaking out to the gardener's shed late at night to meet a boy from the kitchen named Colin, who was unconcerned with the proper placement of fish knives. Colin, fair-haired and pale-skinned, had grown up in the East End of London and had come to Sussex to study furniture making, thanks to the largesse of a trustee of the boarding school, for whom Colin's parents worked as servants. Once Hannah and Colin worked their way up to intercourse, they'd go at it for hours on the stone floor among the rakes and hoes. Until Colin would gasp, 'Bloody hell, luv, I just can't do it anymore, can I?' He made her a beautiful walnut table clock which she kept on the desk in her dormitory room and dusted daily.

Climbing to the second-floor restaurant Simon had selected, a Swedish smorgasbord place above the main shopping street, Hannah was gripped with a sudden fear of tumbling backwards down the steps. She steadied herself with a hand on either wall, reminding herself that it was 'only' menopause. Simon was seated under a hanging spider plant sipping a tequila sunrise. Normally fastidious, he was looking unshaven and unkempt, his blond hair out of place and the vest of his three-piece suit unbuttoned. His wife, Helena, had left him for another man. Hannah studied him sympathetically as she sat down. Bossy little boy and belligerent teenager, he was unaccustomed to not having his own way. Presumably he had to get himself humbled at some point, for the good of his soul, but it was still painful to watch if he'd been your baby. She remembered his agony as a little boy when she'd wash his blanket, how he'd stand anxiously by the machine throughout the cycle sucking a thumb. Once as she passed the blanket through the wringer, he became so distressed at the pain he assumed his blanket was experiencing that he tried to rescue it – and ran his own arm through the wringer by mistake.

When Helena left, Hannah tried to figure out how it was her own fault. She'd married a man who'd died in battle when Simon was barely a year old. She'd followed another man across the Atlantic with Simon in tow. He'd lost a brother and sister, and nearly his own life. He'd had his share of upheaval and insecurity. But who hadn't? There was no way to protect your children from the agony of loss, however much you might wish to.

'So how's it going?' she asked, glancing at the drink list. The only thing that helped when her hormones were bullying her was gin, but too much gin gave her bad dreams and anxiety attacks in the middle of the night.

'Fine,' he said curtly, tossing his head to get the blond hair out of his eyes. He was blessed with the stiff upper lip of both British parents, poor guy. But he'd called her more often since Helena left, set up lunch dates, come to the house for dinner, bringing his laundry.

The waiter appeared, and Hannah ordered gin on the rocks. 'So what's new? Or rather who's new?'

He gave a pained smile. 'Nothing and nobody, Mother.' His eyes were slightly bloodshot.

She patted his hand. 'Courage, my boy. This too shall pass.' She couldn't think how to help him. Maybe you couldn't detach until you had the perspective only fifty years of watching love affairs, marriages, and divorces could give: that there was life beyond 'lurve,' as an embittered client called it. Once during her own therapy, at a time when she was furious with Arthur for being away the night of the accident, she described to Maggie the flirtation she was conducting with Allen Sullivan, presumably to punish Arthur.

Maggie looked at her coolly from her wing chair beside a potted bay laurel tree and replied, 'I'm an old woman now, and I have more important things to think about than whether Hannah Burke is going to seduce her husband's best friend. And so should you, my dear.'

Simon was looking irritated. 'I said I was fine.'

Hannah nodded. She should mind her own business. 'Well, Arthur's not. He has a strep throat.'

'What a drag. Watch out you don't get it.'

'I'm a war horse.' She sipped her gin, hoping to fend off the sensation that the walls were closing in again.

'I know. I hardly ever remember you sick. The rest of us would be flat out, and you'd be bringing us trays and reading us stories.' He clutched his glass in both hands on the table in front of him, gazing into the orange and streaky red concoction like Socrates about to quaff hemlock.

Hannah smiled. He'd been idealizing her since Helena left. Helena was the baddie right now. Mum was the goodie. She was enjoying it, but she knew it would last only until he found another woman, at which point she'd be returned to cold storage, like a mink coat in summer.

She watched him as he itemized her virtues. He was a member of his own generation. Hers, traumatized by the depression and by Hitler, wanted stability, comfort and security, at whatever cost to spontaneity. His, observing the aridity of most of their parents' lives, despised all that. They followed their feelings, hence were always in bliss or despair. They didn't understand that the boring old forms could sometimes carry you through the turmoil and deposit you on the far shores of contentment. Several times in their thirty-eight years together, Arthur had threatened to leave. Because she was bad-tempered before her periods. Because she was a flirt. Because the kids were driving him nuts. Several times she had threatened to leave. Because he was gone too much. Because she didn't know whom he was sleeping with all those lonely nights in strange cities. Because she was tired of washing his socks, or looking at his unshaven face across the breakfast table on weekends. Each time, their tangled web of property, responsibility, shared social life, and mutual concern seemed too complicated to unravel, and they stuck it out. Until here they were, closing in on old age, more in love than even during those first besotted days in the sleigh bed overlooking the Heath. To have been through life with someone, to know all his flaws and failings and he yours, to have done every awful thing two people can do to each other, yet still to be together – it was a pleasure unsurpassed in Hannah's experience. More subtle than those first furious fucks, it sometimes took her breath away just to look at Arthur in the lamplight as he read his *Wall Street Journal*, wearing his moth-eaten green Mr Chips sweater, and to realize what they'd achieved – a lifelong love, like they touted in the *National Enquirer*: 'High School Lovebirds Still Cooing After Ninety-four Years.'

Back at her office, Hannah discovered Mary Beth in her ruffled blouse and Mao slippers sitting rigidly on the tweed couch, which she and Arthur had rearranged the day before so Hannah could have her lake view.

'Are you okay?' asked Hannah, removing her cape, not wanting to hear about it if the answer was no.

'I'm not sure.'

'What's the problem?' There was something demoralizing about therapizing a therapist. If your techniques didn't work for you, why should they for anyone else?

'A client just asked me to go to bed with him. When I said no, he called me the worst names you've ever heard and marched out.'

'What's so terrible about that?' She reminded herself of all the times she went running to Maggie in her early years doing therapy.

Mary Beth looked at her with surprise. 'I must have been leading him on. Or maybe I didn't handle his advances correctly.'

'It sounds to me as though you did fine. Either he'll be back, or he won't. Look, I think you're taking this too seriously, Mary Beth. All you are is a technician. You find out what patterns got set up in infancy, and then you try to point out their recurrence.'

Mary Beth nodded impatiently, as though she knew all that. But clearly she didn't, or she wouldn't be so upset. Hannah recalled the constant anxiety and sense of responsibility she used to feel. Life had gotten easier once she finally realized there was a limit to her power either to help or to hurt. A therapist was, at best, a placebo. This recognition came after a client in a deep depression took a bottle of sleeping pills and climbed into his freezer. She went wailing to Maggie in her office at the university about how it was all her fault. Maggie put on her glasses, looked up from some papers on her desk, and snapped, 'Where do you get off, Hannah? Whose life was it? Not yours. It was his, to do with as he had to. It's a tragedy, but his, not yours. So stop feeling sorry for yourself.' The unexpectedness of Maggie's responses always fascinated Hannah. Looking at her wrinkles and gray hair, you expected kindness. You usually got instead exactly what you needed.

The receptionist buzzed. Caroline had arrived. As Mary Beth stood up and limped to the door, Hannah said kindly, 'Don't take the full weight of human misery on your shoulders all at once, Mary Beth. It'll snap your spine.'

Caroline did a double take as she walked into Hannah's office. The desk and chair had switched places with the couch.

'I've been looking at the parking lot for fifteen years,' Hannah explained. 'I finally got sick of it.'

'But I liked looking at the lake.' Caroline tossed her navy blue parka onto the couch.

'It is nice,' said Hannah, glancing out the window to the vast silver expanse of frozen lake. All morning clients had been freaking out over the new arrangement. They were in such flux that she and her setting were supposed to remain static. But they'd recover, and she'd have her nice new view.

Caroline was circling the office in her white uniform, like a Samoyed unable to lie down. 'I can see it's upset you,' said Hannah. Caroline could do without total predictability from her now. Getting her to accept this would be part of the Great Disillusionment.

'I'd rather look at the lake.'

'Give me a break. I like the lake too. And I'm stuck here all day.' Caroline expressing a preference rather than enduring stoically. Hannah was delighted.

Caroline listened to herself complain with astonishment. 'Well, it is your office.' Hell, she was lucky to have a sofa to sit on, and the leisure to do so. What did the view matter? Sitting on the couch, she glanced all around. Out the window opposite her was a grimy bank of plowed snow and several parked cars. 'Jesus, I can see why you wanted to switch.'

Hannah smiled. 'What have you been up to?'

'I was just having lunch with a friend at Maude's. There was this really old lady, eighty-five or ninety, staring at herself in the rest room mirror. She looked at me and said, "You know, when I look in a mirror, I get scared. Sometimes I wonder what it's all for." '

'What did you say?'

'I said, "Don't look in mirrors, then." '

They laughed.

'Is that something you think about?' asked Hannah. 'What it's all for?'

'Sure I think about it.' A car out the window had a bumper sticker that read, 'Eat More Lamb. 50,000 Coyotes Can't Be Wrong.' Maybe this new view wouldn't be so dreary after all. 'Doesn't everybody?'

'You'd be surprised.' She herself was amazed by the number of clients who assumed the purpose of their lives was to pay off their mortgage. 'What are your conclusions?'

'If there's a God, He's wacko.'

'And we're here because of some complicated chemical accident?' Having eaten a fruit salad at lunch with Simon, Hannah knew there was a God. It would take a genius like God to invent the strawberry.

'Right. Because otherwise you have to see God as a sadist.' What was this, therapy or Sunday school?

'You do?'

'How else are you going to account for all the brutality and suffering in the world?'

'How are you going to account for that pileated woodpecker last month?' Or this incredible lake, Hannah added privately, not wishing to rub it in. She squinted slightly from the glare off the ice.

Caroline smiled, pleased Hannah should remember something she'd said so long ago. 'I saw it again this weekend. It climbed a tree outside my window while I was lying in bed.'

'Oh yes? So how do you account for its existence in such a dreadful world?'

'An apparatus evolved to keep down insects.'

Hannah smiled. 'Why do we need hundreds of varieties?'

'For the hundreds of varieties of insects.'

'What I can't figure out,' said Hannah, lighting a brown cigarette, 'is why, if you hate this world so much, you don't just shut up about it. Instead, you dwell on its horrors in such loving detail.'

'I'm stuck here, aren't I?'

'No. As usual, it's your choice.'

'You mean suicide? I tried that once.' She crossed her legs and put clasped hands around her knee.

'Oh yes?'

'I was married to that doctor in Newton. Jackson. I turned on the gas oven and stuck my head in. It was so dirty I decided to clean it first. By the time I finished, the boys were awake from their naps.'

Hannah smiled. 'Is that really true? Or are you trying to amuse me again?'

Caroline grinned. 'You'll never know, will you?'

Hannah shrugged. 'If you won't let me do my job, don't be surprised when it doesn't get done.' She thought about her own failed suicide. A couple of months after the children died, she walked off across the frozen lake, leaving Arthur a good-bye note. After a couple of hours shivering beside a snow drift, when he hadn't arrived to talk her out of it, she trudged home. Arthur was watching the news, while Simon, Joanna, and the dog staged a loud argument in the playroom. The note still sat propped against a Gordon's gin bottle in the pine dry sink. He hadn't seen it because he hadn't had a drink. She handed it to him. He read it and looked at her. 'I would have come after you,' he said. She shrugged, fixed martinis, and put another log on the fire.

Caroline was indignant. Why did Hannah so consistently refuse to be entertained by her? She sighed and began talking: 'I just couldn't take it anymore. The boys were little, and Jackson was always at the hospital. I didn't have many friends or interests. I'd quit my job at Mass General. My sole purpose in life was to help Jackson save the world.'

'Sound familiar?'

Caroline hesitated. 'My parents, you mean?' She remembered waiting for them to get home at night, just as she had for Jackson. Running their baths, rubbing their temples, bringing them tea. Just as she had for Jackson. She was a fucking automaton.

'So go on. Why did you decide to kill yourself?' Shit, a hot flash was about to hit her. It licked across her body like a grass fire. She trembled with the effort of sitting still as sweat trickled down her chest. The room wavered and receded.

'. . . I used to listen to call-in talk shows on WBZ for company,' Caroline was saying. Was she being polite, Hannah wondered, or did she not notice that her therapist was sitting in a puddle of sweat? Usually clients were too caught up in their own inner dramas to notice if she did a handstand on the desk. Her face must be bright red.

'. . . on this particular day they were discussing office sex. I started wondering if Jackson was getting any on the side with the nurses. It happened all the time at Mass General. It was how he and I had gotten together – those late nights relieving human suffering. So I wondered if that was why he was hardly ever home. This minister phoned in to say he wanted to swing, but his wife wasn't into it, and would it be sinful to do it on the sly. Then the program ended and the news came on. About our tanks rolling into Cambodia, and the slaughter and famine. I had a moment of clarity: There I was in this huge neo-Tudor house, surrounded by all the luxuries I spent my days buying and maintaining, worrying about my husband having affairs – while much of the world was starving and homeless. I walked over to a window that looked out on a marble bird bath. The drapes were crewelwork, handmade in India. I took the edge of a curtain in my fingers and examined all those tiny stitches and realized that some starving woman probably went blind doing them for a few cents an hour. And people came into my house and exclaimed over how beautiful they were. I knew I'd sold out. I did examine the oven, but the boys woke up from their naps.' She didn't add that this was when she took up weaving, as a form of penance. She enrolled in a course at a crafts school, intending to weave blankets for the Salvation Army. But her teacher entered her work in a craft show without telling her, and she won second place. Everything she made someone wanted to buy. And once she left Jackson, she needed the money. She enjoyed weaving, so that even her attempt at penance turned into a sellout.

'Did you tell Jackson how unhappy you were?' asked Hannah, feeling chilled and clammy.

'I tried to. He told me I was too intense, and what about all the patients at the hospital with real problems.'

'Remember the trips to the Salvation Army? Remember Jason at Christmas?' Hannah removed her jacket, hoping her shirt would dry out.

Caroline squeezed the bridge of her nose, marveling at Hannah's memory. She looked up. 'And you think we're not just machines that go round and round?'

'There can be more to us than that. Are you sure it's just the Third World that suffers and hungers?'

They sat in silence for a long time, Caroline studying the tire tracks across the dusting of new snow in the parking lot. Randy Eliot would probably be able to identify the tire brands. She and Brian had had dinner with Randy and Connie a couple of nights ago in their house overlooking Lake Glass. Caroline decided she liked them, despite their passion to know the cost of every object under discussion.

'There's a school vacation next week, isn't there?' asked Hannah, taking out her appointment book. 'Are you and your sons going somewhere?'

'I'm driving them to Newton to stay with their father for the week.'

'Do they get along with him?' Opening the book, she looked for an empty slot for next week.

'They idolize him. But he's very busy and doesn't have much time for them. They usually come home angry and disappointed.'

'It's sad what some parents do to distance themselves from their children.'

Caroline examined this remark. It was true: Just because Jackson claimed he was hostage to his patients' needs didn't make it so. Did that go for her parents too?

'What is Jackson's mother like?' asked Hannah.

'She's a bat out of hell. Nothing he does is ever right. She adores peach ice cream, and I remember one time when we went to visit her in Springfield, Jackson bought several quarts of the stuff from this really fancy place in Boston and packed it in dry ice in a cooler. She took a spoonful of it and announced, "This is disgusting, Jackson. The peaches are icy." I wanted to dump the rest of it on her head.'

'So can you see why he's frightened of closeness with people, and why he stayed away from you and the boys?'

'What?'

'We're all operating from scripts written for us when we were infants. Most of the time we have no idea what other people are really like. You, me, Jackson. We have to treat each other with kindness because we're all laboring under similar disabilities.'

Caroline studied Hannah in her shirt sleeves, pen poised over her appointment book. She was admitting to disabilities. Caroline didn't want to know about them. How come her hair looked damp? 'Mr Right and I went to the Converse Inn Saturday night. I saw you there.'

'Oh yes? I didn't see you. It's a nice place, isn't it?'

'Yes. Was that your husband?'

'Arthur. Yes.' She ran the fingers of one hand through her hair, fluffing it up so it would dry faster.

'He looks nice.'

'He is nice.'

'I'm thinking about trying to make this thing with Brian Stone work.'

'Oh yes?'

'Yeah. Life seems simpler with a man. He throws the spears, and I gather the roots and berries.'

Hannah smiled.

'Besides, my friends have started calling me Saint Celibate. I think it's a bit much.'

Hannah knew she shouldn't let Caroline get away with joking her way out of this one. But the hour was over, and Hannah was drained from the hot flash. Next week she'd put up more of a struggle. 'Whatever you want, Caroline.' She waved her pen hand, wondering if she actually felt as noncommittal as she sounded. Caroline would probably have an easier row to hoe if she could be respectable. But Brian Stone was Daddy and Jackson all over again. Picking him as a partner was like picking Zsa Zsa Gabor as your marriage counselor.

Twisting the claw off her boiled lobster, Hannah looked out the restaurant window to the ocean, which swelled and surged around weathered wooden posts the size of elephant legs.

'The only place I like better than Lake Glass,' she told Arthur, 'is right here.'

'Oh? Why the obsession with water, I wonder?' They both wore plastic bibs with drawings of red lobsters on them.

'Probably that's what growing up in the Outback does to you. Like the Arabs' fascination with flowing fountains.'

'I remember when you arrived in Georgetown from London,' said Arthur, probing a claw with a silver nut pick. 'You acted as though you'd never seen the sun. Every time it came out you raced into the backyard and just lay there. I started thinking I'd married a lizard.'

Hannah smiled.

As she dipped a chunk of lobster in melted lemon butter, it hit her: Wasn't that what her clients did? Overcompensated for whatever they lacked as children? Pursued partners of the same sex as whichever parent had been least available? She began running through client histories in her head. Fathers were hardly ever available. Maybe that was why so many women were heterosexual, and so many men closet homosexuals.

'A penny for your thought,' said Arthur as he split open his lobster tail.

'I don't have this one together yet.' She was chewing on a tiny lobster leg, knowing it was okay to continue this train of thought in silence. After all these years, words between them had become unimportant. Each could gauge the other's mood by the faintest twitch. And when one spoke, it was often the words the other was thinking.

Every few years the hundreds of hours of information from clients would rearrange itself into a pattern she'd never seen before, like the shifting of a kaleidoscope. Lifeless textbook theories with which she nodded in intellectual agreement in graduate school would suddenly take on vivid new life, clothed with her clients' experiences. This could happen at any time – during therapy, but more often while grocery shopping, or while dipping lobster in melted butter by the Maine coast. It felt like what she once observed on Lake Glass: During a spring thaw the ice broke up all at once with a thunderous crack, chunks sailing high into the sky.

As she broke off the lobster's tail with both hands, she examined her new idea from different angles, like a prospector inspecting ore to determine whether it was fool's gold or the real thing. She nodded to herself. Arthur glanced at her and smiled, eating coleslaw from a small paper cup with his fork. Whatever she proclaimed over the years, she'd been prejudiced against homosexuals. She'd accepted homosexuality as a valid response to certain factors in childhood. But she'd privately regarded her monogamous marriage to a man as more 'normal.' But Caroline, say, was no more 'abnormal' than any heterosexual client, or than Hannah herself. She was bright, kind, competent, attractive, and funny. Try as you might, you couldn't dismiss her as a sad sack or weirdo.

Carefully wiping her fingers with a towelette and removing her plastic bib, Hannah remembered wanting to touch Maggie's face with her fingertips during therapy, wanting to bury her own face between Maggie's breasts and feel Maggie's hands on her flesh. And now all these healthy young lesbians sat in her office describing their sex lives in graphic detail, and wanting her sexually as a stand-in for Mummy, whether they were aware of it or not. She'd have to be disembodied not to feel drawn physically to some. Especially toward the end when they were feeling better, and crediting that to her. Probably a sculptor felt toward a completed statue as she did toward a terminating client, proud as hell to observe the serene form that had emerged from a cold gray block of misery. But she'd never acted on these attractions. Caroline had had boyfriends and husbands, yet still sought out women. What was the difference between them?

One difference was that Hannah was an only child whose mother adored her. She knew this from her mother's letters to her grandmother. Her grandmother had also doted, in her own remote way. But her father had deserted her for Trinidad, and her grandfather had spent all his time in the City, so that she could scarcely recall what he'd looked like. Hence her longing for a man. Which had set in very early indeed, in that gardener's shed in Sussex with Colin.

As she and Arthur, encased in sweaters and parkas, walked along a cliff path above crashing waves, icy spray stinging their faces, she thought about Colin with his pale blue eyes and pasty complexion. When she became pregnant from their sessions on the stone floor, he dutifully married her and took her back to Bow, to the horror of everyone she knew. He went to work on the docks, and she decorated their small shabby Victorian row house in a street off Roman Road. Hannah had only ever seen the East End riding through it on the bus loops she took as a girl. Actually living there after Hampstead and Sussex was like living in a foreign country. In Hampstead greengrocer shops were papayas and mangoes, salsify and kohlrabi, delicacies from every corner of that empire on which the sun never set. (Lucky, since the sun was never in evidence in England itself.) In Bow were cabbages, Brussels sprouts, potatoes, and apples. In Hampstead bakeries were cream cakes and scones, croissants and a dozen types of fresh bread. In Bow were white bread and doughy apple tarts. In Hampstead there were small specialty shops whose owners asked in modulated voices about her grandparents' health. In Bow were raucous street markets where people laughed and shouted, argued and bargained, calling each other duckie, darling, luv, and girlie. In Hampstead were Englishmen. In Bow were the dregs of the empire – Cockneys, and one lone Australian whose hybrid accent they mocked.

She enjoyed it at first, once she recovered from the horror of unwanted pregnancy and forced marriage – and her grandmother's fury at both. She hung the mimi spirit on the kitchen wall, and it seemed more at home in Bow than in Hampstead or Sussex. After

Simon was born, she spent long lazy afternoons nursing him by the coal fire in the sitting room. On warm days she'd put him in his pram in the tiny garden, set off from the neighbors by high fences, while she pulled weeds and coaxed flowers. Or she'd push him in the pram to Victoria Park, where she'd nod pleasantly at the other mothers, trying not to open her mouth so they wouldn't discover she wasn't really one of them. Or she and Simon would stroll to the shops on Roman Road to buy things for Colin's tea, when he came home in his high black Wellingtons, his pale boy's face dirty and exhausted, his would-be furniture-maker's hands chapped and grimy.

But Simon had colic and cried a lot, and Colin soon began going to the Duke of Chichester pub at the end of the street in the evenings. Hannah began to nag him, since she longed for someone to talk to after spending all day with a tiny baby. Colin began to long for a woman who didn't nag. He found such a woman, or several, and was gone even more. So that Hannah was lonelier and nagged more. The standard scenario on both sides of the Atlantic, which Hannah had heard from so many clients since. Though at the time, rejected by Colin, isolated from her neighbors, and spurned by her Hampstead and Sussex friends, her misery seemed unique.

Hannah sought comfort from Simon, who picked up her anxiety and howled more loudly. So that eventually Colin was scarcely home at all. And when he was, it was to throw a brick at the screaming Simon, which missed by inches the soft spot on his head where his pulse beat. Another night as she begged him to stay home, Colin grabbed the walnut table clock he'd made for her in Sussex, threw it to the floor, and chopped it to bits with an ax. Later that night Hannah awoke to find the bed covers being pulled off her by Colin, who was urging his drinking mate to go ahead and 'screw the posh bitch.'

Blessedly, the war broke out, ending many such domestic dramas all across Europe. Colin was among the first to sign on to fight the Nazis, and among the first to decay in a shallow grave by the River Meuse. Everyone, even her fierce grandmother, took pity on her, alone with an infant, her man dead in battle. They complimented her on her courage. She spoke to no one of her relief to be rid of him.

She'd earned this peaceful old age, she told herself, slipping her arm through Arthur's and squeezing it. With a little luck and a lot of stamina.

'Are you finished thinking?' asked Arthur, coming to a halt on the narrow rutted cliff path.

She nodded.

'Good.' He turned and kissed her as mewing sea gulls picked through tangled seaweed on the gray rocks below.

Four

Caroline delivered the boys to Jackson's wife at his house in Newton, the neo-Tudor monstrosity with fake half-timbering he'd bought for Caroline all those years ago. It had been a thrill matching upholstery fabrics to carpets, fretting over how many styles of furniture to mix so a room looked eclectic rather than just junky. Jackson had been as thrilled as she to be able to afford all the luxuries he'd done without as a boy growing up in a factory town.

'We love to have Jackie and Jason visit,' Deirdre said from the doorway as Caroline and the boys stood on the herringbone brick sidewalk.

Caroline studied Deirdre's carefully coiffed auburn head and wondered if she'd stuck it in the oven yet. Deirdre would spend the week taking the boys to the Children's Museum, the Museum of Science, puppet shows, movies. Jackson might take them to Durgin Park and an ice hockey game. Otherwise, he'd be at the hospital. The boys, holding their suitcases, looked polite and expectant. Maybe this time their father would be transformed into Gabriel Kotter. By the end of the week they'd be beating each other to pulp in frustration that Jackson was still Jackson.

'I really appreciate your having them, Deirdre,' said Caroline, kissing each boy on top of his head. 'As always.'

Driving down Route 9 toward Boston through the sparse evening traffic, she remembered Jackson's shock when she told him she was leaving. They were cruising Boston Harbor in their sailing yacht.

'But Caroline, I simply don't understand,' he said, pulling down the brim of his dark blue Greek fisherman's cap. 'What is it you want?'

'I don't know.'

'But haven't I always given you everything you want? The house, furniture, clothes, cars, everything.'

'Yes, you have, Jackson.' She sat in a captain's chair sipping a gin and tonic. It was true. The Mercedes, the neo-Tudor house, this yacht. They'd been a kick after all those years of harvesting stunted potatoes with her father.

'Well, what's wrong then?'

'I don't know.' Jackson had brought home the bacon with a vengeance, but she wanted the whole hog.

'Name it and it's yours. Do you want to build a new house? Have another baby? Go to Abaco? Anything, Caroline.'

'But there's nothing else I want.' She was as perplexed as he. How about a deluxe Cuisinart and a complete set of Julia Child cookbooks? No, she was sick to death of all that junk. She'd have sent it to the Cambodians if it would have done any good.

'Then how can what you have not be enough? Is it sex? You seem happy with our sex life.'

'It's not sex.' She bit her tongue. It might be sex. She still liked it fine with Jackson on the rare occasions when it occurred, but it was admittedly more thrilling with David Michael. But possibly because it was illicit and took place in settings like the supply room at Mass General, where she'd begun doing volunteer work two afternoons a week in an attempt to assuage her guilt over the invasion of Cambodia.

'What is it then? Hell, I even let you do those weaving classes and that volunteer stuff. Even though you're sometimes not home when I am. Maybe you should quit. What is it you want?'

'I don't know.' All she had was a vague sense that if she didn't leave, it'd be Oven City. 'I want to do something real.' Something that would still the churning in her guts every time she sat alone at night waiting for Jackson and watching the mayhem on the evening news. Weaving wasn't real, it was fun. Volunteer work wasn't real either. She did the garbage the nurses didn't want to do, but she had skills and training that were going to waste.

'Real! What's more real than two sons who need you? Than a husband who loves you?'

She knew he was right. For a time the movement of his flesh in hers, the memory of past sessions, the anticipation of future ones, had been enough. For a time it had been enough to hold her sons to her breasts and watch their pale tummies swell on her milk like inflatable pillows. For a time matching pot holders to dish towels had been enough. But Jackson was never home now. The babies were little boys, and all she saw of them was the dust their tricycles stirred up as they pedaled away. The wallpaper she'd picked so carefully eight years earlier was now dingy and peeling, but she had no interest in replacing it. It was time to move on. She'd lost her sense of purpose. She needed it back. And David Michael was holding that out to her.

'Maybe I should make an appointment for you with Dr Sauerman. He could prescribe some antidepressants.'

'It's too late, Jackson. I'm already gone.'

'What are talking about, Caroline? You're sitting right here on my fucking boat. Do you have to be so goddam intense all the time? Look, if you think you've got problems, you ought to meet the patients at the hospital I deal with every day of the week. . .' His pager began beeping, and he spun around in his swivel captain's chair to rev the engine for his race to the nearest phone.

As she sat on the pitching deck clutching the arms of her captain's chair and watching Jackson's stern Captain Ahab profile, his set jaw and implacable eyes, Caroline was seized with terror. What was she doing? Was there any way to retract what she'd just said? She'd renounce David Michael, give up the volunteer work, use the loom for kindling. It was her fault this marriage was so dismal. No wonder Jackson never came home. What did she offer him to come home to – a boring, dreary, depressed wimp. She wanted to fall on her knees before his white tennis shoes and crew socks to ask forgiveness, as he savagely spun the steering wheel from side to side dodging the wakes of other boats. If Jackson wasn't in her life, there'd be no one to see her as a boring, dreary, depressed wimp of a housewife and mother. And if she wasn't that, who was she?

Caroline went to a Boston health club Pam had told her about, in the basement of a brick office building somewhere near the Prudential Center. She stashed her clothes in a locker in a dressing room with gray carpeting, showered, and ducked into the empty cedar sauna. Lying on her towel on the top shelf in the dim light, eyes closed, she thought about the day she walked away from that half-timbered house in Newton, loading the boys and several suitcases into David Michael's van, with its scene from Mao's Long March on the rear windows. Jackson stood in the front doorway looking stricken. He had begged her to stay. The pager on his belt was beeping, and he didn't even notice. David Michael put an arm around her shoulders to assist her into the van, eyeing Jackson at the other end of the herringbone brick sidewalk like a rival stag. As they drove away, she kept wondering what she was doing leaving behind a fancy house filled with every object a person could want, and many no one could possibly want. It's not enough, she reminded herself, not knowing what she meant. What she was going to was far less from the point of view of creature comfort. David Michael lived in a squalid commune in a huge white frame house in Somerville with a dozen other people whose idea of a good meal was sautéed bamboo shoots.

When she first encountered David Michael, he was liberating drugs for the People's Free Clinic from the Mass General supply room, disguised as staff in light green scrub clothes, his ponytail tucked under an operating cap, his Fu Manchu mustache damp with nervous perspiration. He grabbed her shoulders and described his clinic with urgency, to dissuade her from reporting him, using phrases like 'the alienation of the people from the health care delivery system.' He talked about the lack of human empathy on the part of the medical establishment, about its members' commitment to a hierarchy that ensured their advantages. Everything he said was an indictment of Jackson. Caroline stood there paralyzed by his hands on her shoulders and his fierce dark eyes gazing into hers. By the end of his presentation she'd agreed to help him.

Week after week David Michael appeared in his green scrub clothes on her volunteer afternoons. She'd let him into the supply room as he glanced nervously up and down the corridor, his mustache damp and quivering. She'd guard the door while he filled his gym bag. Afterwards they'd sometimes sit and chat in the front seat of his forest-green van in the parking lot. She learned he was from a wealthy family in Marblehead and had gone to St Paul's, Harvard, and Harvard Medical School. Now he repudiated his class privilege, which he felt had been seized by a robber baron great-grandfather in the New England textile industry at the expense of thousands of workers. By providing free medical care in the slums of Somerville, David Michael was trying to right a century of family wrongs. He was modeling himself on the barefoot doctors of Mao's revolution.

His family thought he was nuts. Caroline thought he was wonderful. As she listened to him, so intent and dedicated, something stirred deep within her, her capacity for idealism which had been lying dormant during all the years of blind acquisition in Jackson's neo-Tudor palace.

One afternoon David Michael drove her in the van to the People's Free Clinic, in a storefront office on a shopping street in Somerville. The walls were covered with silk-screened posters about Cambodia, South Africa, Zimbabwe, and Chile. Starving children with dull eyes and bloated bellies gazed down from photographs. The row of folding chairs was filled with winos, bag ladies, welfare mothers holding infants. Caroline felt she'd come home. 'It's fantastic,' she said as David Michael showed her the examining rooms. He introduced her to a nurse named Clea, whose long golden hair hung down her back like a satin cape.

Clea said, 'David Michael's told us about you. Are you thinking of joining us? We could use your help.'

Caroline glanced at David Michael, unaware until then that he had plans for her. She wasn't averse to them. She felt an undeniable attraction to people who referred to themselves as 'we.'

Afterwards David Michael took her to his corner room at the rear of the second story of the commune, which they entered through a window after climbing a fire escape. They smoked a joint in the dark cluttered cubicle, then made love on the unmade bed, a mattress on the floor. David Michael took his time – long slow strokes that left her gasping. With each stroke he almost pulled out before starting back in, until she was clutching at his hips to keep him in. He grinned down at her.

Later, as the late afternoon sunlight filtered through the American flags that covered the windows, as their sweat dried and chilled them, Caroline reflected that this might shoot her marriage all to hell. And she was glad.

The next time David Michael came to Mass General, he fitted a chair under the door handle so it wouldn't open. After filling his bag with supplies, he backed her into a corner, removed her underpants, and thrust into her standing up. She was so faint with lust that she couldn't continue standing, so he collapsed into the chair with her straddling him and moving up and down.

After she moved into a room at the commune, with Jackie and Jason in the room next door, David Michael not only supported her wish to reclaim purpose, he insisted on it. Her first night there, as they lay in each other's arms on the mattress on the floor of his room, with the American flags at the windows stirring in the draft, he explained that their relationship, their meals and living quarters, were important only to give them strength to work on behalf of all the people. A certain number of orgasms each week were essential to free them from bodily preoccupations. A certain number of joints and Quaaludes were essential to maintain the peace of mind that enabled them to be effective healers. Caroline was enchanted. She was no longer a boring dreary depressed wimp. Like Clea, she was a skilled healer, a servant of humanity, a Clara Barton who'd found her Civil War . . .

Caroline sat up and dumped a dipper of water on the hot rocks in the corner of the cedar sauna. The water hissed and rose as a cloud of steam. She lay down, inhaling the hot vapor, and recalled how she'd loved working at the People's Free Clinic at first. Her sense of purposelessness faded in the confusion of trying to scrounge rent and supplies for the clinic, rent and food for the commune. When she wasn't at the clinic, she was weaving in her room, or trying to market what she'd woven. Or cooking and cleaning. Or making supply runs to hospitals, food runs to supermarket rubbish bins. Or meeting with welfare workers about various patients. Or making love with David Michael and listening to his plans for a chain of free clinics all across Boston, and then across the nation. Jackie and Jason were tended by whoever was around. Sometimes they went to a community day care center. Her life became one long meeting – house meetings; staff meetings; day care meetings; meetings to organize marches against the Vietnam war, rent strikes against landlords; meetings to discuss alternatives to the nuclear family, alternatives to the health care delivery system, alternatives to capitalism, alternatives to monogamy, alternatives to alternatives. She, Clea, David Michael, and the others were one big happy family. Once again she'd filled the void.

Unfortunately, David Michael's regime for freeing himself from bodily preoccupations eventually involved orgasms with other women. Caroline went numb and silent at night watching him climb the stairs to his room with Clea behind him. Whom anyone slept with was unimportant in the face of the sub-Saharan drought, he maintained. And since Caroline couldn't deny this, she tried to accept it. She and Clea began meeting with Sandra, another woman in the commune, who agreed to facilitate as they processed their hostility. Caroline accused Clea of stealing her man. Clea accused Caroline of bourgeois possessiveness. Caroline accused Clea of intellectual elitism. Once they'd run out of accusations, they sat in strained silence as Caroline began to comprehend why David Michael had wanted to bed Clea. She started having torrid dreams about naked female bodies with long golden hair and large soft breasts. When she was making love with David Michael, she sometimes fantasized that he had breasts, and that his penis was Clea's hand.

One afternoon after several silent meetings, Clea said, 'Look, Caroline, do you really care about that narcissistic bastard?' Caroline smiled with relief, and they went upstairs to Caroline's room hand in hand, Sandra nodding approval from the auto seat in the living room. . . .

Caroline climbed into the tile whirlpool, lowered herself into the scalding water, and propped her feet on the seat opposite. As bubbling water swirled over her chest, she closed her eyes and thought about how it had felt to hold Clea's breasts in her hands, soft, heavy and smooth like bread dough. . . .

When she opened her eyes, a woman with a cap of light brown hair was stepping into the whirlpool. She looked like Caroline's dream counselor from the Quaker work camp in New York State she attended as a girl, at which they helped some Algonquin Indians build a recreation hall. Joyce taught woodcraft. Everyone called her Jo Jo. Long, lean, wholesome and friendly, she wore blindingly white long-sleeved shirts, sleeves turned up twice to display the dark tan and bleached hairs on her forearms. Caroline had tied knots and lashed tripods in a frenzy of concentration, trying to win Jo Jo's approval.

Caroline and the woman smiled and nodded as the woman sat down. She had had an excellent orthodontist, and her eyes were liquid brown like Arnold's. Foamy water washed over the woman's high firm breasts, stiffening the brown nipples. Caroline felt a sharp stab of desire. People came and went, but she could always count on her lust. It had been the only reliable element in her life. She'd endure any amount of abuse as long as the sexual connection with someone was intact. But when that went, so did she. She recalled the evening she told David Michael she was leaving for Diana's cabin in New Hampshire. He exhaled smoke from a joint with a hiss. They were lying on his mattress in the light from a streetlamp. The American flags at the windows flapped in the spring breeze as though from flagpoles.

'I knew you wouldn't stick it, baby, without your fancy house and boat and Mercedes,' David Michael said, handing her the joint.

'That's got nothing to do with it.' She held the remaining half inch of joint between thumb and forefinger, trying to draw on it without searing her fingers.

'Sure it doesn't.'

'But it doesn't.'

'So what does?' She passed the soggy bit of smoldering paper back to him.

'I don't know exactly.' His sleeping with Clea had something to do with it. Her sleeping with Clea also had something to do with it. When Clea wasn't insisting that Caroline's and her nights together were a fluke, Caroline was. They were ricocheting off each other and back to David Michael's heterosexual assurances, where they turned on each other with savagery. The big happy family was falling to pieces. Diana had written from New Hampshire that Mike had walked out to follow his star, and she needed a roommate with a shoulder to cry on. So Caroline fell back on an old solution: numb withdrawal, leaving the struggle to Clea and David Michael.

'Don't know, or won't admit?' said David Michael, handing her the eighth of an inch of joint, which he held between two fingernails. It was like playing Hot Potato; you didn't want to be left holding the joint. 'Won't admit that you miss your Newton comforts? That you're just a boring little bourgeois housewife masquerading as a revolutionary?'

'Whatever you like, David Michael.' It was probably true. She'd ceased to believe in David Michael's revolution. Among her many meetings were some with the nurses at the clinic. If nothing else, they finally figured out that the wounds they spent their days binding – from rapes, knife fights, batterings, and muggings –

were almost entirely inflicted by men. Capitalism wasn't the problem. Racism wasn't. Nationalism wasn't. Men were. Caroline was beginning to want as little as possible to do with them, and with this man lying next to her in particular. She squashed what remained of the joint in the Lincoln Continental hubcap David Michael had stolen from the limousine of some Pentagon official during the March on Washington.

'Damn it, don't waste that shit! Not everybody can affort to run around putting out half-smoked joints.'

'Meaning I can?' she asked. 'The damn thing was nearly non-existent.'

'It requires sacrifice to build a better world. And that's something you know nothing about, sweetheart. Me, I've sacrificed a lucrative practice in the suburbs.'

'That's no sacrifice.' She looked at his body – pale, bony, and hairy in the shifting light, his penis sluglike. In stark contrast to Clea's firm mounds and smooth curves. She could scarcely recall what about him had inspired her to leave Jackson.

'Okay, so you tell me about sacrifice, Caroline. You with your yacht and your Mercedes.'

'I'm not talking about yachts. I don't give a shit about yachts. I don't think building a better world has anything to do with yachts.' What it did have to do with she no longer knew. Not bandaging torn anuses in some storefront slum while your lover balled your friends in the back room.

'Suit yourself.' He got up and shrugged on his light green scrub clothes. 'I've got more pussy than I can handle right now anyway.'

As she watched him walk out, she longed to open wide her arms and call him back. If she wasn't Maid Marion to David Michael's Robin Hood, who was she? A boring little bourgeois housewife, he said, but she'd already been that, and you couldn't retrace an overgrown path. . . .

Caroline opened her eyes to discover the other woman's eyes on her breasts. She looked back for a moment, then concentrated on the water jet pulsing into the small of her back. Why had her lovers always withdrawn? She hadn't given them what they needed so they looked elsewhere? But she'd always tried so hard. What was it they wanted? Diana said she was a taker. Jackson said she was too intense. David Michael said she was a boring bourgeois housewife.

The image of Hannah floated into her head, smiling at her, liking her, telling her she was kind, gentle, and generous. That how other people saw her was their problem, a projection of their own hopes and fears. She sighed and felt the tightness in her shoulders give up its grip.

Then she inspected what she'd done – used Hannah to feel better. She'd become utterly dependent on her. Yet Hannah might die, move away, get fed up with Caroline's neediness. The tightness returned to her shoulders and began to spread down her back.

She climbed out of the whirlpool and went into the steam room, which was like a giant shower stall. Lying on a wooden bench, she breathed deeply, feeling the scalding air move through her nose and down toward her lungs. A long lean female silhouette stood outside the clouded glass door. The door opened, steam rushed out, and the woman from the whirlpool came in. She lay at the opposite end of Caroline's bench. Their feet bumped. Each murmured, 'Sorry.'

Closing her eyes, Caroline pictured the woman coming over to kneel beside her, caress her breasts, and lick her nipples. She jumped up, went out, and took an ice-cold shower until she was thoroughly numb. Then she returned to the top shelf of the sauna.

The woman came in and stretched out on the bottom shelf. Caroline glanced down at the long well-shaped legs, and the triangle of fair pubic hair where the legs joined. The woman opened her eyes and met Caroline's. Caroline looked quickly at the joints between the cedar paneling on the far wall, and tried to figure out if the woman was following her on purpose. Surely someone so wholesome looking wouldn't be on the make.

They dried their hair side by side in front of the brightly lit mirrors. Arranging her hair with her Afro pick, Caroline glanced out of the corner of her eye at the woman in her beige bra and panties. Caroline wanted to run her hand down the curve of the woman's side and up the ridge in the middle of her back. That was all. Nothing fancy.

They dressed in tandem on the gray carpet, studiously pulling on shirts, Levi's, and boots. The woman zipped her down parka as she walked for the door. Hand on the handle, she turned. 'Look, forgive me if I've got this wrong. It's not something I ever do. But would you like to come to my apartment?'

Caroline's heart pounded and her palms broke out with sweat. 'Uh, how far?' As though that were the issue.

'A few blocks.'

'Sure. Okay.'

As they walked down Boylston Street in silence, past darkened stores and noisy restaurants, Caroline wondered if she ought to apologize for having made a mistake. But David Michael did this all the time. A lot of men did. Women too, for all she knew. Just because she always signed over her soul to anyone she was sexual with was no reason to assume it had to be that way. But what would Diana say? Fuck it, if Diana didn't want her, other women did. Besides, who said she had to tell her? They weren't having that kind of relationship anymore.

What about Brian? Jesus Christ, what *about* Brian? She'd dated him a few times and was already worrying about taking care of him. She hadn't even been to bed with him. Let him worry about himself. She'd warned him to find a woman who wasn't a pervert. He simply wasn't her responsibility, however lonely and bewildered he might be.

What about Hannah? Her step faltered. What if Hannah found this behavior sordid and kicked her out? Hannah had a marriage of four decades or something. But who said she was monogamous? But surely she was, she seemed so respectable. But the camp counselor walking beside her with her hands in her parka pockets looked respectable too. What did Hannah have to do with this anyway? If she minded Caroline's going to bed with someone, let her go to bed with Caroline herself. There had to be some way to get that damn woman out of her head.

The apartment was one large fourth-floor room with a kitchen in one corner, a dining table and bentwood chairs in another, and a bed piled with cushions in a third. The floor was polished oak covered with area rugs. Plants hung in elaborately framed windows that stretched along two walls from floor to ceiling.

'What a comfortable room,' said Caroline, taking off her Frye boots on the doormat.

'Thanks. It's ideal for me. Big enough to spread out in, but small enough so I don't have a lot of cleaning. Want some coffee or brandy or something?'

They sat cross-legged among the cushions sipping brandy from snifters as cars passed on the wet pavement below with a hissing sound. Caroline was reluctant to talk. They both knew why they were there, and getting acquainted wasn't the reason. But manners were manners.

'Do you go to that place often?' asked Caroline.

'Yes. A lot. Do you?'

'That was my first time. It's really nice.'

'Yes, it is.' She put her brandy snifter on the floor. Caroline did the same. Looking at each other, they slowly tossed all the cushions off the bed. After undressing, they climbed under the homespun bedspread. Caroline rubbed the spread between thumb and forefinger, automatically inspecting the weave.

'Well, what do you like?' Caroline asked briskly, not knowing how to do this.

'A lot of everything,' the woman replied with her wholesome smile, stretching her long lean body alongside Caroline's. It already felt familiar to Caroline's hands as she touched it tentatively, having inspected it visually from every angle.

Caroline felt a moment of panic. It would probably be better to leave now and spend the rest of her life fantasizing what it might have been like, than to forge ahead and have the reality be awkward and uninspired. It had been so many years since she'd touched anyone except Diana. She didn't know what to do.

The woman smiled her camp counselor smile, then gave Caroline a decidedly unwholesome kiss. It occurred to Caroline she could probably figure this out. With each previous lover, lovemaking had been a microcosm of the entire relationship. All the stresses and expectations out of bed had found their way into bed in stylized form, like a Balinese dance. How someone made love was a template of his or her personality. The ever efficient Jackson was in and out as quickly as possible. David Michael teased, taunted, withdrew, and withheld. Diana gave pleasure unstintingly, but sometimes received it with reluctance. But she and this woman next to her, who was kissing her with proficiency, had no past together, and no shared future. There was only the present moment, and two healthy female animals, who had begun to explore each other with mouths and hands, like lost prospectors finding a water hole in the desert.

There were silver stretch marks around the woman's nipples, Caroline noticed as she sucked and nibbled them. She had a child, or several. But the apartment was one room, and there were no toys. The child was grown, gone, dead? Caroline realized she didn't want to know. Didn't want to baby-sit for her, fight child custody battles with her, only wanted to give and take physical pleasure, for that moment alone.

Eventually they lay with their mouths, tongues, and breasts rubbing together and their hands moving inside each other. Like a blind person reading braille, Caroline felt with her fingertips as the texture of the woman's vaginal walls shifted from velvet to corduroy. Increasing her movements, she felt the woman's vagina grip her fingers convulsively. And her own career as Saint Celibate terminated abruptly in slow shuddering heaves that obeyed the rhythm of the woman's hand.

Later Caroline lay holding the woman and watching headlights from the street sweep across the room. So that was how women settled the issue of who came first – simultaneous orgasm? Diana would be pleased to know. She thought with satisfaction of how annoyed Diana would in fact be. But probably she wouldn't tell her. Caroline needed a few secrets to sustain her in their struggle.

'If camp had been like this,' Caroline murmured, 'I'd have gone every summer.'

'Excuse me?' The woman propped herself up on one elbow and looked down at Caroline questioningly.

'Do you have any idea how wholesome you look?'

'So I'm told,' she replied with a white-toothed smile.

Caroline put her hands under her head and savored the fact that she didn't know or care who'd told the woman that. They didn't have to meet each other's mothers or learn how much sugar to put in each other's coffee. They'd never lay eyes on each other again. But she realized if she stayed much longer, she'd be waking up next to this woman in the morning, which wasn't part of the deal. 'I'm afraid I have to go.'

The woman looked relieved. 'You don't need to rush off.'

'Someone's expecting me,' Caroline lied. 'How would you feel about our not exchanging phone numbers?'

The woman smiled. 'Fine. I have certain . . . complications in my life.'

'Don't we all?'

'You're a marvelous lover. Thank you.'

'Thank *you*. It's been great. Take care.'

Caroline walked along the nearly deserted street to her Subaru feeling fantastic. She'd never known you could go to bed with people without assuming their debts, writing them into your will, adopting their children, folding their laundry, rubbing ointment into their hemorrhoids. She'd had no idea irresponsibility could feel so good. She began whistling, 'Will You Still Love Me Tomorrow?'

Caroline sat down and studied her new view of the parking lot. There was a photo on the wall next to the window that she'd never noticed from where she used to sit. Black and white, abstract. She couldn't tell what it was.

'So what's new with you?' asked Hannah as she looked up from her appointment book, thinking surely something was, because Caroline had perked up since their last session like a potato plant after you plucked off Colorado potato beetles.

'Nothing much.'

Hannah sat back and lit a cigarette. 'You look really nice today.' Caroline wore cords and a flannel shirt, had had her Afro trimmed. The bruised circles under her eyes were less noticeable than usual.

'Thanks. So do you.' There was color to Hannah's cheeks, and she looked rested.

'I was in Maine over the weekend. Eating lobsters, reading, sleeping late, breathing sea air. Wonderful.' It was also wonderful to return and find clients had done fine in your absence.

Caroline studied her. It seemed odd she had this full life Caroline knew almost nothing about. Obscurely threatening. If Caroline had no hold over her, she could come and go as she pleased, even if Caroline happened to need her. She wished she could put her in a freezer, thawing her only as necessary. Then she realized she could, and did, summon Hannah's image in her head whenever she liked. Hannah's physical whereabouts was irrelevant. Unlike Pink Blanky, no one could take that image of Hannah away, not even Hannah herself.

With a faint pleased smile Caroline said, 'I went to Boston to leave the boys with their father.' They'd phoned last night, excited because Jackson had tickets to a Celtics game. Jackson got on the phone, sounding as usual like Sergeant Friday on 'Dragnet.' Neither he nor Deirdre could drive the boys home on Sunday. Deirdre was going to put them on the bus at Park Square, and

Caroline could meet them at her end. They didn't have to change. They'd be fine.

Caroline struggled with maternal terror: the bus would wreck; molesters would abuse them en route; they'd get off at a rest stop and get back on the wrong bus; Jackson was a terrible father, and got worse each year. She listened to these thoughts. From her sessions with Hannah she understood she was railing at Jackson in her head for all those years in which she felt neglected by him, which in itself had something or other to do with her own absent father. The boys would be okay. 'All right,' she said.

'What?' said Jackson, left holding the weapons he'd assembled for her attack.

'I said all right. Fine.' She didn't want to stand in for his perpetually critical mother anymore.

'Did you stay in Boston?' asked Hannah.

Caroline paused, summoning courage. 'Only long enough to get laid.' She felt like a cat placing a dead mouse at its owner's feet. Would Hannah praise her or kick her? Panic tightened her throat. Why had she told her this? Hannah would be bound to be disgusted. She had her wretched marriage.

'By whom?'

Caroline's palms began sweating. Her scalp stung under her Afro. 'By a woman I picked up at a sauna,' she said in a low voice, examining the tread on her snowmobile boot.

'Was it fun?'

Caroline looked up. Hannah was smiling wryly, evidently not appalled. How was this possible?

'Yes.'

Hannah shrugged. 'How nice.'

Caroline sat silent.

'What shall we talk about today?' asked Hannah, looking out the window to the frozen lake and thinking what a pleasure it was not to have to see that orange Le Car anymore.

Caroline's face flushed. If Hannah could pass this off so casually, surely she didn't get the picture. 'The nicest part was that I just walked away afterwards. I don't even know her name.'

'Which isn't how you usually operate?'

Caroline was startled that Hannah realized there were other ways to operate than monogamous marriage. 'How I've always operated is to buy my lovers presents, water their plants, walk their dogs, put coins in parking meters for their cars.'

'To keep them around?'

Caroline paused. Was this why she'd done it? Not just that she was a nice guy? It hadn't occurred to her to do anything else. 'Yes, to keep them around.'

'You felt you had to do nice things to make them love you?'

'Uh, I guess so.' She glanced around for the Kleenex. Where had that damn chest been moved to? Pain was rising to her throat like a creek overflowing its banks. The chest was right beside her. She rested her hand on its familiar polished wood surface.

'Do you see where that comes from?' asked Hannah, watching Caroline.

Caroline closed her eyes and nodded. She grabbed a tissue as a tear rolled down her cheek. 'Damn it,' she muttered through gritted teeth, blotting the tears, her throat aching from holding them back.

'It's all right. Cry if you want to.' As Caroline blew her nose, Hannah thought about the different ways clients did this. Some used the same tissue time after time. Others took a new one for each bout. Some wouldn't stop once they started, using tears to avoid the issues. Some collapsed on the couch and sobbed; others reached out for her. Almost as revealing as a Rorschach test. Some, like Caroline, ground their teeth and struggled against each tear as though it were a drop of corrosive acid.

'What did you learn with the woman in Boston?' asked Hannah.

Caroline looked up, her eyes red and puffy. 'Huh?' She expected some sympathy in return for her tears, but Hannah was just sitting there with her irritating expression of patience.

'I think you can judge whether an experience is worth the effort by what it teaches you.' She glanced out the window to the lake, perfectly still in its straitjacket of ice.

Caroline tried to decide if she'd learned anything. Mostly it had just felt wonderful after so many months to be touched by another human creature. 'I guess I learned I don't necessarily want to keep someone around. And I also learned I don't have to do the laundry for them to want me. This woman said I was a marvelous lover.' She flung down the last sentence like a gauntlet.

Hannah smiled as she lit another cigarette. She enjoyed it when they began feeling their wild adolescent oats, which they hadn't sown when they should have because they were so busy trying to be 'good.' Caroline was looking at her, waiting for her response. Having no idea what that would be, Hannah exhaled smoke, opened her mouth, and heard herself say, 'Well, I wouldn't have any way of verifying that, would I?'

Caroline looked at her speculatively. You could have, she thought. Hannah had a nice husband. But she'd admitted to bisexual feelings. Maybe she was monogamous by default. Maybe no one else had asked her lately. . .

Oh God, though Hannah. Any minute now Caroline was going to come on to her. She had her eyes fixed on Hannah's. Hannah liked them to feel good, but not this good. She'd better head her off before the pass. 'Does anybody in your family have blue eyes?'

Caroline looked startled. 'Uh, I don't know. Yes, I guess my mother does.'

Hannah nodded. 'You notice how you always stare at mine?'

'What?'

'How did your parents react when you started dating?'

Caroline frowned, then began talking in a bewildered voice. 'They watched out their bedroom window when someone brought me home. If we kissed at the door, they'd be waiting at the top of the stairs with a lecture about career options in human services. If we sat too long in the car, they'd flash the porch lights. When I was in nursing school, they dropped by my dorm at all hours. They always ridiculed my boyfriends, except for a couple who were polite and boring. . .'

'And sexless?' asked Hannah, raising her eyebrows.

'What?'

'Do you see what's going on in here?'

Caroline blinked.

'For most of your life you've damped down all these facets to your personality in an attempt to be acceptable. They've been emerging lately, and I'm here to tell you that they're absolutely fine. *You* are fine, exactly as you are – sometimes sad and hurt and wanting to be taken care of, sometimes funny and charming, sometimes sexy, sometimes aggressive, sometimes angry. They're all you, and they're all fine. Just because they weren't fine to important people early in your life doesn't mean there's anything wrong with you.' Her voice was fierce, reflecting the anger she was feeling at the bullies who ran around telling tiny children how to win approval. Many clients at their first session had virtually no personality. Bland robots, identical, antennae extended only to pick up and obey the wishes of others. Until the suppressed emotions made them ill or exploded all over other people.

She thought about the flower border along the base of her house, the dozens of varieties, each with its own scent, color, and configuration. Together, they formed a scene so dazzling one could only be struck with wonder at a world in which such variety and intricacy were not only possible, but evident everywhere you looked. She was certain human beings possessed at least as much potential.

When Nigel was three, she planted the side field above the lake with bulbs – daffodils and yellow tulips. She and Nigel lay in the spring sun amidst the flowers, sniffing, touching, and discussing them. Later that spring Nigel came stumbling up to her, wailing. He clutched a purple hyacinth in one tiny fist. Between outraged sobs he explained, 'Mommy, flowers are yellow. Bad flower!' He flung it to the ground and stamped on it. . .

'Are you monogamous?' asked Caroline with a defiant tilt to her chin.

Hannah started, almost dropping her cigarette. 'What? Oh. Yes.' Did this really have to be part of her job?

Caroline felt her shoulders tighten. So, whatever she said, Hannah actually felt critical of Caroline's promiscuity.

Hannah watched Caroline's sullen stare. Apparently she was determined to feel punished. How many times had she been assigned this role of avenging mother, by her own children and by hundreds of clients? Caroline could have gotten it on with the Queen Mother and the Royal Horseguards for all Hannah cared. 'It's not out of great moral conviction. It's just simpler. And I'm at a time in my life when I value simplicity. I've got a lot of other things to think about. Besides, I get to hear about the exotic escapades of my clients.' She smiled whimsically.

'So you're a voyeur?'

'Very probably.' She laughed. If she didn't engage with the obnoxiousness, sometimes it just fell away, like a discarded stage on a launched rocket. 'You know, I can't keep up with you, Caroline. Last I heard, you were in hot pursuit of a man.'

Caroline frowned. 'Who says I'm not now?' Brian phoned last

night after the boys. She had a date with him Saturday night. The boys would still be in Boston. She'd been making going to bed with him a life and death matter. Why not just do it for fun, as she had with the woman in Boston? It didn't mean they had to spend the rest of their lives together.

'Okay,' said Hannah, gesturing like a flagger trying to slow down highway traffic. 'Just checking.' According to her theory formulated over the lobster in Maine, Caroline should want both men and women, since it sounded as though she hadn't had much contact with either parent, with Daddy off to war and Mummy in despair, and then with them both out saving the world.

'This thing in Boston was just a fling. It's got nothing to do with anything.'

'Yes, but why did you pick a woman to fling with?' asked Hannah.

'Why not?' asked Caroline, jutting out her jaw.

Hannah smiled. 'Indeed. I'm not making value judgments, Caroline. I'm just curious.' Now that she had her lake view, she wondered if she could get away with installing a recliner in place of her desk chair. Would it undercut her authority if she issued observations from a supine position with closed eyes?

'I prefer female bodies aesthetically,' Caroline was surprised to hear herself say. She realized it was true, thinking with distaste of all the hair and hard muscles on Jackson and David Michael, and those ridiculous prongs they were so proud of, that jabbed at you like cattle prods. In contrast to the smooth soft curves and mounds, the warm moist cavities of that head counselor's body Friday night.

'Who doesn't? Why do you think so much pornography and fine art feature women's bodies?'

Caroline looked at Hannah. 'If you really feel that, why are you with a man?'

'Because I love Arthur.'

Caroline blinked, then blushed, then studied her snowmobile boot. 'I see.'

'Choices.'

'Why choose?' asked Caroline. 'Why not have it all?'

Hannah shook her head. 'You must have more time and energy than I do, is all I can say, Caroline.'

Caroline was awakened from a deep sleep by her ringing phone. Flinging out an arm to her bedside table, she found the receiver. 'Hello?'

A male voice said, 'Hello there, darling. I hear you like stiff cock shoved deep into your wet pussy.'

'Wrong.'

After a bemused silence, the man hung up.

'Who was that?' asked Diana, wrapping her arm around Caroline and molding her breast with her hand.

'Some guy who'd heard I like stiff cock.'

'Jesus.' She laughed the husky laugh that had made Caroline fall in love with her over the bed bath in nursing school. 'You said "wrong"?'

'From a deep sleep. Without a moment's hesitation.'

'God, you're such a dyke.' She nibbled Caroline's shoulder.

'I guess I am.' Caroline was remembering the early months in this cabin, after her arrival from Somerville, as she and Diana tried to convince themselves with locker room language that they both wanted a stiff cock. The unacknowledged sexual tension between them could have blown all the fuses in the cabin. For Caroline, exposing vulnerable parts of her anatomy to a member of the male species, who she'd recently realized performed the violent deeds she spent her career mopping up after, seemed about as appealing as suckling a rattlesnake. She and Diana, fed up with men, were spending a lot of time working at the abortion referral center downtown, sick to death of seeing women bear the brunt of male lust and violence. Pam, Jenny, and several of the other workers were lesbians. Caroline and Diana eyed them uneasily when they sat too close at meetings. 'I'm not that kind of girl,' Caroline once said to Pam, who'd hugged her affectionately.

'Tell me about it,' said Pam, amused.

Once she and Diana went to lunch at Maude's with Pam and Jenny. Pam ordered peach cobbler for dessert. When it arrived, Pam picked up the dish and plunged her face into the whipped cream on top. Then she turned to Jenny, who slowly licked off all the cream, gazing into Pam's malamute eyes. Diana and Caroline looked uneasily at them, at each other, and at their appalled neighbors.

One night over a bottle of wine on the couch in Diana's living room, Diana said, 'You know, I really resent how Pam and Jenny think every woman they meet is a lesbian.'

Caroline nodded. 'Yeah. I mean, you can be aware of attractions to women without wanting to do anything about it.'

'Exactly.'

Caroline opened another bottle of red wine. 'What do you think about that new abortion bill before the legislature?' she asked Diana, filling their glasses for the sixth time.

'That guy from Nashua who's sponsoring it is a real hunk,' replied Diana. 'You ought to put the make on him.'

Caroline looked into her wine for a long time, swirling it as though preparing to read tea leaves. 'If I were going to put the make on anyone,' said Caroline, 'it'd be you.'

'What?'

'You heard me.' She looked up at Diana, who'd blushed a bright scarlet.

'I guess I did.'

'Oh, to hell with it.' Caroline began unbuttoning her own chamois shirt.

'What are you doing?' asked Diana in a panicked voice.

'You know perfectly well what I'm doing.' Caroline stared into Diana's green eyes belligerently.

'Yes, I do actually.' Diana started to unbutton her own shirt. 'How come we didn't think of this before?'

'I sure have.'

Caroline sighed with contentment under the down comforter and pressed her back and buttocks more closely against Diana's front. Stiff cocks indeed. 'Why would somebody do without sex for a minute, much less for months?'

'Because she's a fool,' said Diana.

Diana had simply appeared in Caroline's bed earlier that evening, a gift of the night. As Caroline began to comment on her presence, Diana placed her hand over Caroline's mouth and said, 'Let's not talk about it. Let's just do it.' Afterwards, discussion seemed irrelevant. Although she hadn't told Diana about the woman from the sauna, it seemed as though Diana had picked up the message that Caroline might slip away without some enticement to stay. Whatever Diana's reason, Caroline liked the results.

In the morning she'd call Brian and cancel their date. It wasn't fair to lead him on when she was clearly a raving lesbian.

They settled in to sleep. Out the window past the loom, Caroline saw the edge of the new moon, hanging over the lake like a luminous fingernail paring. She started thinking about stiff cocks and what a lot of trouble they caused. She'd changed thousands of diapers on Howard and Tommy, Jackie and Jason. Their tiny penises sprayed all over her. Her goal was to get them covered up again as quickly as possible. That Freud and most men assumed women coveted them always intrigued her. Probably it was impossible for an older sister of brothers, or the mother of sons, to take men seriously. It took a real leap of the imagination after that to regard a penis as erotic. Probably that was why she was such a dyke. Yet you'd better take men seriously, or you'd find yourself with a knife at your throat and a cock up your ass. Wars were fought over which cock got shoved where. Nuclear missiles had been launched by men who couldn't get anything up any other way.

David Michael said his mother used to tell him as a little boy that his cock would fall off if he played with it. Caroline remembered meeting this genius of a mother in her gloomy seaside mansion in Marblehead. She looked like a member of the Addams family, and conveyed about as much warmth.

All of a sudden Caroline understood that David Michael had spent his entire adult life shoving his cock into every hole he could find to prove it was still there. *We have to treat each other with kindness because we're all laboring under similar disabilities*. She felt a stab of remorse that she'd cut off David Michael so abruptly, taking a taxi to the Trailways station with Jackie, Jason, and half a dozen suitcases, without even telling him good-bye.

As she dozed off, she dreamed about David Michael in his green scrub clothes and Fu Manchu mustache. He and she were standing in his cluttered room at the Somerville commune, the American flags flapping at the windows. He yelled, 'You women are all the same. All you care about is stiff cock.' She looked at him. Then she scooped a handful of ashes from his Lincoln Continental hubcap and rubbed them all over his mouth and face, his beard scratching her hand like coarse sandpaper. He looked hurt and confused. Caroline felt awful. She dumped ashes in his hand and knelt at his feet, begging him to rub them into her face.

Caroline jerked awake. What the hell did that mean? Suddenly sad and lonely, she kissed Diana awake and buried her face between Diana's large breasts.

The next morning Caroline awoke before Diana, got up, fixed toast and coffee, and brought them back to bed on a tray. Diana, hidden under the comforter with just her scrambled red head protruding, smiled without opening her eyes. 'You beat me to it.'

'Anything to keep you in my bed,' said Caroline, piling up pillows.

'Actually I have to get up in a few minutes.'

Caroline paused to look at her. She'd been anticipating a morning in bed like in the old days, when magazines, books, food and dirty dishes, cats, dogs, and children had gradually filled the room. Amelia the cat already lay purring in a nest in the comforter at the foot of the bed. 'Are you on duty today?'

'No, I'm going shopping with Suzanne.' She avoided looking at Caroline.

Caroline climbed into bed and took the tray on her lap. 'So cancel it.'

Diana sat up and slipped on her nightgown. 'She wants me to help her pick out an outfit for her sister's wedding next week.'

'She's a big girl. I'm sure she can buy her own clothes. Tell her you're busy.'

'Suzanne's been counting on me to help her.'

'Well, I've been counting on you to fuck me,' said Caroline with a grin.

'We did that already,' laughed Diana. 'Quite a lot as I recall.'

'So what was that charming little interlude all about then?'

'What do you mean?' Diana picked up a piece of toast.

'You waft in here in the middle of the night, seduce me, and now you rush off to your child bride. What the hell are you doing?'

Diana looked at her with surprise, toast halfway to her mouth. 'I wanted you. You apparently wanted me. We had each other. And now life continues.'

'I see.' Caroline's heart contracted into its shell like a turtle's head. This was a fling, not a reconciliation and renewal.

Diana drank the last of her coffee and rolled out of bed.

'Have a lovely day,' snarled Caroline.

'Thanks.'

'Leave the lights on tonight. I've got a date with Brian and may be home late.'

'Why a man?' Diana asked as she picked her terry cloth robe off the floor, where she'd flung it last night.

'Why a teenager?' Caroline sipped her coffee.

Diana whirled around and stalked out. Caroline called, 'And please phone next time before turning up in my bed. I may not be alone.'

Diana returned to the doorway and leaned against it, eyeing Caroline. 'The therapy is definitely changing you, but I'm not sure I like the changes.'

'Too bad.' Inside Caroline was terrified. If Diana didn't like the changes, she wouldn't stick around, even in this attenuated form. But no one had stuck around in any case. *You feel you have to do nice things to keep them around?* Maybe so, but it hadn't worked. She'd knocked herself out doing nice things, and where were all the recipients today? The most appealing aspect to Brian was that maybe he'd stick around. He showed every sign of being prepared to devote himself to her. Maybe she could work up a similar case of devotion to him. The boys would have a father; she'd have a husband; she'd be respectable again; together they'd have plenty of money, even with his payments to his wife. The only thing missing was that spark of excitement that had ignited all her other relationships. She'd been Miss Kitty to Jackson's Matt Dillon; Maid Marion to David Michael's Robin Hood; Cherry Ames, Rural Nurse, alongside Diana. But Brian didn't inspire her. But maybe that was a function of encroaching middle age. Maybe she could no longer fool herself that any mortal could live up to the lyrics of those popular songs on the car radio behind the Stop 'n Shop: 'You are my special angel, sent from up above . . .' But maybe she and Brian could share a mature love, like Hannah and her husband. If the sexual connection worked, maybe everything else would – like boxcars hooking up to an engine.

She leaped out of bed and rushed to the store, where she bought ingredients for a dinner. Roast lamb, scalloped potatoes, spinach salad, apricot soufflé, a good wine. She cooked and cleaned all day, then dressed carefully in her least dykey outfit, a silk shirt and tweed skirt. She splashed herself with Chanel No. 5, rather than the usual Eau Sauvage Diana loved. She stole some makeup from Sharon's room and tried to recall how to apply it.

When Brian appeared at her door, flushed from the cold, she announced, 'I've cooked supper. I thought maybe we could stay home tonight.'

'Fantastic,' he said, eyeing her speculatively. 'It smells wonderful. Or is that you?'

He'd had his children for the school vacation. They'd just returned to Irene in Boston. He'd taken a few days off to go skiing with them at North Conway, and talked about their progress on the slopes, as he and Caroline drank Scotch on the sofa in front of the fire before supper. Caroline studied his profile. He was a very attractive man, especially with his skiing tan, which set off his white teeth.

'I miss them terribly,' he said. 'When I think about them growing up without me around to watch, it kills me.'

'I can imagine.' She reflected on how different Brian's involvement with his children was from Jackson's benign neglect. 'I wish my husband felt the same.'

'Doesn't he want your sons around?'

'He invites them down a couple of times a year. But his wife is the one who spends time with them.'

'Boys need a father,' said Brian, looking into the fire.

'I agree.' Caroline studied Brian's sad eyes and receding hairline, and wondered if she could fan her warm feelings for him into a flame. If only Diana hadn't fucked her senseless last night.

'And a man needs a woman,' he added, looking at her with urgency.

Unable to think of a comeback, Caroline opened her arms. Holding her face with his delicate hands, he kissed her hungrily.

Leading him into her bedroom, Caroline felt her face twitching. It had been a long time since she'd been with a man, and her final experiences with David Michael had been painful and humiliating. But maybe it would be fine. And if it was, her life might take on a new simplicity, stability, and integrity.

'I can't exactly remember what to do,' she said as she and Brian stretched out naked next to each other. She did remember about stiff cocks, one of which was now prodding her abdomen like a doctor feeling for a tumor.

'I think it will all come back to you,' said Brian, putting an arm around her waist and pulling her to him.

And it did. Evidently lovemaking was like swimming. You didn't forget how despite long periods of inactivity. As Brian entered her slowly and lay still for several moments, she recalled the safe feeling of having her hollows filled by a man. With a man around again, maybe there'd be no voids.

'Are you okay?' he asked in a trembling voice.

'Yes,' she gasped. 'Proceed.'

'Do you want some supper?' Caroline murmured afterwards, smelling the lamb burning in the oven. He shook his head no, holding her tightly, face buried in her neck.

The next morning she tossed the charred leg of lamb out the door to Arnold, thinking guiltily of Howard in Chad fighting famine, and took Brian eggs, bacon, and toast on a tray, feeling malicious pleasure at performing one of her and Diana's rituals with him. Diana's Chevette was in the driveway, alongside Caroline's Subaru and Brian's Pontiac; Suzanne's Toyota was missing. Caroline hoped Diana was upstairs glaring out the window at this latter-day hitching post.

'This has been wonderful,' Brian told her at the door as he left to do rounds. He touched her lips with his fingertips. 'For you too, I hope?'

'Very much so.' Caroline took his hand and kissed the fingers, which had functioned with as much delicacy and proficiency last night as at the operating table. Stiff cocks aside, she thought maybe she could fall in love with a man with hands like that. And why not? She'd been in love with practically everyone else.

'I'll call you tonight,' he said.

'Good. I'll look forward to it. Have a pleasant day, you lovely man.'

The phone rang as Brian drove out the driveway. 'That was very cute,' said Diana.

'Oh? Did you think so? It wasn't meant to be cute. It was meant to be fun. And it was.'

'What the hell are you doing?'

'Continuing with my life. Just like you said yesterday.'

'How can you do that to that nice man?'

'Why don't you mind your own goddam business, Diana?'

'I am, and I don't want men in *my* house.'

There was a stunned silence. Ever since they'd been lovers, it had been *their* house.

'You want me to move out?' Caroline finally asked.

'No, of course I don't. I just wish you'd get your act together.'

'Your act, of course, is a miracle of coherence.' Caroline stood in her down bathrobe twisting the phone cord around her arm.

'At least I'm not messing around with men.'

'What if I'm not messing around with Brian, Diana? What if I mean it?'

'If that's true, then yes, I do want you out.'

'Fine.' Caroline slammed down the phone, nearly dislocating her arm with the cord tangled around it.

The bus from Boston pulled in on time, and Jackie and Jason got off, safe and unmolested, each cradling a BB gun like a violinist a Stradivarius.

'What on earth are those?' asked Caroline, trying to embrace them around the guns.

'Rifles, what do they look like?' said Jason, with a Robert Mitchum look of bland superiority.

'Dad gave them to us,' said Jackie. 'Aren't they neat? He couldn't take us to the Celtics, so he gave us these instead.'

'Wonderful,' said Caroline, taking the gun Jackie handed her as though it were contaminated with strontium 90. 'Why couldn't he take you to the Celtics?'

'He had a mergency,' replied Jason, sighting down his gun at Leonard Litter painted on the side of the trash receptacle on the sidewalk.

'I should have guessed. Well, I don't like guns, boys. I want you to send them back to your father. You can use them when you're down there.'

'Ah, Mom!' they howled in unison.

'Never mind. We'll discuss it later.' For the moment there were more pressing problems, such as where to live next.

As they drove out of town along the lake road, Jackie in the backseat and Jason riding shotgun, the boys chattered about their journeys around Boston with Deirdre. 'You know what we saw, Mom?' asked Jason, aiming his rifle at some Holstein cows waiting to be milked lined up outside a barn. 'In the park watching the swan boats. Two lezzies holding hands.'

'It was gross,' said Jackie, leaning on the front seat.

Caroline frowned. What did they think had been going on around them all these years? 'What are lezzies?' asked Caroline, just checking.

'Girl queers,' said Jackie, flopping back in his seat.

'Why is that gross?' asked Caroline. 'Men and women hold hands all the time.'

'Yeah, but they're supposed to,' said Jason.

Caroline felt rage rising into her throat – at the culture that had put these notions into her little boys' heads. 'And women who care about each other aren't supposed to?' The boys were suddenly silent, Jason stroking the barrel of his gun. Caroline looked at them. All her years of effort, and they would still grow into men, and stalk the woods and battlefields with their instruments of destruction.

'Look,' she said in a low, wavering voice, 'the best people you know are lesbians.'

They said nothing for a long time. Finally Jason asked, 'Like who?'

'Like Jenny. Like Pam. Like Brenda. Like Barb. Like Diana.'

'Like you, Mom?' asked Jason, looking at her. Jackie was silent in the backseat. Lake views were flashing by out the windows.

Caroline drove in silence, wondering what the honest answer to this question was. She drew a deep breath, then said, 'Yes, like me.'

'Ah Mom, do you have to be a lezzie?' asked Jason, sighting along his rifle barrel at a dead cat in the road. 'Pow!' he yelled, falling back into the seat from the imagined recoil.

Caroline thought this over, then replied, 'I don't know.'

As she walked in the door, the phone was ringing. It was Brian. 'I've been trying to reach you. Where have you been?'

What's it to you? she thought. Then she remembered they'd made love last night. She was his honey. 'The boys are back from Boston. I picked them up at the bus station.'

'We ought to get together with our ex-spouses and coordinate this. The kids could ride up from Boston together. Get acquainted.'

'Good idea.' He was already taking charge. It was what she thought she wanted, but now that it was happening, she felt colonized. Wasn't it enough that she was allowing him into her body? Did he have to take over the rest of her life as well? But she needed a place to live, and he kept mentioning his big empty lonely stone house.

'When can I see you again? How about tomorrow night?'

'I need to spend some time with the boys, Brian. They've been gone all week.'

'I understand. But we could all spend time together. The four of us.'

'I don't think that's a very good idea just yet, Brian. I think they need me to themselves.'

'How about Thursday night then?'

'All right. Fine.' After hanging up, she stood with her hand on the receiver trying to figure out what she was doing. Three lovers in one week, after none for months, appeared to be addling her brain. She wanted to pick up the phone, dial Hannah, and ask her what to do. But she could already picture Hannah shrugging, smiling wryly, and saying, 'Choices, Caroline.' But to choose, you first had to know what you wanted.

Five

Simon's new woman Estelle was attractive, Hannah supposed, if you went for the Farrah Fawcett look. Cascades of blond hair; made up to look as though she wasn't; well dressed in pleated trousers and a silk shirt that featured birds of paradise. Hannah sneaked glances at her as they ate roast beef and Yorkshire pudding off Arthur's mother's Wedgwood in the circle of light from the Tiffany lamp above the oak pedestal table. Estelle seemed bright and even-tempered, and nice to Simon. Though of course they'd just begun. It was intriguing to try to figure out how each of Simon's girlfriends was similar to herself, since presumably that was why he picked them. They were always attractive, which Hannah took as a compliment. Usually intelligent and competent. And a trifle sharp-tongued, which Hannah was unsure how to take.

Simon, on the opposite side of the table in the spot where he presided as a boy, teasing and bossing the younger children, had the glazed cat-who's-swallowed-the-canary look of the first flush of sexual passion. Hannah was amused to notice twinges of unpleasant emotions in herself. Inappropriate now that Simon was nearly middle-aged, but evidently still operative. Jealousy that another woman was replacing her. Envy toward anyone in that mad state of simple-minded besottedness when nothing that wasn't reflected in the eyes of the beloved even existed. Anger that Simon had brought Estelle here to parade this in front of his aging mother, who'd spent a lot of time being sweet to him during his past months of anguish. Grief that he was withdrawing from her after these months of closeness. Anyone who thought sex united ·people was out to lunch. Simon and Estelle could see and hear no one but each other right now, and not that very clearly.

'So where do you work?' she asked Estelle, cutting her meat.

Arthur's eyes were amused as he listened to the drama being acted out on an airwave higher than the frequency of sound.

As Estelle said something about issuing rent subsidy checks, flipping back one side of her hair with a hand, Hannah glanced at her handsome, horrible son in his suede vest and tweed jacket and recalled his first serious girlfriend, when he was seventeen. Penny had braces, saddle shoes, a ponytail, and Simon's class ring on a chain around her neck. He paraded her similarly, signaling to his mother to back off. He stayed out late with Hannah's car night after night. Once he left a used condom on the back floor. She and Arthur grumbled, as they were supposed to. Though her side of it didn't carry much conviction, since she remembered only too well what she was doing in that gardener's shed with Colin at Simon's age. Simon ranted about how they were stifling and suffocating him, as *he* was supposed to. She figured if he got out his rebelliousness with her and Arthur then, he wouldn't plague some poor therapist in a few years, or some poor spouse for a lifetime. But even with all the practice she'd had relinquishing people dear to her, it had been difficult to let Simon go. And harder still when he wanted to come back emotionally after ditching Penny. Since then he'd come and gone several times, but it still wasn't easy. Each time someone she cared about withdrew, it evoked echoes of all those others who departed and never returned – her parents, her grandparents, Maggie, Colin, Nigel and Mona. As far as Hannah was concerned, intimacy was definitely an overrated experience, considering the inevitable aftermath.

'So where are you from?' asked Arthur.

Hannah shot him a look of gratitude for keeping the conversation going. Simon wasn't helping at all, the bastard. He was behaving just like a client. They'd cling to her while they recovered from a breakup. But when they found a new true love, they'd invent a reason to terminate. Until the new relationship broke up. Unfortunately, she had more to offer than a breakup service. She was pleased if someone stuck around to see what might be found on the far side of passion – rather than burying his head in the shifting sands of sex, as Simon seemed hell-bent on doing. Of course he had a lot to hide out from. For years he felt Mona's and Nigel's deaths were his fault since he'd been in the house when they happened, albeit unconscious and nearly dead himself.

'Why does he do that to me?' she asked Arthur after Simon and Estelle left, explaining self-consciously that they wanted to make it an early evening.

'You're his mother,' he said, clearing dishes from the table.

'Yes, but he could have waited a few weeks until the glow tarnished a bit.' She gathered up the soiled napkins.

'But that's the whole point. You know that.'

She did know that. She knew Simon had to push her away because they'd been so close since Helena left. Though he could have pushed her away more delicately. She remembered Mona's announcing one day when she was seven, as she tried to skip stones on the lake, 'Mommy, I hate you.'

'Oh yes? Why?' asked Hannah, looking up from her book.

'Because I love you.'

As she scraped leftovers into plastic bowls, Hannah pondered the weird mix of attraction and repulsion in a family. Like the competing energies in an atom that bound the electrons together, yet prevented them from collapsing in on each other to form a black hole.

'If I know it and you know it,' she said, wiping counters with a sponge, 'why doesn't he know it?'

'He probably does on some level.' Arthur was washing dishes in the sink, his sleeves rolled to his elbows.

'You ought to be a shrink, darling.'

'I was, in my fashion. What do you think I did all day? Divorces, assaults, the whole bit. Same as you.'

'Funny, I never thought about it that way. Do you miss it?'

He laughed. 'Hell, no. I've done my bit for suffering humanity. Let Simon and Joanna take over. I want to exit with a smile on my face and a par on my scorecard.'

'Simon and Joanna can't take over. They haven't the time. They're too busy getting their hearts broken and mended.' She wondered what it would feel like not to be needed, after a lifetime of it. Marvelous probably. She ought to try it sometime. Or would she feel lost, like an old brick wall stripped of the ivy that had held it together? Certainly on days when she was in a bad mood, doing therapy cheered her up. If she retired early, she might have to subscribe to *Punch* or something.

'I wonder what that poor young woman made of all that,' said Arthur, sitting down on the couch and picking up the paper.

'I doubt if she noticed anything but that lump in Simon's trousers all evening long.' Hannah sat down beside him and lit a cigarette.

'Well, I thought she was charming.'

Hannah glanced at him. 'You think any female under forty is charming.'

'Who said anything about under forty?'

'But you've always gone after chicken, my darling.'

'Just once. And it was the smartest move of my life.'

Hannah smiled and put her hand on the wide-wale corduroy that covered his thigh. 'Well, I didn't like Estelle.'

Arthur smiled. 'You never do, my dear. But that hasn't stopped Simon yet.'

'I am predictable, aren't I?'

'You're just a lioness who can't accept that her cubs are bigger than she is now.'

'I accept it. I just don't like it sometimes.'

Smiling, Arthur shook open his paper. As Hannah watched the open fire in the stone fireplace and listened to waves pound the lakeshore, she recalled sitting in a deck chair holding the sleeping baby Simon as ocean swells on the North Atlantic lifted the gray troop ship to the sky. The wind swirled, tugging at her head scarf. She sat there knowing at any moment a torpedo from a German U-boat could send them spiraling to the ocean floor. The indifferent gray sea surging on all sides would register no more than a few bubbles. When she focused on Hitler, torpedoes, and ocean floors littered with ship wreckage, terror flooded her. And if she kept it up, Simon would wake up, feed on her terror, and whine fitfully. With deliberation she focused on Arthur's smiling face, the bottle of wine they'd soon be splitting, and the sensation of his flesh moving insistently in hers. Panic gradually transmuted into warm well-being. Then she erased Arthur from the chalkboard of her mind and retained the soothing warmth. In that frame of mind, it made very little difference to her whether they wound up on the ocean floor or in port at Bayonne, New Jersey.

As he turned the page of his paper, Arthur leaned over to kiss the side of her neck. She patted his thigh, realizing this was what she tried to convey to clients – that they could use her to achieve tranquillity, but that they then had to recognize the achievement as their own. A plaster cast could allow a broken bone to heal, but if you left it on too long, the leg muscle began to deteriorate.

Exhaling cigarette smoke, Hannah recalled that she'd made it to Bayonne. All happened as she imagined – the wine and the flesh, and the pleasure in both. What wasn't as she imagined was Washington, D.C., where the friends of Arthur and his former wife snubbed her. His children loathed her. His ex-wife was having a histrionic nervous breakdown for which both Hannah and Arthur felt responsible. His colleagues disapproved of the whole scene.

Arthur quit his post with the Department of War and opened a law practice in Lake Glass, his New Hampshire hometown. His parents tried to appear understanding, despite the fact that they couldn't understand how their beloved son could behave so badly. Arthur paraded her in front of them just as Simon had paraded Estelle. Hannah, in an orgy of North Woods loneliness, began her career of baby production, with torrid cocktail party flirtations with Arthur's old friends between pregnancies. After the horrors and heroics of losing Colin in battle, watching the Luftwaffe from Hampstead Heath, evading torpedoes on the North Atlantic, and enduring ostracism by the entire U.S. diplomatic community, simply living and loving with one man in sylvan serenity seemed insupportable. What a fool she was, she reflected. And yet no different from most people. Humans were problem-solving creatures, and where no problems existed, they created some so they'd have something to solve with their much-vaunted brains. Because if they didn't, they were forced to confront the echoing stillness beneath all the hubbub, which was terrifying because it was unfamiliar. It seemed like emptiness at first. Only gradually did you realize it was everything.

Arthur put down his paper and smiled. Sometimes she felt like a hot-air balloon straining skyward. All the ropes had been cut except one – this white-haired man on the leather couch beside her, who'd just taken her hand. When he was gone, what could hold her here?

'Time to hit the sack?' asked Arthur.

'Sounds good to me.' She flipped her cigarette into the fire as she stood up.

Caroline sat on the tweed couch looking out at the parking lot, arms folded across her chest and one ankle resting on the other knee. Hannah studied her with narrowed eyes, wondering what would go on today. Her job required that she take whatever a client dished out. The client didn't usually realize Hannah was the cook.

Caroline was in full-blown adolescence, testing to discover how to control Hannah. Loaves of bread hadn't worked. Now, like a physician poking an abdomen for sore spots, Caroline was looking for ways to earn Mummy's displeasure. Casual sex had been a flop. What would be next? At some point Hannah hoped there would be an angry clash. Maybe today. There was belligerence to the jut of Caroline's jaw and the way she held her shoulders.

'So what's happening?' asked Hannah, propping up her stocking feet and resting her arms along the chair arms.

'Diana and I went to bed together Friday night,' announced Caroline, uncertain whether to add the news about Brian as well.

'Oh yes? Was it nice?'

'For us it was.'

'What does that mean?'

'What?'

'For *us* it was.'

'Well, I know it's incomprehensible to you that two women could prefer each other to men.'

Hannah smiled faintly. 'It's not remotely incomprehensible to me. There've been several women I've felt very close to.' If she were thirty years younger and hadn't met Arthur, maybe she'd have gone Caroline's route herself. Who could say?

Caroline looked at her ironically. She spouted a liberal line, but lived a safe, respectable life. She didn't know what she was talking about when it came to sexual passion between women. Once you felt it in all its fierce poignancy, it was hard to see how you could do without it, whatever the price. Could she herself do without it, was the question she'd been asking all week.

'Do you want to talk about that relationship today?'

'It's not something I feel comfortable discussing with a heterosexual.' There was always the implication hets were doing you a favor, accepting you despite your infirmity. Fuck them. She didn't want her love for women labeled a neurotic symptom that needed treatment.

Hannah shrugged and rested her chin on her chest, thinking what prigs clients could be. Caroline was still struggling with the part of herself that disapproved of lesbianism, and she was calling that part 'Hannah.' Carefully Hannah focused on Caroline as she'd be in a few months, once she gathered together, Bo Peep-like, all the lost black sheep of her own personality. If Hannah managed not to kill her first.

'How are your sons handling all this?'

'All what?'

'Well, your love life seems in flux lately. Does that unnerve them?'

'My sons are fine. Don't unload your issues on me.' Caroline glanced at the blue-eyed children on the bulletin board.

Touché, thought Hannah, feeling herself turn a bit pale.

'Maybe you worry about my kids,' continued Caroline, 'because *you* feel like a flop as a mother.'

There was a long pause. 'You might be right, Caroline. God knows I'm not perfect. If you want to poke holes in me, we can do that all day long. Or we could do what we're here for: talk about what's going on with you.'

'How can you help me if you've got your own problems?'

Hannah was beginning to feel keyed up, as she did when important things started happening. 'I have my blind spots like everyone else.'

'And you don't like me noticing them, do you?'

Hannah laughed. 'Not much. But what you say may be valid. Now do you want to get something done today or not?'

'Now you're angry,' Caroline said hopefully.

'Taken aback maybe. Not angry.' Actually she was a bit excited, and struggling not to let it show. It was a propitious sign when a meek client turned into a brat.

'I almost canceled today.' At lunch with Brian in the hospital cafeteria, as Diana sat across the room laughing with Suzanne, the pressure to make sense of her life seemed too great. She didn't know what she was doing. To explain it to Hannah was impossible.

'It's not too late.'

'As long as I'm here, I may as well stay.'

'It's up to you.' Hannah gazed out the window to the frozen lake, which was covered with a deep new snowfall that sparkled in the sun.

Caroline glared at her. 'I'd like to talk some more about

Jackson. And about David Michael, the man I left him for.' If she could figure out what went wrong with them, maybe she'd know whether something could work with Brian. And whether she wanted something to work. The tug of security, simplicity, respectability was strong. Especially if Diana was going to perform will-o'-the-wisp maneuvers indefinitely. The tug of Brian's empty stone house was even stronger, if she really had to find new living quarters.

'Fine. Shoot,' said Hannah with a gesture of her hand.

'The boys are just back from Jackson's, as a matter of fact.'

'How did it go?'

'As usual. He had tickets to a Celtics game, but he had an emergency at the last minute.'

'Does that sound familiar?'

'Like my own father, you mean? Yes, I'm starting to realize it does.'

'Good.' Hannah nodded.

'Do you know what he did to make it up to them? Bought them BB guns. Yesterday Jason shot the cat. I was so upset I called Jackson and said, "Here you spend half your life removing bullets from people's chests, and you give your sons guns?" He said, "Really, Caroline, do you have to be so hysterical all the time?" '

'Tell me some more about your life with him.'

As Caroline described her standard suburban marriage, and her standard countercultural muddle of an affair, Hannah focused less on the predictable details than on Caroline's aggrieved tone of voice. These two men had ignored, neglected, and betrayed her in all the usual ways. But Caroline's tone of voice indicated a complicated interaction had gone on, that the men in question would have different versions. The closer a client's account was to 'objectivity,' the more detached the tone of voice.

'. . . I've been over this shit a lot lately,' Caroline was saying, 'and it's like a trip to the morgue to identify corpses. I've wasted my life being miserable over idiots.'

'But how nice,' said Hannah, 'to have the rest of your life ahead of you, idiot-free. And misery-free.'

Caroline looked up from her study of her boot tread.

'You've experienced the misery for years. Now you can experience the joy by simply letting go of all that junk you've used to keep yourself feeling shitty.'

'You think I chose to waste all those years feeling shitty?' Caroline glared at her.

'Yes, I do. Not that you knew it. Feeling shitty was comfortable. You were used to it. It was familiar. But now can you face the terror of feeling good?'

The corners of Caroline's mouth were twitching.

'You keep talking about how all these terrible people failed you,' said Hannah. 'Your pink blanket was destroyed, and Marsha was run over by a truck. But it sounds to me as though you left the others. They did things you chose to regard as rejections and betrayals, but you were ready to go. You took on new strength, and they couldn't cope because they wanted someone they could dominate. They failed you. But in their terms, you failed them: you didn't remain submissive and adoring.' Hannah loved summarizing clients' disasters from a different perspective. A judo throw, using their own momentum to turn the tables. 'This pile of corpses you talk about,' she continued, 'you could instead see it as a compost pile. Ask yourself what you learned from each person that allowed you to develop into the fantastic woman you are today. Your parents gave you their sensitivity to human suffering. Arlene helped you become good at your work. Jackson gave you babies and belongings. David Michael taught you about politics . . .' The whole point, it seemed to her, was to figure out that none of these was enough to give life meaning.

'Joy?' sneered Caroline, that word finally registering.

Hannah noted that her entire speech had washed over Caroline unabsorbed. She wasn't ready to see herself as anything other than a pathetic, wronged victim.

'Yes. Joy.' Snow slid off the roof, blotting out the sun through the window for an instant and landing with a thud.

'Joy? While millions of people are starving to death?' Caroline uncrossed her legs abruptly and leaned forward.

'Oh, for God's sake. Look, this life is like a diamond on black velvet. One aspect defines the other. You know the black velvet from every angle. Now allow yourself to see the diamond.'

'Diamonds? Garbage! You're just talking a lot of elitist crap! How much joy do you think someone in a Chilean jail feels? How about the baby I saw in the ER yesterday, whose mother stuffed her in a rural route mailbox because she couldn't afford to keep her? Joy, my ass!' Caroline realized she'd sold out again, sitting here being lulled into passive acceptance of the status quo by this suburban matron, while the world continued to career toward destruction. Deciding to copy Hannah's example and subside into domestic serenity with Brian Stone while the Chinese swept into Vietnam. While entire towns in Utah were perishing of leukemia from fallout in the fifties.

Hannah shrugged and studied her mimi spirit. It was one thing to prod a mimi spirit out from a rock ledge. It was something else again to teach it to dance and make love, instead of tearing the place apart. There was enormous tension in the room. Hannah felt very much on edge. To feed Caroline's flames she said in a bland voice, 'Do you realize every time you feel threatened, you launch into this cosmic number?'

Caroline glared at her and unleashed a diatribe about world hunger, spouting statistics like bubbles from a hooked fish: '. . . twenty-one children somewhere in the world are starving to death *every minute* . . .'

Hannah observed her own irritation flaring like coals on a banked fire. My dear young woman, she said silently, you appear to assume I've never left my own backyard. Can you even conceive of a life that spans three continents and close to six decades? Do you think I'm not aware of what you're saying?

She reminded herself if she engaged on this level, she was done for. The real issue was that Caroline, like Simon parading Estelle the other night, needed distance from her own feelings of dependency. And a focus for the accumulated rage of a lifetime. Her cosmic routine was her number-one defense, an extremely effective one because everything she was saying was undeniably true.

Caroline was now educating Hannah on torture. She felt a driving need to convey to this smug woman in her polyester pants suit that reality was not as she saw it from the window of her cozy ranch house: 'Hannah, your life of comfort and affluence is built on the bowed backs of millions of suffering people. Here we sit in a fascist nation that's looting the world, congratulating each other on being nice people. It's obscene. You're nothing but a suburban sellout!'

Hannah allowed herself only to raise her eyebrows. You didn't lash out at the injured, however provocative their behavior. Anyhow, this harangue sounded like the death rattle of this particular tape. It was about to be erased, which was why it was putting up such a furious struggle.

'. . . ninety percent of violent crimes are committed by men,' Caroline was saying. 'All day long I bandage up women and children whom men have raped, knifed, beaten, shot, strangled. And you yourself live with one of those fuckers, Hannah. You say you love him. You repose under the tent of benefits his white American male privilege provides – at the expense of the rest of us. You try getting through life without a man to protect you from the violence of other men. Then see if you can talk to me about joy!'

Hannah had to stop herself from calling, 'Bravo!' Caroline thought she was locking horns with Hannah. But she knew almost nothing about Hannah. She was actually doing battle with the part of herself that longed for Brian Stone's dubious protection.

'My hour's up.' Caroline stood up abruptly and slapped a check on Hannah's desk. As she stalked to the door, she realized it was all over. She'd just added Hannah's corpse to the pile. Never again would she sit in this cluttered office and study those sharp blue eyes for clues on how to live in such a vile world. She felt a raging mix of pain, loss, nausea – and relief.

'See you next week,' said Hannah.

Caroline did a double take. Hannah stifled a smile. There was hostility in the pleasure she took in thwarting clients' expectations. It allowed her not to retaliate in other ways. Besides, every job needed fringe benefits. She wrote out an appointment card and handed it to a stunned Caroline, who glanced at it and shoved it wordlessly into her jeans pocket.

Hannah lit a cigarette and exhaled with a deep sigh of relief to have Caroline gone. Leaning back in her chair, she used her skills from her drugstore perusal of mystery novels to try to predict what Caroline would do next. Chip continued a similar dispute for several tedious sessions. Other clients were too embarrassed after such scenes to come back for a while. But Caroline's presenting symptom was depression. She responded to her parents at Christmas with depression. Probably she'd plunge into depression. Try to become acceptable to Mummy again by erasing all those nasty emotions, by hanging still and silent in the jump seat. And then what? She might try to kill herself. She said she had once before. The hostility had to go somewhere. She'd be appalled at having turned it on Mummy. She'd turn it on herself. But maybe Caroline trusted her enough by now to ask for reassurance?

Hannah flicked her cigarette ash into Nigel's stone and took another drag. Speaking of suicide, she was killing herself with these damn things. When would she summon enough strength of character to give them up?

She wondered if she'd be able to withstand this junk with Caroline if people hadn't done the same for her. With great dignity her grandmother endured Hannah's endless ways of expressing fury toward her parents for deserting her. Hannah roved the narrow winding streets of Hampstead doing her best to wreak havoc. And Arthur endured her fury toward the universe over Mona's and Nigel's deaths. For years afterwards she raged at him – over his choice of furnaces, his being away that night, his failure to get home in time to save the antiques. But mostly she raged about how he mowed the lawn, or the fact that she always put new rolls of toilet paper on the bathroom holder. Arthur somehow managed never to descend to Hannah's level of rancor. Sometimes he walked away. Other times he inquired coolly, 'Are you finished yet?' A few times he pinned her arms to her sides to prevent her clobbering him. Eventually he suggested she find something useful to do for someone else in trouble, rather than sitting around a messy darkened house all day feeling sorry for herself. Which she did, returning to school for her degrees.

During which she met Maggie, who sat in her wing chair on the wine and blue Oriental carpet by the potted bay tree poking and prodding at Hannah's infected wounds until they broke open again and bled some more. Maggie eventually convinced her to get out photos of all four children and give them to a portrait painter in town. She left the four finished portraits in the trunk of her car without even unwrapping them for several months. When Maggie finally persuaded her to hang them on the wall in her bedroom, she wept and threw the hammer across the room and beat her head against the wall. Then she gathered up the wrapping paper and burned it in the Franklin stove, fixed a martini, and discussed with Arthur when he got home what good likenesses the portraits were.

And now here she herself sat, drawing on cigarettes and absorbing from unhappy people like Caroline exactly what she dished out to her grandmother, Arthur, and Maggie. It was probably the only way to repay that kind of debt.

In the next office Mary Beth yelled, 'Goddam it to hell, Nathan, just pull yourself together or get out!'

Hannah felt a flicker of alarm. Outside her office Mary Beth was so sedate, pinched almost, in her high-necked ruffled blouses. Hannah never shouted at clients, as much as she might want to. They shouted at her. But Mary Beth was fresh out of graduate school. Maybe it was a new technique – Confrontation Therapy or something.

Hannah remembered her first outburst at Maggie, over Maggie's announcement that she was taking a vacation. Hannah amputated her adoration for the woman in an instant, slamming shut the dungeon door of her heart. She told Maggie she was finished with therapy anyway and wouldn't be needing any more appointments. Maggie smiled sourly, put on her glasses, and said, 'My dear Hannah, I'm afraid you've scarcely begun.'

'I've done all I'm doing.'

By the end of that session Hannah had sobbed, shouted, begged Maggie not to go – and begun to gain some clues about her own agony over desertion by loved ones.

Hannah gathered together some books and papers, put on her Berber cape, and left her office. The fiery sun was setting over the lake, the thick blanket of new snow blood red. Big deal. In a few minutes it would all be pitch dark. Goddam fly-by-night sunsets. Tucked under the windshield wiper of her Mercury like a parking ticket was a folded note that read, 'Hannah, please meet me for a drink at Dooley's after work. I'll wait there for you until it closes. I have to talk to you about our relationship. Love, Harold (Mortimer). P.S. I like your new car.' Clenching the muscles in her jaw, Hannah wadded the note into a ball and thrust it into the litter bag on the floor of the car. Relationship? What relationship?

After a supper of Chicken Kiev à la Arthur, Hannah and he sat on the leather couch with coffee and cognac watching the news, an ordeal Hannah put herself through only a couple of times a week. Walter Cronkite was reporting that some Argentine peasants had kidnapped a thirteen-year-old girl, gang-raped her, cut her open, and sewn a human head inside her. Setting her coffee on the coffee table next to a stack of dog-eared gothic romances, Hannah covered her eyes with one hand and felt her stomach churn. Was

Caroline right? Was she a Pollyanna who refused to face the horrors?

With distaste she glanced at Arthur, who sat frowning at the TV. It must be embarrassing to be a man, she decided. All the ghastly deeds your sex performed. Whenever an atrocity was announced on the evening news, Maggie used to close her eyes and murmur, 'Pray God he's not a Jew.' But men rarely had the luxury of discovering the perpetrator of some horror wasn't a man. *Ninety percent of violent crimes are committed by men . . .*

A commercial for Silhouette Romances came on, featuring a dark attractive man carrying a woman in a skimpy bathing suit out of ocean waves and into a thatched cabana. Hannah glanced at the stack of romances on the table beside her coffee cup. The cover on top featured a woman in a clinging gown on the deck of a burning ship. Her soldier rescuer in plumes and gold braid parried the sword thrust of a pirate in an eyepatch, bandanna, and gold hoop earring. It was obscene, she realized. Brainwashing women into viewing their rapists and murderers as protectors. *You try getting through life without a man to protect you from the violence of other men.* She jumped up, grabbed the books, and threw them into the fire. The flames nibbled greedily at the pages.

'What are you doing?' asked Arthur.

Whirling around, she glared at him as he sipped his cognac. 'Darling,' she said acidly, 'would you please explain to me why rape is a man's idea of a good time?'

He raised his eyebrows and pursed his lips. 'Maybe we need to feel in command in order to entrust our precious organs to dangerous places like vaginas.'

'Lovely,' she snapped, plopping down on the couch. 'You only run the damn world. What more do you want?' An earnest young man on TV was explaining why he would never use anything but Preparation H on his hemorrhoids. Hannah tried to remind herself Arthur hadn't raped anyone. As far as she knew. Being with a man you had built-in distance. They were a different species. What would life be like with another woman, a replica of yourself? For a moment she envied Caroline the chance to find out.

She glanced at Arthur, somber in the lamplight. 'The nice thing about war is that it keeps you men off the streets.'

Arthur smiled grimly and sipped his coffee. 'What can I say, Hannah? I'm afraid most men are morally retarded.'

Hannah nodded. 'I'm afraid you're right.' Resolutely she erased the image of the mutilated girl from her mind. If those morons undermined the efficiency of the well-meaning people who heard about them, they'd won. Learn to behave from those who cannot, her grandmother used to intone in the drawing room overlooking the Heath, hands folded beneath her enormous corseted bosom.

Hannah took a sip of cognac, and swirled it around her mouth like Lavoris, feeling the vapors fumigate her sinuses. Studying the snifter with the dark golden liquid in the bottom, she tried to decide if she drank too much. She certainly relished the feeling of oblivion alcohol induced each evening. It cauterized her nerve endings, frayed from a day of listening to such atrocities, and to the despair they engendered.

What about her own despair? It didn't seem to be around much anymore. And when it was, it broke camp pretty quickly, as it had just done. The older she got, the less anything could upset her for very long. Maybe the only real cure for her clients was the aging process. But that could take years.

Six

'I've just done something awful,' Caroline told Diana as they sat on Diana's couch drinking wine and listening to Jackie and Jason play the Incredible Hulk downstairs. Heroes were spinning their autos across the melting snow on Lake Glass in the crimson light of late afternoon. Diana was knitting an Icelandic sweater for Suzanne. 'Are you going to make her matching booties?' Caroline asked when Diana first began. Today was the first time they'd spoken since Diana told her to leave. Caroline felt numb.

'What, for God's sake?'

'I just told off Hannah.' Caroline's muscles were so tight she could scarcely move her shoulders.

'What about?'

'Who knows? She started talking about joy, and I let her have it.'

Diana smiled. 'Not your favorite word. What did she say?'

'See you next week.'

'So maybe you weren't as obnoxious as you think.' She was counting stitches.

'I'm pretty sure I was. She's been so kind to me. I can't believe it. I marched in there and wrecked everything.'

'Well, apparently she's willing to drop it. So why don't you?'

'I wish I'd been struck mute when I walked in her door today.'

'Don't be so melodramatic,' said Diana, getting up and walking to her kitchen counter. 'She's your shrink. She's used to clients acting out. That's what you're paying her for. Call her. She'll congratulate you.'

'You don't understand.' Caroline tossed down half her wine in one swallow. Diana sounded amused. Probably she was pleased.

'Maybe not,' said Diana, tossing the chef salad she'd invited Caroline to share, a gustatory peace pipe.

Caroline decided next week she'd be calm and pleasant. She'd apologize. She'd say she'd thought about a diamond on black velvet and decided Hannah was right. She began shivering and wrapped her arms across her flannel shirt. What if, in the meantime, Hannah became fed up? Nobody had to put up with that kind of behavior from another person. What if Hannah called to cancel their appointment? She took the appointment card from her jeans pocket and studied it.

'God, you look awful,' said Diana as they sat down at her maple butcher-block dining table. 'Your lips are blue. They match your eyes.'

'I'm not hungry.' Her stomach was churning like a washing machine.

'You have to eat.'

Caroline didn't reply.

'Look, call her up. She'll tell you it's okay.'

'But it isn't okay. The things I said. I was horrible.'

'So what? We all are now and then.' Diana studied her, fork in midair.

'I'm going to bed.' Caroline got up and walked to the stairs.

'Is there anything I can do? Do you want a back rub?'

'No, thanks.' Not unless you'd like to pump me full of BBs and bury me in a snowbank, thought Caroline.

'Look, I don't really want you to move out, Caroline,' Diana called. 'I'm sorry I said that. We'll figure this out.'

Caroline turned and looked at her. 'Thanks. That helps.'

She phoned Brian and told him she couldn't go out with him because she was sick.

'You do sound awful. But I'm a doctor. I could make a house call.'

'I'm too repulsive right now, Brian.'

'I'm used to sick people.'

'I need to be alone.' What was this? One lousy screw and now he owned her?

He said nothing for a moment, then replied, 'All right, I'll phone you tomorrow. Feel better.'

'Thanks.'

Telling the boys she was going to the grocery store, Caroline got in her car and drove up the lakeshore, skirting town, listening to David Brinkley on the radio discussing the Chinese invasion of

Vietnam. Her hands on the steering wheel trembled, and her teeth chattered. Her stomach ground like a car that wouldn't start. Each time she tried to calm herself by picturing Hannah's smiling face, her agitation increased. She merely felt the full enormity of her loss.

Well up the lake, she stopped at a Getty station and asked directions to Hannah's house. After several turns down icy dirt roads, she found it. Not the fantasized ranch house at all, but rather a large renovated Victorian summer house, with light streaming out a front greenhouse window onto a wall of snow piled up in the yard over winter by the south wind. Two cars sat in the driveway under a hoopless basketball goal.

Caroline parked behind a bare lilac bush and studied the patch of yellow light on the snow. Could she knock at the door and apologize? Maybe just peep through that window to be sure Hannah was in there? But she'd leave footprints in the snow.

A shadow moved across the patch of light. Someone was walking around inside. What if Hannah looked out and saw her here, huddled in her Subaru? Lucky there were no neighbors to phone the police. What if Hannah had a dog that was barking?

Suddenly Caroline saw herself from a distance: an overwrought woman with a messy Afro and no coat, gazing at Hannah's window with crazed longing. This was insane. Hannah had a home, a husband, children, friends, work. A full complete life that didn't include Caroline. Caroline was nothing to her. A client who ranted at her when she should be thanking her. *You're nothing but a suburban sellout!* Caroline cringed. Hannah wanted nothing to do with her after hours. And probably not even during hours now.

She should get out of the car, sneak over to Hannah's Mercury, find some memento . . .

With a start she realized she'd been here before – stealing yellow Kleenex from Arlene's VW, eyes fixed on her office windows, feeling just as alone and afraid as she did now. What did this mean? Bemused, she continued to sit in the cold car, the frozen lake stretching out silent beside her.

The patch of light on the snow vanished, and another appeared upstairs. Hannah was getting into bed with her husband. When the upstairs light disappeared, Caroline drove home, imagining Hannah holding her white-haired husband in her arms as Caroline had wanted Hannah to hold her. Not only would Hannah never hold her, she'd probably never even speak to her again.

The next morning, having lain awake all night shivering spasmodically despite her electric blanket, Caroline sat in the plaid armchair staring at her phone. At Christmas Hannah gave her her home number and said to call any time. But probably that was just for the trip to Boston. But if she called, Hannah would have to talk to her. Or maybe she'd tell her to go to hell and hang up. But Caroline was already in hell. Her flesh burned as though she were rotating on a spit.

Jackie came in, dressed in a forest-green sweat suit and cradling his gun, which he was polishing with a cloth. 'Hey Mom, what're you doing?'

'Uh, waiting for a phone call.'

'Can I please have some breakfast?'

Mechanically she cooked, then folded laundry, wondering why she was bothering. Life was pointless. What difference did clean clothes make?

The phone rang. Caroline dashed to it. Maybe it was Hannah saying everything was okay. What if it was Hannah telling her to piss off? She sat down and studied the ringing phone. Jackie raced out and grabbed it, looking at her oddly.

'It's for you, Mom.' He handed her the receiver. She held it at a distance, examining it as though it were pinchers used in the Spanish Inquisition. Jackie screwed up his face and tossed his dark hair out of his eyes. 'So answer it, Mom.'

It was Diana, calling from upstairs to invite her out to ski. Looking out the window, Caroline discovered a brilliantly sunny day was in progress. 'Uh, I can't. Thanks very much, Diana, but I'd tied up.'

'How're you feeling?'

'Fine, thanks.' Then she added, 'Not too great actually.'

'You don't sound so great. Take it from me: Call the lady. Unless you enjoy feeling bad.'

Caroline changed the sheets and dusted in a state of terror. She must have been out of her mind. She reminded herself that Hannah gave her an appointment for next week. But probably she'd use it to explain why the relationship was over. Fuck it, if it was finished, it was finished. Why wait around in agony until next week? Why couldn't Hannah level with her?

She picked up the receiver and dialed the first half of Hannah's number. She hung up. If she gave Hannah time to calm down, maybe she'd reconsider the need to end it. Especially if Caroline apologized at the beginning of the appointment. Maybe there was something she could take to say she was sorry. The new sunset shawl? But the bread was a flop. She wasn't supposed to take Hannah presents.

Remembering the orange and red shawl on her loom, she went into her bedroom, sat down, and tried to work on it, thinking the hypnotic motions might calm her. But her hands and feet moved jerkily. She'd mess it up if she kept on. She jumped up and stalked into the kitchen, looking for something more mindless to do.

As Caroline cleaned the refrigerator, she decided she wanted to die. Anyone who behaved like that to someone as kind as Hannah deserved to be dead. It'd be a relief to have it over with. She pictured the pill bottles on her closet shelf. Let the boys take their rifles and go live with their wretched father. She'd had it. This afternoon she'd write good-bye notes. Tonight after the boys were asleep she'd swallow every damn pill in the house. She lay face down on the hooked rug in the living room among hockey sticks and skates. The cabin was still. The boys had gone skiing with Diana, and Sharon was locked in the bathroom talking interminably on the phone. Amelia wandered over and purred around Caroline's head. Caroline was unable to lift a hand to stroke her. Eventually she flicked her tail in Caroline's face and stalked away.

The boys burst through the door. Arnold careened over to Caroline, barking and sniffing her Levi's.

'Go away,' Caroline muttered, unable to move.

Diana stood over her wearing brown corduroy knickers, thick knee socks, and a ski sweater she'd knit, her face flushed from the cold. 'Nothing is worth turning yourself into a nutcase over,' she said, studying Caroline motionless on the floor. '*Please* call the woman. What's the worst that can happen?'

'Maybe she's dead,' said Caroline in a dull voice. 'Maybe I upset her so much she had a heart attack.'

'Don't be ridiculous. Call her. I bet she's fine.'

'What's it to you if I call her? I thought you were jealous of her. You should be glad I've destroyed our relationship.'

'I care about what's best for you. It really bugs me when you get all wide-eyed about her. But I don't want you to be without her. I just want you to have some perspective. Now, tell me her number. I'll dial it for you.' Diana walked over to the phone.

'I can't face her. Not after what I said.'

'Caroline, you're turning into a screwball,' said Diana, going up the steps to the safety of her own quarters.

If Hannah was hospitalized, Caroline realized she could take care of her – give her bed baths, feed her, see that she took her medication, fluff her pillows and water her flowers, answer her call button. This scenario appealed to her: Hannah needing *her*. She sat up. Then she crawled to the phone stand, put the phone in her lap, and dialed Hannah's number. Her repulsive husband would answer. She'd find out what hospital Hannah was at. She wouldn't have to confess that she was the client who was responsible. The phone rang a couple of times. Caroline almost pushed down the button. No one there. They were all at the hospital. Or the funeral home. Her forehead broke out in sweat.

'Hello?' said Hannah in a cheerful voice.

Caroline couldn't speak.

'Hello?'

'Uh, hello. It's Caroline.'

'Oh, hi. How are you?'

'Uh, well, okay, I guess. How are you?'

'Fine, thanks. Drinking a martini and getting ready to cook filet of sole in white wine sauce.'

'Oh. Well, I'm sorry to interrupt you. You said I could call, but I didn't know if that still applied.'

'Sure. Fine. Why wouldn't it? What's up?'

'Well, I was wondering if I could have an extra appointment.' With her thumb she was cracking the knuckles on the same hand time after time.

'Yes, of course you can. Only I'm pretty booked. So why don't we go to lunch on Monday? How about picking me up at my office at noon?'

'What? Oh. Okay. Great. See you then. Enjoy the sole.' She hung up, head falling back against the chair, armpits clammy with sweat. Hannah wasn't dead. She wasn't even sick. She was drinking gin. How was this possible? She sounded the same as always – tough and kind. Not only did she not kick Caroline out, she invited her to lunch. It felt like a last-minute pardon on the guillotine.

Caroline stood up, went to the kitchen cabinet, and filled a Burger King *Star Wars* glass to the rim with Gordon's gin. She

232

drank the whole thing in three gulps, then lay on the couch and felt numbing warmth creep up her legs as Jason in his Darth Vader outfit vaporized her with his BB gun.

When Brian phoned, she could scarcely move her lips.

'Are you all right?' he asked.

'Actually I'm drunk.'

'Do you do this often?'

'Only on special occasions.' She started giggling.

Silence from his end.

'I'm okay really, Brian. I'll see you at work.' She hung up.

Hannah gripped the seat with one hand as Caroline wove her Subaru through the traffic on the highway past the mall like a skier down a slalom course. She wished she'd suggested meeting at the restaurant. Caroline wanted to destroy her, but surely she wouldn't pick kamikaze tactics. Usually a client settled for symbolic destruction. Hadn't the tirade last week been enough?

'Did anyone ever tell you that you drive like a truck driver?' asked Hannah.

Caroline blushed. 'Am I frightening you? I'm sorry.' She moved to the outside lane and slowed down. She'd been pleased when Hannah suggested she drive, and here she was screwing things up again.

Noting the effect of her words, Hannah realized she was being unfair. She didn't like to hand over control of anything to anyone, so she could maintain the fiction that nothing could take her by surprise. She'd been a nervous wreck when Joanna and Simon got their permits, and sat cowering in the backseat as they drove. 'Truck drivers are usually very good drivers,' she said. 'I didn't mean to criticize, just to comment.'

Caroline glanced at her. She was prepared to acknowledge that Hannah was always right. That Caroline had been insane last week. Yet it sounded as though Hannah was apologizing.

Hannah was amused observing Caroline's confusion. She remembered Simon and Joanna as teenagers, calling her a raving bitch, criticizing her fondness for gin, rejecting her meals with contempt – then sidling up to her later in the evening for a guilty good-night hug.

'Aren't you cold?' asked Caroline. Hannah wore no coat, only the navy blue pants suit and blouse Caroline had first met her in.

'No. I have so many hot flashes these days I could probably heat Lake Glass single-handedly. I keep meaning to go to the doctor, but each month I decide I'm finally through menopause.'

Caroline glanced at her as they pulled into the restaurant parking lot, startled to be reminded that Hannah had her own difficulties.

Hannah had suggested Dooley's, which had mediocre food but lots of room between tables, in case Caroline wanted to throw another scene. They sat by a window overlooking the parking lot in rattan peacock chairs, fern tendrils trailing above their heads, and discussed the current angle of the sun to the horizon, the state of the ice on the lake, the imminent return of birds from the south, and the likelihood of another late snowstorm.

Caroline marveled over Hannah's apparent good health and good humor as they ordered sandwiches and coffee from a gum-chewing waitress who withdrew her pencil from her French twist. Had Hannah not heard or forgotten all the awful things Caroline said?

'I suppose you're wondering why I asked you here today,' Caroline said as the waitress sauntered away.

'I asked you,' said Hannah, thinking she probably had a better idea than Caroline herself. She was enjoying chatting away when Caroline expected her to be hurt, angry, or aloof. At such times you could almost see the wires in their brains flaring and crackling as they short-circuited.

'I wanted to apologize for my tantrum the other day.' She played with the prongs on her fork.

Hannah shrugged. 'Why should you apologize for saying what you think?'

'I didn't have to say it so forcefully.'

'You didn't have to, but you did. And so what? It's okay. The globe didn't tilt any farther on its axis.'

'It felt that way to me.' Caroline jabbed the fork through her paper napkin.

'Which way?'

'Disastrous. When I got home, I thought maybe I'd made you sick, or even killed you. That's really why I called.'

'I know.'

Caroline looked at her. 'You did?'

234

'This is my job. Do you understand that on one level you'd like me to be dead? And that's why you were terrified I might be?'

'What?'

'People don't like to need other people.' From Caroline's look of consternation Hannah knew she wasn't ready to face this yet. 'Did you ever get angry with your mother?' Caroline had shredded her napkin with her fork. Hannah wished there were some simple way to let her know everything was all right.

Caroline sorted through the canceled checks in her memory bank. 'I came downstairs one Sunday and said I wasn't going to church since I didn't believe in God. Because if God was so great, how come He'd created a world in which so many people were suffering. She said I didn't know anything about God. I said I could believe whatever I wanted.'

'What happened?' David Dickson, an ex-client whose poorly tied bow ties had riveted Hannah throughout therapy, walked past their table with a woman who wasn't his wife. He pretended not to see Hannah, so Hannah pretended not to see him. Though she did wonder if he was getting it up yet.

'She got upset and went to bed.'

'How did you feel?'

Caroline struggled to remember. 'I kept trying to bring her tea and food and flowers, and she kept refusing them. I think that was when I broke my nose.'

'You what?' The waitress brought their coffee. Struggling to open her cream container, Hannah squirted the cream halfway across the table.

'Ran into the edge of her door and broke my nose.' Caroline tried to blot the cream with the remains of her napkin, and made a swamp of shredded paper.

'Here?' asked Hannah, rubbing the bridge of her own nose with thumb and forefinger. Then she tried to wipe up the whole mess with her napkin. They ought to have a sheet of plastic under their table, like the one she spread under the high chair at home while each child was learning to eat.

Caroline nodded.

'So that's why you rub it all the time?'

'Do I?'

'You aren't aware of it?'

'No.' Caroline copied Hannah's gesture. It felt familiar.

'Well, I am, because I've picked it up from you.'

'You have?' Caroline was amazed she had any impact at all on Hannah. She tried to reconcile this with her conviction over the weekend that her anger had killed Hannah.

'So what happened after you broke your nose?'

'My mother got out of bed and drove me to the emergency room.'

'Was she still depressed?'

'No, she was really nice. She took me out for an ice cream soda, and we joked about how I looked like a pig.' The waitress placed their sandwiches before them, on plates overloaded with potato chips.

'How did you feel?'

'Good. My face was all swollen and purple, but I was really happy.'

'Did your mother go back to bed?' In some ways it was easier to cope with outright child abuse. At least everybody knew what was going on.

'No. She fixed me ice packs. Read me stories because I couldn't see with my eyes all puffy.' She watched Hannah pick up her BLT and take a bite. Gin, sole, BLTs, hot flashes, a husband. Caroline spent so much time consulting the idealized image of Hannah in her own head that it was odd to realize she had a body, needed food and sleep.

'Do you see the pattern?'

'Huh?'

'You assert yourself. Other people depart or collapse. You get frightened and guilty. The world starts looking like a terrifying place. You punish yourself, or try to get them to – in hopes of regaining their patronage.'

'What?'

'Think about it. All right, so you got angry and told me off. Then you got scared. And you worked yourself up into an awful state as an excuse to call me. And what did you discover?'

'That you were all right. That you were drinking martinis.' Caroline realized she hadn't touched her egg salad sandwich. She had no appetite. She nibbled halfheartedly at a rippled potato chip.

'What if I hadn't been all right? What if I'd been in a bad mood? It still wouldn't have been your fault. I might have burned the sole or run out of gin. I have a full complicated life, much of which has nothing to do with you. You simply don't have that much power over me, Caroline. You didn't over your mother. She used your behavior as an excuse to feel depressed. But each of us is author of her own moods.'

Caroline knew this was true. She'd been using Hannah to feel better all these months. 'Like I used my pink blanket.'

'Yes. But you can dispense with people and objects, and feel without intermediary the states of mind you've assigned to them.'

'But that doesn't make sense. If people and events are irrelevant, why would I pick depression?'

Hannah raised her eyebrows. 'Why would you? What did you grow up with?'

'No, that's ridiculous. Horrible things go on. It's no good pretending they don't.' Caroline remembered the word that set her off last week: Joy. Joy to the world. What a joke.

'Things go on. Whether you perceive them as horrible is your choice.'

'Like those Argentine peasants in Sunday's paper, who raped that girl and sewed a human head inside her?'

Hannah closed her eyes and returned her sandwich to her plate, suddenly nauseated. 'Yes, I saw that too.'

'You can choose to perceive that as not horrible?'

Hannah hesitated. She was something more sure of herself than she felt. 'That was horrible. But all you can do is try to maintain your own peace of mind, with the hope that it can soothe the savagery. The way an experienced rider can calm a skittish horse.' Stepping back from her own revulsion, she realized Caroline was doing her cosmic number again.

'Did you ever read *Middlemarch*?' asked Hannah.

'What's that?'

'An English novel I read at boarding school. Anyhow, this one woman tells another character the most important things she's learned during her lifetime is the need to spread the skirts of light in the world.'

'Spread the skirts of light?'

'Yes.'

'Dessert?' asked the waitress, cocking one hip and resting a hand on it. Her glasses had small gold script letters down the side of one lens that spelled 'BABS.'

'Not for me, thank you,' said Hannah.

Caroline shook her head no. She said nothing for a long time, staring out the window past the plant tendrils to the traffic through the parking lot. Lighting a brown cigarette, Hannah pictured that infant in her jump seat, so anxious not to offend that she wouldn't even bounce. 'Don't shut down,' she said gently. 'I'm not your mother. You can disagree with me all you want.'

Caroline looked at her, startled back into the present. 'I don't see how you can sit there feeling serene with horror going on all around. You have to do what you can.'

'But I do. So do you. We both work very hard. All we can do is our best, which often isn't enough. Besides, young girls are being raped by idiots, but there are also pileated woodpeckers.'

'Who're murdering insects. And waiting to be murdered by cats.'

Hannah could feel Caroline's distress massing like floodwaters behind a dam. 'Look, you're a nurse. Think about the human body – the network of neurons that forms the brain. The meshing of the hormones. The miracle is all around you. Stop insisting on loaves and fishes.'

Caroline rubbed the bridge of her nose. She looked up, eyes clouded with pain. 'That diamond on black velvet stuff. I wish I could believe you.'

'But you shouldn't take my word for it in any case. Just open your eyes. See what you see when you're not set to see horror.'

'You make it sound easy, but I can't.'

'Won't?' suggested Hannah.

The waitress brought the check. Caroline reached for it, but Hannah covered it with her hand.

'I'd like to treat you,' said Caroline.

'I think we'd better split it.'

'But I asked you for the extra time.'

'One of these days you can take me to lunch. But not yet.'

'Why not? What would that mean?'

'That you had to pay for people to spend time with you?'

'But that's the nature of our relationship,' said Caroline, taking out her checkbook. 'It's your profession.'

'I don't have rules for how I conduct my profession, so don't make any for me. And please put your checkbook away. I went to lunch with you because I wanted to.' Hannah realized this was true. She liked sessions with Caroline. Her hunger to understand dragged words from Hannah that were news to her as well. Caroline was a serious person. Unlike David Dickson, who gave Hannah a perfunctory nod as she caught his eye while passing his table. David went round and round, a squirrel on the wheel of his own neuroses. But Caroline was halfway out of her cage.

As Caroline drove back to the office, Hannah tried to recall the phase of her own life that was equivalent to Caroline's. One day she was a suburban housewife and mother of four, preoccupied with her flirtations and the proper placement of Tiffany lamps. The next day the pine cupboard, Nigel, and Mona were gone. Her disillusionment with the chimeras of this world had been brutal and cataclysmic. Caroline's had been more gradual. But the end result was the same.

She remembered the months of numb disbelief, during which every cowlicked teenage boy she glimpsed in the street was Nigel, and every plump ten-year-old girl was Mona. Once she found herself changing the sheets on their beds as though they'd be sleeping in them that night.

Then came the months of fury, in which she searched for someone, anyone, to blame – Arthur, the furnace dealer, the rescue squad, the north wind. Then the months, years maybe, when she turned the blame on herself. Daily she dwelt on the ways she failed Nigel and Mona – the arguments over muddy sneakers, the missed opportunities for kisses and kind words, the motor boat they wanted she refused to buy.

Finally, in self-defense, she forged her way into a space in which seeming disaster wasn't disaster, so there was no need for blame. Apparent loss wasn't real loss. Disasters and losses were illusions, products of limited perception. But there was no way to convey this conviction to someone else.

'Have a pleasant week,' she said to Caroline, getting out of the Subaru.

'You too. And thanks.'

'My pleasure.'

'Yeah, I bet.'

Caroline drove up the hill to Lloyd Harris, thinking about Hannah's saying Caroline could take her to lunch 'one of these days.' It sounded as though Hannah thought they might know each other for a while. Or was that wishful thinking? Probably

Hannah was like the plumber, and would stick around only until the drains cleared. But at least she'd stuck around this long, a miracle considering Caroline's behavior. But of course it was her job. But she didn't have to be so nice about it.

As she walked in the ER door, Brian came up in light blue scrub clothes. 'I've been looking all over for you.'

'Hi. I went to lunch at Dooley's.'

'With whom?'

Unzipping her parka, Caroline looked at him, not sure it was any of his business. 'With a friend.'

'I'd hoped we could run over to my house for lunch.'

'Maybe tomorrow.'

'How about a drink after work?' He took hold of her upper arm.

'I have to get home and cook supper.' Brenda rushed by, looking quizzically at Brian's hand on Caroline's arm.

'One hour, Caroline. I want you to see my house.'

Brian's fieldstone house sat in a forest of birches near Randy Eliot's, with equally handsome houses belonging to electronics executives on both sides and across the road. Inside, plush carpeting on slate floors, a huge stone fireplace and cathedral ceiling, colorful Navaho rugs on white walls, antiques mixed whimsically with Danish modern. The eclectic look Caroline had striven for so valiantly in Jackson's neo-Tudor house. From the furnishings Caroline guessed that she and Irene Stone would have a lot in common. As she and Brian inspected the bedrooms, Caroline couldn't stop herself from assigning one to each of her boys. Diana told her she could stay at the cabin. But who knew when she'd change her mind again? The place felt different now that Diana had claimed it. And the deed and mortgage were in Diana's name, whatever Caroline had invested in time, energy, and money over the last five years. She'd been a fool not to get some agreement in writing. But in the grip of passion, such practicalities didn't occur to her.

Out the sliding glass doors in the living room, Caroline could see a swing set, seats filled with cushions of snow. When they reached the master bedroom, Brian made love to her with finesse and enthusiasm on his king-sized bed. Lying in his arms afterwards, she held a pep rally for her heart. Brian was kind and thoughtful, a good lover, a homeowner. Why couldn't she just fall in love and get on with it?'

As she dressed, she said, 'It's a gorgeous house, Brian. Thanks for showing me.'

'I'd glad you like it,' he replied from the bed. 'Will you come spend a night with me soon?'

'Yes, sure.' If she worked at it, she could fall in love with him. Wasn't that the Protestant ethic? With hard work you could realize your aims? Except she was half Catholic . . .

'So?' asked Diana as Caroline walked into the cabin carrying a flat cardboard box from the Pizza Hut.

'What?' Diana wanted to know why she was late?

'So how's Hannah?'

'Oh.' Caroline smiled, stepping out of her snowmobile boots. 'She's fine.'

'And your anger didn't destroy her?' Diana set plates and napkins on her butcher block table.

'Apparently not. Or even affect her.'

'Does that distress you?'

Taking off her parka, Caroline yelled down the steps for Jackie and Jason. 'I guess it does.'

'Your secret weapon is a fizzle?' Sharon came slinking out of her bedroom in an old raw-silk robe of Diana's, doing her Sophia Loren imitation. She'd recently fallen in love with Jimmy Some-body and had scarcely eaten since, in an attempt to turn baby fat into curves no eighth-grade boy could resist. She spent summers in Ann Arbor with her father and his wife, Lauren. She came home caked with makeup and brainwashed into all the standard female affectations. It took Diana and Caroline the rest of the year to debrief her, at which point it was time for her to return to Ann Arbor.

'Right. If it's so ineffectual, how come I've protected people from it all these years?'

Diana smiled. 'Wouldn't it be nice if that were true of Cruise missiles?'

'Jason shot Amelia again,' said Sharon as she took a slice of pepperoni pizza.

Amelia was a calico cat Jackie found one afternoon walking home from school. He begged Caroline to let him keep the gaunt bedraggled creature. She finally agreed, but insisted they name her Amelia Earhart because she hoped the cat would get lost.

241

'Did not,' said Jason, glaring at Sharon.

'How come she ran into the woods howling?'

'I didn't do it on purpose. I missed the target.'

'Sure,' said Jackie, nodding and grinning, holding a piece of pizza to his mouth with both hands.

'That does it,' said Caroline. 'Those guns go back to your father tomorrow.'

'But *I* didn't shoot Amelia,' said Jackie, letting his pizza fall to his plate.

'Oh God,' said Caroline, Solomon of the dinner table, looking to Diana for help.

'I'm not lending Judy any more clothes,' said Sharon.

'I thought she was your best friend,' said Diana, serving the boys salad.

'Not anymore. She's become a humanitarian this year.'

'What do you mean?' asked Caroline.

'Oh you know, she trick or treats for UNICEF. Stuff like that.'

'What's wrong with that?' asked Diana with a perplexed smile.

'It's boring.'

'And that's why you don't want to lend her clothes?'

'She leaves them in a pile on her floor.'

Diana and Caroline glanced at each other. Sharon's room resembled Dresden after the bombing.

'Besides, I don't like to borrow her clothes. They're cheap.'

'Sharon . . .' Diana frowned.

'It's true, Mom. She buys them at Sears. And her jeans are Wranglers.'

'Sharon, you are such a snob,' said Diana.

'Yeah, Sharon,' said Jackie, trying to stab a radish with his fork.

'All I'm saying is that I don't like cheap clothes, okay?' Sharon tossed her head.

'Lots of people can't afford anything else,' said Caroline, studying Sharon's pouty red mouth and green eyelids.

'I don't want to hear all that starvation shit, okay?' Sharon stood up, swept her robe away from the chair, and stalked down the hall.

Diana and Caroline exchanged long-suffering looks. Once the pizza was devoured, the boys returned to their room for homework, and Diana and Caroline moved to the couch. The phone rang. Sharon raced from her room and grabbed it. 'Oh hi, Jimmy,' she said in a voice an octave higher than usual. She shot them a look of contempt as she carried the phone into the bathroom and slammed the door.

'This is going to be our punishment for being lesbians,' said Diana. 'We're going to have to sit here and watch her be transformed into Raquel Welch. You should see what she has on her wall – a Hunk-of-the-Month calendar.'

'But we've set such a good example.'

'Since when did anyone ever benefit from her parents' example?'

'Starvation shit,' said Caroline. Diana gave a husky laugh.

They sipped their coffee in silence. Arnold was chewing the light cord. Caroline was suffused with a sense of well-being. 'Why do you suppose we can't let our life here together be enough?' she asked, looking down into her coffee. 'Why have we created all these complications?'

Diana reached into the basket by the couch for her knitting. 'Maybe if you're accustomed to strife, you don't know how to accept happiness when it camps out on your doorstep.'

'That sounds like something Hannah would say.'

'Do you have to bring her up now?'

Caroline glanced at her. 'I'm sorry. You're jealous. It's so far-fetched I forgot.'

'It's not far-fetched. I know whom you think about to cheer yourself up, and it's not me.' She was arranging strands of yarn.

Unable to deny it, Caroline asked, 'How do you know that?'

'I can feel it. You'd have to be Darth Vader not to.'

'Hannah is important to me. But so are you.'

'Never mind. I can't stand this. Let's stop it. I just love you. I want to be with you however I can.'

'Me too,' said Caroline, wondering if this was true. She didn't know anymore whom she loved, or if she loved. She wasn't even sure what love was. The comfort of being with Hannah, was that love? The physical passion with the head counselor, was that? What about the sense of safety and security with Brian? Or the tender companionship with Diana? She wouldn't swear to it, but she thought she loved them all. Hannah said rather than dwelling on how everyone had failed her, to focus on what they'd given her. But apparently if you did that, if you put aside the anger and resentment and fear, you risked being swamped by love, whatever it was.

She leaned over and gave Diana a gentle kiss. Putting down her knitting, Diana grabbed her head and turned it into a fierce kiss. 'It's your turn to appear in my bed,' said Diana.

'Is that an invitation?' She'd thought Diana was running this show.

'What does it sound like?'

'I will,' said Caroline.

'How about tonight after the kids are asleep?'

'I can't tonight. I need some time alone.'

Diana's face fell. She lowered her eyes, shrugged, and said, 'Suit yourself.'

Caroline went downstairs, anxious at not doing what Diana wanted, but relieved to discover there were limits to her behavior. That she was unable to go directly from Brian's embrace into Diana's without at least a bath in between.

Sitting down at her loom in the corner of her bedroom, Caroline began weaving on her sunset shawl, which was nearly finished. As her hands and feet searched for their rhythm, she reflected that she and Diana were like Scarlett O'Hara and Rhett Butler. Whenever one moved forward, the other stepped back. Diana appeared to want a reconciliation just as Caroline had decided to make things work with Brian. Would they ever meet in the middle, both stepping forward at once?

As her hands and feet finally settled into their familiar groove, the shuttle flying back and forth, thoughts of Diana and Brian and everything else faded.

After putting the boys to bed, Caroline went to bed herself. As she fell asleep, she reflected that Hannah wanted to lunch with her, Brian wanted to live with her, Diana wanted to love her, good-looking strangers in saunas lusted after her. Maybe she wasn't as repulsive as she thought?

She dreamed of wandering lost along a jungle path. A putrid swamp teeming with poisonous snakes and leeches stretched out on all sides. Vines hung from tangled trees, matted foliage blotting out the sun. She walked slowly and fearfully, glancing from side to side, expecting to see a pile of bloated corpses presided over by Jim Jones. As she looked into the dark twisted undergrowth, the scene suddenly trembled. It wavered in and out of focus like a telescope gone haywire. As she watched, everything became sharp and clear. Hundreds of brilliantly colored tropical birds sat in the trees. The tangled vines became snakes of citron, orange, and scarlet, with silly faces like the caterpillar in *Alice in Wonderland*. The forest floor was carpeted with garish flowers. Caroline gasped in amazement.

She jerked awake and lay still, a smile on her face, not moving for fear of dispelling the warm grateful feeling in her heart.

Part Three

One

Dressed in her down bathrobe, Caroline let Brian in the cabin door.

'I'm afraid I'm not ready, Brian. We've had a crisis. My ex-husband gave the boys BB guns, and Jason has been shooting everything in sight. This afternoon I found a dead robin in the yard.'

'That's what little boys are like.'

'Not my little boys.'

Jason sat on the couch staring sullenly at the TV, arms folded across his rugby-shirted chest.

'Jason, can you say hello to Brian?'

Jason gave Brian a surly nod.

'Sorry to leave you alone with Mr Congeniality,' Caroline said to Brian, going into her bedroom to change. She was raising a young murderer. It was all her fault. She'd deprived him of a father. She'd moved him from house to house. She'd had affairs with women. She was about to spend the night with a man she wasn't married to. No wonder Jason was tormenting small creatures. But what else could she have done? Would he prefer a mother dead by her own hand? There were some situations to which there were simply no solutions.

As she walked into the living room in jeans and a silk shirt, she discovered Brian on the sofa next to Jason, fanning open a deck of cards. 'Pick a card, any card,' Brian was saying like a carnival barker. Jason took one.

'All right, young man, now look at it.'

Cupping the card in one hand, Jason glanced at it.

'Okay, now show it to me.'

Jason did so, fighting a small smile.

'Yup, that's the one,' said Brian.

Jason giggled. Caroline kissed him good-bye, then went into

Jackie's room, kissed him and smoothed his dark hair. He didn't look up from his science fiction novel. He was annoyed with her too, but his way of expressing it was her old trick of fake indifference. Upstairs Diana was also pissed off. It was Diana's week to tend the kids, but when Caroline phoned to say she'd be out all night, Diana reacted to Brian's name like a mongoose to a viper. Caroline knew Diana cared for her, but Caroline had to get on with her own life. She couldn't continue to wait around for Diana to tire of Suzanne, because maybe she wouldn't.

As she and Brian walked out, she heard Jason saying to Jackie, 'Pick a card, any card.'

'That was funny,' she said as Brian held open the Pontiac door. 'My kids always used to play that trick on visitors.'

'Jackie and Jason are pissed off at me, as you could probably tell,' she said as Brian started the car.

'They don't want another man in your life?'

'You got it.' Actually they wanted a father, they just didn't want her to have a lover.

Walking into Brian's stone house, Caroline was struck by the silence. In contrast to the cabin, which was usually crammed with battling children, yowling pets, blaring TVs and stereos, endless phone conversations. Waves of emotion were constantly swelling and breaking against the cabin walls. She looked at Brian, who stood holding cardboard containers of Chinese food they'd picked up in town, looking uncertain what to do next. Caroline almost reached out to take the containers and assemble utensils, plates, beverages. But it's his house, she reminded herself.

'Uh, let me take your coat,' he finally said, reaching out. Realizing he held the containers, he searched for some place to set them. He hung up her parka, then led her into the kitchen, where he looked around as though he'd never seen the place. Opening a drawer, he pulled out two forks.

Handing her a container and taking one himself, he said, 'We can each eat half and then swap.'

Automatically, Caroline took the containers from him and said with a short laugh, 'Honestly, Brian, you're hopeless. Where are the plates?'

He pointed sheepishly.

'Do you have any beer?' He nodded. 'Okay, you pour the beer while I set the table.'

She walked across the slate floor into the shadowy dining area, which opened onto the living room. Floor-to-ceiling windows gazed out at the night like blind eyes. Hurriedly she pulled the heavy gold corduroy drapes. Then she turned the dimmer switch until the brass chandelier gave off a warm glow. Opening a drawer in the mahogany breakfront, she was pleased to find some of her own woven place mats from Cheever's. And plaid cloth napkins, undoubtedly chosen by Irene. She had good taste, in accessories as well as in men. There were also candles of many colors. Irene left Brian well equipped. Caroline took a silver candelabra off a shelf, filled it with ivory candles, and lit them.

Walking around the living room, Caroline turned on three lamps. Wood was laid in the huge stone fireplace. She opened the damper and lit the wood, and it flared up as though long awaiting a chance to burn. Kneeling by the stereo, she picked out some Roberta Flack records.

Brian wandered in carrying two bottles of Miller Lite. He looked around the living room. 'Gosh, it looks nice in here. What'd you do?'

She glanced at him. 'Pulled the curtains and turned on some lights.' It did look nice. For the time being, she'd dispersed the ghosts lurking in the shadows.

As they ate moo goo gai pan from Royal Doulton plates and drank Miller Lite from Waterford goblets, Caroline asked Brian about his day. He described removing a lung from a construction worker who'd fallen off a roof beam onto an upright pipe. 'He was lucky to be alive,' said Brian. 'A few inches higher and it would have pierced his heart.'

'Like a vampire, huh?' Brian was looking at her, expecting something. But what? She couldn't remember how to behave with a man. She'd never spent time with men in recent years if she could avoid it. She felt his sad dark eyes fixed on her face, waiting, even though she was busy prodding snow peas with her Gorham Fairfax fork. What did he want from her?

Then she remembered: admiration. He wanted to see himself reflected larger than life in her eyes. That she could provide. She glanced at his delicate hands as he handled his fork. Those hands saved lives, stanched hemorrhages, made incisions, tied stitches. She was filled with admiration. She siphoned some off for him:

'My God, that must have been terrifying, removing the pipe with the heart right there, beating away.'

'Not really,' he said, his ego engorging.

'Well, Brian, you have more finesse and more sang-froid than any other doctor I've ever worked with,' she said, using up her entire French vocabulary in one sentence.

He tried not to smile. His eyes caressed hers with gratitude. 'And what did you do today?'

'Housework mostly. How do you keep this place so neat?' There was a distinct absence of the clutter that threatened to engulf the cabin – candy wrappers, comic books, moldy sweat shirts, crusted dishes.

'A woman comes in two days a week. I keep thinking I should sell this place and move into a condominium at the tannery or something. But at first I thought Irene might change her mind.'

'You've decided she's not coming back?'

'Right. And recently I haven't even wanted her to.' He gave Caroline a meaningful look.

Caroline looked into her beer. The wavering candlelight on the crystal made shifting patterns on the place mat. Roberta Flack was singing, 'The First Time Ever I Saw Your Face.' She realized the first time ever she saw Brian's face, he was wearing a surgical mask, and was removing the broken stem of a wine glass from a woman's abdomen, where her husband had shoved it. She looked up and across the candlelight into his sad dark eyes. He'd been so sweet to Jason. Maybe it would work.

'Let's sit by the fire,' she said.

As she settled into the comfortable corduroy couch, he went to the fireplace and closed the glass doors. As she watched the flames dance behind the wall of glass, a fine chill crept over her. Shaking it off, she poured another beer, and tucked her feet under her.

'Why did Irene leave? She must have been a real fool.' It was all coming back now, the back-scratching that got you asked out on a second date.

'Irene? To tell you the truth, I don't know. It was a total shock. I still don't understand it. She just loaded the kids in the Country Squire and drove to Boston. She hasn't been back since. She used to complain that I never listened to her. But that wasn't true. The minute I'd walk in the door, she'd start talking – about the kids' report cards, the sale on snow tires, the cracks in the bathroom ceiling, the price of avocados. God knows what. Sure, sometimes I'd be thinking about the thyroidectomy I'd just done or wondering what the Dow was doing. But mostly I just listened. Maybe I'd rather have been in the shower or watching the news. But instead I listened. I think I'm a pretty good listener.'

He was looking at Caroline expectantly. He wanted something from her again, but she couldn't say what. 'I agree,' she finally replied.

She told herself to pay attention and flog some romance from her heart. Brian was a lovely man. She could make this relationship work and guarantee herself a lifetime of companionship, security, and Waterford crystal. And she was tired of living hand-to-mouth sexually, never knowing where her next feel was coming from.

As Roberta Flack sang 'Killing Me Softly,' she unknotted Brian's wool tie, then unbuttoned his tattersall shirt. He smiled. She ran her tongue around his ear. By the time she unbuckled his belt and unzipped his zipper, his smile had become more like a grimace. But he did have an erection, which she encouraged with her mouth.

As she removed her underpants, he tried to sit up. 'You're not supposed to move,' she whispered, kneeling over him and settling down on his penis. Slowly she moved up and down. He gave an embarrassed laugh. She could feel him going soft.

'You'll have to excuse me a minute,' he said, rolling out from under like a quarterback from under a rival tackler. She sank into the corner of the couch, chin on her knees, arms around her legs. Evidently he didn't like his women butch. With Diana sometimes one of them ran the show, sometimes the other, sometimes both. She never knew what would go on. But if predictability was what she was looking for, apparently she'd come to the right place.

Brian made a great display of running water and flushing the toilet. Upon his return, he took her hand and led her into his bedroom. In his king-sized bed he lay on top of her saying, 'Let's do it this way until we get used to each other.'

'Whatever you like, Brian,' she said, absorbing his thrusts like cracked pavement a jackhammer.

Stop it, she snapped at herself. This wasn't sex with a woman, but it had its own thrills, such as the anxiety that Brian would lose his erection before she'd come.

Just stop it! she ordered herself. Brian is a sweet man and a sensitive lover. Stop being such a jerk.

She awoke much later, Brian stirring by her side. He rolled over and took her nipple in his mouth. Cradling him in her arms, she rocked him and stroked his hair. Waves of desire washed over her. This man who saved lives needed her. He'd come home after a hard day of heroism, and she'd restore him to life and to warmth. Choices, Hannah kept saying, and Caroline was now choosing respectable heterosexuality just like Hannah's. Maybe if she became half of a heterosexual couple again, Hannah would want to stay friends with her after therapy. She and Brian, Hannah and Arthur could play bridge on a winter evening. They could go on trips together in a motor home. While the guys were out golfing, the girls could take long naps. In the same bed . . .

Resolutely she focused on Brian at her breast, who was sighing with contentment. He held her breast to his mouth with both hands. Nearly swooning with desire, Caroline reached out to his chest, searching with her hand for a smooth round breast. As it settled into a bleak expanse of coarse hair, her desire dispersed. Tears squeezed out from under her eyelids. With Diana, once one finished doing this, the other took her turn. She sniffled, then shook with a sob. Brian gave no sign of noticing or of stopping. She looked down at him, mouth attached to her breast, sucking her dry. Irritation seized her. Her limbs twitched. Still he sucked on. Eventually his mouth fell open, and her nipple slipped out. Like an infant, he had sated himself and was now sound asleep.

Caroline rolled out of bed, went into the bathroom, and washed her face. Fuck it, she'd raised her brothers and her sons, she didn't want a manchild, however rich, charming, and good-looking. Looking into the mirror, she saw an attractive woman with a graying Afro, puffy red eyes, and a perplexed frown. *Mom, do you have to be a lezzie?*

She put on a large terry cloth robe that hung on the bathroom door, and wandered through the silent house, the moon through the birch trees casting shadows on the slate floor, which was icy to her bare feet. Bobby Orr posters on the walls in one deserted bedroom. *Star Wars* posters in another. A beautiful gold and brown Navaho rug hung above the fireplace, another example of Irene's good taste. From the objects Irene surrounded herself with, Caroline felt sure she'd like her. Probably more than Brian.

Caroline stood on the slate floor by the fireplace studying the rug above her head and wondering if she could weave something like it. She'd taken both the sunset shawl and the blue and gray one to Cheever's in the mall. The buyer had been enthusiastic and urged her to weave more shawls, so she started a third in green and blue tones – spring on Lake Glass. But the temptation was strong to keep trying new forms, now that she'd been liberated from place mats.

One thing about Brian's house was now clear to her: He cohabited with ghosts. If they joined forces, he'd provide the cave, and she'd provide the firelight to keep the ghosts at bay. He'd protect, and she'd pretend to be protected, and all would be well. But was bridge with Hannah and Arthur worth it?

Going into the kitchen, she switched on the light and searched the shelves for coffee. Other than a small jar of Nescafé, all she found was a battered box of Tuna Helper. She opened the refrigerator. No milk, only a single orange growing mold. Maybe it was an experiment on home-grown antibiotics. She carried her mug into the living room and sat on the corduroy couch. There were still coals from the fire. She opened the glass doors and added some kindling and a couple of small logs. Leaving the doors open, she sat back down and rubbed her eyes, yawning.

She glanced around the dark room. It had been easy to fill it with light and warmth tonight. Why *not* have that as her job? She was good at it. When distraught families clustered around the ER waiting room, she could soothe and cheer them simply by her manner – by projecting at them like a lawn sprinkler her own confidence. In a patient's room her competent caring presence could elicit smiles from haggard faces. Why not do this for Brian too? It was no credit to her. It was her primordial heritage as a female to create and sustain life. In contrast to males, who dealt in death and darkness, creating disasters and then cooperating in extraordinary feats of heroism to extract people from the destruction . . .

Stop it, she told herself. Focus on the positive, as Hannah had taught her. She pictured Jackie and Jason, each in his own bedroom down the hall, a nursery for the baby daughter she and Brian would have. The cleaning lady twice a week. Brian would come home from saving lives, and she'd serve piña coladas by the swimming pool she'd have built next to the swing seat. She'd learn to cook boeuf en daube for dinner parties with Peugeot dealers. Learn to prune hybrid roses. Read Silhouette Romances all afternoon with a box of Godiva chocolates by her side. Perfect her backhand. Attend medical conferences on cruise ships to Guadeloupe. Dance in a sun dress on the deck under Caribbean stars with native drums throbbing on the shore. Brian would fox-trot her into their first-class stateroom, sweep her into his arms, place her on the bed . . .

She pictured him nursing at her breast, oblivious to her, and was swept with irritation. Brian was attentive now, but once he had her safely installed in his house, he'd work all hours, coming home exhausted and needing succor, if he came home at all. She'd done this tired old trip twice already, with Jackson and David Michael. Her life was merely a poor imitation of 'General Hospital,' a new doctor being written into the script every few years. She was about to do it again, and in less time than it takes to say 'cadaver,' she'd be alone and lonely in an echoing house and an empty bed.

She pictured Hannah raising her eyebrows. *Why would you? What did you grow up with?* And it fell into place. She remembered her father returning exhausted from the office, and herself scurrying around running his bath, shining his shoes, rubbing his temples. But when she needed his attendance at her Brownie Flying Up ceremony, he was posting bail for the underprivileged youth of South Boston. When she needed his presence during her infancy, he was in the South Pacific making the world safe for democracy.

There can be more to us than that. Once you knew you were a gerbil on a wheel, you could refuse to run, or climb down. She'd tell Brian in the morning it wouldn't work.

She began crying, her shoulders shaking and heaving. She'd been entertaining higher hopes for this relationship than she'd known. To give up a present illusion to avoid future pain possibly required more strength of character than she possessed. She lay among the sofa cushions and wept, mourning the unwelcome loss of her comfortable neurosis.

Then she realized Brian wasn't her father. He wasn't Jackson, or David Michael. Maybe it could be different with him now that she was aware of the pitfalls. Whatever, she'd have to decide soon because her hormones were revving up. Soon she'd be sucking his cock and begging to bear his babies. If that wasn't what she wanted, she had to act fast.

When she awoke, shivering among the cushions, it was light outside. A wind was blowing through the birch trees, and the ice-filled swing seats swayed in the yard. She went into the bathroom, washed her tear-stained face, and combed her tousled Afro. Sorting out her jeans and wrinkled silk shirt from the pile beside the sofa, she put them on. Then she made another cup of coffee and sat at the dining table awaiting Brian, uncertain what to do.

'Where'd you go?' he asked when he eventually emerged, in a singlet and boxer shorts with hearts on them.

'I couldn't sleep so I got up.'

'I missed you.' He kissed her neck.

Liar, she thought. You didn't even notice I was gone until you woke up with a hard-on.

'Come back to bed.' He kneaded her shoulders.

'I have to go home,' she heard herself say.

'I thought we had all day.'

'Afraid not.' They could have had all day since Diana was tending the boys, but she'd just discovered she wasn't spending it with Brian. Surely he was picking up that she was upset? Diana could read her mood from a single sentence over the phone.

He got himself some coffee and sat down. 'I don't know how to say this, Caroline . . .'

Oh good, she thought. He's going to call it off so I don't have to. A gentleman to the end.

'. . . but we're so good together.'

She looked at him.

'Look, I know we're both lonely, and looking for someone to share our lives with. We both want someone who's kind and considerate, sensitive, gentle, generous. Someone who can listen. Someone to laugh with. We both want someone who can make the sparks fly in bed and the wheels turn out of bed . . .' He became embarrassed by his fervor. 'Well, you know what I'm saying, Caroline. What do you think?'

She studied his kind face, begging her mouth not to say the words she heard it emitting: 'You're right, Brian: We both want women.'

His lips pressed together tightly. Caroline was filled with remorse. 'Brian, you're a lovely man. I'm very fond of you. And

I've tried. I swear to you I've genuinely tried to make this work. But I guess I'm just a hopeless lesbian. Please forgive me for hurting you. If I could choose, I'd choose to be with you in a minute.'

She could see tears gathering in his eyes. 'But I don't understand, Caroline. We're so good together. And here's this house, ready for you to move in. I'd be a good father to your boys.'

'I know you would, Brian. And I appreciate that more than I can say.'

'What's the problem then?'

She was at a loss for words. 'It's just not me, Brian.' She was beginning to have some idea who 'me' was.

Caroline could see he was getting annoyed. Maybe self-denigrating humor would help. 'I'm a pervert, Brian. Respectability suffocates perverts. It's like putting a lobster in fresh water.'

He shook his head, dazed. 'Well, you were candid from the start, Caroline. I have to say that for you.'

Caroline looked him in the eye, feeling increasingly certain this was the right thing to do. 'Thank you for letting me try, Brian. And I did try. Harder than you might imagine.'

He shook his head again. 'I never knew a woman who'd turn her back on all this so easily.' He gestured vaguely around his house.

'Who said it was easy?'

As Brian dressed to drive her home, Caroline sat with her elbows on the table, head in her hands, feeling terror and loss so acutely that she realized it had very little to do with Brian, whom she scarcely knew. To dispel it, she summoned the image of Hannah. But when it arrived, the head was turned away, no longer looking at her, no longer telling her she was a fine person. She was picking a different course from Hannah's. No bridge, no motor homes, no Caribbean cruises. Hannah would kick her out.

Her hand trembled as she raised her mug to her lips. Resolutely she dismissed Hannah and thought instead about a jungle full of garish birds and gorgeous flowers. Brian, his face a mask, walked out of his bedroom with his car keys, a padre escorting a death row inmate down that long last corridor.

Caroline strode into Hannah's office, glancing around to make sure the furniture hadn't been rearranged. Hannah, holding a mug of coffee, looked up from her chair. 'My, but you look purposeful today.'

'Do I?' Caroline perched on the couch in her white uniform. 'I guess I am. I've been making decisions left and right.'

'Oh yes? Like what?' Hannah sipped her coffee.

'Like that I want a new job. I'm sick of the emergency room.'

'Oh yes?' said Hannah with sudden interest. She set her mug on the desk and swiveled around to face Caroline. 'What kind of job?'

'Still in nursing. But a different specialty. I don't know what. I just decided today.' She'd been standing by the operating table assisting as a knife wound was sutured, neatly tucking yellow fat globules under jagged flaps of skin, when it suddenly occurred to her: I don't have to be here.

'Want some coffee?' asked Hannah.

'No, thanks. Caffeine would probably send me right over the top.'

'So what else have you been deciding?'

Caroline studied Hannah, suddenly afraid. 'I broke things off with Brian Stone this weekend.'

'Oh yes? How come?'

'Well,' she said, studying her hands, 'I guess I realized Mr Right was Mr Wrong.' She'd just bumped into Brian in the hall outside the lab at the hospital. He'd been aloof and efficient. She hoped once he got over hating her, some of the initial friendship would be left. She'd be happy to resume hearing tales of woe about Irene. But she wasn't holding her breath. Meanwhile, it was like Chinese water torture knowing someone wanted something from her that she had to deny.

'What was wrong about him?'

Hannah didn't look or sound particularly disappointed. In fact she was the picture of indifference, sitting there glancing out the window to Caroline's old view of Lake Glass. Did she really not care that Caroline was abnormal? 'It occurred to me in the middle of the night that he's very similar to Jackson and David Michael and my father, and that life with him would probably be just a rerun. I felt like Cinderella's stepsister trying to wedge her foot into the glass slipper.'

Hannah smiled and stopped herself from applauding. It actually worked sometimes, what she spent her days doing. Then she reminded herself not to get carried away. Caroline would probably backslide. What people said and what they were able to carry out were usually two different matters. 'What do you think it would have been like, this life you've decided not to live?'

'Alone and lonely. Taking care of him when he needed it, but not receiving the same from him.'

'You've had a lot of practice at that.'

Caroline nodded.

Hannah looked at her kindly. 'That must be painful to see.'

Caroline nodded again. Then she looked up. 'For a while I thought maybe it could be different with Brian if I was aware of the pattern.'

This came out sounding to Hannah like a question. 'It's possible, but some people just have to stay away from their poison, like an alcoholic from liquor.'

Caroline was dazed. Hannah was not only not critical, she looked pleased. Her face had softened. She was even implying that Brian was 'poison' for her.

'Are you aware,' asked Hannah, 'that you've just made a choice? That you're shaping your life, and not just letting it happen?'

'Yes.'

'And are you aware that you've been doing that all along? Even though you didn't know it?'

Caroline nodded, looking doubtful.

They sat in silence, Caroline idly studying the mimi spirit on the wall by the desk. She'd actually started to like the hideous little creature with its hollow Orphan Annie eyes. It had begun to look friendly and lively, instead of weird and threatening.

Hannah was looking outside to a row of icicles that hung like translucent fangs from the window frame. They dripped in the heat of the sun. For the first time Hannah could recall, Caroline wasn't displacing her inner sense of abandonment onto other people and the world at large. She was leaving Brian, and acknowledging it as her move, rather than his fault.

'I didn't think your heart was in that relationship,' said Hannah.

'You didn't? Why not?'

'Something about the way you talked about him. Calling him Mr Right, for one thing. You always sounded faintly ironic.'

'I thought I was trying to make it work. But maybe I knew it wouldn't.'

'Why did you want it to? You've insisted all along you're a lesbian.'

Caroline looked at Hannah. 'I guess I wanted it to work because I wanted to be like you.'

Hannah smiled faintly, remembering wanting to be Jewish so she could be more like Maggie. 'What stopped you?'

'Being me.'

Hannah studied her, then nodded. Caroline grew up with parents bound together like prisoners on a chain gang. No wonder she felt contempt for all that. Whereas Hannah, her mother dead, her father departed, longed for it as a child and clung to it now.

'Maybe I'd like to be normal and respectable like you,' said Caroline, 'but I'm not. So fuck it.'

Hannah smiled.

'What's so funny?'

'I don't know if I can explain,' said Hannah. 'It's just that I'm not sure we're as unalike as you think. I had an appointment with a friend of yours the other day,' she added, to change the subject. Because Caroline needed to believe in their differences for the moment, honing her sense of who she was by contrasting herself to other people. She pictured Caroline's friend Jenny with her one dangling silver earring, a raised fist inside a woman's symbol. Jenny sat on the couch in a belligerent posture, her legs planted firmly apart. 'So do you think you can handle me?' Jenny demanded at the end of the hour. 'Well, I'm not afraid of you, if that's what you mean,' Hannah replied, watching as Jenny's eyes suddenly filled with tears.

'I know. Jenny told me.'

'She said you suggested she see me?'

'Yes.' Jenny was heartbroken over yet another true love who'd returned to her husband, and had spent an evening weeping in Caroline's arms, her tears causing Caroline's new red chamois shirt to run all over her T-shirt underneath. Expert that she'd recently become on the human heart, Caroline knew Jenny needed to face her inability to steal Mommy from Daddy, and Hannah would help her do that.

'Well, please don't refer anyone else.' Now Caroline was going to start trying to take care of her professionally.

'Why not?'

'Why do you think not?'

Caroline frowned. 'I don't know. I thought you'd be pleased.' Whatever reaction Caroline assumed Hannah would have, she usually had the opposite.

'I have all the clients I can handle.'

'Well, I'm sorry to burden you with another.'

'Don't be miffed,' said Hannah. 'Think about what you're setting up.' She'd done the same thing to Maggie – referred friends to her, then resented Maggie's involvement with them. Just like her children, who begged for baby brothers and sisters, then loathed them when they arrived. Just like herself, feeling stabs of jealousy watching Arthur cradle their new babies and gaze besottedly into their eyes.

Caroline didn't see why Hannah had to turn everything into some Byzantine plot. Some things were as they seemed and nothing more. She imagined what living with her would be like: 'Arthur, you may think this is pot roast, but ask yourself what else might be under that gravy.'

'What's so funny?' asked Hannah.

'You are. I just don't believe everything has all this hidden significance.'

Hannah smiled, glad Caroline could challenge her pleasantly now, tease her even. 'But don't forget how many times I've been through this with other people, Caroline.'

Caroline felt a stab of jealousy. 'Okay. So tell me what I'm setting up.'

'It registers better if you figure it out yourself. But I can tell by the set to your jaw that you're stubborn today.' She watched Caroline nod in agreement, while mouthing disclaimers. 'If you send me clients, you could see me as replacing you with them. As your mother did you with the younger children. As Arlene did you with what's-her-name. As Diana has you with Suzanne.'

Caroline was looking baffled. 'I thought it was a compliment that I'd send my friends to you.'

'It is. But after you're finished, then send people. Not now.'

'I don't understand.'

'I think you're trying to send me a replacement so you can feel rejected. And I don't believe you really want to be replaced because I know I'm very important to you.'

Caroline blushed, her eyes meeting Hannah's. She felt a deep longing for her, in any form she could have her. Therapy, lunch, bridge, bed, anything. She dropped her eyes and said almost in a whisper, 'Yes, you are.'

They sat in silence as Hannah studied the dripping icicles and thought about golf balls. She used to find stray ones among the blackberry bushes on Hampstead Heath. She'd slit open and peel off the tough outer cover to reveal the tangle of cord beneath. Which she'd unravel carefully to expose the small round core, whose smooth surface was scarred like a fossil from the protective cord. Working with a client was similar. You had to penetrate the protective shell, which concealed a maze of vulnerabilities often opposite to what outward appearances would suggest. The bull dykes who arrived on motorcycles and swaggered into the office in full leathers turned out to be frightened little girls. And the Total Women were often as cold and sharp underneath as those icicles out the window.

But once the core lay bare, as Caroline's did right now, Hannah felt awe, and a twinge of fear. You tapped gently for signs of life, aware anything too sudden or forceful could unleash a new landslide that might bury forever anyone still alive in there.

Hannah looked at the photo on the wall over the bookcase, done by an ex-client who was an aerial photographer. At first glance it looked like what it was – patches of snow on a plowed field. But a shift of vision converted the portions of dark field into the silhouette of a veiled woman's head. Her client, convinced it was the Virgin Mary, experienced a conversion, terminated therapy, and went into the priesthood. Hannah was skeptical about the Virgin Mary bit, but was a true believer in the shift of vision. But this shift would probably frighten Caroline even more than all her dependency, anger, and sexuality. And she did in fact look terrified by what she'd just said as she studied her fingernails and tried to appear blasé.

Caroline was thinking about how important Hannah *had* become to her. She'd split with Brian. Who knew what Diana was up to? Hannah had become the focus for her emotional life. She thought about her in the night to quell her terrors. She planned her week around these sessions, thinking over what got said at the previous ones and storing up observations for the next. When she drove to the hospital past Hannah's office, she noticed whether her light was on. When it was, the world felt like a safer place. Here she'd acknowledged Hannah's importance. And her belief since Pink Blanky and Marsha was that once the gods knew what was important to you, they were obliged to take it away, for reasons understood only by themselves. *I know what you want and you can't have it.* Caroline had failed to play it cool. One way or another, Hannah would vanish. Rubbing the bridge of her nose with her fingertips, she felt sweat drench her armpits and stain her white uniform.

'What are you thinking?' asked Hannah gently, watching sweat stains appear under Caroline's armpits. Wasn't Caroline too young for hot flashes?

To explain, Caroline knew, would only make matters worse. You tried not to draw attention to anything you wished to preserve. Even if it was already too late. 'I was just thinking that you're right about Jenny,' she replied in a shaky voice. 'She told me on the phone what a good session she'd had with you. And I said, "Well, just remember she likes me best." '

Hannah laughed. What a charmer Caroline was. 'You're right. I do,' she heard herself say.

'You do?'

Hannah nodded, faintly alarmed by her unprofessional response.

Caroline studied her. How could Hannah like her after all the crap Caroline had laid on her? Probably this remark was another therapeutic technique. Hannah was always pointing out that she was only doing her job. 'What's that photo you were just looking at?'

Hannah glanced at it. 'It's a plowed field covered with snow, viewed from an airplane. But if you look at it a certain way, there's the silhouette of a woman in profile. The man who did it thinks it's the Virgin Mary.'

Caroline smiled. 'I can't see her.'

'Make the white the background.'

Caroline widened, then narrowed her eyes. 'No good.'

'Keep trying. You'll get it.'

As Caroline drove down the lake road through the afternoon sunshine, she could see a large stretch of open water in the middle of the lake, bordered by jagged chunks of softening ice. The ice fishing shanties and the intrepid autos were no longer in evidence.

The dirt road up to the cabin was soggy and deeply rutted. She and Diana had recently switched from complaining about ice on the road to complaining about mud. Before long, they'd be complaining about the dust that sifted through cracks in the cabin in summer to coat the furniture. Soon snow tires, parkas, and storm windows would come off. Doors and windows would be thrown open. The sun would beat down. The children would lie in the grass and identify shapes in the clouds. She decided summer was her favorite season.

But what about autumn – the sky over the lake as deep blue as Hannah's eyes, the air crisp as a bite from a chilled McIntosh apple? To say nothing of the scarlet maples in the woods beside the cabin. The whole point was the juxtaposition, she concluded. Summer was heavenly because it followed mud season. But if you had scorching sun all the time, the vegetation would burn out and you'd sit in the shade dreaming of snow. Each season was perfect in its own way, and in relation to all the others. The point was to know that, rather than to complain about mud in spring, dust in summer, and ice in winter.

Jesus, she was turning into as much of a Pollyanna as Hannah. She smiled.

The smile faded. She'd just admitted to Hannah that she was important to her. Hannah at this very moment was probably feeling burdened. She'd get rid of Caroline in some polite fashion. Caroline felt an overzealous Boy Scout begin to tie sheep shanks with her intestines.

For God's sake, she told herself, wait until next week and see what she does. Don't assume catastrophe before it happens. Meanwhile, she was determined to enjoy this fucking spring. She focused on her dream of tropical birds and felt the knots in her stomach loosen. Anything could happen to Hannah. She could move away, die, go into real estate. She probably would now that Caroline had made her confession. But nobody could take those birds away. Even the pileated woodpecker showed up only when he felt like it. But she could picture the jungle scene any time she liked simply by closing her eyes. And with it came a feeling of warm gratitude – toward what she had no idea – that canceled out the fear and anxiety.

As she waded through the mud to her door, she looked up and saw Amelia perched on the railing to Diana's entrance, balancing on a few square inches of wood. Caroline stood still, boots sinking into the mud, gazing at the cat. Amelia turned her head, met Caroline's gaze, and slowly blinked her yellow-green eyes. Her mouth looked as though it were smiling. Caroline was struck by her gratuitous beauty. Why did such a silly, friendly, aloof, graceful creature exist at all, with her totally unnecessary patches of tan, black, and white? *Open your eyes and see what you see when you're not set to see horror.* Amelia was a miracle. Tears formed in Caroline's eyes.

Amelia stiffened, head snapping to attention. She pushed off from her perch, leaping in an arc of astonishing grace to pursue a small chipmunk that scurried across the yard.

'Amelia, stop it, damn it!' yelled Caroline, robbed of Hannah's vision and plunged into her own. If she'd had Jason's gun, she'd have shot the damn cat herself. She packed some soggy snow into an icy ball and heaved it at Amelia. It landed with a plop in the patch of snow beside the cat, who leapt sideways, back arching and hair standing on end.

Caroline's apartment was silent. Arnold lay snoozing in a patch of sunlight on the hooked rug, flop of a watchdog that he was. The boys and Sharon were at friends' houses. Leaving her muddy boots by the door, she took a Michelob from the refrigerator and collapsed in the plaid armchair by the phone. Taking a long gulp of beer, she felt her spirits descend like an express elevator. Maybe the miracle was all around, but so was the horror. Which was real, she wondered, the graceful insouciance of Amelia on the railing, or the terror in the chipmunk's eyes as it caught sight of that great feline hulk? The air took on heaviness as Caroline tried to breathe, and she felt her shoulders begin to tighten.

As she tossed down the rest of the beer and set the can on the telephone table, she heard Diana moving around upstairs. *Each of us is author of her own moods.* If she wanted to sit down here being depressed over the rapacious personality of her cat, that was her choice, she reminded herself. There were other options, such as accepting Diana's invitation from the other night. Suddenly inspired, she jumped up, raced into her bedroom, and removed her white dress, damp with sweat from the therapy session. She also took off her stockings, garter belt, and underpants, leaving on only her lacy Victorian camisole, which Diana loved. Putting on her down bathrobe, she went upstairs.

'Hi, babe,' said Diana from the couch as she looked out at the melting ice on Lake Glass and knitted on Suzanne's Icelandic sweater. An empty wine glass sat on the shag carpet beside her. 'Have a seat. What are you up to?' She eyed Caroline's bathrobe.

'I'm on my way to your bed. Like to join me?'

Diana smiled, not looking up for a moment. 'Does a hog like to root in swill?' She put down her knitting and stood up, stretching languorously, red hair glowing in the sun like embers.

'God, you're a gorgeous creature,' murmured Caroline, touching Diana's familiar face with her fingertips.

'You're not so bad yourself.' Diana reached out to undo the belt on Caroline's robe. 'Oh my goodness,' she said as the robe fell open to reveal the camisole. Her green eyes narrowed with lust. 'You look good enough to eat.'

'Be my guest.'

Diana's body, so different from Brian's, so similar to her own. Caroline supposed lesbianism was the ultimate in narcissism. She knew what Diana was feeling as she touched her, could feel it in herself, to such an extent that eventually she no longer knew who was doing what to whom. If this was narcissism, so be it. What could be wrong with a little self-love?

Afterwards, as they lay in each other's arms in the sunlight on the shag carpet, the two Eves in Eden smiling down from Caroline's tapestry on the wall, Diana asked in an exhausted voice, 'What do we do when the kids burst through the door?'

'I tell them I love you very much, and hope they're as lucky when they grow up.' Caroline brushed some stray strands of hair off Diana's forehead and kissed one of her closed eyes.

'I see. And then you give them gift certificates for visits to Hannah Burke?'

'Correct.' Caroline wasn't sure she'd ever been this happy. She felt as though she'd returned home after a long stay in foreign lands. Everything seemed suddenly simple. You just walked away from the painful complications you'd concocted, like a hermit crab from an outgrown shell. Brian was out of the picture. Diana would finally finish Suzanne's sweater and get rid of her. The kids would soon be gone, and she and Diana would live out their twilight years in each other's arms and between each other's legs.

'Could I ask a favor?' said Diana.

'Sure. What?' Just then if Diana had wanted Lake Glass siphoned into a thimble, Caroline would have done her best.

'Would you mind not sleeping with that man in this house?'

Caroline felt her heart contract into a tight fist. 'Bad timing, baby.'

'Bad timing or not, it's important to me.'

'Diana, why bring up all that outside junk when right now is perfect between us.'

'*Because* it's perfect between us. I can't bear knowing you're down there doing what we just did with him.'

'If you sleep with Suzanne here, why shouldn't I sleep with Brian?' Why not just tell her it was over with Brian? But a principle was at stake. Besides, if Diana knew Caroline had no one but herself, she'd feel burdened and would withdraw. *I know what you want and you can't have it.* How in the world had this seemed simple a moment ago?

'Because he's a man. If he were a woman, I wouldn't mind. I'd cheer you on.'

'Like hell you would.'

'I would. But I can't bear to have you with a man under my very nose. You'd feel the same if I were doing it.'

'I've paid half the mortgage on this place for five years, and I'll do as I please here.'

'All right, go ahead,' said Diana, standing up and gathering together her tangled clothing. 'But don't be surprised if one day you wake up to find me gone.'

Caroline grabbed her Victorian camisole, ripped it in two, and hurled the pieces at Diana. 'You've been gone for several months already. I wouldn't even notice the difference.'

Back downstairs, furiously pedaling her loom, and banging the beater against her shawl as though against Diana's head, Caroline started thinking about murder – Amelia murdering chipmunks, Jason murdering Amelia, some sexual psychopath murdering Jason as he walked through the woods home from Hank's tonight . . .

Then she sat perfectly still, staring out to the melting lake and realizing what she was doing: shifting her anger at Diana to the world at large and working herself up into an anxiety state. Her hands fell to her sides and her shoulders slumped. *You can't control what happens, but you can control your response to it.* Doggedly she began reviewing her session that afternoon with Hannah. But as she did so, the anxiety amplified. She was going to lose Hannah

266

too. She told Diana she loved her, and Diana informed her she'd wake up to find her gone. You couldn't go around telling people you cared about them. It scared them away. And she'd done that this afternoon with Hannah. Hannah would vanish like all the others. Like Jackson, David Michael, Arlene, Diana. No one was left.

Desperately, she tried to locate the calming jungle scene in her head, but this time she couldn't find the birds and flowers. Only the swamp remained, matted and putrid.

Two

Hannah watched Chip struggle with his need to leave and his need to stay. He was poised above the couch, halfway between sitting and standing. She'd just suggested she was merely a habit, like smoking, that he'd miss their sessions but would soon fill the gap with other people and activities. He looked unconvinced, hovering there in close-fitting tan corduroys and a plaid sports shirt. He'd finally shed those overalls, which he'd been wearing unwashed since the Chicago Democratic Convention. He'd also shaved his full beard, and was about to open a Burger King on the highway near the mall. It was fascinating to watch clients' appearances alter as their self-images altered. Computer programmers became slalom racers, and ski bums became judges. In her wildest fantasies she wouldn't have pegged Chip to open a Burger King. But it wasn't her job to judge the transformations, only to assist clients in achieving whatever bizarre goals they set.

'I don't know, Hannah. I know it's time to stop. But I, like, can't.' He sank back into the sofa.

'Sure you can, Chip,' she said, fighting her own impatience. She felt like a counselor pushing a frightened camper off the diving board. Chip seemed startled by her enthusiasm for his attempts to leave. He was accustomed to females clinging to him when he wanted to sally forth in pursuit of the wild American hamburger, not grasping that her success as a therapist depended on doing herself out of a job.

As Chip sat in deadlocked silence, stroking his beard-free chin, Hannah thought about what a muddle termination usually turned into. Such a decisive word for such a nebulous series of events. Some clients picked a fight so they could leave without missing her. Others dwindled away, skipping appointments and finally not showing up at all. Some expected her to orchestrate a grand finale, like the 'Ode to Joy' in Beethoven's Ninth. Others brought champagne and Tootsie Rolls. Some evaded the issue altogether by hanging on for years, using the sessions as a weekly pep rally for their status quo, until she got fed up and ushered them to the door. Some went away, only to come back again and again. A few really looked at their method of leave-taking, saw how it applied to other areas of their lives, and learned something.

But whatever their style, the only way she could survive was through detachment. Any client could walk out forever at any moment. The couple of times her detachment failed her, she missed them and fretted about what she'd done to drive them away. Probably one reason she did this job was to stay in practice with the skills she'd developed to cope with the deaths of all her dear departeds. Her office was a speeded-up version of the world: people flowed through, and she had to resist entanglements with them or suffer the agony when they moved on, as they usually had to. Every day she felt their allures, and every day she renounced them.

'Come by and I'll give you a free Whopper,' said Chip, finally standing up and walking to the door.

'I might do that.' Hannah stood up.

Chip paused at the door, not looking at her. 'Thanks, Hannah. You saved my life.'

'No. *You* saved your life.'

Chip smiled and shrugged. As he walked out, Hannah closed the door firmly behind him, thinking if she could save lives, she'd have saved Mona and Nigel first.

She ran into clients all over town. Some greeted her warmly. Others nodded and moved away fast. Others spoke of her as their 'friend.' But she hardly ever saw them that way, and felt sad for them if therapy was what they called friendship – a one-way conversation with the focus on themselves.

'Amuse me,' Hannah requested of Harriet Sullivan over seafood salads at Dooley's.

'You look as though you need it. What's wrong?'

Harriet in her silver Marie Antoinette hairdo was wearing color-coordinated everything. Hannah, who wore whatever was on top of the stack of laundry each morning, felt like a slob. 'I had an emergency in the middle of the night, and I'm an ogre today. I let Arthur have it at breakfast.'

'Allen likes it at breakfast too,' said Harriet, holding her fork daintily between fingers with long mauve nails. 'And at lunch and at dinner. Ever since he retired, he likes it whenever he can get it. It's exhausting. I keep telling him to take up a hobby.'

Hannah smiled. 'Sounds like you're it, my dear.'

'So what happened with Arthur?' Harriet patted her mauve lips with her napkin.

'He went out and bought a golf cart. To transport your husband and himself around the course in style. But we owe that money for taxes. He's so impractical sometimes I could scream.'

'Not here, darling.'

'I've screamed enough for one day.'

'Poor thing. But somehow I can't picture you screaming.'

'I didn't actually scream. I complained loudly. The fucker just sat there with that sweet, long-suffering look. So of course now I'm feeling guilty. I wish just once he'd shout back.' Hannah put down her fork, pushed back her peacock chair, and lit a brown cigarette.

'They do seem to feel themselves superior to all those messy female emotions. But you can imagine the impact if Arthur did shout back after all these years?'

Hannah held her lighter to Harriet's Virginia Slim, wondering how Harriet managed to lift her hand to her mouth with so many large rings on her fingers. 'I'd probably fall to pieces.'

'Write it off to spring,' said Harriet, turning her head to exhale smoke away from Hannah.

'You're probably right. My clients are bouncing off the walls. Everyone's either fighting or falling in love like a sheep in heat.'

'As for me,' said Harriet, 'I'm about to buy an expensive new suit.' She placed her cigarette on the edge of the ashtray and sipped her coffee.

'You ought to get together with Arthur. You could ride around in his expensive new golf cart, wearing your expensive new suit.'

'Beats paying taxes.'

'But does it beat going to jail? I've never understood why buying something cheers you people up. To me it's just one more thing to maintain.'

'Face it, Hannah darling, you're not a consumer.'

Exhaling, Hannah realized it was true. Today all she wanted of this world was out.

At Cheever's in the mall Hannah sat in a green velvet armchair and waited for Harriet to change into a handsome gray-green silk suit. Looking around at all the items she didn't want to buy, Hannah noticed a triangular woolen shawl hanging on the wall above a rack of blouses. Strips of reds, oranges, and purples faded into each other like winter sunsets on Lake Glass. She glanced around the shop. A second shawl in shades of white, gray, and blue hung on the opposite wall. Studying it, she thought of cold winter mornings on the lake. Looking back and forth between the two shawls, she considered buying one to hang on her office wall over the couch. Or to wear in winter when a shawl was all she needed to supplement her hot flashes. Maybe there was something to Harriet's Shopping Therapy after all?

She walked over to the sunset shawl, took the corner in her fingers and rubbed it with her thumb. She knew nothing about weaving, but it looked good to her. Glancing at the label, she read, 'Handwoven on the loom of Caroline Kelley.' Hannah let the corner fall back against the wall.

'That's lovely, isn't it?' said the lurking saleslady. Hannah nodded. 'Caroline Kelley is quite talented,' added the woman, who wore green-tinted nylons. 'We've carried her work for years. It's very popular. These shawls are new for her. She usually does place mats and tablecloths. Would you like to see some?'

Good lord, thought Hannah as she examined a stack of place mats. Caroline was gifted. What else could she do that Hannah knew nothing about? How had she developed such problems with self-esteem? How had she managed never to mention her weaving during all these months of therapy?

Shaking her head, Hannah sat down and resumed her study of the sunset shawl. The gray and brown mats were handsome, but this shawl was dazzling. She might have bought it if Caroline hadn't made it. Should she buy it anyway? Whether she did or not, should she speak to Caroline of her reaction? Now or later? What would it mean for Caroline's therapy? What did it mean that she'd switched from mats to shawls in recent months?

Hannah didn't attend the shows of clients who were painters and sculptors, didn't read the writers' books, didn't attend the actors' and dancers' performances because it muddled her clarity. She wanted them to speak to her directly, not via their productions. In any case, they usually wanted to be recognized for themselves, and not for their work. Was this why Caroline never mentioned her weaving? But now that she'd seen the shawls, Hannah couldn't pretend she hadn't. And Caroline was her first appointment after lunch.

She rested her elbow on the chair arm, forehead in her hand. Life was simply too much for her today. Harriet emerged in the green silk suit. 'Buy it,' said Hannah with a dismissive wave. She felt a hot flash coming on. Her throat began to constrict.

'Are you okay?' asked Harriet, pausing in her posturing before the full-length mirror. 'You looked flushed.'

'A hot flash,' muttered Hannah. The walls were starting to close in.

'Come over here by the window.' Harriet took her arm.

'I've got to get out of here. I'll wait for you in the car. Don't worry. I'll be fine. It's only my twelfth for the week.'

As she leaned against the side of her Mercury, awash in a sea of cars, and waited for the hot flash to subside, Hannah was grimly amused. This body and its requirements had dominated so much of her life. But its behavior during menopause had forced her to realize that she and it weren't identical. It was a pillar of flesh with its own schedules and cycles, plodding along toward dissolution. She herself was something else altogether. What, she wasn't sure.

Caroline sat down on the couch, gratified to find Hannah still there, smoking away in her chair, bare feet propped up on the rush stool. She'd evidently not moved away or gone out of business at hearing she was important to Caroline. Caroline would make a point of not letting an admission like that slip out again. She couldn't afford to scare Hannah away. Hannah was all she had left.

Hannah studied Caroline, who was sitting as still as a praying mantis trying to pass for a twig. Now what, she wondered, unable to recall what had gone on last week. At times like this she suspected she was making a mistake not taking notes. She closed her eyes and tried to remember their last session. Her memory was going. Early senility. If she could get her talking, Caroline might give some clues.

'How was your week?' asked Hannah.

'Fine, thanks. How was yours?'

'Okay, thanks.' Caroline's 'Fine, thanks' could mean anything.

Apparently she wasn't giving any hints. 'What shall we talk about?'

'I don't care,' said Caroline. It was better not to talk at all. That way no harmful words could pop out. It was especially important not to tell Hannah about the fight with Diana. If Hannah knew Caroline had no one but Hannah herself, she'd feel burdened and withdraw.

If you don't care, I certainly don't, thought Hannah. She was disgusted with herself for wasting one minute being unpleasant to Arthur. You thought you had all the time in the world with someone, and the next moment they were gone for good. Like Nigel and Mona. She and Arthur had another decade together if they were lucky, and here she called him thoughtless, selfish, a spendthrift. God knows what all, once she got going. Yet he was the most generous person she'd ever known: He'd given up his entire previous life to be with her.

Caroline was glancing at her uneasily. Damn it, thought Hannah, why do I always have to be calm and together for these people? They expected her to play the Rock of Gibraltar so they could be the Dismal Swamp. Let them fucking well take care of themselves. Who takes care of me? Even Saint Arthur ran up debts she had to pay off.

She stopped herself, realizing she was being ridiculous. This was her job. She made her living from it. She was good at it, and she usually enjoyed it. But when she was exhausted, she sometimes lapsed into martyrdom.

She tried a couple more openers, to which Caroline didn't respond. This felt like one of those sessions that was going nowhere, like the Ancient Mariner's death ship. Should she mention the shawls? She hadn't been able to decide, could scarcely decide where in the lot to park her car after lunch. Her judgment was shot to hell today. It was probably better not to try anything fancy. 'If there's nothing urgent, Caroline, do you suppose we could end early today? I was up all night, and I'm not in very good shape.' It was good for Caroline to discover the laws of nature applied to her authority figures too. She'd cancel this afternoon's appointments and go home. She was useless in this state anyway.

Caroline looked at her and said nothing, her face a mask.

Shit, thought Hannah, yearning to apologize to Arthur, drink a martini by the fire, and drag him off to bed. But Caroline was resorting to her tired old jump-seat trick of numb withdrawal.

'Sure. Fine.' Caroline felt the globe totter beneath her boots. Her assessment had been correct: You couldn't go around telling people you cared for them. It scared them away.

'It doesn't look fine with you at all,' sighed Hannah. 'What's wrong?'

'Nothing's wrong.' Brian was gone. Diana was gone. Hannah was gone. No one was left.

Hannah studied her, struggling to set aside her own exhaustion and irritation. 'What's going on, Caroline? Your face has gone blank. Tell me what's wrong. I'm not a mindreader. I can't know if you won't tell me.'

Caroline felt her blank expression crumple into anxiety like a bashed fender. None of the old tricks worked with Hannah. 'I feel as though you're kicking me out.' Shut up, she snapped at herself. Don't make demands or complaints. Be still and quiet and good. Then she'll let you stick around.

'I swear to you that wasn't my intention, Caroline.' Each child had gone through this phase, wailing that she didn't love them. She'd gone through it with Arthur and Maggie. Once she yelled at Nigel, 'For God's sake, you little brat, what do you want from me? I only devote my entire life to you!' He just stood there, staring at her and sucking his battered pink bottle. One of the moments she was least proud of, and now there was no way to make it up to him. She probably should have bought that shawl, hung it on the wall. Then Caroline would know Hannah regarded her highly – except on days like today when she regarded no one highly, least of all herself.

'Why in the world do you think I'd kick you out?' asked Hannah, attempting a smile.

Caroline drew a shaky breath. She might as well tell her. The worst had already happened. In a trembling voice she said, 'I told you last week you were important to me, and this week you aren't even really here. And now you kick me out. I guess I've scared you off.' She shifted her eyes from Hannah's to the abstract photo over the bookcase. Squinting, she tried to locate the Virgin Mary. All she could see were meaningless blobs of black and white.

Hannah heaved a sigh of relief finally to understand what was going on. She'd forgotten about that exchange last week. 'Please believe me that I'm not kicking you out, Caroline. You're entirely accurate when you say I'm not all here this afternoon. I've had an exhausting week, lots of emergencies. This morning Arthur and I had an argument. I've been having hot flashes all morning. It's nothing to do with you.'

Caroline studied her, wanting to believe this. Hannah did have dark circles under her eyes.

'Does it occur to you that I felt *you* weren't all here? You didn't seem to want to talk. And you're sitting as still and stiff as a statue. Why are you sitting like that?'

Caroline was surprised to hear herself say, 'I'm waiting for the ax to fall.'

Hannah gave a startled laugh. 'What color is the ax?'

Caroline's doomed expression broke up into confusion as she addressed the issue of whether axes come in different colors.

'I'm not going anywhere, Caroline. You'll have to leave this time. That's what I am here for – to be left.' It occurred to her this was what life was all about – learning to leave it. My, what dreary thoughts spring brings, she mused, glancing out the window to the melting ice on Lake Glass and feeling exhausted at the idea of witnessing another tedious round of new life.

'Why would I want to leave?'

'Don't you see that if you decide to go, of your own accord, it'll break your pattern of waiting around to feel rejected?' True, Caroline had left Brian Stone. But she hadn't been fully engaged with him. She needed to renounce someone who was as dear to her as her own life – and in doing so, to find herself. As Hannah had been forced to do time after time. She'd gotten acquainted with herself by default. At various points there'd been no one else left.

Caroline looked bewildered. Hannah realized she was going too fast. This talk of anybody's leaving was frightening her. 'How did people in your past react when you told them you cared about them?'

Caroline couldn't open her mouth. She was preoccupied with the color of axes.

'For next week will you please think about that?'

Caroline nodded.

'And for today, can we please call it quits? I'm a mess.'

Caroline nodded again, looking bemused, with glimmers of sympathy around the edges.

As Hannah sat finishing her cigarette and summoning the energy to drive home, she figured out why old women in other cultures were reputed to be wise: because they were. She'd just realized she felt ghastly today because it was time for her period. Her hormones hadn't gotten the message after several years that she wasn't any longer having periods. They continued their monthly polka through the parlor of her emotions. She really ought to see her doctor. But one thing a woman could learn from this ordeal was not to take her emotions too seriously. Hence the wisdom. She only hoped she could survive menopause first.

Jonathan appeared in her doorway, his face flushed and tense, his impeccable gray Afro tangled and spiky. 'I'm afraid I have some bad news.'

''Tis the season,' said Hannah, stubbing out her cigarette in Nigel's stone.

'Mary Beth's killed herself.'

Hannah stared at him.

'They found her in her apartment a couple of hours ago. In the bathtub with a razor.'

Lowering her gaze, Hannah said nothing.

'I guess it was just a question of time. She tried twice before.'

'Jesus, the perfect end to a perfect week. Sit down, Jonathan. You look frazzled.' She was picturing Mary Beth with her strained smile and nervous patting at her hairdo, her Miss Muffet outfits. A razor? What a messy death for such a neat creature. She visualized her pale bony body sprawled in the bathtub smeared with blood.

'Several times I heard her yelling at clients,' said Hannah, shaking her head. 'I should have done something. At least realized she was falling apart.' She'd been irritated by Mary Beth's 'novice nerves.' She was ashamed.

'That's bullshit, lady, and you know it,' said Jonathan, sprawled on the couch. 'Her father raped her when she was three. She had all kinds of difficulties that had nothing to do with you. She wasn't your responsibility.'

Hannah gave Jonathan a grateful, sheepish look. The same words she was always saying to clients. Usually she could say them to herself as well, but today clearly wasn't her day. She kept thinking about Medevac helicopters crashing on battlefields. The way she felt today, Mary Beth's solution to the problems of living had an undeniable appeal. 'Probably it was yelling at clients that kept her alive this long,' said Hannah.

'Probably.' Jonathan stood up wearily. 'I'd better go spread this cheery news.'

Hannah was shaken. It was dangerous, this spelunking in the caverns of the psyche. She lit another cigarette and wondered what her own disowned qualities were, and whether she was foisting them off on her clients similarly. If she was, she'd be the last in town to know, that being the nature of dissociation.

Oh, do shut up, she snapped at herself. You could tell if you were dissociating by the intensity you brought to a client's situation. Whenever you felt unusually angry or supportive, you could be pretty sure you had a personal stake. And you'd damn well better drag it out and look at it or you'd join Mary Beth in the bathtub.

Exhaling with a sigh, Hannah considered her seizure of martyrdom during Caroline's session. Such an unattractive stance, and one she'd witnessed in herself before. Yet why did it emerge then? She was exhausted, reason enough. But she'd been exhausted all morning. Caroline was accustomed to eliciting irritation from people when she wanted reassurance? Or did she want reassurance? Maybe she wanted what she got – space. Hannah suddenly recalled telling her last week that she cared about her too: *You're right, I do like you best.* Evidently Caroline hadn't absorbed this. Caroline said she was afraid she'd scared Hannah off. Did their warm exchange scare Caroline off? But maybe it had scared Hannah. Why didn't she remember it until now? She knew she wasn't too crazy at the time about having said that. She wasn't being paid to like clients, she was being paid to shrink their heads. Was there some truth to that remark, or was it just what Caroline needed to hear at the time?

Oh, fuck it. It was too confusing after a fight, a sleepless night, hot flashes, and a suicide.

'I'm sorry,' she said to Arthur as she walked into the living room. Arthur stood on the carpet putting a golf ball into the plastic hole.

'For what?' He looked up, knees bent.

'For calling you a spendthrift this morning.' She plopped down on the couch.

'I probably am.'

'Maybe you are. Maybe you aren't. Who knows? Who cares? But I'm sorry for being such a raving bitch about it.'

'You're not a bitch.' He walked over to the couch and rested his putter against the end table.

'Liar.'

He smiled.

'If you wouldn't be so damned forgiving, we could make up properly.'

'Since when have we needed an excuse?' he asked, pulling her by the hand.

As they strolled across the living room towards the stairs, arms around each other's waists, Hannah pictured Mary Beth sprawled in her bloody bathtub. She'd tell Arthur later. Meanwhile, she was someone who'd always done her best grieving in a horizontal position.

Three

Holding a Dixie cup of rum and Coke, Caroline sat on the smooth red plastic bench watching Brenda in her orange Lake Glass Kennels shirt flex the arm that held her bowling ball. Lucille was telling Barb about the French triceps extension exercises she was doing with five-pound weights at Gloria Stevens to tone up the undersides of her upper arms. 'You'd think heaving patients on and off stretchers all day would take care of it,' said Lucille, patting her finger curls. 'But you can see for yourself that it doesn't.' She poked the pale slack flesh that hung from her underarm.

Munching a powdered doughnut, Caroline was thinking woefully of what happened when she let people know she cared about them. Marsha got run over by a truck. She tried to show her parents via presents. But her father always returned his for a refund, and her mother exchanged hers for something different. She changed Howard's and Tommy's diapers and wiped their tears for years. But now they catalogued the times she made them play cannibal to her medical missionary, lynched Howard's teddy bear, let the air out of their bicycle tires. When she invited Arlene to supper, Arlene told her to get lost. *I know what you want and you can't have it.*

Brenda sat down, elated by her fifth strike. 'Hey, how come Dr Stone is always hanging around your desk?' She punched Caroline lightly in the arm.

'He isn't anymore.' Caroline dusted powdered sugar off her orange team shirt. Brian had a new woman, a scrub nurse named Audrey with curly black hair. They sat together at lunch in the cafeteria and during coffee breaks, heads close together. No doubt Brian was regaling her with tales of Irene's departure. Caroline was grimly amused that he'd recovered from her more quickly than she from him. Evidently Brian, like nature, abhorred a vacuum. And any woman could fill it.

Brenda glanced at her. 'How come he was then?'

'We dated a few times.'

'You and Dr Stone?'

Caroline smiled. 'I had a brief seizure of respectability last month, but I've recovered.'

'You and Dr Stone?'

'Diana and I have been having troubles.'

'I noticed she was spending a lot of time with that new kid up on the children's ward.'

'Kid is right.' Caroline stood up and went over to the return rack.

As she studied the distant triangle of pins and speculated on the unlikelihood of getting the ball down there in a straight line, she recalled the first time she told Jackson she loved him. During their maiden argument, in the living room of his Back Bay apartment, over whether to leave the cellophane on new record jackets. She accused him of warping the Beatles album she'd given him for his birthday.

'Well, if I'm so dumb,' he said, 'why do you stick around?'

Realizing she didn't care if his records were warped, Caroline replied, 'Because I love you.'

He blushed. He tossed his dark hair off his forehead with one hand. He laughed harshly. He glanced around the room like a trapped bird in search of an open window. 'You love me? What do you mean? Define your terms.'

'I don't know what I mean. Forget it. I'm sorry. I lost my head.'

'All I asked was what you meant. We may mean different things. You may want more of a commitment than I'm prepared to make.'

'I didn't mean anything. It just slipped out.'

'That's exactly what I mean about you, Caroline. You're so goddam . . . intense, or something.' His pager went off, and he raced out to the hospital, leaving her worrying over how to be more relaxed. If Jackson didn't like her intensity, he'd leave her. So she'd get rid of it. She'd be still and quiet and good, she promised him silently, as she lay motionless on the carpet.

Drawing back the ball, Caroline moved forward, sliding to the foul line and releasing the ball with a clunk. It rolled into the gutter and barely made it to the other end of the lane. She'd better concentrate on what she was doing. Last fall she'd been in despair over the idiocy of bowling. Now the idiocy entertained her. Progress?

After picking off seven pins with her next roll, she sat down and took a drink of rum and Coke, recalling that when she first told David Michael she loved him, his erection melted like a stick of butter at room temperature. He rolled off her and turned his hairy back. The American flags at his windows stirred in the night air leaking around the window frame.

'What's wrong?' asked Caroline.

'Jesus Christ, Caroline, that's like holding a knife to someone's throat. You say, "I love you, David Michael." What can I reply except, "I love you too, Caroline." And what if I don't feel like it?'

Caroline stared at his hunched back in the light from the street. 'So don't say it.'

'Yeah, and then you get all upset.'

'You're the one who's upset.' Stroking his back, she wondered how to get him to finish what he'd started with her body.

'You're the one who made me upset.'

'But I was just trying to tell you I think you're a fine person.'

'So who asked you?'

'Nobody.'

'I'm not a fine person, and I get sick of hearing you say it all the time.'

'Okay, so you're not a fine person.' She'd say whatever he wanted to hear. If she didn't, he'd leave.

'Oh yeah? Why not?' he demanded. 'What's wrong with me?'

'Dr Stone, huh?' Brenda sat down and draped her beefy arms along the bench back. 'You don't seem like his type.'

'I wasn't.'

'Did you ever meet his wife?'

'Irene? No. Did you?'

'Yeah. She's not at all like you. A real wimp. Phoning him during a thyroidectomy because she'd lost her checkbook. That kind of thing. He ate it like candy.'

Caroline glanced at Brenda. 'Wimp' was one of the words on her list for Hannah last fall. But Hannah didn't see her like that, and apparently neither did Brenda.

'So tell me about this kid on the children's ward,' said Brenda.

'Suzanne Sanders is her name. She's always bringing Diana cups of coffee and Reese's cups. And asking her simple-minded questions, and acting impressed when Diana answers them.'

Brenda shook her head. 'There's no competing with that stuff. We all love admiration.'

'I walked into the bathroom today, and Suzanne was standing there looking in the mirror, adjusting her cap. I went into a stall without saying anything. And she said, "You know, Caroline, all this would be a lot easier if I could just dislike you. But you seem like a nice woman to me." '

Brenda grimaced. 'What did you say?'

'I said, "I *am* a nice woman." '

Brenda laughed. 'Speaking of the bathroom, would you excuse me?'

As she got up, Caroline reflected that when she and Diana first acknowledged their love, life together became an arms race, each struggling to find more forceful ways to express devotion. Ever since last week's Camisole Caper, the arms race was escalating again, as they tried to gloss over their argument like paperhangers concealing gaping cracks in a plaster wall. Diana mailed her a sexy French postcard in a plain brown envelope. So she left a badge on Diana's dresser that said, 'Trust Your Lust.' So Diana put a quart of coffee ice cream in Caroline's freezer. So Caroline left some shasta daisies in a vase on Diana's table.

Brenda plopped down on the plastic bench and unwrapped a Mars bar. Glancing at her, Caroline said, 'Brenda, I think you're a fine person. I like you a lot.'

Brenda looked down at her half-eaten Mars bar. She reached up and touched the '*Plus que hier, moins que demain*' medallion at her throat. 'Uh, well, I like you too, Caroline.' Her eyes darted around the vast bowling alley. 'But I'm really happy with Barb.'

'That isn't what I meant.'

'My turn at the foul line!' Brenda leaped up and raced to the ball return.

Why did I do that, Caroline wondered, having figured out it scared people off? She wanted to scare them off? But why?

After leaving Lake Glass Lanes, Caroline stopped in at the mall to shore up her depleted stockpile of treats for Diana. Wandering through the brightly lit shops, she selected silk stockings and the March issue of *Penthouse*. St Patrick's Day was coming, so she bought green eyeshadow and a card that said, 'Knock, knock. Who's there? Irish. Irish who? Irish I hadn't had that last drink.' In the liquor store she bought some Chartreuse liqueur. At Baskin-Robbins as the clerk hand-packed pistachio ice cream, Caroline flipped open the *Penthouse* to Miss March, who lay masturbating in black stockings, high heels, and lacy garter belt. In real life she was an accountant, who attributed her success to her friendly personality. A teenage boy, whose wide leather belt had a silver buckle shaped like New Hampshire with 'Live Free or Die' embossed on it, stood next to Caroline. He was also studying Miss March, and Caroline's own interest in Miss March, so she shut the magazine.

Glancing over her armful of packages, Caroline suddenly realized: This isn't love, this is psychosis. Both she and Diana were coming down with another case of Terminal Thoughtfulness. They would pamper each other to death. What was it all about? *You feel you have to do nice things to make them love you?* Each felt herself inadequate to maintain someone's interest without showering that person with the entire inventory of several small shops.

She handed the *Penthouse* to the startled teenager and left the clerk holding the half-filled carton of ice cream. She dumped all her packages into a Leonard Litter trash can in the corridor like an alcoholic pouring liquor down the drain. If Diana didn't want her just as she was, without props, then to hell with it.

Driving back to the cabin, she wondered if anyone would want her unadorned by gifts and services, least of all Diana. Something in her was insisting she find out. But she felt naked and afraid empty-handed.

She pictured Hannah's face. But it was strained and tired, as Hannah had been at their last session. *That's what I'm here for – to be left.* To please Hannah she'd have to leave her. Besides, she couldn't lean on her indefinitely. She'd have to lean elsewhere. But where? Brian was gone. Probably Diana would soon be gone without gifts to hold her. Hannah would be gone.

Frantically she summoned the gorgeous jungle birds and flowers. *The miracle is all around you.* The strange feeling of warm gratitude began to creep over her, like the numbness that rose up her legs when she had too much to drink. Was it possible she didn't need another person to feel happy and safe? That the contents of her own head, which no one could take away, were sufficient? Surely not.

Caroline sat in her Subaru watching two men in rust-colored ski patrol parkas load a gray metal desk into a small moving van that stood in the parking lot of the therapy center. Maybe Hannah really was going into real estate. Maybe she'd lied last week when she said Caroline would have to do the leaving. But surely she'd give her clients some notice? Caroline's stomach felt queasy, as it had the day she arrived to find Hannah's office rearranged. Nothing here was supposed to change. Caroline was the one who was changing.

'What's up?' she asked as she walked into Hannah's intact office.

'What do you mean?' Hannah swiveled in her chair to look up at Caroline, who stood shifting nervously from boot to boot.

'Who's moving out?'

'Oh. The woman in the next office killed herself. Her parents are clearing out her stuff.'

Caroline sank down on the couch.

'Does that distress you?' It could be part of the Great Disillusionment to let Caroline know that therapists sometimes had worse problems than clients. Hannah had been seeing some of Mary Beth's clients, trying to discourage them from copying Mary Beth's example. 'It makes all my months with her one big joke,' wailed a woman student in a blue jean jacket covered with badges that said things like 'Fuck Authority' and 'Chaste Makes Waste.' But if Mary Beth helped her, and she apparently had, did it matter how?

'I guess it does.' Caroline rubbed the bridge of her nose.

'Do you know why?'

'I guess I want you all to have it all together. I want *someone* to.'

'Why not yourself?'

'I'm working on it,' said Caroline.

'Yes, you are. You're working hard. You listen, and you hear, and you apply what you hear. It's impressive.'

'Thanks,' said Caroline, smiling faintly, wondering what wrecks other clients must be if she herself was impressive with all her fear, anger, and longing. She studied that damn photo over the bookcase. She simply couldn't find the Virgin Mary. Maybe she wasn't there. Maybe it was a ruse to check clients' honesty, like the emperor's new clothes.

'What shall we talk about today?' Hannah propped her feet up on the stool and settled back in her chair.

'I'd like to talk about Diana.'

Hannah refrained from commenting on Caroline's previous reluctance to talk about Diana to a heterosexual. Now that Caroline had accepted herself more fully, maybe she didn't need to pin her own lack of acceptance on other people. 'What about her?'

'We had a bad fight a couple of weeks ago. And we got so scared of losing each other that we started trying to outpamper each other again. So last night at the mall buying cards and candy and stuff, I suddenly got fed up. I thought, fuck it, if me as I am isn't enough, then it's no good anyway. So I dumped everything I'd just bought into the garbage can.'

Hannah laughed. 'That was courageous.' Also extravagant. This woman ought to meet Arthur.

Caroline hesitated. 'At first I felt as though I'd been let out of a cage. But the closer I got to home, the more frightened I became. Because maybe she really won't stick around if I don't do nice things for her.'

'I trust by now you see where that feeling comes from?'

Caroline nodded. 'But maybe she won't.' She wanted to be assured that she would.

'Maybe she won't. That's the risk you take if you change: that the people you've been involved with won't like the new you. But other people who do will come along.'

Caroline's hand trembled as she stroked the tweed sofa cover with her fingertips. She didn't want other people. She wanted Diana.

'What did you fight about?'

'We'd just made love. I was feeling peaceful and happy, as though maybe we'd make it after all.' Caroline blushed and studied her fingernails. Could you really say these things to Mother? 'Uh, I told her I loved her. And she asked me not to sleep with Brian Stone at our house, so I flipped out.'

'I thought you ended it with him?'

'I have. It was the principle of the thing. I pay half the mortgage. I can do as I like there.'

Hannah studied Caroline's indignant face, wondering if it was really so difficult just to hug Diana and tell her Brian was out of the picture. The games everyone played were exhausting. 'Principles start wars.'

Caroline said nothing. Hannah had just betrayed her.

'So you told her you cared for her, and she let you have it,' said Hannah. 'Just as you thought I'd do last week because you told me I'm important to you?'

Startled, Caroline said nothing, looking out the window to the moving van in the parking lot. 'I guess so,' she finally said. 'Oh yeah, I did that assignment. Thought about what happened when I told people I cared about them.'

'Oh yes? What have you remembered?'

As Caroline described her routs on the battlefield of affection, Hannah recalled her own experiences. The one time she told her father she loved him, he laughed with embarrassment and returned to Trinidad on the next plane. When she told Colin she loved him, he threw her walnut clock to the floor and chopped it up. But with Arthur it was the other way round. When he told her he loved her, she kicked him out of bed. And whenever the men she used to flirt with at parties proclaimed their devotion, that was her cue to get rid of them. What was everyone so afraid of?

When Caroline stopped talking, Hannah asked, 'Do you see why they reacted like that?'

Caroline shook her head no, her glance sullen. 'I guess I'm too intense. Just like Jackson always said.'

'No, you're not too intense. You're not too anything. You are who you are. But other people don't want to hear what doesn't fit with their own view of themselves. If Diana is accustomed to feeling unloved, she won't want to hear that you love her, and she'll try to reinstate her unlovableness. It's like a heart transplant: A body often rejects the very thing that would keep it alive because the immune system won't accept it. I didn't have to flee when I heard I was important to you, because I'm important to me too.'

Laughing, Caroline said, 'But I don't understand why someone wouldn't want to hear she's loved.'

'Ask yourself that. How come last session you seized on my request that we leave early as proof I didn't care about you? When I told you the previous week I do.'

Caroline could scarcely hear Hannah. She saw her mouth moving, but she couldn't pick up the words.

Hannah tried to think of a different way to make the same point. If she could come up with five or six versions, sometimes later in the week it would fall into place for clients. Or later in their lives. 'Caroline, someone important to you is telling you she cares about you. Do you know why you aren't hearing me?'

Caroline sat in confused silence.

'You can't hear me because you've had no experience of an authority figure who wasn't aloof and rejecting. Either you have to classify me with the refugee maids and your little brothers, who were nice to you because they had no choice. Or you have to see me as rejecting. But I'm neither. Can you face that?'

Caroline didn't even understand what she was supposed to be facing. She studied one of the men in green work clothes and ski patrol parkas, who was hefting a cardboard box into the van. If Hannah killed herself, Caroline would kill her.

'Look, the people you really wanted – your parents – were absent or aloof. So you yearn for affection from such a person now. But if such a person gives you affection, he or she ceases to be unattainable. So you try to get the person to withdraw. Or you start looking around for a new unattainable. Do you see what I'm saying?'

'Uh, I don't think so.'

'The point is,' Hannah said with urgency, 'most of us have had difficult childhoods, and we have to learn to accept acceptance.'

Caroline noted the 'us.' 'Did you have a difficult childhood?'

'My mother died of typhoid when I was four, and my father deserted me when I was five.'

Caroline studied Hannah. A dead mother, dead children, a rejecting father. *You think you've got problems?* How come Hannah was so cheerful most of the time?

The movers were stomping down the hallway slamming doors. 'All right, think about Jackson,' said Hannah, pursuing another tack, the way Nigel used to when landing his sailboat against the north w nd. 'What did he say when you told him you loved him?'

'He asked me what I meant.'

'What did you mean?'

'That I loved him.'

'What do you mean by love?'

Caroline studied her. 'Uh, that I liked being with him. Thought he was a nice person. I don't know.'

'When some people say, "I love you," what they really mean is, I want to go to bed with you. Or I want you to support me financially. Or please don't leave me all alone.'

Caroline was remembering the songs on the car radio when she necked with Kevin behind the Stop 'n Shop – 'Young Love First Love,' 'When Will I Be Loved,' 'When I Fall in Love,' 'I Can't Help It If I'm Still in Love with You.' The songs took for granted that everyone knew what love was. 'What is love?'

Hannah laughed. 'I asked you first.'

'Well, you just said what it isn't. So what's left?'

'Why don't you figure that out for next week?' Hannah smiled, since most people spent their entire lives trying, and failing, to figure it out. Because they assumed love was something that had to do with other people.

'Nothing's left, as far as I can see.'

'Maybe love is whatever's left once you've eliminated everything else.'

'What?'

As Caroline walked out, Hannah lit a cigarette and reviewed Caroline's dilemma as a child. If she expressed need, she got taken to the Salvation Army. If she expressed anger, her mother took to bed with depression. If she expressed love, everyone got up and left. What remained except to stay as still as possible and hope her mere existence wouldn't offend? A suicide of the emotions.

Watching a moving man pass her open door with a box of books, Hannah reflected that Caroline was in the most difficult phase of therapy. The dependency, anger, and sexuality Hannah could handle fine, but the alternative was so nebulous it defied description. Either a person felt it or she didn't. If she didn't, no amount of discussion would help. Besides, love wasn't something a client could experience in any depth with a therapist. The unequal nature of the relationship precluded it.

In the parking lot the van revved up, spewing black exhaust, and rolled away. Farewell, Mary Beth, thought Hannah. May you finally find some peace. Though she suspected suicide wasn't a long-term solution. Mary Beth would probably have to come back as a barber, until she learned the proper use for razors.

As she tapped her cigarette into Nigel's stone, a stick of incense to ward off evil spirits from next door, Hannah thought about her first lunch with Maggie after ending her own therapy. They met at a restaurant overlooking the lake and sat in the sun at a table on a wooden deck.

'I'm afraid I'm in a rush,' said Maggie, studying the menu, which had drawings of nautical knots all over it. 'I have a two o'clock appointment.'

Hannah was miffed. She was also relieved. Never at a loss for words in Maggie's office, outside it she felt like a teenager on her first blind date.

After they placed their order, Hannah took a deep breath and said, 'You remember that fight Arthur and I had over whether to go to Maine or the Cape for our vacation?'

Maggie nodded without enthusiasm.

'We decided to go to the Cape.'

Maggie said nothing, lips pressed tightly together.

'I discovered once Arthur agreed to go to Maine, I didn't really care anymore.'

Maggie put on her thick-lensed glasses. Hannah couldn't see her eyes.

'I guess what I really wanted was for Arthur to defer to me.'

Maggie continued to sit in silence.

'What do you think?' asked Hannah, feeling anxious and irritated by Maggie's sphinx imitation.

Maggie pursed her lips, put an elbow on the table, and rested her chin on her fist. 'I think it's a pity I can't just order you to treat me as an equal.'

'What?'

Maggie turned her head and appeared to look across the lake, where white sails dipped and swooped like gulls.

It began to dawn on Hannah that there was a difference between being Maggie's client and being her friend. For the rest of the lunch, Hannah confined her conversation to jokes, gossip, and summaries of movie plots, to convey to Maggie that she no longer wanted Mummy, or free therapy. Though she felt sudden anxiety:

Not only could she no longer run to Maggie with all her problems, Maggie might even want to run to *her*.

Over the months, each relaxed into a new way of interacting, until they eventually became real friends. But then Maggie went and died.

On the whole friendships with clients weren't worth the effort, although, thought Hannah, she'd done it a few times herself. She had enough people in her life as it was. In fact she wanted to let go of the old friends who were left, before they could be snatched away like all the others. Some days her heart felt like Flanders Field. She lacked the energy to add new names to her address book.

Putting out her cigarette, she glanced out the window and discovered a sunset in progress. She studied the bare white wall above the couch. If she hung Caroline's shawl there, she could lie in her recliner and watch the sunset out the window, seeing it reflected in the shawl. But was it psychotherapy?

She was suddenly confused. She thought she didn't like sunsets anymore.

Diana cut the broccoli quiche she'd made for St Patrick's Day and put pieces on everyone's plate.

'Quiche! Yuck!' said Jason. Caroline glared at him. He met her glare with a look of defiance.

That afternoon Caroline had had a meeting with the guidance counselor at his school, who informed her Jason was throwing erasers in class and getting the shit beaten out of him on the playground.

'What's going on at home?' asked the burly young man. His desk was cluttered with color photos of his own no doubt well-behaved children.

His mother has been trying to get her head together, she thought. It couldn't be easy for a kid to have his mother in the same developmental stage as himself. 'Nothing much.'

'Try to give him some extra special attention right now,' he suggested in a voice copied from Mr Rogers.

The important thing was to get out of that office without revealing anything of significance, so she nodded. Thinking, have you ever tried to cuddle up to Darth Vader, young man?

'Don't you think John Travolta's gorgeous?' sighed Sharon, prodding her quiche with her fork.

'That fag?' said Jackie.

Diana and Caroline glanced at each other, trying to decide whether to wreck the dinner hour with a lecture on the term 'faggot.'

'Don't you think he's yummy, Caroline?'

Caroline opened her mouth to say she wasn't into men, but managed not to. 'I like Mick Jagger better.'

'He's cute,' said Sharon. 'But he's so old.'

Laughing, Diana asked, 'Hey, how come you took all my Rolling Stones and Janis Joplin albums?'

'Mother, that's not your kind of music.'

Diana and Caroline smiled at each other.

'Jackie has a girlfriend,' said Sharon, using the backs of both hands to flip the sides of her hair into the sleek wings fashionable with her set.

Jackie glared at her, fork poised and ready to plunge into her recently formed breast. 'That's a lie.'

'He sits next to her on the bus.'

'At least I don't tongue kiss her in the woods at lunchtime,' said Jackie.

Diana and Caroline glanced at each other, trying to figure out what role to play in the nascent love lives of their heterosexual offspring. Caroline recalled what sweet little children the three had been, prancing through the woods and fields playing elaborate games about being members of a circus troupe. Soon they'd be sweating with lust and suffering over loss just like their parents.

'I don't have to listen to this,' said Sharon, getting up and flouncing down the hall in her tight orange-tag Levi's.

'Sit down and finish your supper, Sharon,' called Diana.

'Forget it!' Sharon slammed her door.

Diana sighed. 'She'll do anything to avoid eating vegetables.'

'If Sharon doesn't have to eat this shit,' said Jason, 'neither do I.'

'Jason!' said Caroline. 'That's not very polite when Diana's cooked you this nice supper.'

'I hate quiche, Mom!'

'Shove it up your ass then,' suggested Jackie.

Jason held up his middle finger. 'Rotate, Jackie.'

'Just go downstairs, you two,' said Caroline. 'But don't ask me to fix you something later.'

As they clomped downstairs, Caroline said to Diana, 'I think the quiche is marvelous.'

'I've long since ceased to care what those three think about anything.'

'You'd slit your throat if you did.'

'Can you imagine what our parents would have done if we'd behaved like that?' Diana put Sharon's plate atop her own and started in on Sharon's quiche.

Caroline chuckled. 'Instant death.'

'Secretly I like it. They must feel well loved if they think they can afford to be so obnoxious.'

'Agreed,' said Caroline, eating Jason's quiche. 'I always felt I was walking on eggs around my house.'

'Me too. And even so, my mother was never happy with me.'

'You realize we do that with each other?' When she got home from work, Caroline found a St Patrick's Day card and a pair of lacy green underpants on her bed. She felt a stab of panic, just like a junkie without a syringe: She had nothing to give Diana.

'What?'

'All the gifts and favors. It's how we behaved with our mothers, and we still do it with each other. I think it's time to stop.'

'Stay out of my head,' said Diana, putting down her fork.

'Sorry.' They sat in silence. Caroline began absently pulling petals off one of the shasta daisies she'd given Diana, which sat in an earthenware vase between two gold candles.

'Thanks, by the way,' said Diana, 'for not having Brian here.'

'It's required no special effort. I broke up with him several weeks ago.'

Diana looked up, candlelight glancing off her red hair. 'What was that fight about then? Why didn't you tell me?'

'It was the principle of the thing.'

'Oh, Jesus, Caroline. What do you think this is – *High Noon*?'

'Well, it's lucky someone around here has some principles.' Don't say that, she said to herself too late.

'What's that supposed to mean?'

'Nothing.' Caroline had just pulled all the petals off the daisy, coming out with a 'loves me not.'

'You mean Suzanne?'

'Never mind.'

'What's unprincipled about that?'

'Other than the fact that she's nearly Sharon's age.' Shut up, Caroline, she pleaded.

Diana's green eyes blazed in the candlelight. 'And Hannah's your mother's age. So what?'

'Hannah's my shrink, not my lover.'

'No thanks to you. If she were queer and willing, you'd have her in the sack in a minute.'

Caroline considered this remark, unable to deny it. 'What do I have with Hannah? One hour a week that costs me thirty-five dollars. Big deal.'

'But you think about her all the time. It's practically the same thing.'

Somehow Diana had turned the tables. They were supposed to be discussing her child bride. 'Now *you* get out of *my* head.'

'Can you deny it?'

Caroline was suddenly sad and exhausted. 'I need her. I need someone I can count on.'

'And you can't count on me?'

'You're off with Suzanne half the time. And when we're together, you're usually hating me. Like right now.'

'You need someone who thinks you're wonderful? Because you're paying her to?'

Caroline squeezed the brown center of the daisy until it fell to pieces on the butcher block table. Abruptly the image of Hannah shrugging floated into her head. She shrugged and said, 'Well, I understand that's how you see it, Diana.'

Diana sat with her mouth half open, unable to find anything in Caroline's statement to refute. 'You've become so remote since you've been in therapy,' she finally said. 'Sometimes when we're together it feels as though you aren't even here. Maybe I need Suzanne because I can't get through to you anymore.'

Again Caroline shrugged. *That's the risk you take if you change: that the people you've been involved with won't like the new you.*

'Well?' said Diana.

'Well what?'

'Goddam it, Caroline!' She banged her fist on the table so the dishes clattered. 'That just illustrates my point.' She did an exaggerated version of Caroline's shrug. 'Would you please engage with me? At least Suzanne listens to me and takes me seriously.'

From her months with Hannah, Caroline suspected Diana wasn't talking to her, she was talking to her own mother. But this wasn't something you could say to someone else. For one thing, they'd never believe you. Cloying, a taker, remote. It had very little to do with Caroline. She sat in a perplexed silence, unable to think of anything to say. Diana was looking at her expectantly. Now that Caroline knew how to fight on the playground of life, she also knew almost nothing was worth fighting about. But she didn't know what to do instead, and there was no time to call Hannah and ask. So she stood up and walked toward the stairs.

'Jesus Christ,' gasped Diana, 'you're just going to get up and walk away in the middle of a discussion?' A plate went sailing like a Frisbee past Caroline's left ear and crashed into the wall. They both stared at the shards on the floor.

Diana and Caroline lay on cushions on the hooked rug in each other's arms, watching the fire flicker in Caroline's darkened living room. The children were asleep, and the only sound was the snapping and crackling of the flames. They hadn't spoken for an hour or more. Caroline could scarcely feel her own body, although vivid mental images were flashing through her brain like a returned tourist's slide show. She was picturing the households she'd been a part of – her parents' in Brookline, Jackson's in Newton, David Michael's in Somerville. In each case, a house filled with people, possessions, furnishings. Different foods had appeared on different types of plates on different styles of tables. She'd called each variation 'love,' just as she'd been calling this scene with Diana love. Just as she'd been prepared to call the setup with Brian love. But what she called love wasn't love – it was survival. Food, shelter, protection, sex, procreation. Hannah suggested love might be what was left after you discarded all that. But what was left? Nothing, as far as she could see.

She tried erasing from her awareness the cabin, the sleeping kids, the flickering warmth of the fire, the broccoli quiche in her stomach, Diana's slow-breathing body in its chamois shirt and Levi's, her own similarly clad body that lay entwined with Diana's. What was left? Something. If only the clear sharp awareness from which she'd erased everything else.

Diana stirred in Caroline's arms, just enough for Caroline to see her face. Her green eyes were wide open, staring into the fire. She'd arrived downstairs an hour earlier, sheepishly bearing a shamrock-shaped cake with green frosting.

Caroline shifted her hand slightly so it lay on Diana's full breast, which rose and fell as Diana breathed. No doubt Diana had within herself an area of empty awareness just like Caroline's. This area in Diana was connected to its counterpart in Caroline at that very moment. They were one, more now than during lovemaking, when physical sensations and sexual fantasies stole the show. This is it, Caroline decided, this current between two patches of empty awareness that made them no longer two. *Stop looking for loaves and fishes . . .*

Diana sat up abruptly, removing Caroline's hand from her breast. 'I can't go around throwing things at you, Caroline.'

Caroline sat up. 'That was my fault, Diana. I'm sorry. I realized too late I didn't want to fight, but I didn't know what to do instead.'

'I'm sorry too, but we may as well face it: It isn't working anymore.'

Caroline shut her eyes, warding off a blow.

'We've got to stop being lovers. If that means one of us moving out, then that's how it has to be.'

'But I was feeling so close to you just now.'

'Me too, and it scares the shit out of me. Every time we get close, one of us lashes out.'

'But now that we know that, maybe we can stop. Let's keep trying, Diana.'

'We've tried and tried. I'm sick of trying. I want some peace. I'm too old for all this agony.' She stood up and went to the steps. 'We can discuss what to do tomorrow.'

Caroline lay back down and put her forearm over her eyes as tears seeped between her clenched eyelids. She caused her lover agony. She failed to buy St Patrick's Day presents. She picked fights and walked away in the middle of them. She was a horrible person.

But Hannah saw her as kind and generous, she reminded herself. But she was going to leave Hannah soon.

She blotted out the whole room, and Diana and Hannah with it, envisioning jungle birds until the ache in her heart subsided enough for her to go to bed.

Four

Dressed in wool slacks and a parka, Hannah was walking along the rutted dirt road beyond her house, looking at the night sky over the melting ice on the lake. Thousands of pinpoints of light shone like the reflection of a moonbeam off a new snowfall. Hannah had been entranced with these stars ever since her move to North America. The English cloud cover was usually too thick to allow a child there to develop much interest in stars. But someone must have fostered enthusiasm in her for the broad clear night sky in Australia, because sitting looking up at stars felt familiar.

She came to a shale beach where she'd often sat with her children, tracing the constellations to help them with scout merit badges. Reading up on the constellations, she first realized what arbitrary configurations they were. The Big Dipper was known elsewhere as the Great Bear. Shepherds in different countries, each Indian tribe, connected the same stars like numbered dots in children's puzzles to form different pictures – and then concocted stories to explain their inventions. These stories elicited fear, delight, the whole range of emotions.

She could think about Mona and Nigel, Colin, Maggie, her parents, her grandparents; picture their faces, recall the endearing things they used to do; dwell on the times she'd failed them; and soon feel awful. But she could connect the events in a different pattern and generate different emotions. The underlying reality was those pinpoints of light labeled Nigel, Mona, Maggie, Mummy, Gran, who'd moved into her life for a time, and then moved away. For reasons she didn't entirely understand but had come to accept.

In the woods a dog barked, as though it had cornered a porcupine, the sound echoing out across the lake. She only hoped it wasn't her dog. Pulling the quills out of his nose and mouth was such an ordeal.

Observing what she'd just done, she realized she didn't have to dwell on those people who had inspired such joy, exasperation, and anguish in her. She could instead picture a dog bristling with porcupine quills. Or the mocha walnut torte Arthur had baked for supper. When she was intent on mocha walnut torte, it was impossible to feel anything other than greed, impossible to feel the confused welter of warring emotions associated with that platoon of ghosts that marched in hobnail boots around the parade ground of her heart. And once you figured this out, you could erase the whole show, as though the night sky were a giant blackboard covered with the incomprehensible scribblings of an insane scientist. Or you could sit on this rocky lakeshore and wait for dawn, when individual stars would fade in the light from the sun.

Hannah sat down on a log of driftwood, stretching her legs out in front of her. Her fingers automatically began searching the beach around her for small smooth stones appropriate for skipping. Noticing what she was doing, she folded her hands in her lap. Even if she found any stones, there were no children to hand them to. Dead or grown. Gone.

Abruptly the night sky over Canada lit up with flares of eerie green. Hannah watched in astonishment as the northern lights throbbed and flickered above the White Mountains, swelling and receding time after time. A Martian light show that shot her sunrise metaphor all to hell. That was the thing that bugged her most about life: You thought you had it figured out, and then you got socked with something you hadn't bargained on.

Hannah studied how Caroline was sitting. She no longer perched tentatively on the edge of the tweed couch in her white uniform, a sea gull about to take flight. Nor did she sprawl helplessly, as in her early weeks. She sat squarely today, legs crossed, arms by her sides. But not as though she owned the room, as she had a few times in recent weeks. She looked calm, confident, and a little sad – like someone on the verge of finding the balancing point to her personality.

Caroline felt Hannah's eyes on her and wondered what she was seeing. Those sharp blue eyes, which had seemed intrusive on the first visit, still seemed penetrating, but in the kindest possible way. There was almost nothing they hadn't seen, but very little they condemned.

'So how are you today?' asked Hannah.

'I'm okay.'

'Just okay?' Hannah propped up her stocking feet on the footstool.

'That's pretty good, considering.'

'Considering what?'

'Considering Diana doesn't want the sexual part of our relationship anymore. Again. Considering I may have to move out of her house. Considering I have nowhere to go.' Caroline had spent the days since Diana's pronouncement fluctuating between terror of the unknown and excitement over new possibilities. She finally landed smack in the middle, one canceling out the other, leaving her ready for whatever happened.

Hannah's eyes widened with surprise – that Caroline should look so well after sustaining such a body blow, so to speak. 'That's the bottom line, isn't it? When someone feels powerless in a relationship, he or she cuts off the sex.'

'Powerless? Diana's one of the least powerless women I've ever known.' That small red-headed frame issued proclamations at a rate even medieval popes would have admired.

'Apparently that's not how she sees herself.' Hannah lit a cigarette.

'How could Diana feel powerless? It's her house. She has Suzanne. I'm the powerless one.'

'Not anymore you aren't.' Hannah exhaled with a hiss. 'You're a powerful lady now. I'm sorry, but it's written all over you.'

Caroline smiled. Praise from Caesar was praise indeed. 'But I thought Diana would like me better if I were less of a wimp.'

'What did she say a long time ago: If you realized what a neat person you were, why would you stay with her? I think you've begun to realize it. She's probably terrified you'll move on.' Hannah glanced out the window to the lake. There was a broad patch of open water in the middle of the soggy ice.

'So she moves on before I have a chance to?'

'Why not? Probably she feels you've already moved on. You're not the same person she fell in love with five years ago, are you?'

Caroline shook her head no. The woman who'd seduced Diana had been homeless, jobless, disillusioned in love, in despair over the state of the world, friendless in a new place, staggering under the responsibility of two young children. Diana herself had been lovelorn and alone with a child. They'd glued each other back together like cracked teacups. 'But I'm so much more fun now,' said Caroline with a smile.

'Diana's a nurse. Nurses tend the diseased. Sometimes they don't know what to make of the healthy. People who don't need them make them insecure.' Maggie used to insist, 'To really help someone, you first have to recover from your own wish to be a helper.' Caroline was looking baffled.

'So how have you been feeling through all this?' asked Hannah.

'Not bad. I seem to have lost my taste for suffering.'

Hannah laughed. 'Congratulations.'

'I know I can find another house. I can find other lovers. Brian Stone wanted me. So did that woman in Boston. I have a job, good friends, nice kids. I feel as though I can cope with whatever I have to.'

'What would you look for in a new lover?'

Caroline thought it over as she studied the aerial photo on the wall over the bookcase. She grinned and looked at Hannah. 'The first thing I'd look for is a good eye-hand coordination.'

Hannah gave a startled laugh. She usually got a couple of good laughs out of an hour with Caroline. She'd miss that when Caroline stopped coming. Most sessions in here were as humorless as a Wagnerian opera. But Caroline mostly kept her sense of humor under wraps. Just like her weaving.

'Hey, how come you never told me you're a weaver?' asked Hannah.

Caroline blushed and looked down at her hands. 'How do you know that?'

'I saw your shawls in Cheever's. They're gorgeous.' She eyed the bare wall above the couch.

'Thanks.'

'But why have you never mentioned it?'

'It never seemed relevant.'

'Everything you do is relevant in here. Speaking of power, it's interesting you never brought up something you're so good at.'

'Why is that interesting?'

'You've insisted on portraying yourself as helpless and pathetic. When clearly the opposite is the reality. You're a fraud, Caroline.'

Caroline smiled and resumed her study of the aerial photo. All of a sudden the white dropped into the background and out popped a veiled head. 'Hey, I just saw that head! It does look like the Virgin Mary.'

Hannah turned to look at it, cigarette between her lips. 'Hmmm yes, it does a bit, I'm afraid.'

Their eyes met, and they looked at each other with mutual approval for a long time. This is it, thought Caroline, that connection between patches of empty awareness I felt with Diana on my living room floor. She was suddenly afraid. Diana felt it too, and walked out on her. Maybe Hannah was about to clobber her.

'I thought about love this week,' said Caroline abruptly.

'Oh yes? Are you for it or against it?' The art of silence was hard to master. Hannah remembered sitting as a small child with the family of an aboriginal playmate in their shack on the sheep station, in utter silence for an hour at a time. Eventually the children ran out to play, but the adults kept sitting, far more connected than people who insisted on discussing their connectedness.

'That it's not something you can really talk about.'

Hannah smiled. 'I agree.'

'Because that interrupts your ability to experience it.'

Hannah nodded noncommittally.

'So I have nothing further to say on the topic.' The one additional thing she wished to say – that now that she had some clue what love was, she loved Hannah – she couldn't. Hannah was always warning that she was looking for a way to get rejected, and she didn't want to back her into a corner. Hannah was a professional, a plumber of the psyche. She wasn't there to care about clients, she was there to unclog the backed-up drains of their hearts. Obviously she couldn't get personally involved with all the people who crawled through her office. But the longing to have her affection remained. As one person to another, not as plumber to sink hole.

'What are you thinking about?' asked Hannah. Caroline's blue eyes had gone vague and dreamy.

'Clogged drains.'

'What?'

'I'm wondering how I'll know when this is over.'

'Probably one morning you'll wake up and not feel like coming.'

Hannah felt a stab of regret, but promptly slipped into her coat of chain mail and grabbed up her shield. Caroline had to go, and Hannah had to help her go.

Caroline was sure this would never happen. She might not feel like being a client anymore, but she couldn't imagine not wanting time with Hannah. But she was being unreasonable. That wasn't the nature of their relationship. 'Well, I have a feeling it's almost over. But I can't bear it.'

'So how do you want to phase out?' asked Hannah. 'Do you want to come every other week for a while?'

Caroline was taken aback. She'd only begun thinking about this. She had no idea Hannah would be so eager. Probably Hannah was bored and couldn't wait to be rid of her. Recognizing her tired old pattern of anticipating rejection, she sidestepped it. 'What I'm really trying to say is that I wish I'd met you around town. Because clients have to leave, but friends don't.'

They sat inspecting this statement like a meteorite from a distant galaxy. Caroline hadn't withdrawn or gone numb. She'd stepped forward.

Caroline felt fear knot her stomach, tense her shoulders, and furrow her forehead. She'd done what she meant not to – shown Hannah her hand. And it contained only hearts, no clubs. Like all the others, Hannah would feel burdened or suffocated, get angry or flee. *I know what you want and you can't have it.*

'If you hurry up and get this over with,' Hannah was alarmed to hear herself say, 'maybe we can go out to lunch and start all over again.'

Caroline studied her. Was it possible Hannah wasn't just doing her job? That she really did like the person she glimpsed under all the misery and confusion? In this complicated tango of the emotions, neither had stepped back. Caroline felt such bafflement that she devoted herself to an intense scrutiny of the books on Hannah's shelves: *Sex and Masochism in American Society*, *The Neurotic Personality in Our Time*, *The Inner World of Mental Illness*, *On Death and Dying*.

'So do you want to skip a week?' asked Hannah, getting out her appointment book.

Caroline said nothing, trying to imagine a week without this hour in it.

'You look terrified. Is it really that frightening?'

'I feel like a Flying Wallenda in a windstorm without a safety net.'

Hannah laughed. 'Let's hope the results are more successful. Aren't they always crashing and dying?'

Caroline nodded. 'Yeah. Okay. Let's skip a week.'

Hannah handed her an appointment card. Taking it, Caroline walked to the door. Hand on the handle, she turned, suddenly swamped with loss.

'You're going to be fine,' said Hannah, reading in Caroline's eyes the panic of a shot doe.

Caroline nodded doubtfully, opened the door, and walked out.

Hannah watched her go, wondering why she said that about lunch. The last thing she needed was another ex-client hanging around, watching her feet turn to clay. They always seemed disappointed that in real life she wasn't the Earth Mother of their dreams. Her ability to play that role hinged on their seeing each other for only an hour or two a week; their ability to see her like that was based mostly on their own yearnings. And she had to confess, as Maggie always insisted, that the hardest part of termination for her was giving up their adoration. Because it felt so accurate . . .

Oh well, probably there was a reason for having said that. She rarely knew what would come out of her big mouth, but usually the results were okay. Many ex-clients wanted lunch dates, but a couple convinced them she didn't order more exotic meals than anyone else in their lives. But occasionally someone slipped in under her guard, and it was like finding a cockroach in her kitchen. To allow someone new into her real life was to open up another avenue of eventual loss. And she needed that like she needed an income tax audit.

Unlocking her car door in the parking lot, Hannah heard the cries of Canadian geese returning from the south. Searching the sky, which was mottled with small puffy clouds, she finally detected their wavering V, heading across town and up the lake to the Canadian border. How did they manage to travel like that for thousands of miles? If they got too close, the whole formation crashed. If they got too far apart, there was no formation, only some lonely geese wandering around the skies.

As Hannah climbed into her car, she saw the orange Le Car creep up the street beyond the parking lot. She started her engine, pretending not to hear its horn honking at her, and backed out of her parking spot. Then she stepped on the gas and flew out of the lot and down the street, as the orange Le Car turned around in a driveway to pursue her.

Feeling like one of Charlie's Angels, she took a circuitous route through the streets lined with electronics executives' houses, hoping to shake the Le Car. As she turned onto the lake road, no orange Le Car in sight, she figured out why she responded like that to Caroline. Caroline issued a genuine invitation, straight from her heart, unsullied by hidden client games, and Hannah felt no choice but to respond in kind. Like called forth like. (Except when opposites attracted.) Once she tried to drag out of Maggie her reasons for becoming friends with her after therapy. Maggie looked over the top of her glasses and said brusquely, 'Sometimes people come into your life to whom you simply can't say no, however unwelcome their arrival.'

Turning onto the dirt road to her house, Hannah recalled her stab of regret that afternoon when Caroline brought up termination. Unprofessional. What personal stake did she have in Caroline's behavior? It was usually easy to help clients go, a pleasure even, because it spelled her success as a therapist. Mona would have been close to Caroline's age had she lived. . . . But a bit of countertransference could be a useful thing. Because she identified with Caroline's struggle, she knew how to help her. Because Caroline reminded her of Mona, she wanted to help her, as she'd been prevented from helping Mona.

Yes, all right, she admitted it: Her detachment was wavering. Did Caroline embody qualities undeveloped in herself, as she was always explaining to clients about their choice of acquaintances? She did admire the energy, courage, and integrity that drove Caroline's generation to keep reshaping their lives, however messy the results. She envied them the sense of security that allowed such exuberant experimentation. Those who had faced German torpedoes on the North Atlantic had very little interest in rocking the boat.

As she pulled into the driveway behind Arthur's car, it hit her what Caroline was doing. Hannah told her she'd have to do the leaving, to break her pattern of waiting around to feel rejected. So she was now doing just that – leaving, not by riding off into the sunset, but by asking to be accepted as an equal. Breaking

Caroline's pattern involved letting lunch happen a few times. She was pleased with Caroline for challenging her pattern, pleased with herself for responding appropriately, and pleased finally to figure it all out.

Climbing out of the car, she smiled at herself. Whatever happened was okay if she could fit it into a therapeutic context because then she was the boss. Face it, pal, she notified herself as she dropped her car keys into her pocketbook: You just like this woman.

Five

Driving home from Hannah's office, feeling queasy at the thought of two weeks without a fix, Caroline spotted a V of Canadian geese flying over the open water in the middle of Lake Glass. She stopped her Subaru by the roadside, overlooking a soggy plowed field that sloped down to the shore. Wet snow lay in the furrows like stripes on a zebra. Climbing out, she heard faint honking as the geese gossiped in mid-flight.

Picking her way through the mud down to the lake, Caroline pictured the dead Canadian goose on her doorstep last fall. What maniac would aim a gun at that V and pick off one of those majestic birds? Probably the same maniacs who'd inject poisoned Kool Aid into little children.

Standing at the edge of the lake, poking the toe of her boot into the soft ice, she observed herself. If she kept this up, she'd soon be feeling awful. You didn't have to look at geese over a lake and think about jungle murders. Unless you enjoyed feeling horror. Which she no longer did. If she ever had. She felt anxious leaving Hannah; she turned that terror out on the world. It was as simple as that, and always had been, as Hannah had been trying to make her realize. Yet she'd see Hannah in two weeks, and lunch with her once therapy was finished. No need to be anxious, therefore no need to see this world, which contained such gratuitous wonders as wavering V's of flying geese, as a horrible place in order to explain why she felt anxious.

Breathing deeply of the muggy spring air, she studied the returning geese, moving slowly up the lake with the undulating mountains behind them and the cloud-mottled sky overhead. Rather than harbingers of jungle horrors, she could see them as heralds of spring. She could be grateful to have survived the drifts of winter. She took a few steps out onto the melting ice, which creaked ominously. A pattern of cracks formed under her boots like a mirror shattering. Soon the kids would be racing down the green field in front of the cabin to fling themselves into this water.

Back at the car, Caroline could no longer hear the geese and could just barely see them, a flying wedge heading for home. Those geese knew effortlessly how to conduct their lives, and she felt dawning in herself a similar ease. All would be well.

As she climbed into the car, she wondered if she was turning into a fruitcake. All these dreams, signs, and portents were things she'd always made fun of. What if she found herself putting a bumper sticker on her car that read 'I Brake for Unicorns'?

Alarmed to find she was whistling John Denver's 'Sunshine on My Shoulders,' Caroline shoved a cassette from the hospital library on 'Deaths from Self-Induced Abortion Among Adolescent Females' into her tape deck. Although she tried to concentrate on hemorrhages from knitting needles, she kept thinking about Hannah's willingness to lunch with her. Unexpected. As usual. What Caroline had come to expect from Hannah was the unexpected. She'd been bracing herself for never seeing Hannah again, knowing she couldn't stay now that she felt better. To stay would require new crises so they'd have something to deal with. Yet the whole point was to get rid of her atmosphere of crisis. She'd known it was time to leave and had carefully not asked to stay in touch so Hannah wouldn't have to refuse her. And now Hannah was suggesting lunch. *I know what you want and you* can *have it?*

Caroline was uneasy. She wasn't even sure she wanted to lunch with Hannah. What would they say to each other? Hannah knew too much, had seen her weep and grovel and rage. None of the standard social ploys would work with her. Yet they couldn't continue as therapist and client outside the office. But what if Caroline had a crisis and needed a therapist? Maybe it would be better to preserve Hannah as a monument in her memory, rather than to lunch with her again and discover she liked tofu.

As she turned up the dirt road to the cabin and revved the engine for a race through the mud, Caroline realized if Hannah hadn't been willing to go to lunch, it would have thrown the whole therapy into question. If Caroline was as likeable as Hannah kept saying, of course Hannah would wish to lunch with her. If she wasn't, Hannah was a liar. Hannah was a smart lady. Presumably she was aware of this, since it was her job to be, as she was always pointing out. Therefore, she suggested lunch under duress, not because she really wanted to. She regarded Caroline as a pain in the ass. Lunch was a way to get rid of her more quickly. She practically forced Caroline to skip a week. Hannah couldn't wait to replace her with a more interesting client with real problems, like a split personality or something. What had she said about Diana? That caretakers sometimes didn't know how to behave with healthy people. Yet Hannah herself was a caretaker, and Caroline was now healthy. Hannah didn't want her around any more than Diana did. The only way to keep them both would be to relapse. Caroline's optimism leaked away like air from a punctured tire.

Parking in front of the cabin, Caroline saw Diana, dressed in bib overalls and a parka, removing a wooden cover from an evergreen beside the cabin foundation. Diana looked up, waved perfunctorily, and began clipping away the rust-colored winterkill. The most they'd done since Diana's pronouncement by the fire was to wave in passing. It was unclear how long this could continue. They seemed locked in a pointless stalemate neither knew how to break. Caroline wondered if she should go ahead with plans to move. But she still harbored a faint hope Diana would change her mind and they'd live happily ever after. It was worse than simply losing a lover. Diana was also her best friend. With men you retained your women friends to see you through the breakup of romances. But Diana was one of those women friends to whom she wanted to run for comfort after fighting with Diana as a lover. No Diana, no Hannah, and no one to take their place.

Caroline looked around the car for things to carry in. Her appointment card lay on the dashboard. She picked it up, intending to tear the goddam thing into tiny pieces. She might not even keep the appointment. Better to go ahead and get it over with. She glanced at the card. Then she stared at it. The date was wrong. It was for next week. Hannah had failed to skip a week. A smile crept across her strained face. Good lord, was it possible Hannah was reluctant for her to stop coming too?

'I really don't understand you two,' said Jenny, as she and Caroline sat at a table in Maude's Corner Cafe under a wooden ceiling fan. Jenny wore her navy blue Mao cap with the red star on front. There were dark circles under her eyes and deep frown lines between her eyebrows.

'That makes two of us,' said Caroline. 'Probably three of us.'

'I don't think you ever decided on a form for your relationship. Are you a standard couple, or roommates, or co-parents, or sometime lovers, or best friends who sleep together, or what?' Jenny scooped up hummus with pita bread and sprinkled bits of Bermuda onion on it.

Caroline laughed. 'I'm stunned to hear that coming from you, Jenny. Why should we have a form for it?' She took a bite of her BLT.

'No reason. But it can get pretty confusing if even you don't know what you're doing. I mean, I tell every woman I'm with that I can't be half of a couple. So we all know where we stand. But you and Diana are all over the place.'

Caroline shrugged. 'Well, I understand that's how you see it, Jenny.'

Jenny paused in mid-bite to look at her. 'What's that supposed to mean?'

'It means I don't want to argue with you.'

Jenny laughed. 'I wasn't criticizing, just commenting. In hopes of being helpful.'

'Diana's and my relationship has a logic all its own. We went along with whatever the other person needed at any given time. But the logic has broken down now that we're both happy. That desperate need that keeps lots of couples together is gone. It may be hard on you, Jenny. I'm sure we'll both be harassing you for sympathy.'

'No problem, darling. I love you both. Harass me all you like. And if you ever want to share the bed of a woman who can't be half of a couple, just let me know.'

Caroline smiled. 'Thanks, I'll remember that.' She leaned across the hummus and kissed Jenny on the mouth while the mouths of Maude's other patrons gaped. 'But I suspect our styles wouldn't suit each other. You've specialized in multiple relationships, and I've specialized in multiple orgasms.'

Jenny laughed. 'You're probably right.'

'So how's it going with Hannah?'

'Good. She's really something.'

'She sure is. I envy you. I wish I'd just begun.' Caroline looked at the circles under Jenny's eyes. Jenny was miserable and got to see Hannah. If Caroline became miserable again, she could

309

continue with Hannah too. They might go to lunch, but lunch was voluntary. Hannah could refuse lunch as she couldn't a therapy appointment. The price of happiness was high.

'But don't forget how grueling it is,' said Jenny.

'Wait till you try stopping. It feels like self-amputation.'

'Well, I've never seen you so together. I always knew there was a John Wayne beneath your Mother Teresa act.' Jenny grinned.

'Friends like this I need?' laughed Caroline.

Walking down the main shopping street to her car, Caroline passed a florist's shop. Many pots of blood-red tulips sat on the sidewalk, basking in the spring sun. Caroline stopped. Having looked out on white snow, gray skies, and glaring ice for so many months, she was dazzled by the red. Squatting, she touched the waxy petals with her fingertips. *This world is like a diamond on black velvet*. She went inside and paid for two pots, one for Hannah and one for Diana, her two favorite women. Which didn't mean she wouldn't give serious thought to Jenny's invitation. Though it seemed unlikely Caroline would accept. The challenge for her parents' generation had been to find people to go to bed with. The challenge for Caroline's was to stay out of bed with people.

Setting the tulips on the front seat floor, she remembered she'd forsworn gift giving. She intended to find out if anyone could like her for herself alone. Besides, she wasn't supposed to take Hannah presents, and Diana and she weren't speaking. She studied the newly orphaned tulips. She could keep them for herself. Why not?

To hell with it. Hannah wanted her not to bring presents, but she was no longer doing things to please other people, and *she* wanted to give Hannah presents. En route to her appointment, she stopped at Cheever's in the mall on the highway and retrieved her sunset shawl, despite protestations from the manager.

Walking into the office, Caroline thrust a pot of tulips at Hannah. 'You have to let me act out my need to bring you gifts. I know you don't enjoy them, but it's your job.' She tossed the bag containing the shawl on the couch. She'd give it to Hannah later, once she saw her reaction to the tulips.

Hannah laughed. 'Thank you. They're beautiful. I love tulips.'

'You can plant them in your garden to remember me by.' Hannah didn't seem displeased. Maybe the rules had changed now that they were almost finished?

'I will.' Just what I need, thought Hannah, someone else to remember.

'Speaking of which, why am I here today?' Caroline plopped down on the couch beside her package and studied Hannah. She felt oddly buoyant – despite the estrangement from Diana, despite the need to leave Hannah. It had something to do with that screwed-up appointment.

'What do you mean?'

'Last week I decided to skip a week, but you gave me an appointment for today.'

Could this be true? Hannah swiveled around and studied her appointment book. Caroline was right. 'So why didn't you cancel?'

Hannah sounded irritated. Caroline smiled mockingly. 'I didn't want to cancel. I was delighted. I thought it showed you don't want me to stop either.'

Hannah looked down. Damn. You taught them your tricks, and then they used them on you. She looked up and met Caroline's steady blue gaze, marveling at the transformation of the anguished little girl who sprawled helplessly on that couch last fall. 'All right. Yes. You're right. I'm going to miss you. Our sessions have been a pleasure for me, professionally and personally.' She realized this was true. She was glad on days when Caroline's name was on the appointment book. She wasn't just doing her damn job.

'Thanks. For me too. I so rarely meet someone smarter than myself.' She grinned. It was real, what had gone on all these months, not just a shadow show manipulated by a master puppeteer from a sense of professional duty.

Hannah laughed. 'Well, now that we've gotten this love feast out of the way, what would you like to talk about?'

'I'd like to tell you a dream I had last night.'

'Okay. Shoot.'

'You and I were shopping in the Grand Union at the mall. I went over to the meat cooler and took out a leg of lamb. I unwrapped it and picked up a carving knife and trimmed off all the fat. Then I handed what was left to you. You seemed pleased. I felt . . . sheepish.' They laughed.

'What do you make of it?' Hannah eyed the red tulips on her desk. They were lovely. She ought to stop discouraging clients from bringing gifts. She could use some new plants in here. And she had no big objection to candy, jewelry, perfume . . .

'I started thinking about getting rid of the crap, getting down to bare bone.'

'That's what I was thinking. See? You don't need me anymore. You can do it yourself.'

Caroline felt a stab of panic and began casting around for a problem? Jason was still shooting small animals with his BB gun. Jackie had become secretive about his girlfriend. Suzanne was hanging around the cabin more than ever. But she didn't much care about any of these.

Hannah watched Caroline's eyes dart around the room. 'You'll be surprised how easy it is to get along without me,' she said. 'Millions of people do.'

Caroline laughed despite her terror. Damn it, she felt able to cope. Surely there was some disaster somewhere for which she required Hannah's help? What about the Harrisburg meltdown? The Yorkshire ripper? *But all we can do is our best, which often isn't enough.* And Canadian geese were still flying up the lake in orderly V's. Tulips continued to bloom.

'Remember your list when you first came here? asked Hannah, glancing at her stone Venus. 'How would you describe yourself now? List your ten most characteristic qualities.'

Caroline sat in silence, words marching through her brain like a color guard on parade. *Wimpy, devious, malicious,* she'd written last fall. But they didn't right anymore. 'Bright, imaginative, generous, serious . . .'

'Talented?' Hannah pictured those shawls. 'Funny?'

Caroline nodded with an embarrassed smile. 'Modest.'

They laughed. Hannah looked her in the eye and said, 'You are all those things.'

They sat in silence for a long time, listening to the first faint chirps out the window of birds back from the south. Hannah looked down to the rippled lake, veined with gold by the spring sun.

'So what do you want to do?' asked Hannah. There didn't seem a lot left to discuss. If Caroline continued, they'd just be marking time until Caroline summoned the courage to leave. But that of course was reason enough to continue.

Caroline was unable to answer, knowing it was time to end, but not wanting to. It had been so difficult to accept Hannah last fall. Now it felt impossible to give her up. But it was up to Caroline.

She knew Hannah would sit there until the Second Coming, if that was what it took to get Caroline to take the initiative – and in doing so, to break her old pattern of waiting to feel dismissed. Finally she said in a low voice, looking across the parking lot like a lone astronaut surveying the dark side of the moon, 'Okay. I'm ready. I know it's time.'

Hannah studied Caroline, who looked a bit green around the gills. But apparently once she made up her mind, she didn't mess around. Just as well to get it over with quickly. 'Sometimes I do a follow-up after six weeks. Do you want that? Or would you prefer to go cold turkey?'

'Yes. Good. In six weeks.'

Caroline stood up and took the appointment card. 'Thank you. You've helped me so much,' she said in a choked voice. She reached out and patted Hannah's forearm, like touching wood for luck.

'You did all the work. I was just the excuse.'

'Bullshit.' Caroline thrust the Cheever's bag at her.

'Thanks. What's this?'

'Nothing much.' Caroline walked quickly to the door, feeling as though she were wandering the streets of Hiroshima after the blast. But she'd made it to the door. She had to keep moving, or she was done for.

Holding the unopened bag, Hannah stood up to watch Caroline depart, thinking about Mona when she was five and learning to ride a bicycle. She started out with training wheels, careening up and down the driveway. Once she came over in tears to Hannah on the porch, wailing, 'Mommy, the bicycle keeps leaning over.'

After the training wheels, Hannah loped alongside, holding the bicycle steady. The afternoon Mona caught on, all in a rush after so many crashes and scraped knees, Hannah was trotting along holding her arm. Finding her balance and pedaling faster, Mona grabbed Hannah's hand. As she pulled away, Mona loosened her grip. Until only their fingertips touched, Mona's exerting a downward pressure, her eyes fixed on the road ahead.

Hannah saw Mona needed only to realize she was now riding the bike on her own, so she lowered her fingertips and fell back. As their fingertips touched for the last time, and brushed apart, Hannah felt a pang of joy and pride, mixed with anguish – at the loss of the little girl who couldn't ride a bicycle. As Hannah and the other children cheered, as Mona rode back, her eyes bright with triumph, Hannah first understood that parenting was a series of such small daily deaths, and that learning to let go of your charges was as crucial as learning to take them on.

She hadn't been prepared, however, to let go of Mona and Nigel so soon or so completely. Sometimes she dreamed about that last moment with Mona as their fingertips brushed apart, and woke up to find her face wet with tears.

Which was why she now tried to make sure that nothing and no one was ever that important to her again. Call it self-preservation. If you attached your heartstrings to people and objects, you were dooming yourself to heartbreak, because they all eventually vanished.

But she still felt twinges as clients departed, and sometimes a genuine pang, such as at that very moment watching Caroline cut off an oncoming car to pull her Subaru into the line of traffic up the street. Hannah shrugged with less aplomb than usual, feeling irritated with Caroline for being a menace on the streets. For coming into her bloody life, and then departing like all the others.

The brakes squealed on the tan Maverick Caroline had just cut off. Her body was seared with a blaze of physical fear. But her numb brain didn't give a shit. Let him crash into her. What did she care? She'd as soon be dead as face the upcoming weeks without Hannah.

As she glanced into the rearview mirror at the incandescent face of the enraged driver, she reminded herself that Hannah was willing to go to lunch once the therapy was finished. But probably that was just her way of easing Caroline out. Why would Hannah want to lunch with an insect? Then Caroline recalled today's extra appointment. People would say anything, but could rely on what they did. Besides, if she couldn't get along without Hannah, she had no business stopping.

Turning onto the lake road, she tried to visualize pileated woodpeckers, Canadian geese, tropical plumage. But her stomach continued its dull grind. She might have to pull over and throw up. She remembered vomiting in the storm sewer as Arlene climbed on the trolley that last time. How in hell had thinking about dumb birds helped her feel better? All these things she thought she'd been learning – they were mirages. The whole therapy was one big farce. She felt better because she had Hannah to lean on. Without Hannah, she felt as awful as the first day she walked into her office, all those months and all those dollars ago. She felt *more* awful because emotions she used to have under control had been stirred up like some hideous witches' brew. Frog eyes and lizard tails kept swirling to the surface.

Pulling up in front of the cabin next to Suzanne's Toyota, Caroline pounded the steering wheel. That damn Hannah had a hell of a nerve, coming into her life, eliciting all these feelings and then departing, leaving Caroline stuck with them.

Plunking the second pot of tulips on her table, she realized she placed the first pot on Hannah's desk just as she had placed the plastic hydrangeas on Marsha's grave. Broiling chicken, she brushed her hand against the oven coil. 'Goddam motherfucking son of a *bitch*!' she screamed, shoving the hand under the faucet and turning on the cold water. The odor of burned flesh filled her nostrils. Her stomach churned with nausea. She might as well die along with Marsha and Hannah. She could put one limb after another under her broiler. MOTHER FOUND BROILED TO DEATH, the newspaper would read.

'Are you all right?' Diana called down the stairs.

'No!'

A long pause. 'Is there anything I can do?'

'Yes. Stay out of my way.'

'With pleasure.'

At supper Jackie asked, 'Hey, Mom, what did you do to your hand?'

'Burned it.'

'Does it hurt?'

'Yes.' As she studied the white blisters and angry red skin, she began to cry.

'What's wrong, Mommy?' asked Jason, holding a drumstick in one hand.

'I guess I'm sad tonight.' She wadded her napkin in her fist. Her shoulders began to shake. Burying her eyes in the napkin, she gave herself over to wracking sobs. It was no use. There was a yawning void in her heart, which Hannah used to inhabit. What was she supposed to do about it? She didn't even have next week's appointment ahead, at which she could discuss with Hannah how much she minded not seeing her anymore.

Jason was standing beside her, patting her shoulder and pleading, 'Don't be sad, Mommy.' His world was tottering, just as her own had tottered on days when Hannah was down or tired. More so, because Jason couldn't even drive a car, or write checks. But she couldn't hold it together for him any longer. She lay her head on her arms on the table and wept. It was all over. She couldn't do it anymore.

Now Jackie was standing on her other side, also patting her. Jason was saying, 'I love you, Mommy. So does Jackie. Don't you, Jackie?' Somehow she had to pull herself together. 'So does Amelia,' said Jason, shoving the struggling cat into Caroline's face. 'Arnold too. Don't you, Arnold? Here, boy!' Arnold leaped up and down barking. On his last bounce he grabbed the chicken breast off Caroline's plate.

Caroline sat up with a deep sigh. 'Would you get that mutt out of here?' She blotted her eyes with her crumpled napkin.

'Are you okay?' asked Jackie, studying her with his dark serious eyes.

'Yes. I'm all right now. I've had a hard day. Please don't worry. Whatever happens, I'll always take good care of you two.' They looked simultaneously relieved and bored, as though this were what they needed to hear, but they couldn't afford to let her know how badly. 'Tell me some jokes,' she said weakly, getting herself another chicken breast as Arnold splintered bones on the hooked rug.

The boys dragged out every bathroom joke they'd ever heard. They also summarized the plots of *Star Wars*, *Raiders of the Lost Ark*, and *The Muppet Movie*. Pretending to listen, Caroline reached out and touched the waxy red petals of the tulips with her fingertips. Yes, they were beautiful. They were a fucking miracle. But in a couple of weeks they'd be withered and dead. Like everything else in her life. Just as Hannah said many weeks ago, her parents, Marsha, Arlene, Jackson, David Michael, Hannah herself had given her wonderful experiences, helped her develop skills and strengths. But where were those bastards now? Never more would she sit on that tweed couch, opposite Hannah in bare feet, choking on Hannah's smoke, watching her sharp blue eyes and kind smile, listening to her lousy jokes and wise words.

Jackie's voice as he explained something about R2D2 was cracking. He had some scraggly hairs in his armpits, and a girlfriend who saved him a seat on the school bus. Jason spent his spare time in the woods stalking birds and chipmunks with his BB gun. Soon they'd be gone. Never again to burst through the door and show her the garter snake they'd just trapped. Never to turn her living room into a space capsule or the interior of a submarine or a hockey rink.

Caroline could hear the rumble of Diana and Suzanne conversing upstairs. Soon Diana would be gone. Never again to lie in Caroline's arms all morning watching snow swirl out the window. Never more would they run through sunny green fields together, walk through fiery stands of maples, ski through new snow, make love through a balmy spring night.

Even Amelia, who was sitting watching Arnold crunch chicken bones, having curled up on Caroline's bed all winter, now preferred to stay out hunting all night. Where did this leave Caroline? Alone.

Reassured, the boys departed to their room for homework. As Caroline washed the dishes, her burned hand hurting so much that tears filled her eyes, she tried to think positively. Like the aerial photo in Hannah's office, what you saw depended on how you focused. Her life was in ruins, true. But somewhere in the wreckage surely a daisy bloomed? She still had friends to play poker with, to bowl with. She still had a badly paid job, a healthy body. She could add new ingredients now that she knew she was the chef. Maybe she should take up macramé. She could weave a shroud of many colors. Or a new Pink Blanky. What about smoking? Even Hannah smoked. Somehow the void had to be filled. But with what?

She fixed herself some coffee, turned on the TV, and sat on the couch for the news, hoping to fill the void for the time being with familar routines. Some nights Walter Cronkite appeared to have the world under control, and one could go to sleep relatively confident of waking up the next morning still alive. Unfortunately, not that night. Walter's henchman was describing Idi Amin's predilection for filet of small child. Caroline felt the slow grind in her stomach rev up like a B52 taxiing for takeoff. But this time she was ready for it: She felt undefended without Hannah, and was shifting her terror onto the world at large.

Abruptly she stood up and switched off the TV. She could choose not to engage with this madness. She'd phone someone. Who? Not

Hannah, not Diana, not Brian. Her father hated long distance calls because they cost money. Marsha was dead. She had no number for Rorkie or David Michael. Jackson already felt she was hysterical. Jenny! Maybe she'd even take her up on the invitation to share her bed. Anything not to sleep alone tonight. She dialed Jenny's number. No answer. She dialed Pam. No answer.

'Hi, babe. What's up?' asked Brenda.

'Nothing much. I'm just feeling crummy and wanted to hear a friendly voice.'

'What's wrong?'

'Diana and I have called it quits again, and I've just ended therapy.'

'Both at once? Don't you and Diana ever get tired of breaking up? And why are you stopping therapy so soon? God, it's a wonder you aren't in the loony bin. Look, Barb and I are going to Maude's for supper. Want to meet us there? Have a few drinks, a few laughs?'

'Thanks, but I can't. I have the kids tonight.'

'Well, we'll stop by on our way then.'

'That's okay, Brenda. Really. I'll be fine.'

'We'll be there in ten minutes.'

Caroline forgot she was dealing with an Emergency Medical Technician. By the time she fluffed cushions and picked up baseball cleats, Barb and Brenda were at her door carrying a bottle of rye and a plate of brownies.

'Jeez, you don't look so great,' said Brenda, ushering Caroline to the couch and handing her a brownie. 'Eat this. It'll raise your blood sugar level.'

As Caroline ate the brownie, Barb mixed drinks on the kitchen counter. Brenda told about a burly man who'd been brought into the ER from a rowdy bar the previous night, dead drunk with a broken leg. When she cut off his trousers, she found he was wearing lacy bikini briefs and had a sausage taped to his inner thigh. Barb laughed so hard she spilled rye all over the counter.

After a couple of drinks, and Brenda's description of every accident in the area for the preceding week, Barb said to Caroline, 'Are you sure you won't have supper with us?'

Caroline said, 'No, thanks. I'm in charge on the home front tonight. But thanks for coming over, girls. You've cheered me up.' Saying it, she knew it was a lie.

'Take two aspirin and go to bed with a friend,' said Brenda, exiting with a hearty laugh.

As their car pulled away, Caroline wondered if she herself would ever laugh like that again. Brenda had done her best, but there was nothing she could do. There was nothing anyone could do. It was finished. She'd tried everything. All that was left was to take a hundred and two aspirin and go to bed alone. She carried a glass of water into her bedroom and set it on the nightstand. Then she went into the closet, collected all the pill bottles from the shelf, and grouped them next to the water.

Methodically she removed and folded her clothes. Then she put on her flannel nightgown. After brushing her teeth, she went into the boys' room. Intent on homework, they scarcely glanced up as she kissed them good-bye and smoothed their hair.

As she climbed into bed, eyeing her pill bottles, she remembered promising the boys at supper that she'd take care of them. Damn. She studied the Luke Skywalker glass full of water. She never broke promises. It set a bad example. Shit. She couldn't even weigh the options and decide to stay alive. She was stuck here. She swept the bottles off the table and into the wastebasket on the floor.

With a disappointed sigh, she scooted down in her bed, turned out the light, and pulled the covers to her chin. She began to examine her void from every angle. Eventually she realized it wasn't really new at all. She'd carried this feeling of emptiness with her all her life. Like malaria, it flared up periodically. She pictured that toddler trying to find her way to the bathroom through the dark hall, pink blanket clutched around her shoulders for protection against the monsters and Japs lurking in the shadows. She felt the same terrified emptiness on the bus carrying flowers to Marsha's grave. And looking out on her lawn covered with Rorkie's toilet paper. And standing on the street watching Arlene in her office with Dusty. And entombed in Jackson's neo-Tudor house, to which he rarely returned. And hearing David Michael's headboard clatter against the wall on his nights with Clea. And listening to Diana by the fire the other night saying their relationship wasn't working. In a flash she understood that her feeling of abandonment and despair had almost nothing to do with those other people. They were just ordinary flawed mortals, doing their clumsy best to get through life with some measure of pleasure and meaning. Her void was hers and hers alone.

Let them go, it suddenly occurred to her. Let them all go. Let them all go in peace. Her parents, Marsha, Rorkie, Arlene, Jackson, David Michael, Diana, Hannah – they all had to go. She'd revolved around each of them like an Israelite around the golden calf. Whomever she turned the searchlight of her soul on had become instantly deified. But now they all had to go. All the persons, places, and possessions; all her memories, imaginings, and desires. They caused her too much pain. The only solution was to give them up voluntarily, before they could be wrenched away. There was more than one way to kill yourself off, and she proceeded to do just that, slashing through the tangled jungle of her past with a machete of renunciation.

When the mayhem was over, Caroline looked around and found this void she'd cleared wasn't empty. It was full of the dark healing stillness she felt when she dreamed of jungle birds. She felt it on the floor by the fire with Diana, and sitting in silence with Hannah. But the birds, Diana, and Hannah were no longer present. She had given them up, along with everything else. And had just discovered there was no need to fill the void because it was already full.

A plop at the foot of her bed caused her to start. Sitting up, she saw Amelia's yellow-green eyes blinking as she settled into a nest in the comforter. Caroline could hear steady purring.

Lying back hoping to recapture the state of mind Amelia had startled her out of, Caroline closed her eyes. And suddenly she saw that terrified toddler rise up to her full height and fling off the pink blanket, like Wonder Woman her cape. The toddler stood there in the dark, frozen, waiting for monsters to attack. When nothing happened, she looked around and found there were no monsters, only shifting shadows from the play of moonlight through the trees outside the window. Not only were there no monsters, there was no longer a terrified toddler. Through Caroline's head ran the thought: The strength you've insisted on assigning to others is actually within yourself.

Six

'I feel like a failure.' Caroline sprawled on the tweed couch in jeans and a work shirt. What was the point of that seizure of renunciation last month, Caroline wondered, if here she was weeping in Hannah's lap again?

'Forget it. We don't use that word in here.' Although Hannah had to admit, at least to herself, to feeling disappointment at hearing Caroline's anguished voice on the phone that morning asking for an emergency appointment. Were they going too fast? Hannah had been through this with so many people that she sometimes forgot it was the first and only time through for each client.

'Well, anyhow, thanks for seeing me.' Caroline had held the phone receiver to her ear that morning like a pistol to her temple. It was her last resort.

'You can come back any time you want.' Hannah studied her, trying to figure out if this was what Caroline needed to know, or if there was a real issue. She had dark circles under her eyes, and the same clenched mouth and pained squint as when Hannah first met her. She slunk into the office and plopped down on the couch like a beaten dog, not even noticing her shawl, which was hanging over the couch.

'You look pretty awful,' said Hannah. 'What's wrong?'

Caroline sighed. 'I did great for three weeks. Felt good. Handled everything that came up. But a few days ago I fell apart. Finally I decided to call you because I'm supposed to go to Boston for this two-week course, and I don't see how I can go feeling like this.'

'Like what?'

Caroline rubbed the bridge of her nose. 'I'm terrified.'

'What of?'

Caroline tried to decide what label to put on the grinding in her stomach this time. 'Of leaving the boys.'

'Whom are you leaving them with?'

'Diana.'

'Has she kept them before?'

'Lots of times. It's always been fine.' Diana was their second-string mother, just as she herself was Sharon's. Whatever else went on between Diana and her, this was never in doubt.

'Are things bad between you?'

'No. Everything's okay. Ever since we gave each other up for good, we've been getting along great.'

Hannah smiled. 'So what's the problem?'

'This is going to sound screwy, but you're used to that with me.'

Hannah shook her head vigorously. 'Don't put yourself down in here.'

'Yeah, okay. Anyhow, I read in the paper last week about this creep in Vermont who raped and killed an eight-year-old boy. They haven't caught him yet, and I keep thinking he'll turn up at the cabin and hurt Jackie or Jason. Or abduct them as they walk home from school. Last night I dreamed a carload of men broke down the cabin door and tortured them.'

'I don't think that's screwy at all,' said Hannah. 'Most mothers feel anxious when they go away from their children. It's perfectly normal. It's what's kept the race going all these eons. But once you're on the road and no longer the adult in charge, you'll probably feel fine.' For years after Mona's and Nigel's deaths it had been impossible for her to leave Simon and Joanna, and she turned down vacations with Arthur all across the Caribbean.

'I guess my imagination is too vivid. I can picture the whole scene with that little boy in hideous detail. And I get so . . . furious.'

Hannah felt tension building in the room. 'That's understandable. It was awful. I read about it too. I murdered the motherfucker in my mind, slowly and painfully.' Actually, she castrated him, then murdered him. First things first.

'I started thinking if little kids can't rely on adults, who can they rely on?'

'Did you hear yourself? Do you remember what you said our first session, when I asked what was the most painful thing that had happened lately?'

Caroline struggled to recall.

322

'You said the Jim Jones thing.'

'How can you remember when I can't?'

'It's my job. You should instead ask yourself what's preventing you from remembering. Anyhow, you talked about how his followers adored him and called him Dad, and he turned around and killed them. Betrayal by parent figures has been one of your themes all along, hasn't it? Daddy went off to war, and Mummy took to bed with depression. Marsha died. Arlene took up with a new student. And what's just happened between you and me?'

Caroline looked pained and perplexed as she rubbed the tweed sofa cover with her fingertips.

'I didn't betray you. But we've been ending our therapeutic relationship. That could feel like betrayal.'

Caroline frowned.

'But who's doing the leaving this time?' Hannah shook a cigarette from a pack of Mores.

'I am,' said Caroline.

'And in truth, who's always done at least half of the leaving?' She put the cigarette between her lips and lit it.

Caroline frowned again.

'The painful part about growth is the need to leave behind whatever you've outgrown.' Simon and Joanna had knocked themselves out trying to make their need to move out her fault. They accused her one day of being a suffocating busybody. And the next, of being a rejecting witch. She observed their fluctuating assessments of her with a fascination that annoyed the hell out of them. But Nigel and Mona departed so abruptly. This endless nonsense with Simon and Joanna was a real luxury.

'You're making it too complicated,' said Caroline. 'I have to go to Boston, and I'm scared stiff some psychopath will murder my sons. It's as simple as that.'

Hannah shrugged. Hardly anything was as simple as that. 'Well, it's certainly a valid fear, given the globe we inhabit. Whether you want a valid fear to incapacitate you is another question.' She glanced at the shawl above Caroline's head, the many shades of purple, red, and orange fading into each other. Hard to believe the talented woman who wove it was the same woman who now sat on Hannah's couch trembling with terror. Probably they weren't the same woman. This Caroline was an impostor. Hannah had to get rid of her so the real Caroline could return.

'What I want,' said Caroline, rubbing the bridge of her nose, 'is not to live in a world in which maniacs murder the children they should be caring for.'

As she tapped her cigarette into Nigel's stone, Hannah shook her head. Caroline had just gone cosmic. Hannah had offered an interpretation. She'd offered sympathy. It sounded like time to get tough: 'Well, my dear friend, you've been feeling pretty good for a long time now. I'd say you're casting around for an excuse to feel bad again.' She paused, alarmed at her words. Caroline might get annoyed enough to throw off the mounting depression, or she might stomp out and kill herself. Hannah fought to maintain her composure and waited to hear what dreadful thing she'd say next. 'Look, to make sense of this world, you have to have faith and humility. And I'm not sure you have either.' Wow, thought Hannah, watching Caroline carefully.

Caroline glared at Hannah through narrowed eyes. Where did this woman get off? Caroline came in crisis – to her therapist, to her potential friend – and Hannah kicked her in the teeth. This was what you could expect from people. They all failed you in the end. She'd known Hannah would eventually turn on her like all the others . . .

The healthy part of her, the part that had been uncovered and strengthened during the past months, listened to these thoughts and recognized them as The Pattern, as repulsive as last year's leftovers found moldering in a discarded refrigerator. Hannah had just put responsibility for Caroline's state of mind right where it belonged – with Caroline. If she wanted to feel better, she should proceed to feel better. Because she now knew how to. Otherwise she should shut up, enjoy feeling bad, and stop wasting Hannah's time.

Hannah watched Caroline's face contort with some kind of inner struggle. Caroline's eyes rested on the stone Venus. Maybe Caroline would throw it at her. Nobody had tried that yet. Hannah felt determined to provoke a definitive reaction: 'Nobody ever said life was supposed to be easy.'

Hannah watched with surprise as a small smile spread across Caroline's strained face, like the sun peeking through massed storm clouds. 'What's so funny?' Hannah felt herself smiling in response. The real Caroline had just returned from the gloom. The tightness around the mouth and eyes let up a bit.

'I'm trying to keep from saying, "I Never Promised You a Rose Garden," ' said Caroline.

'You didn't succeed, did you?'

Caroline laughed. 'You know, I always thought it was a question of achieving some permanent state of tranquillity.'

'Nirvana or something?' Even Caroline's voice sounded different from a moment ago.

'Right, but it's not. It's more like learning to surf. The waves keep rolling in, each different from the last, and you have to ride them, instead of getting pounded to bits.'

'I agree.'

'Good. It must be right then.'

'Think carefully before you answer,' said Hannah. 'What's the next question I'm going to ask?'

Caroline frowned, sorting back through the session, through past sessions. Hannah raised her eyebrows. 'You want to know if I ever tried to go back home once I left.'

'You may have your Junior Therapist badge.'

'Junior?'

'Don't get carried away or I'll reject you. So what's the answer?'

'I was just trying to remember. One night at Mass General I was in charge of the ER. I was terrified. Arlene had just ditched me, and I felt as though I'd lost my magic amulet. Here I was, responsible for all these potential crises. A five-year-old girl was admitted with meningitis or something. She died in my arms at dawn, before the doctor on duty could get there. I still don't know to what extent it was my fault. If at all. I guess I had a nervous breakdown. Stopped working, stopped eating and sleeping, lay in my apartment all day with the shades pulled down listening on the news about the ghettos all across the country going up in flames. I developed this rash all over my body. I phoned my father and said I wanted to move back home. He said no because I'd already paid a half year's rent on my apartment. I called my mother, and she said my father knew best. Then she went to bed in a depression.'

'So Arlene failed you. Then you failed that child. Then your parents failed you. Adults failing children. Do you see how that relates to the Jim Jones thing? And to your fears about leaving your sons? Leaving them evokes your own terror of being left.'

Caroline nodded doubtfully.

'When you were an infant,' said Hannah, 'Daddy went to war, and Mummy withdrew into anxiety and depression. Leaving you feeling undefended in a threatening world. Leaving you feeling all this disaster was somehow your fault. And you've lived in that atmosphere ever since. But Caroline . . .' Hannah looked at her with urgency. 'That's *all* it is. It's over now. You're no longer a helpless infant. You're a strong, competent woman who can defend herself.'

They sat in silence. Caroline looked across the parking lot, which was bordered by small dunes of the sand that had been spread on the ice that winter. During her months here nothing much had changed on the surface, yet underneath everything was different. She glanced at the aerial photo over the bookcase, isolating the veiled head from the cow pasture with ease. What a surprise to find you could shift the contents of your head like rearranging furniture in a room.

'So what have you discovered today?' asked Hannah.

'That I can come back home to Mommy if I want.'

'Yes. Good. And?'

A smile returned to Caroline's face. 'Now that I know I can, I don't want to.'

'How do you feel?'

'Great.' Caroline stood up. 'I can't believe it. I'm fine.'

'No kidding?' Hannah couldn't believe it either.

'You do good work.' Caroline stretched luxuriously, feeling her body relax for the first time in several days.

'I guess I do.' Hannah studied Caroline with amazement. Like Caroline's waves, each person was different. She never knew exactly what would happen. This whole session was unexpected, but right. Caroline had just come full circle.

Caroline did a double take as her eyes took in the shawl on the white wall above the couch. 'It looks nice there,' she said with a pleased smile.

'It does, doesn't it? I've had a lot of compliments on it.'

'Thanks.'

'Thank *you*. So when are you off to Boston?'

'Day after tomorrow.'

'What's the course?'

'Didn't I tell you? I've switched to the delivery room. It's a refresher course.'

'That must be fun.'

'It's only two floors up from the emergency room, but it's like another world. Everybody's so happy.'

'Do you think you can handle it?'

Caroline laughed. 'It's been a strain, but I'm getting there. I just got another job offer, so I can always leave.'

'Oh yes? What job?'

'My old weaving teacher in Boston wrote and asked me to come teach at her craft school.'

'How nice.'

'Yes, it is. But I like Lake Glass.'

Hannah nodded, trying to be impartial on the topic of Caroline's whereabouts in upcoming years. 'Are you staying with your parents in Boston?'

Caroline nodded.

'How will that be?'

'Fine, I think. It'll be interesting to see if I can behave like an adult around them now that I'm nearly middle-aged.'

Caroline paused at the door. Would Hannah still want to have lunch, or had Caroline just failed the friendship test? She looked at Hannah, the blue of her eyes exaggerated by a blue turtleneck. Caroline wanted a chance to know the woman underneath all the roles Caroline had imposed on her. But probably she blew it by crawling in here in pieces. She recognized The Pattern revving up. Just because she'd asked for help didn't transform her into a repulsive toad.

'I want to point out,' said Hannah from her chair, 'that you stood up and are walking out my door before your hour is up. Once again, I'd like to ask who's doing the leaving.'

Caroline paused, hand on the doorknob. She turned to look at Hannah with a wry smile. 'A bit more practice and I'll have it down pat.'

Hannah grinned. 'Why don't you call me in a few months?' She wondered who Caroline would become now that she was giving up trying to be how she thought other people wanted her to be.

'I will. But for lunch or for an appointment?'

'We could do either. But I can't do both at once. So you'll have to decide which.'

'Lunch,' said Caroline hesitantly. Lunch was the point of no return, but what if she needed to return?

'Okay. Fine,' said Hannah with resignation. The last thing in the world she wanted was someone else to miss. But it would be like not drinking from fear of a hangover. And she was never one to pass up a martini. She stood up and slipped on her shoes.

They walked outside into the yard together. The lake spread out below them, a soft pewter color under the overcast sky. All the ice had melted. Summer was coming. They heard a clamor in the trees bordering the yard. Looking up, they saw that the branches, swollen with new buds, were filled with chattering yellow evening grosbeaks, fresh back from more balmy lands, sporting their jaunty masks like revelers returning from a Caribbean carnival.

MORE ABOUT PENGUINS, PELICANS, PEREGRINES AND PUFFINS

For further information about books available from Penguins please write to Dept EP, Penguin Books Ltd, Harmondsworth, Middlesex UB7 0DA.

In the U.S.A.: For a complete list of books available from Penguins in the United States write to Dept DG, Penguin Books, 299 Murray Hill Parkway, East Rutherford, New Jersey 07073.

In Canada: For a complete list of books available from Penguins in Canada write to Penguin Books Canada Ltd, 2801 John Street, Markham, Ontario L3R 1B4.

In Australia: For a complete list of books available from Penguins in Australia write to the Marketing Department, Penguin Books Australia Ltd, P.O. Box 257, Ringwood, Victoria 3134.

In New Zealand: For a complete list of books available from Penguins in New Zealand write to the Marketing Department, Penguin Books (N.Z.) Ltd, Private Bag, Takapuna, Auckland 9.

In India: For a complete list of books available from Penguins in India write to Penguin Overseas Ltd, 706 Eros Apartments, 56 Nehru Place, New Delhi 110019.

A CHOICE OF PENGUINS

☐ *Further Chronicles of Fairacre* 'Miss Read'   £3.95

Full of humour, warmth and charm, these four novels – *Miss Clare Remembers, Over the Gate, The Fairacre Festival* and *Emily Davis* – make up an unforgettable picture of English village life.

☐ *Callanish* **William Horwood**   £1.95

From the acclaimed author of *Duncton Wood*, this is the haunting story of Creggan, the captured golden eagle, and his struggle to be free.

☐ *Act of Darkness* **Francis King**   £2.50

Anglo-India in the 1930s, where a peculiarly vicious murder triggers 'A terrific mystery story . . . a darkly luminous parable about innocence and evil' – *The New York Times*. 'Brilliantly successful' – *Daily Mail*. 'Unputdownable' – *Standard*

☐ *Death in Cyprus* **M. M. Kaye**   £1.95

Holidaying on Aphrodite's beautiful island, Amanda finds herself caught up in a murder mystery in which no one, not even the attractive painter Steven Howard, is quite what they seem . . .

☐ *Lace* **Shirley Conran**   £2.95

Lace is, quite simply, a publishing sensation: the story of Judy, Kate, Pagan and Maxine; the bestselling novel that teaches men about women, and women about themselves. 'Riches, bitches, sex and jetsetters' locations – they're all there' – *Sunday Express*

A CHOICE OF PENGUINS

☐ *West of Sunset* **Dirk Bogarde** £1.95

'His virtues as a writer are precisely those which make him the most compelling screen actor of his generation,' is what *The Times* said about Bogarde's savage, funny, romantic novel set in the gaudy wastes of Los Angeles.

☐ *The Riverside Villas Murder* **Kingsley Amis** £1.95

Marital duplicity, sexual discovery and murder with a thirties back-cloth: 'Amis in top form' – *The Times*. 'Delectable from page to page . . . effortlessly witty' – C. P. Snow in the *Financial Times*

☐ *A Dark and Distant Shore* **Reay Tannahill** £3.50

Vilia is the unforgettable heroine, Kinveil Castle is her destiny, in this full-blooded saga spanning a century of Victoriana, empire, hatreds and love affairs. 'A marvellous blend of *Gone with the Wind* and *The Thorn Birds*. You will enjoy every page' – *Daily Mirror*

☐ *Kingsley's Touch* **John Collee** £1.95

'Gripping . . . I recommend this chilling and elegantly written medic-al thriller' – *Daily Express*. 'An absolutely outstanding storyteller' – *Daily Telegraph*

☐ *The Far Pavilions* **M. M. Kaye** £4.95

Holding all the romance and high adventure of nineteenth-century India, M. M. Kaye's magnificent, now famous, novel has at its heart the passionate love of an Englishman for Juli, his Indian princess. 'Wildly exciting' – *Daily Telegraph*

A CHOICE OF PENGUINS

☐ **Small World** **David Lodge** £2.50

A jet-propelled academic romance, sequel to *Changing Places*. 'A new comic débâcle on every page' – *The Times*. 'Here is everything one expects from Lodge but three times as entertaining as anything he has written before' – *Sunday Telegraph*

☐ **The Neverending Story** **Michael Ende** £3.50

The international bestseller, now a major film: 'A tale of magical adventure, pursuit and delay, danger, suspense, triumph' – *The Times Literary Supplement*

☐ **The Sword of Honour Trilogy** **Evelyn Waugh** £3.95

Containing *Men at Arms, Officers and Gentlemen* and *Unconditional Surrender*, the trilogy described by Cyril Connolly as 'unquestionably the finest novels to have come out of the war'.

☐ **The Honorary Consul** **Graham Greene** £1.95

In a provincial Argentinian town, a group of revolutionaries kidnap the wrong man . . . 'The tension never relaxes and one reads hungrily from page to page, dreading the moment it will all end' – Auberon Waugh in the *Evening Standard*

☐ **The First Rumpole Omnibus** **John Mortimer** £4.95

Containing *Rumpole of the Bailey*, *The Trials of Rumpole* and *Rumpole's Return*. 'A fruity, foxy masterpiece, defender of our wilting faith in mankind' – *Sunday Times*

☐ **Scandal** **A. N. Wilson** £2.25

Sexual peccadillos, treason and blackmail are all ingredients on the boil in A. N. Wilson's new, *cordon noir* comedy. 'Drily witty, deliciously nasty' – *Sunday Telegraph*

A CHOICE OF PENGUINS

☐ **Stanley and the Women** Kingsley Amis £2.50

'Very good, very powerful ... beautifully written ... This is Amis *père* at his best' – Anthony Burgess in the *Observer*. 'Everybody should read it' – *Daily Mail*

☐ **The Mysterious Mr Ripley** Patricia Highsmith £4.95

Containing *The Talented Mr Ripley*, *Ripley Underground* and *Ripley's Game*. 'Patricia Highsmith is the poet of apprehension' – Graham Greene. 'The Ripley books are marvellously, insanely readable' – *The Times*

☐ **Earthly Powers** Anthony Burgess £4.95

'Crowded, crammed, bursting with manic erudition, garlicky puns, omnilingual jokes ... (a novel) which meshes the real and personalized history of the twentieth century' – Martin Amis

☐ **Life & Times of Michael K** J. M. Coetzee £2.95

The Booker Prize-winning novel: 'It is hard to convey ... just what Coetzee's special quality is. His writing gives off whiffs of Conrad, of Nabokov, of Golding, of the Paul Theroux of *The Mosquito Coast*. But he is none of these, he is a harsh, compelling new voice' – Victoria Glendinning

☐ **The Stories of William Trevor** £5.95

'Trevor packs into each separate five or six thousand words more richness, more laughter, more ache, more multifarious human-ness than many good writers manage to get into a whole novel' – *Punch*

☐ **The Book of Laughter and Forgetting**
Milan Kundera £3.95

'A whirling dance of a book ... a masterpiece full of angels, terror, ostriches and love ... No question about it. The most important novel published in Britain this year' – Salman Rushdie

A CHOICE OF PENGUINS

☐ *The Philosopher's Pupil* **Iris Murdoch**   £2.95

'We are back, of course, with great delight, in the land of Iris Murdoch, which is like no other but Prospero's . . .' – *Sunday Telegraph*. And, as expected, her latest masterpiece is 'marvellous . . . compulsive reading, hugely funny' – *Spectator*

☐ *A Good Man in Africa* **William Boyd**   £2.50

Boyd's brilliant, award-winning frolic featuring Morgan Leafy, overweight, oversexed representative of Her Britannic Majesty in tropical Kinjanja. 'Wickedly funny' – *The Times*

These books should be available at all good bookshops or newsagents, but if you live in the UK or the Republic of Ireland and have difficulty in getting to a bookshop, they can be ordered by post. Please indicate the titles required and fill in the form below.

NAME _____ BLOCK CAPITALS

ADDRESS _____

_____

_____

Enclose a cheque or postal order payable to The Penguin Bookshop to cover the total price of books ordered, plus 50p for postage. Readers in the Republic of Ireland should send £1 R equivalent to the sterling prices, plus 67p for postage. Send to: The Penguin Bookshop, 54/56 Bridlesmith Gate, Nottingham, NG1 2GP.

You can also order by phoning (0602) 599295, and quoting your Barclaycard or Access number.

Every effort is made to ensure the accuracy of the price and availability of books at the time of going to press, but it is sometimes necessary to increase prices and in these circumstances retail prices may be shown on the covers of books which may differ from the prices shown in this list or elsewhere. This list is not an offer to supply any book.

This order service is only available to residents in the UK and the Republic of Ireland.